Siren in Bloom

Other Books By Lexi Blake

ROMANTIC SUSPENSE

Masters and Mercenaries
The Dom Who Loved Me
The Men With The Golden Cuffs
A Dom is Forever
On Her Master's Secret Service
Sanctum: A Masters and Mercenaries Novella
Love and Let Die
Unconditional: A Masters and Mercenaries Novella
Dungeon Royale
Dungeon Games: A Masters and Mercenaries Novella
A View to a Thrill
Cherished: A Masters and Mercenaries Novella
You Only Love Twice
Luscious: Masters and Mercenaries~Topped
Adored: A Masters and Mercenaries Novella
Master No
Just One Taste: Masters and Mercenaries~Topped 2
From Sanctum with Love
Devoted: A Masters and Mercenaries Novella
Dominance Never Dies
Submission is Not Enough
Master Bits and Mercenary Bites~The Secret Recipes of Topped
Perfectly Paired: Masters and Mercenaries~Topped 3
For His Eyes Only
Arranged: A Masters and Mercenaries Novella
Love Another Day
At Your Service: Masters and Mercenaries~Topped 4
Master Bits and Mercenary Bites~Girls Night
Nobody Does It Better
Close Cover
Protected: A Masters and Mercenaries Novella
Enchanted: A Masters and Mercenaries Novella
Charmed: A Masters and Mercenaries Novella
Taggart Family Values
Treasured: A Masters and Mercenaries Novella
Delighted: A Masters and Mercenaries Novella
Tempted: A Masters and Mercenaries Novella

Courting Justice
Order of Protection
Evidence of Desire

Masters Of Ménage (by Shayla Black and Lexi Blake)
Their Virgin Captive
Their Virgin's Secret
Their Virgin Concubine
Their Virgin Princess
Their Virgin Hostage
Their Virgin Secretary
Their Virgin Mistress

The Perfect Gentlemen (by Shayla Black and Lexi Blake)
Scandal Never Sleeps
Seduction in Session
Big Easy Temptation
Smoke and Sin
At the Pleasure of the President

URBAN FANTASY

Thieves
Steal the Light
Steal the Day
Steal the Moon
Steal the Sun
Steal the Night
Ripper
Addict
Sleeper
Outcast
Stealing Summer
The Rebel Queen
The Rebel Guardian
The Rebel Witch
The Rebel Seer

Siren in Bloom

Texas Sirens, Book 6

Lexi Blake
writing as
Sophie Oak

Siren in Bloom
Texas Sirens Book 6

Published by DLZ Entertainment LLC

Copyright 2018 DLZ Entertainment LLC
Edited by Chloe Vale
ISBN: 978-1-942297-05-5

Sign up for Lexi Blake's newsletter
and be entered to win a $25 gift certificate
to the bookseller of your choice.

Join us for news, fun, and exclusive content
including free short stories.

There's a new contest every month!

Go to www.LexiBlake.net to subscribe.

Dedication

For Shelley Bradley—who is sitting somewhere plotting revenge...I hope I caught your bratty, sweet, lovingly loyal spirit. My life would be so much less without your friendship.

Prologue

Deer Run, TX

Leo Meyer stared at her, the one woman who'd ever tempted him beyond measure, the one he couldn't help but open himself up to. Unfortunately, Shelley McNamara Hughes had already opened herself up to another man—her husband.

She stood in front of Aidan O'Malley's desk, leaning against it, her lovely body tense. Her glossy black hair hung in a long wave over her shoulders, her brown eyes tired. She was fucking gorgeous, but he couldn't believe the words that had come out of her mouth. "What did you say?"

Her eyes slid away from his as they often did when he put that hard tone into his voice. It was one of the sure signs of a submissive. He'd taken one look at Trev's sister two years before and his fucking heart had flipped. And then he'd found out she was married.

"I said you should leave." The words came out quietly, but there was power behind them. "You should go back to Dallas."

Leo crossed his arms over his chest and stared down at her. What the hell was she thinking? The last couple of days had been hard. She was worried about her brother, and Leo believed she had every right to be. Trev McNamara had come back to Deer Run after a long absence, and someone wasn't happy about it. "You think I should leave when someone is obviously after your brother? You're the one who called me down here. You got me up in the middle of the fucking night because you were sure Trev was slipping."

She'd called two nights before when her brother hadn't come back to her place. Trev was a recovering addict and it had been his first time on his own. Leo had hopped in his car and gotten his ass down to Deer Run. He hated to admit it, but his haste had been as much about Shelley as it was about Trev. He'd been willing to leave the search for his wayward patient to the McKay-Taggart employee he'd brought with him. He'd gone to be by Shelley's side. It looked like she didn't want him there.

Dark, midnight-black hair shook. "No. Trev is strong. You did an amazing job with him. He won't slip up. I know that now. I trust him. I was wrong to bring you here. You should go back to Dallas."

"When all these people are harassing Trev? Sweetheart, I don't think that's a good idea." He softened, everything inside him responding to Shelley's obvious despair. It was there in the slump of her shoulders, the tightness of her eyes. He'd made a study of this woman. He'd greedily taken her in every time he got near her. When she would visit her brother, he would make excuses to see her, and then he would stare at her like a student studying a work of art.

She sniffled, and he couldn't handle another second of it. He reached out and pulled her into his arms. God, it felt like the right thing to do.

She was stiff for a moment, but then she melted into him, her arms going around his waist.

It was the first time he'd touched her in this way. He inhaled her scent, the citrus of her shampoo, the clean smell of the soap she used. He sank his hands into her hair.

He was done. He'd seen what her husband was really like. He wasn't going to let her marriage vows to a man who behaved like Bryce Hughes hold him back. He was crazy about her.

Fucking hell. He loved her. After all these years, a failed marriage, and countless flirtations, he'd finally found the right woman.

"Shelley." He whispered her name. God, he even fucking loved her name. "Baby, it's going to be all right."

Her head tilted up, her eyes bright with tears. What the hell had that monster put her through? Bryce Hughes was a son of a bitch who was about to get the full treatment. He would call in some investigator friends, and by the time Ben and Chase Dawson were done, Leo would know everything about Bryce Hughes. He would know every dirty secret, and he was damn sure there were many. Something about the man was filthy right down to his core.

Her lips trembled. Leo knew he shouldn't, but his decision was made. Her marriage didn't matter. Hughes had given up rights to his wife by treating her like shit. He would have Lucas start divorce proceedings immediately, so it wouldn't matter if he had this one moment with her.

He lowered his lips to hers. A gasp escaped her, a soft, submissive sound that had Leo's cock tightening. She was everything he could want. And all he had to do was take her.

His fingers sank into her hair, pulling it back slightly. He took her mouth, letting his tongue run across those plump, sensual lips, demanding entry. Her body pressed to his, and her mouth opened with a sigh. Leo invaded, the taste of her heady and encompassing. He inhaled her. After years of longing, this was what he needed. He needed to sink into her, to know that she was his. His tongue found hers and he dominated, taking over, slanting his mouth again and again. He thrust his tongue deep in a naked imitation of what he wanted.

She gave as good as she got. Her hands tightened on his shoulders, fingers sinking in. If he hadn't been wearing a shirt, he would have half-moon indentions on his flesh, and he would have shown them off proudly. He wanted to bear her mark, even as she would bear his. Her ass would be red from his hand, his paddle, his whip. He would make her his submissive, his wife.

Oh, she was going to be his wife.

"Baby, I'm going to take such good care of you." He ran his hands down her back and found the round globes of her ass. He cupped that gorgeous rear and pulled her close, letting her feel how much he wanted her. "I won't let him touch you again. Lucas can draw up papers today. As soon your divorce is final, we can get married."

She seemed to come out of her daze, her eyes widening and those chocolate brown orbs glistening. "Leo, no."

He pulled her closer, slightly afraid that if he let her go, he could lose her. "You have to leave him."

Her head shook, and her hands came down from his shoulders to press against his chest. "No. I'm not leaving Bryce. I'm sorry. You completely misunderstood me."

The words didn't penetrate. He couldn't quite make himself let her go. "He's not good for you."

She sniffled, but an air of resolve descended over her. Her shoulders straightened and set, her chin coming up in a stubborn tilt. "He's my husband."

"He doesn't have to be. Baby, I know you're scared, but I'm going to take care of you." She had to understand. Bryce had her terrified.

But she didn't look terrified. She looked annoyed. "You have to stop. This was a huge mistake. Please let me go."

She pushed at his chest again, and he had no choice. He released her and took a step back. What the hell was going on? For years he'd watched her. He'd caught the way she'd looked at him. He couldn't have been mistaken. She felt the same way he did. Didn't she?

He forced his hands to his sides, and took another cautious step back, hoping distance would bring some sanity back to the situation. "Tell me you don't want me."

He wouldn't believe it until he heard it.

"I can't." She smoothed back her hair. "I want you, Leo. I just don't want to leave my husband."

"You want an affair?" The thought turned his stomach. The reason he'd never laid a hand on her was his deep distaste for cheating. He flirted. He flirted all the time with unavailable women, but he would never actually touch one. His own wife had divorced him after she'd had an affair with a coworker. Shelley couldn't be asking him to be the other man.

"No." She turned away, staring out the window that overlooked the vast O'Malley Ranch. "I don't want that. I've never cheated on Bryce, and I never will."

Thank god he hadn't misjudged her. He took a deep breath. "I understand. I'm sorry. This got out of hand. Look, it's my fault. I had a rough night. Let's take this slow. The first thing we can do is sit down and talk to Lucas about your options. He isn't a divorce lawyer, but he knows enough to advise you. When the time is right, we'll find an excellent divorce attorney for you. And we won't touch again until you're comfortable."

It was better this way. Everything would be aboveboard.

She didn't turn, merely stared out the window. "I'm not getting a divorce."

"Bryce is dangerous. Something is going on with him. I don't know what it is yet, but I will find out."

Now she turned, and there was a cold look on her face. "Don't. Leave him alone. I'm not one of your patients. Stay out of my marriage."

"Did he say something to you?" Had Bryce threatened her? "He can't hurt you."

"He has never raised a hand to me. Get that through your head. You're seeing what you want to see. You're a good-looking man. I can't help but be attracted to you, but I'm not going to ruin my marriage over what would only be a short-term fling. We're from two different worlds."

"Are you telling me you *want* to stay with Bryce?" He couldn't believe it. Bryce was a douchebag, and Leo was pretty sure he was involved in something criminal.

"Is that surprising? I married him."

"Do you love him?" He searched her face. It was as blank as a doll's.

"That doesn't matter. I have to live in this town. I'm not leaving here. Bryce and I make sense. I like our life. I'm certainly not going to give it up. What could you offer me? Do you want me to live at a BDSM club? I can't do that."

He felt like she'd punched a hole straight through his chest and ripped his fucking heart out of his body. This was about money? This was about the lifestyle? She didn't want him because he worked in a club? "I guess you're right. I can't offer you what Bryce can. Bryce is rich."

She nodded. "Yes, he is. I'm in a good place. I would be a fool to throw it all away. I have a big house and the respect of everyone in the community."

He doubted that. Oh, the house was big enough, but he'd heard rumors about Bryce's infidelity. He would bet there were a lot of people in this tiny piece-of-crap town who felt sorry for her. But if this was what she wanted, who the fuck was he to take it from her? After all, he was an idiot with a PhD who worked in a BDSM club.

He took a deep breath, seeking that place where he found peace. He'd learned long ago to let go of the things he couldn't control. He couldn't force Shelley McNamara to love him. Hughes. He had to start thinking of her that way. She was Bryce Hughes's wife. And that was right where she wanted to be.

He was going to stop making a fool of himself.

"I wish you well. Please let your brother know I'm always here for him." He let the real meaning lie there between them. He would always be there for Trev McNamara, but they were done. He wouldn't take her phone calls. He wouldn't answer her e-mails. He was through.

She nodded and turned back to the window, dismissing him utterly.

Leo walked out of the room, a coldness settling around his heart. He wouldn't try again. He'd been wrong to try this time. He would go home and do what he did best—help others find peace and happiness.

There was neither in the world for him.

* * * *

The minute the door closed behind her, Shelley broke down. She thrust her fist over her mouth to muffle the sound or the sob would have echoed through the house, giving away the game she was playing.

She'd lied. God, she'd lied about everything.

Tears coursed down her face.

She wanted to run after him, to beg him to stay, to take her away with him. She'd never loved anyone the way she loved Leo Meyer. She'd known it the minute she'd met him.

And she loved him enough to keep him alive.

Bryce was a monster. She knew that now. She could still feel his hand punching her gut. He'd laughed when she'd fallen to the floor and explained that he wouldn't touch her face because it was too pretty. He needed a pretty wife since she'd been useless in every other way.

And he'd explained that he would kill Leo Meyer if he caught her even thinking about him again.

Shelley let herself sink to the floor.

She'd done what she had to do.

Chapter One

Dallas, TX
15 months later

"No. Absolutely not. Can't you see this is a very bad idea, Julian?" Leo Meyer looked at his boss trying to convey his deep belief that impending fatherhood was obviously affecting Julian's brain. Ever since Danielle Lodge-Taylor had announced her pregnancy six months before, Julian's brain had gone soft, and his current request was merely proof that the situation was getting worse.

Julian looked up from the papers he was studying, that single eyebrow arching. He could tell a lot from his boss's eyebrow. Where most people wore their expressions on their mouths or their eyes, Julian was all about that single arching brow. This particular time, that brow told Leo that Julian was getting frustrated with his stubbornness.

"She's merely put in a simple request, Leo."

There was nothing at all simple about Shelley Hughes. "I thought you hired Mrs. Hughes to redecorate the penthouse. Not to play around in The Club."

Julian leaned back, a frown on his hawklike face. Despite his money and privilege, Julian had come up the hard way. Leo had made a long study of his boss, but the last few years had shown a deep and abiding change in Julian Lodge. Loving Danielle and his partner, Finn, building a life with them, had turned Julian into a meddling old matchmaker. "You know The Club is a place for exploration. I'm a bit shocked that you think I would turn down a woman in need."

Leo felt his jaw drop open. Julian didn't run a soup kitchen. He ran a BDSM club, and a ridiculously exclusive one at that. "She's not a member of this club. Have you started a pro bono fund? Because I don't think Mrs. Hughes can afford the membership fee."

Julian's eyes rolled. "Good lord, you're transparent, Leo. She's not married anymore. And she's taken her maiden name again."

He was well aware of that. Her husband, Bryce Hughes, had been killed a year before. Did she still mourn him? She said no, but then she'd lied before. "Good for her. It doesn't explain where she got the money to buy her way into this club."

"Sometimes I allow people in for other reasons than simple money. Lexi couldn't afford this club. Neither could Aidan. Your new charge certainly can't."

Logan Green. He was coming in this morning. The big guy from Colorado had some serious problems, according to his brother. God. He had to deal with Wolf. The last thing he needed was Julian trying to force him together with Shelley. He'd let it go. He'd let her go. Why had she come to Dallas? She'd made herself plain enough that day at Aidan O'Malley's ranch. She didn't need anything he had to offer.

"Wolf thinks Logan needs this place," Leo said absently.

"And I think Shelley needs it." Julian tapped a file folder in front of him. His desk sat in front of a large window with a spectacular view of the Dallas skyline. "I want you to be honest with me. I trust you, and if you tell me differently, then I will deny her request. I'm going to give you a scenario. A smart woman, who happens to be related to a man I respect greatly, comes out of a difficult marriage. She was used by her husband to cover his many crimes. She's utterly disillusioned and heartsick. She watched the man she'd married be brutally murdered. She was taken hostage herself and was only saved by the actions of her brother. She's been in a deep depression. Her husband was the only man she's ever had a relationship with. She married young and never explored her own sexuality. She's obviously submissive but has had no chance to discover this part of her personality. She's sweet and kind and I worry that if something doesn't change for her, she will fade away. If you had no idea who I was speaking of, if you merely had these facts in front of you, what would you recommend?"

Fuck him. Julian was putting him in a corner. "It's not the same."

"How is it not the same? You came to me two days ago and laid out the case for allowing Logan Green to become an ancillary member of this club. He doesn't have the funds with which to join, but you feel he can benefit from training."

Leo felt a stubborn look settle on his face. "You know my methods include impulse control. I believe Logan has a stress disorder brought on by an incident where he was almost killed. He was tortured. He needs to feel like he's in control."

"And Shelley wasn't tortured?"

Julian was missing the point. "She chose to marry that man. She chose to stay with him."

"I am asking you to put aside your own strong feelings for Shelley and answer the question. Would you recommend that woman I described for training?"

Leo felt his fists clench. Julian wasn't going to give up. He could lie, but Julian would see right through it. He was damned no matter which way he went. "Yes."

"Excellent." Julian looked back down at his paperwork. "That is all."

What? "We're not going to talk this through? You're simply going to tell me to train her and that's all there is to it? Don't you think you owe me more than an order?"

Julian's eyes came back up. "I wasn't ordering you to do anything."

Leo huffed. "Then you're not going to put Shelley into training?"

"Oh, I'm putting her in training."

Frustration threatened to choke him. How the hell was he going to put impersonal hands on her body? The very thought of finally seeing that petite, curvy body naked had his unruly dick standing at full attention. He couldn't walk into a room with her without his cock threatening to take over. She was dangerous. She'd burned him once, and he was not going to allow it to happen again. She'd made it plain she didn't need a white knight. Not that he'd ever been good at that. His history with women proved it. "And she agreed to have me as her trainer?"

What kind of game was she playing? She couldn't kick him out of her life and then turn around and draw him back in simply because she suddenly found herself without a husband. Guilt gnawed at him. Bryce Hughes had been a monster. Maybe he wasn't being fair. Maybe she truly had come here to explore herself. Maybe she had come here because she knew she'd made a mistake.

Julian shook his head. "Not at all. She was horrified at the thought. It was the one thing she required before she would agree. She wouldn't have you."

A kernel of hurt flared to life. Well, he had his answer. He'd been pining for her, but she certainly hadn't done the same for him. "I'm the resident Dom. Her training falls under my purview."

"Are you?" Julian asked, standing up. He was dressed in his day clothes, a perfectly tailored suit and tie. Julian was immaculate, every stitch in perfect position, as though the clothes wouldn't dare do anything so gauche as to wrinkle. "A Dom usually takes a sub."

Fuck, they were going into this? "Do you have a problem with the way I run this club?"

Julian held out a hand. "You're perfect. You're wonderful and you know it. I have no idea what I would do without you. I simply worry that you aren't getting what you need. For the last year, you've held yourself apart."

Because no one needed him. Julian was happily married. Most of the members of The Club he'd grown close to in his first years were settled and content. Everyone was moving into a phase of their lives that he hadn't gotten close to yet. "I've kept up my duties."

Julian's voice became hushed, softer. It was a tone Leo knew he only used on his family and friends. Julian's circle was tight, but he would kill for someone he loved. "I know you, my friend. Don't think I don't know what I owe you. I wouldn't be the man I am without you and Jackson. The two of you have had an enormous influence on me. I truly consider you my brothers. And that's why I worry. You loved that woman."

"No." He wasn't going to admit that to anyone. "Shelley was merely one in a long line of unavailable women I became attracted to. I hit on Abby Barnes, too. Hell, I hit on Dani."

Julian smiled at the mention of his wife. "Please continue to do so. She's worried the baby is making her unattractive."

Leo smiled. "Do you have any idea how far you've come? A few years back, you would have beaten the shit out of anyone who hit on your sub."

"But I trust my Danielle. That's the difference. Don't mistake my trust in her for a change in my possessive nature. I trust Danielle, and I trust you. You can hit on Danielle and Abigail all you like because you don't mean anything by it. It was different with Shelley Hughes. She's different. Tell me something, and I'm asking as a friend, not a boss. Have you slept with a woman in the last year?"

His stomach churned. "No."

He'd thought about it, but it had seemed like cheating because he loved her. *Fuck.* He had to get over that woman. He couldn't let his life be ruined because one woman couldn't love him.

"Let her go, Leo. I don't know what happened between the two of you, but you're both miserable and neither of you is willing to deal with the situation. Are you willing to go after her?"

He shook his head.

"Then let her go," Julian said. "You'll both be happier for it. Shelley is a lovely woman. You're family. I want you both happy, and I think this is the way to do it. I've found the perfect man to train her. You have another sad-sack freak to fix. Let each other go."

"He isn't a freak."

Julian shrugged. "I think I can joke about it. I was one of the sad-sack freaks you helped. Concentrate on your new charge. Shelley's new Master will help her."

It was an excellent plan. Perfectly logical. So why did the thought of another man laying hands on her put him in a killing mood? "Who? Which Dom did you pick? Because I can't think of a single one we have here who will work. Ben is too easy. Chase is too hard. And they like to work together."

"She did mention that ménage was one of her fantasies," Julian offered.

That was not happening. "Fuck no. Chase is hardcore. And he'll be far too distant. She needs someone emotionally available or you're putting her in the same position she was in before. She's going to require a patience neither of those men has."

"As it so happens, I agree with you," Julian explained.

But he was on a roll now. "Dane is a part-time Dom, and quite frankly, I hear he's about to start on a big murder case. He's not going to have time. Are you planning on setting her up with one of the married Doms? Greg would be perfect." Greg was madly in love with his wife, Heather, but he enjoyed training a new sub from time to time. He wouldn't fuck her. Actually, Greg was his best-case-scenario Dom. "It's Greg."

Julian shook his head. "No. I think she needs someone who is going to be utterly focused on her needs. I'm afraid I'm playing matchmaker here. I'm looking for someone who wants a permanent sub, who will go into this with an open heart. She's been talking to him over the web and on the phone for a few weeks now. I think you'll find these two are very suited to each other. I was careful." Julian reached back and hit the button on his intercom. "Candice, you can send him in."

He was here? Who the hell was he? Who was this Dom Julian was talking about? Had he put up a fucking classified ad? *Seeking candy-ass Dom who will take sub under his wing and into his heart*? Vomit. No Dom in his right mind went into a training contract hoping to find a goddamn soul mate. And she'd been talking to him? She'd been sitting up late at night talking to some damn Dom while he'd been making himself sick over her?

"I would, sir. If he were here, I would absolutely send him right in." Candice was Julian's longtime assistant. At one time she'd been his nanny. Candice was, in many ways, the mother Julian had needed after his own had died. Julian had managed to build a family out of nothing.

Why couldn't he do the same? He had a family, and yet he felt far away from them.

Julian growled a bit. "The little shit. I had this perfectly timed. I said my line, and now he's supposed to make his grand entrance. Does he understand the meaning of the word timing?"

Over the intercom, Leo could hear the dinging of the elevator.

"Ah, he's here now, sir."

"Well, hello, pretty lady."

Leo froze. That wasn't…fuck, no. It was a coincidence.

He could practically hear Candice smiling over the intercom. "I'm old enough to be your grandmother."

"My granny didn't look like you, sweetheart. Can you tell the big guy I'm here?"

So many things fell into place. The laid-back Western accent. The cowboy-lothario treatment Candice was getting. The shit-eating grin on Julian's face.

Only one person in the world would truly annoy the hell out of him.

"Tell me you didn't hire him." Leo gritted the words out.

The door opened, and sure enough, there was Wolf Meyer.

"Hello, brother."

Leo was sure in that moment that he'd landed in hell.

* * * *

And he'd done it again. That much was plain. Wolf forced his face to remain placid. He wasn't going to let Leo know how much the lack of greeting cut through him. He hadn't seen his brother in almost a year, but this was what he got. His brother stood there looking at him like a mangy dog who had walked into the room. Which was a bad example because Leo would have petted the mangy dog and tried to figure out what the mutt needed. He wouldn't do the same for his own brother. "Something wrong?"

"I thought you were driving Logan down," Leo said, his voice tight.

"I did. He's sitting in the lobby."

Leo moved in. "I didn't realize you were planning on working here. This isn't a friendly visit, is it, Wolfgang?"

"Well, no, it doesn't feel friendly at all, Leonardo." If his brother wanted to get snippy, he could give as well as he got. Why the fuck had he thought this could work? What was he doing here? He'd had a decent job in Bliss. He'd been close to his mother. Why was he here when it was obvious that his brother didn't want him around?

Because he was still five fucking years old, clinging to his older brother because he didn't have anything else. He'd left Bliss because he didn't want to spend his life riding herd, and his mother was perfectly happy with the craziest guy in town.

And he missed his brother.

The trouble was, his brother had never once missed him.

Leo frowned. "I didn't mean it that way. I'm sorry. Julian didn't mention he'd hired another Dom."

"You didn't tell him?" He looked to Julian, who had seemed like a nice guy, but then Wolf wasn't the brightest bulb in the light socket. He was a dumb grunt who shouldn't trust his instincts.

"I didn't think I had to." If the big boss was at all uncomfortable with the tension in the room, it didn't show. "It is my club, after all."

Wolf thought about the phone call he'd placed before he'd left Bliss. Leo had sounded happy. He'd said he had the guest rooms all made up. No wonder. He hadn't thought Wolf would be staying more than a night or two.

His first instinct was to turn and walk out the door. If Leo didn't want him here, then he would go home. He would get in his truck and march his ass right back to Bliss. He would find a job. Surely he was good at something. The trouble was the only two things he'd ever been good at were being a soldier and being a Dom.

He wasn't allowed to be a soldier anymore. There wasn't much call for professional Doms in a place as small as Bliss. He'd talked to the owner of the only other club in Dallas. Sanctum already had a Dom in residence.

Fuck. He needed this job. "I'm sure we can work it out so you don't have much interaction with me, Leo."

"That would be difficult," Julian offered. "He's going to be your boss."

Double fuck. "I thought you had a client for me?"

"No," Leo said, his mouth a flat line.

"Yes," Julian insisted at the same time. "But Leo is the resident Dom. He'll oversee your training with Shelley."

Shelley. *Damn.* He was a dumbass. Ever since that first conversation with Julian about coming to work at The Club, he'd thought about this woman who would be his submissive in training. He'd heard about her background, though she didn't like to talk about it. Her background had been one of the things she had shied away from in their conversations. She'd been in an abusive marriage. She'd witnessed a horrible crime. She was alone in the world. She had a brother, but he was happily settled down on the very ranch Wolf had just left.

So why hadn't he talked to Trev about his sister? He'd had the opportunity, but he'd avoided it. He'd told his friends that he would be working at The Club, but he hadn't mentioned that he would be topping Trev's sister.

"And she's agreed to it? Has she signed a contract? Does she want to meet me in person first?" Despite the fact that he'd spent hours getting acquainted with her over the phone, there was a lot he didn't know about her, and she, him. Julian had placed many things off-limits. No exchanges of addresses. No discussions of family in anything but broad terms. All there to protect them both, but it left some pretty big holes. And they hadn't exchanged pictures. She could take one look at him and run. It seemed to be what most women did these days.

How was he supposed to act as her Dom when he was down on himself? He shook it off. He could handle it because he would be doing it for her. To give her what she needed. To get what he needed. The power exchange didn't only work for perfectly confident people. But when it worked well, it gave a man confidence. And he was fucking confident. He was a man who'd survived Hell Week with the SEALs. He was a man who didn't give a shit what most people thought.

Except the minute he got near his brother, he turned into a needy kid again, longing for the approval of the man who had raised him.

"She doesn't need to meet you, Wolf. There's been a mistake." Leo took a step forward, but Julian blocked him.

Julian pulled a file off his desk. "She's already signed a standard contract. I've attached a set of hard and soft limits for you both to discuss and agree to. Sexual contact is up to you, but she seems open to it if the two of you click."

"Are you fucking high?" Leo practically roared. "This is not happening. Wolf is not working here. He's not topping Shelley. He's going to get back into his truck and drive right back to Colorado where he can take care of our mother."

"She doesn't need me." He felt his whole body flush with humiliation. God, why had he thought this would work? It wouldn't. Not if Leo didn't want it to. "Ma's happy, Leo."

"With Crazy Mel. Yes, she's happily awaiting the next alien invasion. She needs someone who can take care of her."

"Mel's a good guy." Where was this coming from? Leo had never had a problem with Mel before. Leo had laughed with Mel the last time he'd come home. He'd joked and played golf and drank some of Mel's special tonic. And gotten slightly trashed since Mel's special tonic happened to be rotgut whiskey.

Leo took a long breath. "I know he is, but they're both getting older. Have you thought of that? And you don't have any formal experience."

"He passed Stefan Talbot's tests. I like Mr. Talbot. I trust his judgment," Julian explained, but it didn't seem as though Leo was listening.

"I don't care what some guy in Colorado thinks. I run the Doms here and I say no, or are you letting me go, Julian?"

The question dropped like a mine waiting to go off.

Julian's face went perfectly blank for a moment. Then he looked up, and Wolf knew he'd lost. "I apologize for the inconvenience, Mr. Meyer. It seems I've made a mistake. Please let me offer you a room in the hotel portion of The Club. Candice will make sure you have a suite at your disposal tonight."

Wolf stared at his brother for a moment, but Leo's face was a stony mask. The urge to put his fist through his brother's nose was riding him, but it wouldn't fix anything. Somehow, Leo had gotten it into his head that he was useless, and nothing he'd done seemed to be able to fix it.

It was time to move on.

Without another word, he turned on his heel and walked out.

Logan Green sat outside the door, which had been left open. It seemed his friend had heard the whole humiliating scene.

"Are we leaving?" Logan asked, his big body coming out of the chair he'd been perched on.

"I am." Just because he wasn't welcome didn't mean Logan shouldn't get what he needed.

Logan's mouth curled down. "Uhm, that guy sounds like an asshole. I'll go with you. We can be back in Bliss by morning."

And Logan would continue down the same self-destructive path he'd been on for over a year. No. He couldn't let that happen. Logan had been through too much to throw away this opportunity. "Stay. He's a good guy."

"He didn't sound like it."

Wolf shook his head. "It's only with me, man. I'm telling you, he's great with his patients. You won't find a better shrink. He won't give up on you. He'll stick with you until you make a breakthrough, and then he'll stand by if you falter. Ask Trev. Ask anyone who's worked with him."

Logan's eyes slid toward the elevator, seemingly looking for an escape route. "I don't know."

How did he explain this? How did he let Logan know what kind of a person his brother was? "Our dad left when we were kids. I was a baby, but Leo was five. As you know, our mom has some issues. She worked, but it was hard. We barely managed to keep our cabin. Leo had to grow up fast. I think that's why he doesn't want me around. I remind him of how crappy it was. When Ma lost her job, we didn't have enough to eat. Do you know what that asshole in there did? He would put half his plate on mine. He was eleven years old. Do you understand what it takes for a hungry eleven-year-old to give up half his food? He sacrificed for me. I didn't turn out as good as he thought I should. That's on me, not you, man. He will help you."

Logan nodded after a long moment. "Okay."

Wolf slapped him on the arm. "And I'll buy the first round when you get back to Bliss. You're going to be fine."

He turned to go, and Leo stood in the doorway.

"It wasn't so bad. Our childhood, I mean." He looked down at the floor suddenly. "I don't resent you, Wolf. At least I didn't think I did. Julian surprised the hell out of me with this. I had no idea you were coming to stay. Julian's manipulating everyone. It's his weird version of love. Look, I sort of had a relationship with the woman he's asked you to top."

"Fuck, I didn't know." That explained a lot.

"It doesn't matter," Leo insisted. "It didn't work. There was nothing intimate between us. We were friends, nothing more. But she does need you. I apologize. Please stay."

He should go. He should walk the fuck out the door. He'd wanted to come to Dallas to have a relationship with his brother, not to step into the middle of a shit storm. If Leo said he was involved with this woman, then it had been serious. Leo wouldn't use those words on someone he felt casually about. Could he top his brother's ex? Fuck. He should walk away and be satisfied with e-mails and the occasional visit. It's what most brothers had.

"Sure. I'll stay."

He'd never been satisfied with ordinary.

Chapter Two

Shelley McNamara stared out the window at the city streets. The Dallas skyline rose all around her like some giant enfolding her in its arms. She'd grown up in the country with wide open spaces and nature all around her. She'd thought she would hate it here, but she loved the city.

It had been right to come to Dallas. She'd needed the change, needed to get back to work. But was she making a horrible mistake with the personal side of things? She was waiting, counting down the minutes until she met with this man, this Dom who would guide her while she explored the BDSM lifestyle.

"Getting nervous?" Danielle Lodge-Taylor walked through the hallway of the penthouse she shared with her husbands. She glanced over at the new furniture that had arrived hours before. "This is lovely. Oh, Shelley, it's beautiful. What a transformation."

She smiled, feeling confidence grow inside her. Pleasing her clients was the best part of her job. "I'm glad you like it."

"The old room was elegant, but there was no warmth to it. I think Julian told the last designer to simply buy the most expensive stuff possible with no regard to comfort."

Decorating this glorious penthouse had been her reason for living for the past several months. It had been the perfect project to sink into while she made the transition from angry widow to something…more.

"I think this has a much warmer feel to it. I'm anxious to get to work on Julian's office."

"You'll do a fabulous job," Dani assured her. "Now, I'll ask again. Are you getting nervous?"

The gorgeous blonde smiled as she took a seat, carefully lowering her very pregnant body into the chair.

Pregnant. Shelley was almost thirty. She'd thought for sure she'd have kids by now. Of course she also thought she would be happily married. Unfortunately, she'd picked an asshat, douchebag, drug-dealing, blackmailing son of a bitch as a husband.

Dani pointed her way. "Oooo, you were thinking of him. That's your 'I hate my ex' face."

Shelley smiled. She couldn't help it. Something about Dani eased that anxious place inside of her. In the time she'd been at The Club, her friendship with Julian Lodge's wife had blossomed into something she held dear. "Sometimes I wish I'd been the one to shoot him."

"I know the feeling," Dani said. "It would have given you closure. But he's gone now. You know if you let his memory hold you back, then he wins."

This was an old argument. Since she'd come to work for Julian three months before, she'd heard a lot of this from Dani. She'd poured her heart out to the gorgeous blonde and found a willing ear and a stubborn mouth. Dani was firmly in the "move on" camp.

Dani had been the one to finally convince her she should give BDSM a serious try. "I know, sweetie. And yes, I'm nervous. Terrifically nervous. Even though we've talked and sent a bunch of e-mails back and forth, it's different to meet him in person. Were you this nervous before you met Julian?"

Dani's mouth came open slightly, and she shook her blonde hair. "Oh, I didn't meet him the way you're meeting Master Wolf. This is very traditional. My meeting with Julian was not. I met Julian when I jumped into his car as I fled my wedding to a man named Jimbo."

Shelley couldn't help the giggle that escaped. She still had a hard time reconciling the elegant, educated woman in front of her with the redneck girl she claimed to have been at one point in time. "Jimbo?"

Dani nodded. "Jimbo Smart. It's a misnomer. And he's now

married to my sister. They both work out at the spa I opened. You have absolutely nothing to be nervous about when it comes to the meeting. I think you're going to like him. I saw him earlier, you know."

"Master Wolf?" God, she was curious. Master Wolf. Who was named Wolf? She had to wonder if it was a nickname. She would feel more comfortable with someone named Bob or Randy. Why wasn't any damn Dom named Master Bob? No, they were Julians and Wolfs and…Leo.

"Yes, I meant Master Wolf," Dani said.

Dani didn't seem to have noticed her mental drift off. Shelley was happy she didn't have a "pining for Leo" face.

"And?" Maybe he would be ordinary looking. Or much older. A nice man who would lead her on this journey but who wouldn't tempt her. Yes. She could use a friendly, kind mentor.

Dani's eyes lit up. "Don't you ever tell Julian I said this, but I think my eyes almost popped out of my head. He's gorgeous. I mean it. I actually drooled."

"Are we talking about Wolf?" Finn Taylor asked as he walked into the room. One hand was on his tie, pulling it off. He set his briefcase down. Finn Taylor was Dani's other husband. She found herself surrounded by happy ménages.

But she only wanted one man. Leo. And she could never have him.

"Yes," Dani said, flushing slightly.

"Don't feel bad, baby," Finn assured her. He leaned over and brushed his lips across hers, his hand caressing her round belly. "That man is sex on a stick. Holy hotness. You would have to be blind not to notice him. But I get the feeling there's something Julian's not telling us about him."

Dani looked up at her husband, her eyes narrowing. "Is he plotting again?"

"The Master is always plotting. I haven't figured this one out yet." Finn sat on the arm of the comfy seat and turned to Shelley, his hand never leaving his wife's belly. "Welcome to sub world, Shelley. Doms never let you in on their plots. You have to be sneaky."

"It's called topping from the bottom. We've made an art of it."

Dani leaned her head back. "We'll figure it out."

"So he's attractive?" Would she think so, or was she so caught up in Leo that no other man would ever quite do?

Finn gave her a brilliant smile. "Take it from a bi-guy, he's gorgeous. I would guess he's ex-military, but I think I see some cowboy in there, too. And he was nice. I only talked to him for a minute, but I got a good vibe. Some Doms are real assholes, but Master Wolf seemed like a genuine guy."

And he would be her Master. Well, for training purposes.

What was she doing?

Putting her life back together. That's what she was doing. She straightened her shoulders. She wasn't going to sit around any longer. She'd moped for long enough. It was time for Shelley McNamara to figure out who the hell she was. She'd been Bryce's wife. Before that she'd been Trev McNamara's sister and her parents' daughter.

It was time to find out if she could simply be Shelley.

"When is your meeting?" Dani asked.

She glanced up at the clock. Too soon. Way too soon. Could she rethink this? Get out of this? She could tell Julian Lodge that she'd reconsidered and realized that it was ridiculous to think she really wanted to get tied up and spanked and forced to call some stranger Sir.

Especially when all of her fantasies didn't involve a stranger but a man she'd dreamed of every day since the moment she'd met him. She'd made horrible decisions that had led her to being forced to throw the only man she'd ever truly loved out of her life, and she didn't deserve a second chance. Not that he seemed to want to give her one. He wouldn't even look at her. She'd been here three months and all she'd gotten from him was a cold nod as they'd passed each other in the hall.

As if she didn't really exist. As if he'd never kissed her, never offered to take her away.

She needed to forget Leo Meyer.

"She's got her 'pining for Leo' face on," Finn whispered.

Shelley laughed. It felt good to laugh again. It felt amazing to be able to laugh at her own ridiculous self. How many years had it been since she'd simply laughed without thinking about how her husband would take it? "I was hoping I didn't have one of those."

Dani shot her a sympathetic look. "No, sweetie, it's totally there. Are you sure you want to do this? Julian could talk to him. Julian is excellent at manipulating people. If Leo was your trainer, I seriously doubt he would be able to keep his hands off you. It could bring you together."

Leo had made it plain that whatever had been between them was over. She was self-aware enough to admit that she'd hoped she would walk in and Leo would fall all over himself to get to her, but that wasn't what had happened. He wouldn't talk to her. He would smile and make chitchat with all of the other employees. Leo Meyer was like the life of the party until the moment he realized she was there. Then he would shut down like someone had unplugged him.

She didn't want that for him. "No. Maybe I should go somewhere else. I think I'm making Leo miserable. That wasn't my intention. I heard there's another club."

Finn leaned forward. "I don't think Julian is going to allow you to go somewhere else, and certainly not to Sanctum. You know it blew up, right? No one's working there right now. It will be months before Taggart gets it up and running again. Come on, Shelley. You can't cut off a piece of yourself because Leo has a stick shoved up his ass."

She shrugged. She had cut pieces of herself off for a long time. "Maybe I'm not submissive."

Lie. Her husband had used her gentle nature against her for years. It was why she'd been attracted to him in the first place. She was incredibly attracted to a commanding presence. Bryce simply hadn't had the soul to back it up. She longed for a man who knew how to give back.

"Perhaps you aren't ready."

Four words proved how submissive she was. Not the words, precisely, but the way Julian Lodge said them. She turned and found Julian standing in the doorway, his eyes pinning her where she stood.

Julian Lodge was one amazing-looking man, but it was his presence that moved her. And Julian knew how to love his partners. She wanted what Dani had found. Hell, she wanted what her brother had. Trev had found himself in this place. This place, and the man in front of her had transformed her brother from an addict who thought only of himself to a man she was damn proud of. Trev had gotten over his guilt to become the kind of man who everyone relied on.

"I am ready, Sir. I'm sorry. Sometimes I let the past weigh me down." But she couldn't drown under it. She couldn't.

Julian's face softened. "I understand that. I truly do. Would it help at all if I told you I think Leo is being stubborn?"

"No. He has his reasons to be stubborn. Please, if he's against this, let me know. I'll finish my work here and I'll go. I owe that much to him."

"He's agreed. And he's agreed to my choice of Dom." It was said with the slightest tightness to his tone. Shelley had to wonder exactly what had happened. "Everything is in place for you. Leo will be fine. He's excellent at seeing other people's issues, and not so good at seeing his own. But he is dear to me. I can't force him to do something he doesn't want to. I know he will never believe me, but I truly selected this Dom because I think he's what you need. And I believe you will be good for Master Wolf. He's different."

"All right," Shelley said, her mind made up. She would meet Wolf. She was intrigued by the man. He'd seemed smart and funny and sweet over the phone. A bit like Leo. She would be grateful for all of the amazing gifts Leo had given her. She loved him. Loved him deep and true and forever. She would go to her grave with Leo Meyer on her mind, but she wasn't the right woman for him. Maybe Julian was right. It would be good to bring some joy to someone. "I'm looking forward to finally meeting him in person, Sir."

Julian smiled, an uptick of his lips. "Excellent, because he's ready to meet you. Please find something appropriate to wear. The jeans and paint-splattered T-shirt are fine for working on the condo, but I expect your new Master will want something a bit more feminine."

Shelley looked down at her clothes. She'd brought a tote bag with her best slacks and a pretty silk shirt. It was professional with a hint of sex appeal. She hoped it hadn't wrinkled. She'd spent the day with the painters working on the mural for the baby's room before the furniture had arrived. She must look horrible, and she didn't have much time.

"Stop panicking," Dani said, hoisting herself up. Julian and Finn both hurried to give her a hand. "Guys, I don't need a crane to get me out of a chair. Not yet."

"Danielle, you will allow your husbands to help you." There was no mistaking the command in Julian's voice.

Dani softened, letting her men help her from the chair. She went up on her tiptoes and kissed Julian. "Yes, Julian." She turned to Shelley. "Come on. We'll get you all gorgeous for Master Wolf. I'll dress you up since I can't dress myself up anymore. I have a ton of beautiful clothes I can't wear since none of them were made for a woman who swallowed a watermelon."

"That's ten, Danielle. I can spank you without harming our baby," Julian promised.

"He's been practicing," Finn said with a smile. "After this, he can write a book. *The Dom's Guide to Maternal Discipline* or *Getting Your Freak on With Child*."

Julian sighed. "Your sarcasm grows by the day." He sank a hand in Finn's hair before kissing his partner. It was a sweet kiss of deep longing. When Julian let Finn go, he stared down. "Sex on a stick? Really? Holy hotness?"

Finn grinned. "It was all a lie, Master. I didn't want Shelley to know the new Dom was hideously unattractive."

Julian laughed, ruffling a hand through Finn's hair. "You keep it that way, Finn. Go on, ladies. Finn and I will have a drink while we wait. I'll walk you down, Shelley. Master Wolf would like to go over the full contract before you both sign."

She was going to sign a contract with a man. A contract that detailed all the things he could do to her. It was weird but exciting. She was starting a new chapter in her life.

The Shelley chapter. She followed Dani. There was no way she started her new life in a dirty T-shirt and jeans. She would walk into it with her head held high and hope in her heart.

And her love for Leo would always be there, but in the background. She would go on. She would find someone who needed her.

These were her baby steps, and she would take as many as she had to until she found her peace.

* * * *

Senator Mitchell Cross stared at the man in front of him. He was a fit man, though Cross doubted he'd perfected his physique in anything so tame as a gym. His eyes were a cold, flinty gray, his hair cut in a precise military style. He wore simple, generic clothes, khaki pants and a T-shirt, well-worn boots. It was easy to picture him in fatigues. Steve Holder looked exactly like what he was. A mercenary.

Of course, he was a mercenary with several government contracts that could blow up in all of their faces. Holder's danger potential went far beyond his ability to kill a man.

"You say you know this guy?" Cross slid a picture across the desk toward the soldier of fortune. And fortunate he was. Holder was a millionaire because of under-the-table deals he'd made with Cross himself. He had a lot to lose, too. It was precisely why Cross had called the man in.

Holder stared down, his expression closed off. He had a long scar running down his face beginning at the side of his left eye and running down to his chin. Cross wouldn't like to know what had happened to whoever had given him that scar. "I served with Lieutenant Leo Meyer for about two years. He was in my SEAL unit."

Before Holder had stopped serving his country and started serving himself. Cross couldn't blame the man. The Navy paid shit. So did the Senate. His yearly salary barely paid for his wife's cocaine habit, much less for his mistress. And his investments were drying up. Old money wasn't what it used to be. He'd had to set up a network of lobbyist money and selling favors to men like Holder in order to keep up a proper standard of living.

Shelley McNamara Hughes could bring down his entire house of cards.

"Were you close to him?" Units like the SEALs tended to forge strong bonds between the men who served in them.

Holder shoved the picture back toward him. "As much as I got close to anyone. But we weren't on the same squad. We were in the same platoon, but sure, I knew him. He was younger than me, but he was a solid sniper. I heard he went back to school after he left. That didn't surprise me. Meyer was a do-gooder. He was one of those true believers. He was obnoxious, but he didn't know I couldn't stand him. There was an incident with a translator in Afghanistan. He left the unit after that."

"Really?" Maybe there was something he could use against this guy. It would be easier if Meyer was dirty.

"A girl he was fucking got killed. She worked as a translator in the area. It wasn't smart to get involved with the locals, but that didn't seem to bother Meyer." Holder sat back in the wing chair. He could have been talking about the weather for all the emotion in his voice. "She was butchered. He found the body."

Cross was interested in that. "Did he kill her?"

Holder shrugged. "Who knows? The Navy didn't think so. Look, it was fucking Afghanistan. Do you know what the locals do to a woman they decide is a whore? They can still legally stone a woman in that part of the world. She could have been killed because some Taliban freak caught her with a man who wasn't her husband or because they didn't like her working for the Americans or because she looked at someone wrong. Who the fuck knows what those people think? The Navy cleared Meyer, but he wasn't the same, and when his time was up, he left. I lost track of him."

"He wasn't someone you tried to recruit?" Cross had heard that Holder and his company liked to recruit as many Special Forces soldiers as possible.

Holder waved him off. "Nah. He left. He went back to school. He wasn't a viable candidate, though I hear his brother recently got his walking papers and he didn't want to leave. I haven't talked to him personally, but I've been following him. The last I heard Wolf Meyer was still trying to get back in. He would be an excellent addition, but his brother makes me nervous. So does the fact that he's here in Dallas. There's a whole group of ex-military here in Dallas I don't like to mess with. What does Leo Meyer have to do with the fact that you let some asshole bug your office?"

He hated the superior way Holder looked at him. But it was the truth. Fucking Bryce Hughes had been a blackmailing son of a bitch. Bryce Hughes was the reason Cross was in this position. He'd been a discreet drug dealer. Bryce had been smooth, friendly to work with. He'd given the senator a good deal and even offered his lovely wife's design services.

Which was exactly how he'd gotten caught on tape fucking his mistress on his senatorial desk. It wasn't that particular episode that worried him. It was the fact that he'd made a deal with White Acres Security that effectively sold out US interests in the Middle East.

"I don't need your sarcasm, Holder. You're involved in this, too."

The tape in which he proved he had problems with premature ejaculation would only get him voted out of office at the midterm election. The second tape, if it existed, could get him brought up on treason charges.

"I wasn't the one who was friendly with a blackmailer. I thought the fucker died."

It was good to know the mercenary kept up with the news. "Oh, he's dead. Hughes owed a Colombian cartel some cash, and they don't give extensions. Fortunately, he'd hidden a lot of his blackmail tapes."

"How do you know he hid them?" Holder asked.

"Because if the cops had those fucking tapes, we would both be in jail." Cross took a deep breath. "Look, I can't be sure the tape even exists. I only know that we had a few meetings during the same time that Hughes was bugging this office."

He had to find that fucking tape, and only Shelley Hughes could give it to him. Despite the fact that the cops had cleared her of her husband's wrongdoing, Cross had to make sure she didn't know about the White Acres deal. He had to.

And it looked like Leo Meyer might be involved.

Holder's expression didn't change a whit. "Where does Meyer fit into all this?"

"Leo Meyer is employed by a man named Julian Lodge. Lodge runs a business that caters to men and women with certain proclivities." Cross tried to put it delicately.

Holder's eyes flared. "What? He's a pimp? Meyer runs girls? Are you fucking kidding me?"

"No. It's a BDSM club."

Holder sat back. "Bondage and shit. Yeah, I can see that. What does he do? Spank women for a living?"

Cross didn't know and wouldn't give a shit if Meyer didn't figure into Shelley Hughes's life. "No idea. I have some friends who are members. They say Leo Meyer is the big guy at The Club. According to my sources, Shelley Hughes is working for Julian Lodge and has a past with Meyer."

"So you want me to look my old buddy up and see what I can find out. I can do that. But, Senator, the next time you treat me like your fucking lackey, I'll show up at your bedside with a knife to your throat, and no amount of security will keep me out. Don't think for a minute that I'm your employee." Holder stood up, his ridiculously intimidating six-feet-five-inch body towering over Cross.

He swallowed and then nodded. Fuck, he hated this shit. He never should have taken the Armed Services committee post. He should have gone for the cushy Veterans' Affairs job. Then all the soldiers he would have to deal with would be old fuckers in wheelchairs and sad sacks who had gotten their limbs blown off for their country. But, no, he wanted the big job. He forced himself to stay strong. After all, he was the elected official here. He wasn't without power. "I understand. This is for both of us. We're both at risk here."

Holder put two hands on the desk and leaned forward, the scar on his face whitening as his expression tightened. "Yeah, well, I'm not the dipshit who invited the blackmailer's wife to decorate my office. Now what's the name of this club?"

"The Club." There wasn't a website or a listing in the phone book, but he had an address.

Holder stared at him for a moment. "Seriously? That's the dumbest name I ever heard."

"Lodge believes in simplicity."

Holder straightened up with a derisive snort. "He sounds like an idiot."

"He's a rich idiot with a lot of important connections. Meyer has a listed phone number, and I e-mailed you the address of the building The Club is in. I'm going to go to The Club with a colleague of mine in a couple of days. If you can gather whatever intel you can on what Shelley Hughes is doing in that club, what her relationship is with

Meyer, and where she's living, I would be grateful."

Holder nodded, turning without saying another word. He crossed the office in a few neat strides and opened the door. The door closed behind him, and Mitchell Cross could breathe again. His brain ached and his stomach was in fucking knots. He hadn't gotten into politics so he would have to deal with the trash of the world. Yet here he was.

And now he had to basically go undercover in a BDSM club. *Fuck. Fuck. Fucking fuck.* He was supposed to be relaxing, but he had to play bondage games because apparently his former drug dealer's widow was some kind of a pervert freak.

He put his head in his hands. If he survived this crisis, he was going to get clean.

But until then…he opened his drawer and found his small stash of cocaine. Until then, he really needed some relief.

Chapter Three

"Have you looked over the contract, dear?" Julian asked as he pressed the buttons that would take them to the club level of the building. Julian owned the entire downtown property, and Shelley had decided weeks ago that it was something like his own private kingdom. Everything Julian could want was in this building. His offices were here. His club was here. He had designated several floors as a luxury hotel for his friends and guests. She'd learned several of his employees also lived in the building. Leo was on the sixteenth floor, below the penthouse. He shared the floor with the brothers, Ben and Chase Dawson, and two part-time Doms named Brandon and Dane.

But they were going to the club section.

To meet her Dom.

"Yes. I read the contract before I signed it." She'd stared at that three-page document for days. She'd read *Anna Karenina* in less time than it had taken her to finally get through the contract that would bind her to a man she didn't know.

"Well, Master Wolf will now want to go over your hard and soft limits. Danielle explained those?" Julian's voice was soft, his eyes on the numbers overhead, watching as they descended.

He was treating her with kid gloves. She rather thought it was a sign of affection. Julian could be terribly cold when he wasn't involved. He'd terrified her at first until she'd become close to his wife and his partner. They softened him. "I understand. I'm still probably going to giggle when he asks me about butt plugs."

Julian turned down to her, his face lighting with a smile. "See, I knew I had chosen well. Many Doms would be insulted, but I believe Master Wolf will laugh along with you."

"He seems nice."

"He reminds me of an overly large Golden Retriever," Julian mused. "I'm actually a bit worried he won't be strong enough to truly discipline you, but I have a friend who claims he's the perfect mix of Dom and mentor."

"Why doesn't he have a sub?" He sounded too good to be true.

"He recently left his post in the military. It wasn't his choice, as I understand. He was injured in the line of duty. He's struggled a bit with that. I suspect he hadn't thought about his future past his military career. He returned to Colorado and found a job, but when I offered him a position here, he jumped at the chance. I think he's looking for his place in the world."

Then they were well matched. Despite her longing for Leo, she felt a spark of hope. Julian had put some thought into this. "And he's going to be working for you, too?"

A sly smile crossed his face. "Yes. I got to him before Taggart did. I happen to know that Taggart was planning on sending Wolf's old CO to talk to him in a few weeks. Apparently the man now works for Sean Taggart at his new restaurant. Anyway, Eric Vail was set to call Wolf and convince him to interview with Taggart, though the bastard knew he would hire him. Joke's on him."

"I thought Taggart worked for you." She'd heard the name of the security company. A nice man named Jesse had come out to ensure that her design choice to move the lighting fixtures around hadn't disrupted the electrical input to the security monitors. They apparently were on some super high-end grid that switched to a backup if someone cut the power to the system.

"He does, but over the years he's less and less an employee and more of a rival in ways," Julian allowed. "Like Jack Barnes, I saw something in the man. When his start-up company needed funding, I stepped in. When he had a bit of cash, I brought him into my investment group. I like a man who knows who he is and what he wants. I also like a man who takes care of the people around him. Taggart is very much like that. But I will admit that it's always fun to get one over on him. I also believe Wolf will be much better off being close to his brother. Those McKay-Taggart employees are always jetting off to exotic parts of the world. More so now that Taggart married. Remarried. I don't know. It's a quandary with him. I had to figure out what the proper gift is when the bride has been dead for five years but came back. Does one purchase wood, as one would for a fifth-year anniversary gift? Or perhaps a case of Valium, because the bride will likely need it. In the end I went with a lovely set of paddles. Wood and kink. It worked, I think."

She had to laugh at the thought of Julian worrying about the perfect gift for his friend's wedding. And she realized something. "I'm ready."

"Are you truly?"

She nodded. "I am."

The doors opened, and Julian gestured for her to enter in front of him. "I'm glad. I've set you up in one of the offices. There's a two-way mirror. I'll be watching the whole time."

"Why?" Shelley asked, a bit disturbed at the thought.

"Because Wolf is new to me, and I take your safety and happiness seriously. You've been a good friend to my wife. I admire your brother. Trevor's years at The Club made me very fond of him, and quite frankly, Leo is part of my family. Despite his stubbornness, I know he wouldn't want you hurt."

Because he was a good man. "And I wouldn't want him hurt, either."

Julian stopped in front of a door. He'd given her a tour of the facilities weeks back when he'd decided to let her redecorate the entire building. She knew that if she turned left, she would be in the hallway that led to The Club. Here in this part of the building, the floor was a very elegant marble, but down the hall it gave way to a decadent rich, burgundy carpet that her shoes sunk into. She'd wondered what it would have felt like on her bare feet. Of course that was only the lounge area of The Club. The dungeon floor itself was covered in rich hardwoods that would be cool against bare feet and knees.

If she agreed to sub for Master Wolf, she might know. Some Masters wouldn't let their submissives wear shoes.

"If you think you would like to try to get through to Leo, perhaps you shouldn't walk through that door, dear."

She shook her head. "No. Julian, do you honestly think I haven't tried? I broke trust with him. I lied to him. I had what felt like a good reason, but it doesn't matter now. He can't forgive me, and I need to move on."

"Trust is important. It's everything in a relationship like this, but if there's enough love, sometimes a breach of trust can be overcome. I would have told you that I would dismiss any submissive who broke trust with me. It changes when you truly, deeply love the person. I doubt I could dismiss Danielle and Finn for any reason. I could make their lives miserable, but I couldn't let them go."

Her heart ached, but she was resolute. "Then there's your answer. He let me go. It's all right. I knew what would happen. I knew I was giving him up. But I have to find my own place in this world, and I think it starts by meeting Master Wolf."

Julian opened the door. "Know that I'll be watching. If you need anything, you have only to ask."

Her heart raced as she stared through that open door. She could see the long conference table and the back of a man sitting at the end. His shoulders rose above the chair, dark hair cut in a neat military style. He was a big man. His shoulders looked like they went on for miles.

Doubt crept in. Did she want to place her body and her safety in the hands of such a large man? Bryce hadn't been big, but the one time he'd hit her, she'd felt it. She'd been smaller than him, and he'd used it to his advantage. How much worse could it potentially be with a man this big?

And then he turned. And her jaw dropped open.

Master Wolf was absolutely the most glorious-looking man she'd ever seen in her life. She prayed, prayed she wasn't actually drooling. Dani was right. Finn was right. Holy hotness.

"Hello. It's nice to finally meet you in person." He stood, his huge body graceful as he moved. He had to be six and a half feet tall.

47

He was dressed in jeans and a T-shirt that couldn't quite hide the tight muscles of his torso. He really worked out. Like a lot.

God, she felt like she was thirteen and staring at a rock star. She managed to get out a breathy "Hi."

He smiled, and his hotness went up twenty degrees. That was a movie-star smile right there. Even, white teeth gleamed from between his impossibly sensual lips.

She was supposed to sub for this man? She was ten pounds overweight. She had cellulite on her thighs. Her eyes were starting to get fine lines around them. She was a normal, average woman, and he was a Greek god.

"I'm Wolf," he said, holding out a hand.

She held out her own, and he took it in his. His big palms embraced her, making her feel small and delicate. She was enveloped in heat. "Shelley."

"It's good to meet you, Shelley. You're more beautiful than I was told."

And this was ridiculous. "And you're so far out of my league, it's silly." She turned to the large, rectangular window that dominated the far wall. "Are you kidding me, Julian? Seriously? Do you see him? He's...oh, my god. I couldn't handle Leo, and you think I can handle him?"

She slipped her hand out of his. He was too much. There was no way she could do this. She'd thought she could ease into the lifestyle, but Master Wolf was more like jumping off a cliff into the deepest part of the ocean. She'd hoped for someone like Julian. Julian was a gorgeous man, but somehow she saw him as a kindly mentor, not a potential lover. Master Wolf was an orgasm on two incredibly sculpted legs. She was already thinking about kissing him. There was no way she could hold herself apart, and there was damn straight no way she would ever be able to keep him. He would break her heart, just like Leo.

God, he reminded her of Leo.

"Sit down."

His previous relaxed manner utterly disappeared. She turned to him, his body seeming to grow larger in front of her eyes. His smile was gone, and in its place was a steely gaze and a frown that had her eyes sliding away from him.

Yep. He was a Dom, and she was responding to him.

"I said sit down. You may sit or you can walk out the door. Those are your choices, and you should make up your mind in a hurry. I drove all night to make this meeting. If you're going to walk out, I would prefer you did it now so I can get some sleep."

The words came out in a staccato barrage, but there was a current underneath them that she detected.

He'd driven all night? She certainly would have waited until tomorrow. "I wasn't going anywhere. You could have rescheduled the meeting."

His mouth was a flat line. "I didn't want to. I wanted to be here. I wanted to meet you. Now I'm not so sure. When Julian described you, he talked about your sweetness and your vulnerability. He didn't mention what an egregious brat you are. Do you have a checklist for the Dom you require? Will you dismiss every one he finds for you until you get exactly what you want?"

"Isn't this supposed to be about finding what I want?" Shelley asked, but the tone of his voice was sinking in.

"It is supposed to be about exploring the lifestyle. I can plainly see we have two different visions of how this works." He sat down, slumping into his chair and running a hand through his hair. He took a deep breath and rubbed a place on his forehead. When he finally looked back at her, she could see the weariness in his eyes. "You may leave. I'll explain to Julian that you would prefer someone else."

He closed his eyes again, obviously dismissing her. It hurt, but he'd been a bit kinder to her than she'd been to him.

"He knows. He's watching." And Julian was probably horrified at the way she'd reacted. She'd been exactly what Wolf had said. A brat who saw what she wanted to see. She'd seen a gorgeous body, and not once had she thought about the man inside it. She'd never considered his feelings, as though no one who looked like that could possibly have feelings.

"Well, naturally. I'm sure he's not the only one." His mouth turned down, and a grimace came over him.

"Are you all right?" She should probably leave, run away and tend her wounds. She wouldn't try this again. She couldn't handle it.

But she didn't want to leave him like this.

"I'll be fine. It's the start of a headache. If I handle it now, it won't turn into a full-blown migraine." Wolf ground the words out. "If you don't mind, turn off the lights as you leave."

She got up and turned off the front light, bringing the brightness down. A single line of illumination was left, and she stared for a moment at the man who could have been her Dom. He was only a man with all the troubles that went with being a man. She was tired of being afraid. She wanted to find the woman she'd been before Bryce, and that Shelley would never have treated anyone the way she had.

She walked behind his chair. "Let me."

She touched his scalp, running her fingers all along it with a firm pressure. She ran her hands across his skin, feeling the silkiness of his pitch-black hair and a raised, puckered scar that wove across his head. "Is this okay?"

"Took some fire a while back on an op."

The scar felt somewhat new, probably not more than a few months old. "It feels bad."

"No, love, it feels really good." He groaned and gave over to her. His shoulders relaxed and a deep sigh rumbled through him. "The wound, on the other hand, was really bad. They had to crack my skull open. In the field. It wasn't a pleasant experience. Luckily, I don't remember a lot of it. They say I never will, and I'm okay with that. I woke up at Ramstein and was told I would live, then some bureaucratic asshole handed me my walking papers."

Her heart went out to him. "Did you like the Army?"

"The Army sucks." He chuckled. "I was Navy."

Again, exactly like Leo. But this man wasn't Leo Meyer. Leo would never have allowed her to comfort him like this. Leo was always strong. Wolf seemed sweeter, the tiniest bit lost. "Did you like it?"

Leo had left the Navy on his own, and when she'd asked about it, he would always turn the conversation to something else.

"I loved it. I guess I'm still having a hard time reconciling myself with the fact that my career is over."

She took a deep breath. God, she knew how that felt. She ran her hands to his temples and rubbed, feeling a deep connection to this man who had terrified her. Men were just men, even the beautiful ones. His good looks hadn't spared him from heartache, hadn't ensured that his life had turned out perfectly.

"So they dumped you because you got injured?"

He groaned again as she rubbed the top of his head. "Right there, love. Yeah. That's it. I can't tell you how good that feels. Yes, that's what the Navy does. I was no longer useful. In addition to my head injuries, they had to put a titanium rod in my leg. I can't make it through a metal detector. That makes me useless in undercover work. I wasn't cut out for a desk job, so I went home and then came here."

And then a bratty sub had given him more hell. God, would she ever stop screwing up? "If you wouldn't mind, I'd like to start this meeting over again, Sir."

He would probably toss her out, but at least she would have tried. "I don't know that that's such a good idea. I might be a dumb grunt, but I can put two and two together. Leo mentioned he'd been friends with you. It was more, wasn't it?"

"Sort of," she said, confused. Why did he care about the fact that she'd been involved with Leo? "We didn't have an affair or anything. I was married. He helped my brother, Trev. My brother spent a couple of years here in this club after he lost his career."

"Julian," Wolf called out, never once opening his eyes. "Did you bother to tell her anything? You knew I spent the last couple of months working with Trev. You didn't mention that to her? You really are a manipulative bastard."

He knew her brother? Wolf had mentioned he was in Colorado, but not that he'd been in Bliss.

The intercom came on, and Julian's voice came over. "Or perhaps I am simply smarter than everyone else. Make your decision, Wolf. If you won't do it, I'll have to find someone else for her."

His eyes came open, and his hands came up to cover hers. "It's up to her, but she should know."

"Know what?"

"Well, at least you should know my last name. I don't suppose Julian told you that."

"What's your last name?" But she had a sneaking suspicion.

"Meyer. Leo is my brother. I know yours. He bought into the

ranch I was working at before I came here. He's a good man."

Yes. He was a good man. A much better man for having known Leo Meyer. Wolf turned his chair around and took her hands in both of his, warmth enveloping her. Now she could really see it. Wolf was different than his brother, but the similarities were unmistakable. It was there in the long, cut line of his jaw, the cheekbones any male model would kill for, the beauty of his eyes.

But this man seemed more...vulnerable than Leo. Much more open. He obviously needed something, someone, where Leo was a citadel. Leo Meyer was a castle with fortified battlements. Wolf had let down his drawbridge.

"And Leo knows?" She was certain of that. If Leo had wanted to block this, he would have.

Wolf nodded.

Leo Meyer had brought her brother back to life. He'd shown her a world outside the narrow confines of her small town and a bad marriage. She'd burned him. She hadn't meant to, but she had, and it couldn't work between them now. She owed him so much.

What if she could help his brother? If Leo didn't care, why should she turn Wolf down?

Especially when she was so intrigued.

"Okay. What do we do now, Sir? If you'll forgive me for my tantrum from before."

A slow, ridiculously sexy smile crossed his face. "With hands like yours, sweetheart, I think I can forgive a lot. Now sit down and let's go over a few things."

Her heart actually fluttered in her chest. It occurred to her for the briefest of moments that this was still a horrible idea. He was too gorgeous. He was Leo's brother.

But Leo had basically thrown her his way. Wolf himself had told her that Leo was perfectly okay with the scenario. If he didn't have a problem, why should she? Perhaps this was actually what Leo wanted for her. Leo could be every bit as manipulative as Julian.

But in the end, it all came down to one thing and one thing only. Was she ready to move on?

Shelley took a seat across from Wolf. "I'm ready, Sir."

* * * *

Fuck it all, she was gorgeous. He had no idea what his brother was thinking allowing this woman to get away, but Wolf wasn't going to make the same mistake. No one had bothered to tell him that the woman his brother had been involved with was the same woman he would be topping. No. No one had thought that was at all important until Leo had made his announcement. Julian had allowed him to fall half in love with a woman who had been involved with Leo.

Julian Lodge was definitely a manipulative bastard, but he wasn't willing to walk away from her. Leo had said it hadn't worked out, that they had only been friends. Wolf wasn't sure he bought that, but it got him thinking. Maybe he could be just as manipulative as Julian Lodge.

"Do you understand the basic contract?" Wolf asked as his brain replayed the last few minutes. He started to go over it, but all he could think about was the fact that she was still here.

He'd been sure she was going to leave. And he would have let her. He wasn't going to force himself on someone, but he wanted her. Hell, he'd wanted her from the first time Julian had described her.

Lovely. Sweet. Submissive. Smart and sassy. The other three didn't work for him without the smart and sassy. He didn't want a slave. He wanted a partner, a lover.

And according to Julian Lodge, Shelley McNamara needed a lover, too.

"What does this mean?" Shelley asked, pointing to a paragraph that described high protocol.

He wasn't about to make her speak only when spoken to. He drew a line through that. "It's not something we need to worry about right now. We'll come up with our own protocol. I want you to be able to ask questions and tell me how you're feeling. I only ask that when we're in public, you treat me with every politeness. You are to call me Sir and attempt to obey me."

She frowned. "In public. So, I have to call you Sir if we're in a restaurant?"

He hid his smile. He liked the fact that she was already thinking of him outside the club setting. He was damn straight thinking of her.

Dating, however, wasn't covered in the contract and never would be. "This contract only covers The Club, sweetheart. It's a training contract. If we decide to see each other outside The Club, I wouldn't expect you to call me Sir. I'm not a twenty-four-seven Dom. I enjoy the lifestyle, and I would love it if you felt comfortable enough to allow me to help you with any problems you might have, but outside of this club, I won't hold you to any rules we don't agree on. The only rule that's not up for discussion is the rule where you call me when you're in actual physical trouble. You read that clause?"

It was an important one for him. If she found herself in danger, there were protocols that involved him. He'd insisted on it.

She nodded. "So the rest of this is only for…for sex stuff."

She couldn't possibly know how that soft Texas twang made his groin tighten. "Not necessarily. It's about pushing your boundaries and discovering discipline."

Her nose wrinkled up. "I don't know how much I like that word."

Yeah, most people didn't, but then they didn't understand what he meant by it. "Then I'll have to change your mind. You see, you hear the word 'discipline' and you think punishment, but I hear it and I have a different definition. Discipline is the art of getting what you want. I wanted to be a Navy SEAL. I didn't enjoy Hell Week. It was the most miserable I've ever been in my life. But it was necessary. We don't get the things we want by allowing life to happen to us. We have to take an active role."

She nodded, and he would have sworn he could see a sheen of tears in her eyes. "Yes, I can see that. I allowed things to happen for years. It seems odd to hear a Dom saying that. I don't know. I guess I would think you want me to be submissive."

Another common misconception he was happy to clear up. "You *are* submissive. I can see it. Julian can certainly see it. I suspect you've allowed a man who was more dominant than you to walk all over you before. That isn't what a Dom should do. A Dom should be your partner in helping you reach your potential, even if you never have a moment's sexual contact. You understand that, right? And this isn't a one-way street. You'll help me reach my potential, too."

She sniffled slightly, and it took everything he had not to pull her onto his lap and try to soothe her. "You're right about getting walked all over. I should be honest with you. I spent years in a marriage I shouldn't have stayed in because it was easier than dealing with the fallout. I want to be stronger than that. I want to be in control."

"And I can help you."

Julian had mentioned her marriage. It hadn't taken much to look the story up. Bryce Hughes had been a very bad man. He'd run drugs and a blackmailing ring that used his wife to get dirt on politicians. According to everything he'd been able to discover, Shelley had been exonerated. The feds didn't believe she knew anything, but that hadn't stopped them from seizing all of the assets she'd shared with her husband. She'd lost her house, her bank accounts, her reputation.

She needed a steady hand. He would have to put aside his own desires. He really wanted to inhale her. She was exactly the type who flipped his switch, but she needed more than one more man who rubbed his dick on her and gave her nothing in return. She needed someone in control. He could do that.

His dick protested mightily, but he could control that, too.

"So, let's go over your hard and soft limits." Yeah, because talking about all the dirty games he loved would get his libido under control. He should have picked up a woman last night to share with Logan, but taking Logan into a bar had seemed like a bad idea.

And he hadn't been able to stop thinking about Shelley. Even before he'd seen her.

She bit her bottom lip as she looked over the long list he'd handed her. "Uhm, I don't know what some of these are, to tell you the truth."

"What do you have a question about?"

"I understand the bondage part, and I'm fine with that. I'm willing to try all the toys." Her skin flushed. "I'm…I'm curious about spanking."

And he was totally ready to spank her. He'd gotten a glimpse of a round ass before she'd gone on her slightly manic tirade. Her skin was pale. He would have to be careful with her, but he could get that alabaster skin a lovely hot pink in no time at all. And when she was panting and her pussy was dripping wet, he'd find her clit and rub her until she cried out, begging for his cock.

Or he would simply spank her because he'd promised to not take advantage of her.

Maybe *he* was the masochist.

He forced his voice to remain calm and even, so she hopefully wouldn't guess that his cock was pounding against his jeans. "I think you'll enjoy a good spanking. Let's talk about the bondage for a minute, though. You understand I like to practice an elaborate form of bondage called Shibari, correct?"

She smiled, a bright thing. "Trev is obsessed with it. I walked into the barn at Aidan O'Malley's ranch at the wrong time once. My sister-in-law was fully suspended in some insane getup my brother had bound her to. Bo was sitting there reading a book to her. He said she'd been a bad girl, but he didn't want her to be bored so he was reading her one of her favorite romances." She sobered. "Beth is so much stronger now. She's happy. She was perfectly happy in what she called her Bondage Barbie wear. Yes, I'm willing to give it a try."

"Good. One hurdle gone. I prefer not to engage in blood or fire play, but I could find a Master to introduce you to that if you're interested." He'd seen enough blood for a lifetime. He didn't want to cause her to lose a single drop.

She shook her head, a shiver running through her. "No. No blood. I wouldn't even want to watch that. I think that might be a hard limit."

He nodded and handed her a pen to mark it off the list of acceptable play. He'd read that she'd been in the same house when her husband had been shot. Had she seen it? Had she watched it and wondered if she was next? He changed the subject. They would get to all of that later when he'd earned her trust. "No extreme play. But I will bind you to a St. Andrew's Cross, and I will make punishment public if I think it will help."

She would be beautiful, her arms and legs spread, waiting for the crack of his whip.

She smiled, her lips tugging up enigmatically. "We have different definitions of extreme, but I understand. I'll try not to earn any public punishment." Her eyes worked down the page. "What is this? What do they mean by scat games? Please tell me that has something to do with jazz."

He laughed out loud and marked that as a hard limit. "Not at all, sweetheart. That's exactly what it sounds like, and neither one of us is going to engage in that. Doms have hard limits, too."

She breathed a sigh of relief. "And puppy play? Pony play?"

He was going to have to convince her of that. "It's role playing, sweetheart."

She shook her head. "I don't think I want that."

And it was his job to make her change her mind because he definitely wanted to play with her. "Let me give you a scenario. It's nothing more than a game where you're my soft, sweet pet. You eat from my hand, treats I'll have to reward you for good behavior. You'll sit at my feet. If I decide you're a good puppy, I'll pull you up on my lap and lavish you with affection. And everyone loves a good puppy. Everyone would want to pet you. All those hands, rubbing across your body. Under the watchful gaze of your Master, of course. But a good Master knows a puppy needs love."

"You're evil," she said with a grin, but he could see her flush had changed from embarrassment to arousal. She was starved for affection. Puppy play was an easy way to get many hands on her without having to share her in a sexual way. He wasn't sure he could do that. Not with strangers.

He'd spent too much freaking time in Bliss.

"That's my job, sweetheart. Let's give it a try. There is nothing you can't stop. I know I'm the Dom, but you're in control."

She put a hand to her mouth and laughed. "Yes. Oh my god, I agreed to be a puppy."

"Yes, you did, but that's a little down the road." He would ease her into rougher play. "For tonight, we'll watch and see what intrigues you. Let's talk about contact. At this stage, I think it's best if we agree to no intercourse, but I would like the opportunity to touch you, to bring you to orgasm, to teach you pleasure."

Her face turned bright red, and he was worried for a moment that he'd pushed too far, but it was important. He wouldn't take anything for himself, but he needed to teach her to equate chosen submission with pleasure.

"Yes."

"Excellent." It was a good first step. He couldn't wait to get started. "Then we'll start tonight. We'll go to The Club and we'll play it by ear. No pressure. We're going to have a nice meal and then watch some scenes and talk. I'll have clothes sent to your room."

"I have a townhouse," she said. "I decided to go for broke and move up here. Dallas is going to be my home from now on."

That worked for him. Dallas was going to be his home if he could make things work. He was ready to settle down. Roots. A man needed roots. He'd spent most of his adult life jetting around the world on missions. If that part of his life was over, then he wanted a real home. "Give me the address, and I'll pick you up. Dress casually. I'll have clothes waiting for you in The Club's locker room."

Her hand came up in a flighty wave. "Oh, I can take the train. No problem."

He stared at her.

"Or you could pick me up," she said quickly.

Excellent. She was learning.

"And you will wear the clothes I select for you." It wasn't a question.

"Yes."

"Then I will see you at eight this evening."

And then the real fun would begin.

Chapter Four

Leo tried to let the tranquil sound of his wall fountain soothe him, but for once it was failing.

His stomach was in knots. He'd stood behind that glass with his rat fink bastard boss/ex-friend and watched as his brother made a visible connection to Shelley. There had been that one glorious moment when she'd tried to dismiss Wolf. Leo had found himself unaccountably happy until he realized she was threatening to not accept him because Wolf was so damn attractive.

Awesome. Great. She was drooling over his brother.

And then he'd actually looked at Wolf.

Fuck it all. His brother was lonely, and Leo hadn't exactly welcomed him home.

"Uhm, is this part of the therapy? Like the quiet game?"

And he'd nearly forgotten Logan Green was sitting across from him. He was losing it. He turned to the young man in front of him. Logan Green, according to his file, was twenty-four years old. His eyes made him look older.

Older. Leo was five years older than Wolf. Maybe she liked younger men. Now that he thought about it, Wolf was closer to her age. They probably had more in common.

Logan shifted in his seat and cleared his throat.

Damn it. He had to get his head in the game and off the way Shelley had stared at his brother's chest. "Why are you here?"

Logan's eyes rolled, the fallback gesture of the young and sarcastic. "Uh, because I'm twenty shades of fucked up and everyone's sick of dealing with my shit."

Leo sat forward. He wouldn't take a ton of crap off of anyone. He stared at the young man, letting the silence go for longer than was comfortable. He tried to put Shelley out of his mind. After all, he would have to deal with her tonight. When she walked into The Club. With his brother. "It's plain to see that you're fucked up. I was referring to the inciting incident. I take it you've been going downhill for a while. You've been in how many bar fights in the last year?"

"A couple," he muttered.

Logan obviously wasn't going to simply admit to his problems. Well, it had been a while since he'd had a real challenge. "According to a man named Nathan Wright—I believe he's the sheriff you work for—it's more like five. And one of them caused serious damage to the bar. Almost ten thousand dollars' worth."

"I paid for that," he said, sitting up and pointing as though he'd been accused of something.

Leo wasn't accusing, merely stating the facts. It was best to get everything out on the table, but it did bring up an interesting point, one many of Logan's friends had voiced concern about. When Leo had talked to a few of the people worried for the young man, they had wondered about the incident. "Did you? How does a sheriff's deputy come up with ten grand?"

His eyes slid away. "I have a friend. He fronted me the cash."

And Leo could plainly see Logan didn't like that, but Leo bought that the kid was telling the truth. "That was months ago. You didn't seek help then. You continued on your way. What made you decide to come to Dallas now?"

Logan's arms crossed over his massive chest.

Minutes went by. Leo sat and waited. There was no use in pushing a patient to say something he wasn't ready to say. Besides, he'd discovered long ago that silence bothered most people. They were willing to fill the void with anything, even truths they didn't want to admit.

Of course, the silence was bugging his ass now because every second that Logan didn't speak had him going over and over what had happened between Shelley and Wolf.

Had she gone completely insane? Wolf wasn't *that* attractive. He was fine. Wolf wasn't unattractive. He was maybe above average. But it wasn't like he himself was chopped liver. He worked out. Probably way harder than Wolf. Wolf looked like he'd lifted one too many weights. Who the hell was that muscular?

Flexible. Leo was flexible. In many ways. Well, not many now that he thought about it. Physically he was flexible, but god, his life had become one rigid regime of working out, working with his patients, and walking the dungeon halls at night, never truly joining in. He'd given up on meditation. Meditation always brought about images of Shelley McNamara Hughes and her beautiful face laughing up at him as he took her hand.

Fuck. When was the kid going to break?

"I shot someone."

Thank god. He could get back to someone else's tortured soul. "Are you talking about the incident at the Movie Motel?"

Logan nodded shortly. "Yeah."

Interesting. Logan's face was blank, but guilt seemed to hang on him like a cloud. "That was in the line of duty. You were protecting your town."

He shrugged. "The dude died. He deserved to die. He was a paid assassin. He was willing to kill anyone to get to his target."

But Leo could see plainly that there was more to this. "Lots of police personnel need treatment after they kill someone in the line of duty. It's nothing to be ashamed of. Military, police, anyone working in a high-stress job, especially one protecting the public, needs routine therapy in my opinion. And yet the very personalities that make them excellent protectors make them reticent to seek the therapy that would make their lives better."

Logan laughed, a bitter huff that came out of his chest. "I'm not some born protector, Doc. God, that's a laugh. You know why I applied for the deputy job? Because there wasn't any other place I wanted to work, and it seemed like an easy way to make some money for college. Not that I really wanted to go to college. I never wanted to leave Bliss, but I sure as hell didn't want to work for Stella. She scares the crap out of me. And I don't know anything about cars so

Long-Haired Roger was out. The very idea of working for my moms. God. I love them. I do, but no. When Rye Harper told me he was looking for a deputy, I jumped at the chance. Man, I took it because I could nap and I got a county vehicle. I'm not some fucking hero."

That wasn't what his file said. His file stated clearly that Logan Green had performed valiantly in the line of duty. And he'd sacrificed. "Why didn't you quit after you were held hostage by the Russian mafia?"

That was the crux of the problem. A year before, Logan had been taken captive and tortured by a member of the Russian mafia. He'd been sacrificed to save two women. He'd gone with his captor and kept his mouth shut about Alexei Markov's true intent. He'd been tortured for hours. He'd barely made it out alive.

And, according to his loved ones, the sweet young man he'd been had died that day. It was Leo's job to see if he could bring that man back to life.

"I don't talk about that."

The wall had come up. Too soon. If Logan wouldn't talk about the incident, then he would veer it back to what the young man seemed willing to talk about. "This wasn't the first time you've been in a dangerous situation. What was it about this time that caused so much anxiety?"

"I killed a man." Logan shifted again.

He wasn't buying it. "Is that what sent you over the edge?"

Logan shook his head, his face flushing. "No. That man deserved it. He was willing to kill a friend of mine and the town doc, the man who stitched me back together."

"Then what's wrong?" There was definitely something here other than simple anxiety disorder.

"I thought about not shooting him at all."

Leo felt his brows raise. "Because you didn't want to hurt someone."

A hard chuckle came from Logan's mouth, a sound that didn't begin to resemble humor. "Because I thought he might actually get Alexei Markov, and for a couple of minutes, I was okay with that."

Now they were getting somewhere. "Markov was the man involved with the mob? He was there when you were beaten?"

Logan's eyes came up, and there was a blankness that Leo had seen before in men and women who had survived unimaginable things. Sometimes he saw that look in Shelley's eyes. "Markov fed me to them to give himself time."

"I can see where you would want revenge," Leo allowed.

"But that wasn't what really got me, Doc."

Leo was silent, allowing Logan to come to his own decision to speak.

"What scared the crap out of me was the fact that when I shot that asshole, I liked it."

Yes, that was the heart of the problem. And it was definitely something they needed to work on. He sat back and sighed. "It's a good thing to admit that."

"Really? It's a good thing to admit that I'm some kind of a freaky killer?"

Leo shook his head. "No. We have to talk about these things so these feelings and impulses have no power over us. We learn to control them. My brother and I served in the Navy. We both saw heavy action. Do you honestly believe I never high-fived after I sniped a target? That my heart didn't race and I didn't find some sense of satisfaction in killing the man I was charged with taking out? I did. Wolf did. I'm sure your boss has. It's not having the feeling that creates the problem. It's giving in to it. We can talk about this. And we'll begin working on your impulse control and your trust issues."

"I don't have trust issues."

Leo laughed.

"I don't," Logan insisted. "Look, if you're looking for some deep, dark secret, you're barking up the wrong tree. I was raised in a loving family. I love my moms. I adore them, and don't you dare tell me that having two lesbians for moms fucked me up."

"I would never say that," he replied, wanting to put that issue to a quick rest. "It wouldn't be true. Having loving parents is important no matter their gender."

Logan leaned forward, his face flushing with obvious emotion. "I loved my town. I still love my town. I trust my friends and my boss. I hate that fucker Markov. If he wasn't around, I would have been fine."

It was obvious the deputy was fooling himself. "Because you didn't have any problems before he came back? That's not what this file says."

"I don't have issues with trust when it comes to anyone but that Russian asshole." Logan practically snarled the words.

"But you do. You have trust issues that run so deep you can no longer function, and it's not Markov who is the problem. You might not trust him, but that's not the core of your issues. Alexei Markov is not the person who broke trust with Logan Green in such a deep way that you can't come back from it on your own."

Logan threw his hands up in obvious disgust. "Who? Oh, great and mighty fucking Oz, who? Tell me because you seem to know so fucking much. You can't even get along with your brother, who's one of the nicest guys I've ever met. You seem to have some problems of your own, but obviously you know what I don't."

He didn't react to the bile. It was common at this stage. "You, Logan. You don't trust yourself anymore. You don't trust your dreams or your hopes. You don't trust the world you built for yourself. We have to get you back to the place where you trust the Logan Green who lives inside you."

Logan stopped, his head going down. His hands were on the arms of the chair, and they tightened before he finally looked up. "How the fuck do I do that, Doc?"

Now he had him. Yes, he could work with Logan Green. "I'm going to show you. We start tonight. I had the staff send a pair of leathers to your room. You'll wear them with boots. A shirt is optional. You're a Dom-in-training. Included with the leathers is a training contract. Please read through it and sign it before we begin."

Leo stood. This session was over, and he was pleased with the results.

Logan stayed where he was, his eyes coming up. "How is spanking women going to make me trust myself?"

This was the part most people didn't get. "There's trust between a Dom and a sub. It has to run deep. The power exchange can be a compelling thing, but there's beauty even in the small exchanges with a submissive. Over time, after training, you'll learn discipline and how to control yourself because you wouldn't ever, ever want to abuse the trust they place in you. And when you reach that place where some lovely, soft woman trusts you with her body, with her life, you'll learn that you're worthy of that trust, and you'll believe in yourself."

Logan stared for a moment, the words seeming to sink in. "Wolf was right. You're not an asshole."

Guilt gnawed at him. "I can be."

"But you know what you're doing."

Leo nodded. "When it comes to this, yes."

Logan shook his hand and walked out of the room, promising to meet Leo at eight.

And Leo was alone with the soothing sound of his fountain.

He wasn't unattractive, damn it. He just wasn't an overgrown freaking male model. What the hell was she thinking?

And why hadn't he known about Wolf's migraines? His brother had looked weary, and Shelley had known exactly what he'd needed.

There was a knock on the door. Excellent. Maybe someone had gone bonkers in the dungeon and needed intense therapy. Yeah, that would help. He opened the door to his office. Kitten stood there, biting her bottom lip, her eyes sliding away from his as though her shoes were suddenly very interesting.

Kitten. The secretary Julian had foisted off on him. Kitten, who barely managed to answer a phone without crying she was so damn shy.

"You have a call, Sir."

"You don't have to call me Sir outside the dungeon, Kitten. My name is Leo." He'd explained it to her before, but she simply continued. She was here because she was Finn's cousin, the only member of his family he still spoke to, and Julian was a sucker.

Note, he hadn't hired Kitten to work for him. No, the bastard had foisted the wretchedly shy girl off on Leo. Still, she was a sweet girl and she'd been through something unimaginable.

"Yes, Sir Leo. You had a call. He knows you. He said he knows you. He could be lying. Kitten doesn't know. Kitten is not good at catching lies. Kitten believed it when the Prince of Nigeria wrote Kitten and wanted this one to trade checks with him. Did you know he was willing to pay millions of dollars to get his money out of the country? Kitten thinks Nigeria must be a dangerous place. Luckily Kitten didn't have any checks to send him. It was a scam. That's what Finn told Kitten. Can you believe it?"

And Kitten had serious self-esteem issues. In the months she'd been at The Club, Leo still hadn't heard her refer to herself in anything but the third person. "Shocking. Now, who called?"

She blinked a couple of times and then the light came into her eyes. "Oh, the phone call. Yes. You had a phone call. His name was Steve Holder."

Leo did a double take. Seriously? Steve "Madman" Holder was calling him? It had been years and years. God, it had been forever since he'd talked to anyone from the Teams. When he'd walked away from the Navy, he'd cut himself off.

A vision of Ada assaulted him.

Fuck, there was a reason he'd left it all behind.

"I'll call him later." He turned and walked back to his office. He didn't want to talk to Holder. Holder would bring back a million bad memories, but he did have someone he wanted to talk to. He picked up the phone.

"Hello?"

"Hello, dear," Leo said, his voice filled with warmth for the woman on the other end of the line. Seeing Kitten had made him think of Janine. She was Kitten's therapist, but she'd been much more to Leo. They'd been a horrible married couple, but they turned out to be pretty damn good friends.

"Leo, it's good to hear from you. I was going to call you to let you know Harry and I will be at The Club tonight. I think I have enough of my figure back to feel decent about shoving my body into some PVC. Not so sure about the heels, though. I think pregnancy ruined my feet. How weird is that?" Janine Halloway asked with a laugh. She and her husband had recently had baby number three.

Janine was happy. Without him. Three years of marriage to him had been enough to throw her into the arms of another man.

"Wolf is in town," Leo said.

There was a long pause. "I'll be there early."

The phone clicked, and he looked at the clock. Hours. She wouldn't be early enough.

* * * *

Shelley hopped onto the Blue Line going toward Mockingbird Station, slightly tired after the long, emotional day. It was crowded, the press of bodies reminding her that it was rush hour, but still a nice man offered her his seat. She smiled gratefully and took it, placing her laptop bag at her feet and her purse in her lap. She settled in by the window as the train took off.

Why had she listened to the denizens of Deer Run? Everyone in her tiny hometown had been against her coming to Dallas. She'd heard time and time again that she'd be raped and killed the minute she entered Dallas County. Apparently that was what happened to small-town women who dared to go to the big city. Well, that or she would become a drug-addicted prostitute.

What they didn't say was that she'd gotten herself into trouble in a town like Deer Run, so how the hell would she stay out of it in Dallas?

She loved the city, and she'd almost never had to stand on the train. Dallas was filled with gentlemen. And almost no one knew about her past as the wife of the drug dealer and blackmailer. It had made a small splash in the press when Bryce's blackmailing activities had come to light, but it had quickly been replaced when the next scandal came along.

But sometimes she wondered if it would always follow her around, like a stain that wouldn't go away no matter how many times she washed it.

She sighed and stared out the window. The train stopped at the next station, and there was a general jostling as people got on and got off. A large man stepped in and looked around. He waited as the women on the train moved into the open seats.

She was going home to her small townhouse where she would shower and maybe have a fortifying glass of wine before fixing herself up and heading to The Club. Not on a tour. Not as a designer getting ideas about a space.

As a sub. Wolf's sub.

She smiled as the door closed, and the train jolted forward. Well, she'd been worried that maybe she would never be able to look at another man, but Wolf Meyer had put that thought firmly out of her mind.

Every hormone in her body had lit up and screamed like a teen at a pop concert. He was unbelievably masculine. Wholly beautiful. And kind.

And Leo's brother.

Yeah, that was bugging her.

"Hi."

She glanced up, pulled out of her thoughts by a masculine voice. She looked up and smiled back. The man was big, almost too big for the seat he was squeezed into. He sat directly in front of her, and a well-dressed woman settled into the seat next to her, a gorgeous designer bag in her lap.

The bag caught her eye. She loved beautiful things. It was why she'd become a designer. She couldn't sew for crap so she'd put her eye for fashion into making living spaces lovely and comfortable, but she still loved clothes and bags and shoes. It took all she had not to drool over that handbag. Quilted and black, with gold braided satchel-like handles, it stood out on the dreary train. Versace. Handmade. She'd seen it at the Versace store the week before when she'd walked through NorthPark Mall looking for inspiration. She'd taken pictures of the straps, thinking she could use it as a takeoff place for decorating the bar that served as the entryway to The Club.

That was one amazing-looking bag. Her own paled in comparison. And the laptop bag at the woman's side was a work of art, too.

"Well, I can see I have nothing on a pretty purse." There was a wealth of masculine deprecation in the words.

She looked up into laughing gray eyes. Damn. She'd been terribly rude. "Sorry. It's a stunning bag."

"Thanks," the woman beside her said, patting the expensive bag. She'd checked the price tag and remembered that she didn't have her husband's blood money to rely on anymore. Not that he'd shared it. She'd been forced to work in a bar in order to pay her mother's medical bills.

"I saw it a couple of days ago on display in the store. I couldn't help but admire it," Shelley said, trying not to think about a life that hadn't been real in the first place.

The cool blonde nodded and held the bag to her chest. "Normally I wouldn't carry it on the train. My ride got stuck at the firm, and I had a long day in court. I wasn't willing to wait, but now I'm wondering. I feel like I need an armed escort."

The handsome man in front of them gave her a jaunty salute. "I'll be happy to apply for the job, ma'am. Steve Holder. Non-active duty Navy SEAL."

The woman next to Shelley blushed and muttered something about feeling safer.

"Hi. I'm Shelley McNamara. I seem to be surrounded by ex-SEALs these days," Shelley said, shaking her head as a young man in a hoodie took the seat across from Designer Bag Lady. He kept his head down, bobbing to music only he could hear.

Holder laughed a bit. He had a jagged scar that ran down his cheek, but his smile seemed genuine. She could definitely buy that he was ex-military. He looked like he'd kept up the workout regime. His shoulders were massive, his neck corded with muscle. "There's no such thing as an ex-SEAL, ma'am. A SEAL's a SEAL. We old guys don't get to play anymore. But it's funny you should say that. I can't seem to find any. I was in town talking to some clients and tried to look up an old teammate of mine. He works at a club now as a therapist."

Seriously? No. She sighed and asked the question anyway. "Leo Meyer?"

Holder pointed at her, his eyes widening in surprise. "Yeah. Wow. You know Leo?"

Leo seemed to be everywhere today. "We work for the same man."

"Julian Lodge." Holder nodded his head. "Yeah, I read up on him when I found out Leo was working for him. He's an interesting man. He's got quite the reputation, though I wonder how much is hype and how much is true."

Designer Bag Lady looked up, her perfectly painted mouth dropping open. "You work for Julian Lodge? The infamous Julian Lodge? Tell me something—is that man as hot in person as he is in pictures?"

Shelley smiled and nodded. Her boss was a lovely man. "I'm redecorating his building. Yes, he's gorgeous, but he's also happily married." *And to more than one person.* She didn't say that out loud. Julian jealously guarded his privacy. "And his wife is pregnant."

That was one he hadn't been able to hide. Pictures of Dani had made the society pages the week before.

"Damn it. All the hot ones are taken." She grinned. "It doesn't hurt that he's also a billionaire."

Her cell phone rang, and she picked it up, leaving Shelley alone, talking to Holder.

"How is Leo doing?" Holder asked, his big, callused hands on his knees. He leaned forward, curiosity on his face.

How was Leo? He was gorgeous and remote and impossible to forget. "He's fine. He's made a good life for himself. He was my brother's therapist. I can safely say the man is a miracle worker."

She didn't mention that the club he worked at was an infamously private BDSM club. She glanced out the window as the train stopped again. Two stops left, and then she would get out and walk the block and a half to her place and try to convince herself she wasn't making a horrible mistake. She didn't have long until Wolf would knock on her door.

"I can believe it," Holder continued. "He was the go-to guy when you needed a good talk. He would listen to everyone. Man, I remember Leo. He was always a flirt. He was a great guy, but he was all about the chase, you know what I mean? I was surprised when I found out he got married."

Her heart nearly stopped. She turned back to Holder, praying she wasn't flushing. Leo had been married? He'd never once mentioned he'd been married. And she'd never noticed him flirting with other women. He'd always been so focused on her when he'd been around her. "I never thought of him as a flirt."

Holder snorted. "God, he was the biggest flirt on the team. We called him Casanova. And he preferred his women to be unavailable. I don't think he ever actually cheated with any of them, but he liked to play around when there wasn't any possibility of commitment."

She felt her whole body go hot with embarrassment. She was

torturing herself over a man who hadn't bothered to mention that he was divorced. She'd told him almost everything. She'd spent hours on the phone with him. Ostensibly they had been talking about Trev and how to handle him and how to deal with his drug and alcohol problems, but she'd found herself telling the handsome counselor everything about her life.

And he hadn't really talked about his life. Maybe because she wasn't important.

"And he was great at riding in and saving women," Holder continued. "He was a white knight, if you know what I mean. I remember this town we were liberating from the Taliban. There were bombs going off everywhere. We were taking crazy fire and Leo's running through the flames of a house carrying a woman and her baby. I admire the hell out of him."

She'd been in trouble, and Leo had tried to ride in. He was a Dom with deep protective instincts. She'd been everything he couldn't resist. She'd been right. If she'd laid her problems at Leo's feet, he likely would have gone straight to Bryce and gotten himself killed.

She had to let him go. He'd been good to her. She couldn't blame him for not loving her back. It wasn't his fault, but she could damn well blame herself for not moving on. She'd been standing still for over a year. Everyone thought she'd been mourning her marriage, but it had been Leo she'd mourned.

And it was time to move on.

She gave Holder what she hoped was a gracious smile as the train began to slow. "This is my stop. It was nice to meet you."

Holder held out his hand and she shook it. He passed her his business card. "You, too, ma'am. And if you see Leo, give him my card. Let him know I'd like to have lunch, catch up. His secretary seemed a bit confused, so I'm not sure he got my message."

Kitten Taylor. Yeah. She was a trip. She was absolutely the subbiest woman Shelley had ever met. Kitten made Beth look like a warrior princess. She'd probably gotten flustered at Holder's commanding voice. "I'll let him know."

She slipped the card into her purse. She nodded to Designer Bag Lady and stood as the doors opened.

And immediately was back in her seat as the young man in the hoodie shoved out, his hands slamming against her chest. There were startled gasps as the young man grabbed the beaten-up leather laptop bag at her feet and leapt off the train, shoving passengers aside. Shelley scrambled to get up, reaching for the bar at the end of the seat. He'd taken her bag. She clutched at her purse, her heart pounding, a rage starting to take over. She got to her feet and pushed her way out. Her heels hit the concrete and she looked around, searching for the jerk who had her bag, and more importantly, her laptop.

He was rushing down the stairs, pushing aside anyone in his way. A woman got knocked down. He simply leapt over the railing and ran toward the street.

She had to catch that little shit. Why was she wearing three-inch heels? She was going to try anyway.

"Don't." A hand held her back. Holder stood behind her as the train rushed away.

"He has my laptop." It had all her work on it. All her designs. All her thoughts. All the pictures she'd taken and sketches she'd made. *Damn it*. Her life was on that laptop.

"He also might have a knife or a gun," Holder said, his grasp on her arm tightening. "I've already called the cops. They're on their way."

She could hear the sirens, but it would be too late. The thief was gone. She searched the crowd below, but he'd run toward the shopping center with its stores and restaurants and businesses. It was thick with rush-hour traffic. She couldn't see him.

She clenched her fists and waited for the cops.

Chapter Five

Wolf slammed the door to his massive black truck and looked at the townhouse Shelley was living in. According to what he'd heard, it was much smaller than the huge, rambling near-mansion she'd shared with her husband before the feds had seized most of their assets.

Did she miss it? The wealth? The standing in her community? He couldn't give her either.

He was a guest in his brother's condo.

And it looked like she had a guest, too.

Her door opened, and a man stepped out. He was a large, bulky man. Even from his place in the parking lot, he could see that the man was at least former military if not still in the service. Shelley nodded at something he said and then he patted her shoulder and turned.

Fuck all. Steve Holder. What the hell was Holder doing with his sub?

Holder's gaze seemed to focus, and a smile came over his harsh face. "Wolf fucking Meyer. Small world."

Holder walked toward him, his hand out.

Yeah, it was way too small a world. What the hell was Holder doing here? Everyone in the military knew Steve Holder had set up a "security" company named White Acres based in Atlanta. He loved to recruit special ops guys, though it always had seemed shady to Wolf. If he'd wanted to hop around the world working on security issues, he would have called up his old CO and gotten an interview with McKay-Taggart. Though the guy had been Army, his company was beyond reproach.

He turned to Shelley and saw telltale signs that she'd been upset.

"Sweetheart, you want to tell me what's going on?" Wolf asked, checking his first instinct to get in Holder's face.

"My laptop bag got stolen," she said, her hand on the doorsill. Her warm brown eyes were wary as she looked between the two men.

"I was sitting across from her on the train. I saw the whole thing happen. I tried to help her out," Holder explained.

"You didn't stop the thief?" Wolf asked, surprised. Holder might not be a SEAL anymore, but he knew damn well the man had kept up his training.

Holder chuckled, shaking his head. "You obviously have never been on DART at rush hour. I couldn't get to him. Too many people around. And, honestly, I've been behind a desk for too long." He turned back to Shelley. "I'm sorry. I should have been able to catch the fucker, but my knees aren't what they used to be."

Wolf seriously doubted that. And why the hell was he hearing about this now? It had been several hours since Shelley had left The Club. He'd walked her out himself, standing on the platform with her until the train had come. He should have driven her home, but he'd had a meeting with Julian.

Holder pulled out a card and held it out. "Look, man, I'm sorry. I had no idea you were involved with her. If I had, I would have found a way to call you. Actually, I was trying to get in touch with Leo, but he was in session apparently, whatever that means."

Wolf took the card. "He's a shrink."

"Yeah, I'd heard that he made it through some serious school."

In an amazing period of time. Leo had gotten the majority of the brains in their family. Wolf could still remember the call he'd gotten when he'd announced he was skipping college to follow his brother into the Navy.

Why the fuck do you think I'm here, Wolf? So you don't have to be.

"I'll let him know you're in town," he said, pocketing the card.

"And I'd love to talk to you, man. How long have you been out?"

74

Holder asked.

He didn't have to ask out of what. "Almost a year since I got the boot."

Holder shrugged. "Your career doesn't have to be over. I'm always looking for good men, and I don't give a shit that you have a plate in your head. I think there's a lot of good time left in you, Wolf. Give me a call. We can talk. Shelley, nice to meet you."

Holder nodded and walked away.

"Is that man what I think he is?" Shelley asked, her eyes trailing after Holder.

"He's a soldier of fortune, if you want to use a romantic term. I would call him a mercenary."

"And he wants you to be a mercenary, too. I don't think that's a good idea."

Oh, so the sub wanted to put her two cents in? He took a step forward, crowding her. "What happened?"

Her eyes flared for a minute, and then she backed up. "I was on the train and this punk jerk-face stole my briefcase. The idiot didn't even have a good eye. There was a Versace bag right in front of him. My bag was worth crap. I sincerely hope he enjoys my crappy laptop and all the things he'll find inside. He must have needed emergency tampons and cinnamon gum. And my energy drink."

He followed her inside, not giving an inch. He was satisfied that she seemed aware of him finally. "Did he take your phone?"

She backed up a bit, her legs finally meeting with her coffee table. "No. I was lucky. I had it in my purse. I'm glad I kept them apart today. I went to lunch with Kitten earlier, and I didn't want to haul my laptop bag around so I brought my purse. He didn't get my wallet, thank god. Just my computer, which good luck with that, buddy. It's on its last leg. I bought that sucker from a pawn shop because…"

She stopped, her face flushing.

"Because the feds took yours?"

She nodded. "They haven't seen fit to get that back to me. Anything, really. I guess this isn't my first time getting robbed."

"But it is your first time getting robbed with a contract in place. Would you like to explain to me why you've already violated our contract not three hours after we signed it?"

"What are you talking about?" Shelley asked, her voice going low. "I didn't do anything."

And that was the problem. He leaned in. She didn't have anywhere left to go. Her chest brushed against his. "The emergency clause. In the event of an emergency, the submissive will make every attempt to get herself out of immediate danger by calling the proper authorities, but the submissive will call the Dominant the first chance she gets in order to give the Dominant every opportunity to perform his main role—to protect and shelter the submissive."

Her lip trembled. "I forgot."

"Yes, you did, thereby taking away my right to perform my main duty."

"To protect and shelter me?"

He could feel the heat of her body, but he wasn't about to give in and do what he wanted to do. They had a few things to work out. "Yes. Instead, I discover you here hours after the crime was committed. And I find you with another man."

She shook her head. "But he offered to stay with me when I talked to the cops, who, by the way, were fairly useless. And then I was still shaky, so he walked me home."

All things that should have been Wolf's responsibility. "Thereby taking away my right to perform my main duty."

"Crap." Her face fell. She looked down. "Am I in trouble?"

Finally she understood. "Oh, yes. Unless, you've changed your mind and you don't wish to be protected and sheltered. If you want me to leave, tell me to go."

Her eyes widened. "That's not fair. I'm finding my feet with this. I want to try it."

He took a long step back, giving her the space she would need. "Then we begin as we mean to go. Pull down your pants and lay your hands flat on the coffee table, ass in the air."

"Why would I do that?" The question had an air of hushed horror to it.

"The better to spank you, my dear."

She frowned. "Big, bad Wolf, huh?"

"That's me, sweetheart," he shot back. "And I'm not happy right now. I'm very much pissed off that you didn't even think to call me."

"How is spanking me going to fix that?"

"Well, first off, it will make me feel infinitely better. Second, it might serve as a reminder that the next time something bad happens, you're supposed to call your Dom right away."

Her mouth pouted in the sweetest, sexiest way. "I know I should have called you. I'm sorry. I'm not used to relying on someone."

She batted those big brown doe eyes. It wasn't going to work on him. Oh, he wanted to haul her in his arms and promise everything would be okay, but that wouldn't make his point. "It's a count of ten right now. Would you like to go for twenty, sweetheart?"

"Damn it, Wolf. I've been through a lot today." She practically stomped her foot.

"Twenty it is, then."

She pushed at him, and for a minute he thought she would shove him out of her townhouse and tell him to go hell. But she frowned and her hand went to the clasp of her pants. Her eyes teared up. "Can I go change first?"

Odd request. "No. Pull them down."

A sniffle came from her. "I'm not wearing anything pretty. I…I have a girdle on."

He checked his laugh. She was worried about that? "Do you need help getting out of it?"

Her mouth firmed in a stubborn pout. "No. I think I can handle it."

Her hands went to the waistband, and she unbuttoned her slacks. They fell to her ankles but she wasn't on display yet. A nude colored form of underwear covered her from high above her waist down to her thighs. She hooked her thumbs under what looked to be some feminine torture device. She pushed at the spandex that wrapped around her waist.

"Stop."

She stopped, her eyes widening. "You don't want to spank me anymore, do you?"

He was going to have to work on her self-esteem. He could see the red marks the way-too-tight girdle left on her skin. He reached into his boot. "No. I simply don't want to watch you try to wiggle out of that for the next five minutes. Why are you wearing that thing, woman? I'm pretty sure we used something like that on Taliban prisoners to get them to talk."

He pulled a knife out and flicked open the blade.

"What are you doing?" Shelley asked.

"Helping you." He pulled at the band and made quick work, filleting the girdle off of her.

She sighed in relief and then frowned. "That was not cheap, Wolf."

He traced the lines the device had left on her skin. Angry-looking red marks covered her hips where the seams had bitten into her flesh. "It doesn't matter. You're not allowed to wear it again. No more, Shelley, not while our contract is in force."

"I need it," she argued. "I'm not exactly slender."

She didn't need to be stick thin. He'd seen enough women in the world who were starving. He wanted her gorgeous and healthy. "You're beautiful. And I find these marks vulgar. No more. You're a gorgeous woman with amazingly sexy curves, and I don't want you hiding them."

"My pants won't fit," she said stubbornly.

"I'll buy you new ones." Why was he arguing with her? Because she didn't seem to notice that he could see her pussy. Pretty little pussy. *Fuck.* How was he going to keep his dick out of her? He allowed his hands to trace the line of her hips. "You don't need that thing."

She put her hands on his shoulders as though she required some balance. "I don't like it, but I want to look nice."

"You look nice, sweetheart. Very nice." He stared at her nest of dark curls. It took everything he had not to let his fingers roam down and sink into her pussy, rubbing until he got her cream flowing, until she begged for something bigger than his fingers. "But we need to talk about grooming, love."

She huffed. "I know. I was going to shave, but then jerk-face hoodie guy stole my laptop."

And they were back to the point of the lesson. *Damn it.* He had a job to do. "You can have a shower after your spanking. Turn around and grab hold of that table."

She squeaked, trying to turn on her heels. He caught her and turned her to properly face the opposite wall. He watched with a smile as she tried to settle down to the right position. She was endearingly clumsy.

Her head turned back, a grimace on her face. "I hope you're enjoying this."

"No sarcasm. Five more."

She grumbled but didn't say anything else. Her ass came up in the air as she leaned over.

Heart-shaped. Round. Juicy. That ass was a work of art, and she'd tried to hide it behind punishing spandex. He touched her, needing to show her how gorgeous she was. He ran his hands over her flesh and then did what he'd wanted to do the moment he'd seen her. He pressed his pelvis forward and let her feel the hard line of his cock. "Does that feel like I'm not interested in you? That I don't find you sexy? Now, I have zero intention of using anything but my hand on your pretty backside, but you need to understand that I greatly prefer you in your natural glory."

"Yes, Sir."

He was content with her breathy reply. "Now, pick a safe word. I'm serious about safe words. I don't want you to be afraid to use it if you're hurting or you're really afraid."

"I have a safe word. It's Gucci. I like their bags. I used to have one."

"I don't know what that is, sweetheart, but I can remember it." He stepped back and felt a sweet contentment overtake him. This was their first play together.

He meant to make damn sure it wasn't their last.

* * * *

Shelley took a deep breath, waiting for the first strike.

What the hell was she doing? Her ass was naked and in the air and her slacks were around her ankles, and a man she'd barely met was touching her and making every cell in her body ache for him.

She had to hand it to him. She wasn't thinking about being robbed anymore. She was one hundred percent focused on Wolf

Meyer.

Well, maybe not one hundred because there was also a piece of her that couldn't let go of Leo. When she'd chased after the man, one of her first thoughts hadn't been to call the police. It had been to call Leo. But he didn't answer her anymore. She had to move on, and god, she wanted Wolf.

Wolf, who was a taunting bastard because he'd left her standing there for what felt like forever, her naked ass in the slightly chilly air.

And then a loud smack roared through her.

Shelley gasped, whimpering at the pain that rushed through her system.

"I need a count, sweetheart."

He wanted her to count? *Asshole.* And yet her mouth opened, and she managed to form the word. "One."

"Thank you." He sounded as though he was thanking her for passing the salt, not for counting out her own punishment.

A second smack hit her like a freight train. Tears blurred her eyes. "Two."

She could barely breathe as he continued. Torture? Wolf Meyer seemed to understand the word. He smacked her ass again and again. She thought about using her safe word. When he hit her a tenth time, it was right there on the edge of her tongue. "Ten," she said, and then she was going to say, "Gucci," but the word didn't come out.

"You're doing amazingly well." Wolf's hand rubbed her ass, and for the first time, she felt something beyond the pain. Heat and languor were starting to sink in, flushing her flesh with an odd pleasure. His words sank in, too. He talked about how lovely her backside was, how strong she was.

And she felt it. She could handle this. The pain settled into her bones and somehow she turned it into something more, something sweet. She was in control even as her Dom smacked her an eleventh time.

"Eleven," she said. "Twelve." The count was easy now. She gritted her teeth against the pain, knowing all the while that it led to something better. Twelve through twenty-four flew by, each smack pushing her to someplace that was just out of reach. She breathed, letting every sensation flow in and out of her body.

"Sweetheart, that was twenty-five. Can you say it for me?"

They were already done? How had that happened? She'd forgotten where she was. She'd simply been. All of her cares had flown away. Even Leo hadn't been there in the back of her head. She'd been a creature of sensation, and it had been remarkable.

"Twenty-five," she said with almost a sad sigh. This was what her brother gave Beth, a safe place to forget herself and simply be. This was how Beth had finally managed to find her strength.

Strong hands soothed over her flesh. "You look so pretty like this, sweetheart."

She felt pretty. Strange. The horrible self-consciousness that had plagued her before seemed to have floated away on a haze of pain and pleasure.

"You didn't use your safe word."

She shook her head.

"Did you think about it?"

Honesty. She was supposed to be honest with him at all times. She'd signed a contract that had promised him honesty and openness. At the time, it had seemed an odd thing to do, but now she found it freeing. She had to be honest. "Yes, Sir. I did."

"And why didn't you?"

Wretched honesty. "Because I decided I liked it."

She felt something soft press against the small of her back. God, he'd kissed her. He'd kissed her right above her tailbone, his lips as hot as the smack of his hand and even more devastating.

"Thank you for the honesty. Now go and take a shower. We need to be at The Club soon. I'll run out and grab us some food." He helped her up.

She kicked out of her shoes. It seemed a silly thing to pull her pants back up when she was about to get into the shower. She stared up at him. His gorgeous face was hard as a rock, the only softness there in his eyes and the slight uptick of his lips. She wanted him to kiss her.

But he simply pulled her in for a hug. "Be a good girl. Dress comfortably. We'll change at The Club."

And he turned and walked to the door. Damn him. He'd left her all hot and bothered. And she could plainly see that he wasn't unaffected. His cock was a huge bulge against his jeans, as though the thing was trying its damnedest to get out and get back to her. Well, she could take care of herself in the shower. Yes. She wouldn't walk into The Club with her pussy aching and dripping wet. That would be a bad idea.

Wolf turned at the door, his eyes narrowing as if he could hear her thoughts. "No touching. Leave that pussy alone with the singular exception of shaving it. And don't put on any underwear. Not if you want to keep it."

He winked and slipped out the door.

She stared for a minute, her body aroused and her mind in a pleasant, fuzzy state.

The door opened again. Wolf's head popped back in. "Lock the door behind me."

The door closed again.

"Bossy." But she locked the door.

She wasn't thinking of anything but Wolf while she showered. The night, despite the stress of the day, was looking up.

* * * *

Holder shut the door behind him, making almost no noise as he entered the small room. The motel was not his usual. After years of roughing it in the most dangerous parts of the world, he greatly preferred a suite at the Fairmont, but he was trying to keep a low profile.

And his cohort would definitely look out of place in an expensive suite.

"Give me an update." He shrugged out of his jacket and neatly placed it on the hanger. Just because he was in a piece-of-crap motel didn't mean he had to act like an animal.

"She's got shit on this system, boss. It looks like it's all crap." Kyle Nelson's young face was illuminated by the light of the computer screen. The hoodie he'd worn earlier had been tossed on one of the beds. Kyle had been halfway decent as a purse snatcher. He'd kept his head down and the hood over his brow. Holder was pretty sure Shelley McNamara wouldn't recognize him even if she was introduced to the man who had stolen her bag. She'd seemed much more upset about the loss of her work than the man who had taken it. She had given the cops only the vaguest of descriptions.

Of course, he'd kept her attention focused on him until the time was right. She'd done exactly what he'd wanted her to do.

"You have any trouble getting around her password?" Holder asked, opening the mini fridge and pulling out a beer. Shelley McNamara was a pretty piece of fluff. If that overgrown ape Wolf hadn't shown up, he would have given serious consideration to attempting to seduce her. It had been a while since he'd played a woman for information, but he wasn't exactly unattractive. Even the scars could be used right. A lot of women loved that "wounded warrior" shit. But Wolf had practically growled at him. The last thing he needed was a former SEAL getting pissed off because Holder had touched his shit.

He needed the Meyer brothers' goodwill to get into that club.

"The dumb bitch didn't have a password." Kyle looked up over his screen. "Hey, pass me one, boss."

Holder popped the top and then smacked young Kyle upside the head. "Watch your language when talking about a lady."

His eyes went wide. Kyle had gotten the old naval boot for getting too interested in certain websites. Holder didn't have a single problem with whatever the idiot wanted to hack in his spare time as long as he did the job at hand. But he needed to show some respect. The mercenary business wasn't what it used to be. The insanely wealthy people they worked for expected their highly paid killers to have some manners.

The young man took a deep breath and proved he had a brain in his head. "The very nice lady did not properly protect her computer, sir. I got into it without a single problem."

"Better. Nothing incriminating?" Holder looked over Kyle's shoulder. Shelley's background was a soothing landscape that slowly turned into Manhattan at night and then a sunny, calm beach.

Kyle shrugged. "She does a lot of shopping online, but she doesn't buy anything. She likes to look at shoes. I mean a lot. What's up with women and shoes? I mean, you got two feet, right? Why should you have more than one pair of shoes?"

Holder barely managed to not roll his eyes. "Anything besides the shoes?"

"Uhm, she doesn't clear her cache. Besides her preoccupation with something called Louboutin, her latest searches go to a lot of kinky stuff, if you know what I mean." Kyle's voice went low, as though he was telling a secret.

"I don't. Tell me." God, why had he decided to take care of this himself? He could be in some shithole war zone getting his balls blown off, but no, he got to hang out with a twenty-two-year-old hacker.

"Bondage and shit."

Well, of course. They were back to the bondage. It made sense. It's what Leo Meyer had been into. Everyone had known that. Meyer had a taste for tying women up and playing some kinky games with them. It was what had gotten Ada into such trouble. It wouldn't surprise him at all to find out baby brother Meyer was into the same shit. "It's not that mind blowing. Shelley works for that Lodge guy and apparently he runs a secret club."

Cross was trying to get into The Club. He had a friend in the Senate with privileges there and would be in town in a few days. Holder didn't want to wait that long.

Kyle's eyes lit up. "Oh, yeah. Lodge is into a lot of shit, boss. And hacking into his system wasn't easy. I couldn't actually get into his business system. Well, I did, but then I had to do the online equivalent of jumping out of the window of a house I was robbing and running like my pants were on fire. Pretty sure I covered my tracks. But I managed to find out a lot. Rumors mostly, but enough to make me think they're true. He's a pervert."

He didn't give a crap about the guy's morality. "Aren't we all? So he's personally into bondage, too? It's not merely a business for him?"

"Yes, the club he runs is a BDSM club, and he's definitely a member," Kyle explained. "I think he's got a lot of people in his back pocket. You're not going to like his security firm."

He gritted his teeth because that could only mean one thing. "Tell me it's not Taggart. I know that do-gooder is here in town."

"Oh, from what I can tell Lodge bankrolled Taggart in the

beginning. McKay-Taggart has a hand in every security issue Lodge has," Kyle said. "And it's worse. There are rumors that Lodge even has some mob contacts."

Fuck. That was all he needed. Shelley McNamara, wife of an infamous blackmailer, was working for a man with mob connections and whose security firm was known for being ruthless about protecting their clients. Cross was right. They had a serious problem, but if he couldn't find the files with the taped meetings, it would always be hanging over their heads.

"Anything that looks like a blackmail file?"

Kyle shrugged. "Not unless she's blackmailing people for their design tastes. She's got a bunch of weird sketches and something called virtual swatches. What the hell is that?"

Nothing he could use. "Dig deeper."

"I'll try." Kyle went back to his work, his fingers flying across the keys.

Holder stepped to the window, looking out over the spectacular view of the parking lot.

If he had to bet his life on it, he would bet that Shelley McNamara was exactly what she appeared to be—a sweet, slightly kinky woman with a shoe fetish.

But then there was the problem of Julian Lodge. How did a woman go from a blackmailer/drug-runner husband straight to a boss with possible mob connections? She'd made it out of the investigation into her husband's practices smelling like a rose despite the fact that she'd placed many of the items that had caught the incriminating activities Bryce Hughes had used against her clients. And yet the feds had bought her "I didn't know anything" story because she'd had a lawyer she shouldn't have been able to afford.

Finn Taylor. Julian Lodge's lawyer.

Appearances could be deceiving. He needed to get into The Club. And he definitely needed to know how Leo and Wolf Meyer were connected to Shelley McNamara. If they were involved in her scheme, then he would need some serious backup.

The sun went down while Kyle worked, and Holder wondered how he was going to kill not one but two former SEALs.

Chapter Six

Shelley stared at herself in the mirror. She didn't hate the way she looked, though Wolf might have been nicer and given her some actual underwear. The miniskirt didn't count. It barely covered her butt cheeks. God, was her cellulite hanging out?

She was too old for this. She couldn't walk out into a club filled with young hot bodies. Why had she thought this could work? She'd been fine until she'd walked into the locker room and seen all the gorgeous, younger subs getting ready.

Any one of these women would probably look better with Wolf.

Was one of them getting ready to play with Leo? Would she be all right watching Leo sexually dominate another woman?

"You okay? You have that newbie, 'am I going to survive this' look." A gorgeous amazon of a woman with strawberry blonde hair stepped up to the mirror and glossed her lips. "Did you meet this guy over the Internet? Did you answer his 'Dom who's definitely not a serial killer seeks submissive with no ties to the outer world' ad?"

Oh, she was a sarcastic one. "No. I met him through a friend."

"Is your friend a serial killer?"

"He's Julian Lodge."

A brilliant smile crossed the redhead's lips. "Ah, definitely a killer, but the best kind. You're safe then. If the Dom you're meeting gives you hell, Julian will take care of him. Buck up, honey. This is all about fun." She frowned. "Unless he's an asshole who's trying to seriously dominate you. Does he try to get you to clean shit you don't want to? Because I draw a serious line there."

From what she could tell Wolf was pretty neat. He didn't look like he was a slob. "Uhm, I'm pretty much a clean freak."

"Yeah, you need a military Dom. Let me tell you, they teach those boys right," the woman said. "My husband can't stand things being out of place, and a dirty kitchen is his nightmare. I'm going to start trying to convince him that if we ever have kids, they'll be like the cleaning staff of our home."

"He was a SEAL. But he's out now. He didn't want to be, though. I think he wanted the military to be his career."

The woman obviously had an interesting marriage. All the D/s relationships she was acquainted with were fairly typical. There didn't seem much particularly subby about this woman.

"Excellent. Then all you have to do is be super subby in the bedroom and make him understand that you are the CO of your house. It works for me and I've got the world's hardest-ass sarcastic bastard as my Dom. He's my husband, too." She held out a hand. "Charlotte Taggart."

"Shelley McNamara." She shook the redhead's hand. "And Wolf is kind of my training Dom, and by kind of I mean he is. My training Dom."

Charlotte chuckled. "And you are one scared newbie. I haven't met Wolf yet but I know his old CO. Eric thinks the world of him. My husband's kind of upset with Julian because he stole Wolf right from under his fingers. I told him he should have hauled his hot ass to Colorado and talked to the guy, but Ian wanted to slow play it. I think he thought if he looked too eager, Wolf would have known he could get a lot of money out of him. Of course, once he realizes Wolf is linked to a submissive, he'll say he was smarter than the rest of us and he always knew. He didn't."

She was confused. "Why does having a sub mean McKay-Taggart wouldn't hire him?"

She knew enough to know the name Taggart and how it was connected to Julian. He'd mentioned that he liked pulling one over on his security team.

Charlotte leaned against the counter top. "Ian's looking for man meat. We do a lot of investigations that require undercover work. He needs a couple of hot guys who can chat a woman up without freaking out that his wife is going to get pissed off. Because we do, even if it's for work. He's taken on a couple of new guys, but they don't have the experience Wolf has. However, if he's attached, Ian won't send him in, so it's for the best."

She was kind of happy Wolf wouldn't be globe-trotting. And definitely happy he wouldn't be dealing with undercover investigations. That sounded dangerous. "Well, I hope he enjoys working for Julian. Julian's a nice man. I've had fun with the redesign on the penthouse. I'm going to work on The Club soon."

Charlotte's eyes widened. "You're the designer?"

Shelley nodded.

"The one whose asshole ex used her designs to hide cameras in high-profile politicians' offices so he could blackmail them?"

Shit. Maybe she should have kept her mouth shut. "That's me."

Charlotte practically vibrated. "Oh, my god. I saw some of those designs and they are stunning. Please, you have to help design New Sanctum. If Ian has his way, it will be a concrete floor, a bar he picked up at a garage sale, and stunningly beautiful bondage equipment. That's what he'll spend all his money on. I'll have the most gorgeous spanking bench and the lounge will be folding chairs. Mama needs some luxury."

Had she just gotten another job? "I heard something happened with your club. Did it actually blow up?"

"Yes, in spectacular fashion," she agreed. "A sleeper agent with a vendetta against one of our employees drove a bomb into the place. Took out about half of it. Ian was pissed off because it disturbed his lunch. I'm okay with it because Old Sanctum wasn't what I would call luxurious."

Wow, she was really happy Wolf wasn't working there now. "I would love to help out. Though I should warn you, I'm new to this."

She shook her head. "But you're not new to gorgeous things. You're not new to taking a space and making it both functional and comfortable." Charlotte's eyes narrowed. "Is that why you're standing here looking at yourself like you should run the other way? I was joking about the newbie thing. It's an awesome thing to be. Everything is new. You get to experience it all for the first time."

"It's also uncertain."

"What's life without a little uncertainty?" Charlotte grinned and looked impish despite the fact that she was a gorgeous amazon of a woman. "What scares you about this? I'm going to give you a big old hint. If you say something like I'm worried I'm not pretty enough or too old, you've gone the wrong way."

"I'm allowed to have my insecurities."

Blue eyes rolled. "I'm too tall. I weigh too much. My boobs sag when they're not hoisted up by a way-too-tight corset. But you know what? I'm enough. None of this is going to work if you can't figure that out. I read about you. You came out of a pretty bad marriage and you're here. You are allowed to have your insecurities, but don't make them a security blanket. I should know. I did my time in that particular cage. Come out. The world is way more awesome when you aren't locked in."

"That's easy for you to say," Shelley shot back.

"No, it's not and it never was." Charlotte stood up to her full height and checked herself in the mirror again. "But I get it. It's hard when you're in the cage to see that there's a cage at all." She smoothed over her corset, adjusting it slightly. "Let me know if you're interested in the Sanctum job."

She winced. "I am. I'm sorry. I didn't mean to be a bitch."

Charlotte grinned. "That wasn't bitchy. That was what I like to call being un-self-aware and bratty about it. It's cool. I can handle it. Have fun tonight and try to get out of your head. From what I hear Master Wolf is hot as hell."

"That's part of the problem."

"Having a hot guy is part of the problem?"

"I don't know that I'm in the same league."

She nodded as though immediately understanding the issue. "We're back to the cage again. Okay, have you spent any time at all with this guy?"

"I've talked to him a lot." She flushed, remembering how they'd spent the afternoon. "And we played."

"I'm going to ask you a very invasive question because I have no filter at all. What did his dick do?"

A laugh escaped because she thought it might be fun to be this woman's friend. "It got hard. I got naked. Well, my bottom was and he spanked me and he got hard."

Charlotte pointed her way like her argument had been made. "Dicks don't lie." She frowned. "Well, dicks totally lie. A lot. But penises do not, Shelley. Trust your Dom. He's going to think you're hot as hell. Now I'm going to find mine and enjoy a particularly nice evening. The lounge here is like heaven. Plush carpet helps when you spend a bunch of time on your knees. Make note of that."

"Carpet in the lounge area. Got it." She might have a job. A huge job.

Charlotte gave her a thumbs-up and then she was gone.

And Shelley was left alone with that image of herself in the mirror.

Maybe it was time to open the cage door and see what it looked like on the outside.

* * * *

"Are you sure I have to wear this? I'm not wild about leather." Logan Green shifted uncomfortably, his tall body moving in a graceless manner. For once his face wasn't tight, but instead Leo could see the kid Logan Green really was.

"You'll get used to them." Leo himself had spent so much time in leathers he often thought of them as his second skin.

He looked out over the dungeon floor wondering if Wolf would bring Shelley here on their first training night or if he would keep her to the playroom section of The Club. If he knew Wolf, she would be here, and Leo would have to see her in fet wear.

"So when do I start spanking girls? That one looks like a bad girl. Yeah, she's probably done something exceptionally naughty." There was a healthy leer in Logan's voice as he zeroed in on the object of his desire.

Well, at least he didn't have to deal with the kid's inhibitions. As far as Leo could tell, Logan didn't have any. When they'd gotten dressed in The Club's expansive locker room, Logan had shed his clothes without batting an eye and walked around naked for a while, as though he actually preferred to be without the encumbrance. Logan had sat his naked ass down on a towel and started asking him all kinds of questions.

He hadn't been able to miss the scars on the deputy's body. There were rough scars where someone had used a knife on him and neat, surgical scars left over from the operation that had saved his life. But they all formed a road map of the trauma that should have Logan twitching in his boots.

"You aren't even close to spanking girls. There's a training process involved. It doesn't consist of throwing you out there with a paddle and whip. Tell me something. You seem comfortable here. The idea of these people being tied down doesn't bring back bad memories?" He'd rather expected Logan would have a bad reaction to the dungeon.

Logan shrugged. "Nah. I'm cool with it. I've hung out with enough pervs to be okay with a little kink."

Yes, the deputy seemed perfectly comfortable, but if he wasn't bothered by anything, then why was he here?

"Are you sure I can't spank her? Maybe I'll let her spank me." Logan watched as a lovely blonde made her way through the crowd. She was full figured and definitely older than the young man.

But he certainly wouldn't call Janine a cougar. Leo smiled as his ex-wife made her way toward them. She was bigger than she'd been when he'd married her, three children in six years having taken a bit of a toll on her figure, but she glowed with happiness. She was beautiful. He understood why Logan would want a piece of that.

But the fact that the deputy was still joking about spanking after what he'd been through made Leo suspicious. Logan Green put up a great wall. It was Leo's job to bring it down.

Logan straightened his spine, his chest puffing out a bit. "Hey, Doc, she's coming my way."

"She's coming my way, but I like the positive attitude. Logan, meet Janine, my ex-wife."

"Oh, I'm so much more than that, darling." Janine smiled and held both hands out. Leo gave her what she wanted, drawing her into a hug. He'd married Janine straight out of college, before she went to med school and he began working on his PhD. They had lived in this very club, working their way through school thanks to the largesse of Julian Lodge. "I'm his past. The one who won't go away."

"I don't want you to go away, dear." He took her hand in his. He wasn't looking forward to this conversation, but he needed it. He sent Logan an authoritative glare. "Stay here. Don't get into trouble."

He led Janine to the hallway where the stairs began that led up to the playroom.

"Damn, this must be serious. Is Wolf all right? Did the Navy damage him? Does he need help?"

Even years later, Janine still cared about Wolf. His brother made an impression. "I want to know if I was a good husband."

Her eyes widened. Her hand tightened on his. "Oh, sweetie, what's going on?"

"Wolf showed up today and I was kind of a dick, and he made me question a few things." Leo ran a hand across his head, pushing his hair back. "I started to think that maybe I haven't been the best brother."

Concern showed in her eyes. "What did he say?"

"He said something about me being harder on the people close to me than I am on people who don't mean as much. Like I sacrifice my relationships for my patients because it's easier to sink myself into them."

"Smart man," she replied. "Wolf always claimed he didn't have a brain in his gorgeous head, but he was emotionally intelligent."

Leo felt his eyes roll. "He's not that gorgeous."

Janine's lips curved up. "Oh, baby brother is one hot hunk of man, but he's also right. Do you really want the truth? As your ex-wife and a psychiatrist?"

No. He didn't want either. He wanted her to tell him that he'd been perfect and it was all her fault that she'd fallen in love with another man. But he knew deep down that was wrong. "Give it to me, Janine. Come on. Haven't you waited years for me to ask you for your professional opinion?"

Two shrinks should never marry each other. They never stopped the psychoanalyzing long enough to have a relationship. Yet, when he'd gone into the marriage, he'd gone in with his eyes open. He'd been pretty sure it would fail.

Janine turned her blue eyes up, and that piercing intelligence pinned him. "You're right. You always have paid more attention to your patients than your personal life. You do it for the same reason you greatly prefer to flirt with unavailable women. You have a deep-seated fear of responsibility."

"I sure as fuck don't," he shot back. He hadn't been prepared for that. He'd been ready to listen to her talk about his commitment issues, but no one ever claimed he didn't take responsibility. He preached it.

She shrugged, not at all upset by his hostility. "You do, Leo. Oh, you're committed to your patients, but that's a professional thing. It doesn't involve your heart and soul. It's an intellectual exercise that brings you pleasure. You enjoy fixing people, and when you've fixed them, you move on to the next damaged soul. But here's what you don't understand. Your brand of therapy is very personal for patients. You make them your friends. They come to trust you and love you, and when you're done, you move on."

Fuck. Had he really done that? He didn't take on many patients, but now that he thought about it, he hadn't talked to Trev in months. He'd been Trev McNamara's rock for three years, and he'd not once called to see how the man was. Leo was working with Ian Taggart. Oh, they mostly shot hoops and talked about Charlotte Taggart's issues. Janine ran a women's support group for victims of abuse. Leo helped the men in their lives support and understand them.

Tag wasn't a patient. He was a friend Leo counseled. So why hadn't he gone to dinner with the man when he'd invited him? Big Tag had wanted to show off his brother's new restaurant, but Leo had held back, giving him some bullshit excuse.

"Julian misses you."

Leo stared down at her. "I haven't left Julian. I'm right where I've been for ten years."

She shook her head. "No, you're not. I had lunch with him the other day. I asked about you, and we talked. He misses his friend. Before he got married, you spent time with him. Now you've waved a wand and declared him fixed and moved on to the next person who needs attention, but Julian misses you. He finally gets the lesson about how to truly care about the people around him and you've moved on."

He hadn't meant to. It had simply been easier to do his job. Julian hadn't needed him anymore. Except maybe he had and Leo was too self-absorbed to see it. "Why did you leave me?"

Her smile turned sad. "Because you fixed me, too. You took a woman who had been abused and helped turn me into a fully functional human being capable of great love. But I wanted to be loved, too. I wanted someone to be passionate about me, and that was never going to be you. I'm not sure why you married me. Maybe because it seemed like the only way to gain my trust and set me free, but I had to repay the favor. You think I left you for another man, but he was a convenient excuse. I needed to let you go or you would have gone on the way you were going. The only true passions in your life would have been intellectual."

"But you married him." He could still remember the day she'd told him she was leaving him. He'd said all the right things, but if he was honest deep down, he'd been relieved. Their marriage had been a mistake.

"Yes," she said with that glowy smile of hers, one she'd never had when she'd been married to him. "A happy accident. It turns out that when I did something good for the man I loved, I found the one who loved me, and that's been the joy of my life. I woke up one day and realized that bald lawyer was the best thing that ever happened to me. And you made that possible. I'll love you until the day I die for that. But I wish you would wake up and see what you're doing. You're running away by standing still."

He'd called Julian a manipulative bastard, but manipulation was the language of Julian's love. What if he'd been doing exactly what he'd said he was doing? Trying to make things better for both Leo and Shelley? Guilt assailed him. He'd railed at the man who had given him so much.

And Wolf. *Fuck*.

Julian had asked him earlier to step back and give his professional opinion of what Shelley needed. What was his professional opinion of himself? If he had a patient with his background and history, what would he think?

He had a deep disconnect that had begun in childhood. Despite the love his mother had managed to give him, the scars of his father's abandonment ran deep. He'd taken on responsibility for Wolf. He'd been everything to his kid brother, and it had been a relief almost to go into the Navy and only have to worry about himself.

He blamed Wolf. *God*. Deep down, he blamed his brother for their father walking away.

"You know your relationship with Wolf could dissolve. Do you want that?" Janine asked.

Wolf had been the one he'd sacrificed for. Wolf had been the one who threw it all away by going into the goddamn Navy instead of college.

"I'm still mad at him. Crap, Jan. I didn't even see it until now. How could I blame him for all that? He didn't make our dad walk out."

"Our emotions aren't logical. You know that. What did you always tell me?" Janine asked, her eyes deep with sympathy.

He knew what she meant, but now the words sounded hollow, though he'd preached them for years—like a pastor who didn't honestly believe in God. "That sanity is the ability to give and receive love."

And he'd done neither.

"Leo." Janine put her hands on the sides of his face, pulling him back to her. "The fact that you're asking these questions means you might be ready to deal with them. Is this about that woman? Trev McNamara's sister?"

Damn, Julian had turned into a gossipy old lady. "She was one of my unavailable flirtations."

Except that he'd offered to take her away. He'd thought of marrying her, and not in the lackadaisical way he'd gone about convincing himself to marry Janine. Passion. Shelley McNamara had been the first time he'd felt a deep and abiding passion for a woman.

"I doubt that," Janine said. "But no one can make you admit it. Leo, know this. I'll always be here for you. And I'll always want the best for you."

But he could clearly see he'd disappointed her. And she wasn't the only one.

Shelley stood on the bottom step dressed in a tight miniskirt and a black and crimson bustier. She wore no shoes, and her hair hung down in long, shimmering black tresses. But it was the hurt in her eyes as she looked between him and Janine that had his gut churning.

"Janine? Oh my god!" Wolf didn't seem to notice the ocean of despair that stretched between Leo and Shelley. He had a huge grin plastered on his face, and he reached out, swinging Janine into his oversized embrace.

Janine laughed, her voice filling the dungeon. "Wolf Meyer, you're more gorgeous than ever, little brother."

"Hah, I'm getting old and out of shape. I ran into Big Tag and he told me he's glad I took the job with Julian because he didn't hire operatives with potbellies. Such an asshole." Wolf grinned as he set her down. His hand went back and brought Shelley forward, pride evident in his stance. "Janine, this is my submissive, Shelley. Shelley, this is my sister-in-law, Janine."

Shelley nodded, her lips curving but without the normal vivaciousness that made Leo's heart ache. "Nice to meet you."

"He's Shelley's trainer. She's investigating the lifestyle," Leo said, the words coming out of his mouth with a stubborn bent. It wasn't like she'd signed a permanent contract with his brother. They weren't married or anything. Not even close. As far as Leo knew, there wasn't even sex written into the contract.

Fuck. Wolf wanted to have sex with her. Jealousy, pounding and nasty, took up root in his gut. But it was all right because Shelley was only training with Wolf.

Except when Wolf's hand curved around her hip, she leaned into him as though his presence was comforting to her.

"Shelley as in Shelley McNamara?" Janine breathed the words on a hushed, awed sigh.

Shelley nodded. "Yes. I'm sorry. Do I know you?"

Janine smiled, reaching out for Shelley's hand. "No, dear, but I get the feeling we're going to have a lot in common. And if the three of you need some therapy after all this, I'll give you a group rate. Good luck, dears. I'm feeling toppy tonight. I think I'll give the hubby a few whacks."

She winked, and he was left alone. With his brother and the only woman he'd ever loved.

Wolf grinned, his oversized paw wrapping around Shelley's waist. Shelley leaned into him, but her eyes found Leo's. Silent. Accusing.

"This is going to be a fun night," Wolf said.

It was definitely going to be a long one.

* * * *

Shelley pulled at the top of her bustier, all of the bravado she'd found while talking to Charlotte gone now. Wolf obviously didn't understand women's cup sizes. Or he'd totally misjudged the size of her boobs.

"Stop," he said, using that dark voice on her. "You look beautiful."

"My boobs are hanging out. I need a bigger top." She wouldn't even go into the micro mini he'd put her in. She could practically feel the cheeks of her ass dropping past the nonexistent hemline of the leather Band-Aid he'd dared to call a skirt.

And to further her humiliation, he looked like some kind of Greek god. Tall and powerfully built, Wolf Meyer stood at least two inches above every other man in the room. His torso looked like Michelangelo had come back from the grave and sculpted it in one last burst of divine inspiration. Charlotte Taggart's husband was totally wrong about his abs. He didn't have a six-pack. Oh, no, nothing so ordinary for Wolf. His washboard stomach boasted a full-on outrageous eight-pack, and she wanted to cry over the perfection of the notches at his hips. She could see them because Wolf wore nothing but a pair of low-slung leather pants and his boots.

She looked across the room where Leo stood with someone Wolf had introduced as Logan. Her heart ached at the sight of Leo. Leo was slightly smaller than his brother, but she loved his graceful lines and the way Leo's long hair hit broad, muscled shoulders.

But she'd heard too much. Leo didn't want her.

"Hey," Wolf said, his hand cupping her chin and drawing her face up. She stared into deep, dark-blue eyes. She could get lost in those eyes. "Are you all right? I don't know what happened between you and my brother, but if this is too much, then I can take you home.

Sweetheart, this should be good for you. If I'm some kind of reminder of him or if I'm keeping you from what you really want, then tell me, and I'll let you go."

She opened her mouth to say something, but he put a finger on her lips. "Hush. Let me finish. I don't want to hurt you or Leo. And I don't want to hurt me, either. I haven't had a lot of luck lately, and I would rather avoid the craptastic whammy of getting to know you and liking the hell out of you only for you to tell me you're not interested because you have a thing for another guy. Especially my brother."

She got the feeling things weren't easy between Wolf and his brother. She looked over at Leo, who was involved in what looked to be a teaching moment. It was exactly as Janine had said. She'd walked down ahead of Wolf, who had some paperwork to fill out before they entered the dungeon. She'd heard a lot of the talk between the exes. Leo had saved her. Oh, it hadn't been complete. He would have preferred to have whisked her away, but he'd tried, and now he thought she didn't need him.

Was she willing to let Wolf go when what she had with Leo had been more in her head than anywhere else?

"I never dated your brother," she admitted.

"That doesn't mean you're not in love with him."

True. "I don't want to be. I let him go a long time ago. There's nothing between us." The words hurt, but they were the plain truth. Seeing him with his ex, the sweet way he'd held her hand and talked to her, made everything clear. Leo hadn't even smiled at her in four months. He was done, and she would be twelve kinds of a fool if she didn't try with Wolf. "Please, Sir. I want to try this. I can't promise it will work out. I can only promise that I'll be open to the experience."

The smile that crossed his face nearly blinded her. "I will, too, sweetheart. That's all we can ask. And you don't need a bigger size." He looked down, his eyes on her breasts, the heat nearly palpable. "This is perfect. So fucking gorgeous."

She had the sudden urge to reach up and sink her hands into his barely there hair and pull his head toward her breasts. Where had that come from? Wolf Meyer was doing crazy good things to her ego and her libido.

"Now, let's get to the fun part of the evening. I want to show you

98

a couple of scenes. You're going to watch, and then we'll talk about them and how they made you feel." He took her hand, threading his fingers through hers. Her small hand was engulfed in his big one. "Come on, sweetheart. Julian's getting ready to whip Finn. I've heard the boss can be hard on him. It should be interesting."

He started to walk toward the far end of the dungeon, taking her away from Leo. She could breathe again. It was odd how much easier it was to concentrate on Wolf when she wasn't directly in the same room with Leo. She found herself unaccountably positive for the first time in over a year.

A good portion of the crowd in the dungeon had gathered in front of the raised stage that dominated the far end of the floor. She'd seen it, but never in use. Julian had walked her through the dungeon when he'd given her a tour, but it was different when filled with a crowd of scantily dressed Doms and subs. Wolf made it to the front of the crowd, tugging her along. Though she was jostled back and forth, it seemed that everyone got out of Wolf's way, as though his stature and presence ensured his status as the alpha male.

"Here we go, sweetheart." He brought her in front of him, his big body a bulwark against the rest of the crowd.

"Hello," a deep voice said from just to her left.

She turned slightly and saw a gorgeous man. Times two.

Twin Doms stood to her left, their lovely chests on display. Dark hair hung right below their ears and four perfectly blue eyes stared at her. Well, at her chest. Still, it made a girl feel like she still had it.

"Hi," she replied, smiling. She noticed a small female between them dressed in a PVC mini dress that covered her from her shoulders to the middle of her thighs. It was fairly circumspect for a skintight dress, with the singular exception of the fact that there were holes cut out of the garment accommodating her small but nicely rounded breasts. She had a thick collar around her neck with a long chain attached. "Hello, Kitten."

"We're in charge of her tonight," the Ken Doll she decided was Dom Number One said. He held Kitten's leash in his hands but passed it off to his twin.

Kitten turned her pretty green eyes up. They widened as she looked up and up and up at Wolf. "Wow. You're a very large man.

Kitten would love it if you hurt her."

"Down, Kitten!" Dom Number Two barked, pulling gently on the chain. Kitten whimpered and fell to her knees. Dom Number Two sighed. "Sorry, she gets aggressive when she's in the dungeon. And if she isn't good, we'll make her cover her breasts and take her out to the bar where no one will play with her."

She didn't look aggressive. She'd fallen to her knees, her legs spread and her head down. She looked deeply submissive. Dom Number One petted her hair.

"It's all right, Kitten. Calm down."

"And while Kitten is de-stressing, you can tell us your name, gorgeous," Dom Number Two said with a wink.

"Her name is Mine, asshole." Wolf put an arm around her waist, pulling her back toward his body.

"Nice, brother. I thought you were a boy who liked to share your toys," Leo said, moving to Wolf's right.

Damn, she was surrounded by hot guys. Even that Logan fellow had a perfectly cut chest and lovely face. He grimaced and shrugged toward Wolf. "Sorry, man. I bragged about last summer and you and me and James."

Wolf's arm tightened. "No problem, man. I don't mind a good ménage, but I'm not about to offer up my sub. A ménage is something between friends, and they're not my friends."

Dom Number One smiled, an easy curling of his fabulous lips. "We could be friends."

Dom Number Two seemed to be the surlier of the two. "Probably not. I'm not very friendly. Kitten, up."

Kitten popped up and immediately smiled at Leo. "Hello, boss."

Leo nodded. "Good evening, Kitten. Are Ben and Chase treating you well?"

Kitten's eyes slid away as she replied. "Yes, Sir. But they won't hurt Kitten. They say Kitten hasn't been good enough. This big man looks like he could hurt a sub. Kitten would like to try fire play, Sir. Would you talk to the large, attractive man about burning Kitten?"

Yeah, Kitten had issues.

"Sorry, man. I tried to tell her she wasn't cleared for that. Big Tag and Charlotte are all about the fire play right now," Dom Number

One said. "I thought they were doing private play parties while New Sanctum is being built."

"Charlotte doesn't want to hang out in Li's garage or something, so they're sneaking in here," Dom Number Two explained. "I sent a text to Adam about Tag cheating. Didn't say anything else, so that should cause some chaos. And I tried to explain to Kitten that he's not actually burning his submissive. He likes his balls too much to do that to Charlotte."

Leo leaned forward. "Kitten, until Miss Janine clears you for play, all Julian will allow is two spankings a night. You know the rules. You don't want to upset Finn, do you?"

Kitten's head shook. "No. Kitten loves Finn. But you're all wrong, you know. Kitten is not crazy. Kitten is just more perverted than the rest of you. One day you'll see." She turned her eyes up to Wolf. "And Kitten really would like to play with you, Sir. What's your name?"

"His name is Mine, Kitten." The words came out before Shelley could think about them. But they felt right. Kitten apparently got chatty when she chucked her day clothes. She'd never heard Kitten able to put so many words together without stammering.

She could practically feel Wolf's satisfaction. "Sorry, Kitten. I have a sub. And the name is Wolf. Wolf Meyer. Though I do go by Mine where Shelley is concerned."

She thought she heard Leo say something about vomiting.

Julian Lodge stepped through the crowd, Finn and Dani at his sides.

"I love it when all my boys get along," Julian said. He nodded Shelley's way. "You look lovely, dear."

Finn winked. He was wearing leathers but no shoes. "That top fits you perfectly."

"By perfectly, he means it makes your boobs fall out." Dani wore a modified version of fet wear that showed off her lovely belly. And her boobs did, indeed, seem to be falling out.

But now that Leo was close, she felt a bit self-conscious again.

"Oh, little one, if I've properly judged Master Wolf here, before long she'll simply be naked," Julian said with a smile. Her whole body flushed at the thought, but Julian continued. "Master Wolf seems to be a man who likes to share the beauty of his sub with those around him."

Wolf's hands cupped her shoulders. "I don't think she's ready for that, Julian."

"Oh, but one day she will be," Julian assured him. "She'll find that sharing her beauty is a wonderful thing."

Dani grinned. "Yes, sharing is good, Master. And from what I've heard, Master Wolf is a 'sharing' kind of person."

Shelley looked up, and Wolf had flushed slightly, his eyes narrowing on Logan.

"Sorry, man. I thought it was fine to talk about it. I mean, have you seen where we are?" Logan asked.

"Dude, discretion," Wolf shot back. "Have you told everyone?"

Logan shrugged. "I'm surrounded by crazy threesomes, man. It seems normal to me. When Dani there asked about my life in Bliss, I thought she was asking about the kinky stuff."

"You're in a threesome?" Shelley asked, her jaw dropping open. And he hadn't bothered to mention that?

"No. I've never had a permanent threesome," Wolf replied quickly.

"Just a whole bunch of short-term ones," Logan supplied helpfully.

"Wolf, you've spent too much time in that town," Leo said, his mouth firming to a flat line.

"I like Bliss," Wolf admitted. He looked down at Shelley. "And your brother is in a happy threesome. You probably shouldn't judge."

"I wasn't judging, Sir." But she was thinking.

"And she did put down ménage on her list of sexual fantasies," Julian added. "It was one of the reasons I decided Master Wolf would be perfect."

"Julian, hello, perfect sharing twosome right here," Dom Number One said.

Julian turned to the twin Doms, bowing slightly. "I apologize, Benjamin. I hadn't heard you and Chase were seeking a permanent submissive. I will immediately begin looking for the perfect woman."

Dom Number Two, who she'd figured out was named Chase, turned a nice shade of green. "Don't you dare, Julian. Monogamy.

The word makes me sick."

"Well, it wouldn't be monogamy, would it?" Julian pointed out. "The two of you can't have a separate thought, much less claim a woman on your own. I believe the word you're looking for is polyandry."

Ben shook his head. "Nope. Don't like that one either. They both mean the same thing. One pussy for the rest of my life. I intend to live a long time."

Chase was quietly petting Kitten, who had gotten back to her knees. Chase held her leash in his hands. "My kitten doesn't want commitment, does she?"

Kitten shook her head. "No, Sir. Kitten would like to try as many Masters as Kitten can."

"Good, Kitten." Chase stared at Julian like the man had threatened to hang him.

Julian waved it all off. "Come along, my loves. Let's play until we can't anymore. I suspect our littlest one is going to curb our playtime when he comes along," Julian announced with a grin.

"Julian, it's a girl. The doctor said she's a girl," Dani insisted. "We had a sonogram last week, but Julian hasn't gotten the message yet."

Now Julian was the one who looked a bit green. "No. This child is going to obey me, not some sonogram." He got down and spoke directly to his wife's belly. "You will be a boy. Girls scare Papa. Grow a penis and quickly."

He stood and sighed, seemingly satisfied that the fetus would do his bidding. Then he turned and walked up to the stage.

Finn covered his laugh. "You'll have to excuse the Master. He's in denial. The thought of having a daughter has, well, scared the crap out of him."

"I'm worried he'll try to exchange her," Dani said.

"No, baby," Finn replied, taking her hand. "He'll take one look into her perfect eyes and fall madly in love, and then the world had better watch out because he's going to be a scary-as-fuck father. I fear for the teenaged idiot who tries to date our daughter."

"Finn!" Julian's bark had the whole room silent.

Finn straightened up quickly. "Come on, baby. He's going to

need a little something, if you know what I mean."

"Really, Wolf?" Leo asked the minute they were gone. "Didn't I teach you properly?"

Wolf grinned his brother's way. "Yes, you told me to share my toys when we were kids."

"Well, I certainly didn't mean it that way." Leo crossed his arms over his chest. He finally looked directly at her, though there was a blank expression on his face. "Is he treating you well?"

Her heart ached. He was so beautiful and so remote. "Yes. He's been perfect, Sir."

Sir. Not Leo. It was easier this way. Yes, Julian had been right. This was the right path.

Leo's face tightened. "Good. Wolf, you have a key?"

Wolf shook his head. "Nah. I'll find a motel. No problem. In a couple of weeks, I'll start looking for an apartment. Don't worry about me."

Leo wasn't having it. "You'll stay at my place. Logan already moved his stuff in. I have another bedroom ready for you, unless, of course, you want to share with Logan."

Shelley stared at Leo, about ready to tell him off, but there was a smirk on his face.

Wolf shot his brother the bird. "Fuck off, man."

Leo's smile grew. "Well, I know you like to share, brother."

"You're such a fucker."

They seemed to be having some sort of brotherly moment. The kind no woman could understand.

Leo sighed. "Come on, Wolf. If Ma finds out you're not staying with me, she'll give me hell."

Wolf turned away, his eyes going back to the stage. "Fine. I'll stay with you until I find my own place."

"Good." Leo nodded her way and turned back to Logan as Julian strapped his partner to the St. Andrew's Cross.

The crowd hushed, and the show began. She forced her eyes to the stage, forgetting about the fact that she might be able to give up Leo, but it didn't look like he would be out of her life anytime soon.

Chapter Seven

She watched as Julian Lodge's perfectly formed body wielded the whip. There was a crack through the air and a snap back, and then a thin, red line welled on the white flesh of Finn's back.

Shelley took an unconscious step away from the stage and right into Wolf's chest.

"Shhh, it's all right, sweetheart," Wolf whispered against her ear. "Finn loves this. From what I understand, Finn has been Julian's submissive for years. They know what they're doing and what it takes for Finn to find his subspace."

She gasped as the whip cracked again, the sound violent, like a snake striking from nowhere. She kept her voice low. "I don't see how Finn isn't screaming."

"It sounds worse than it is."

She looked over and Leo was standing right beside them. She thought he'd walked away, felt more comfortable with him walking away. But he was standing right there beside his brother, dressed almost identically. Two amazingly gorgeous men.

Yeah, if she hadn't had ménage fantasies before, she sure as hell had them now. Why had she ever put that down on the questionnaire?

Because there was a part of her that wanted what Trev had found. Because there was a part of her that wanted the balance of two men just in case one of them turned out to be a criminally minded

Lexi Blake

douchebag. Because she didn't trust herself anymore.

And because the whole month she'd spent talking to Wolf, she'd had fantasies about Leo suddenly turning around and both men wanting her. But that was all it was, a fantasy.

"Don't be afraid, sweetheart," Wolf said, his arms encircling her. He was so protective, but could she trust him?

"She isn't afraid. She's worried. That's her worried face. Her brows wrinkle, and she gets this deep line right in the middle of her forehead."

Trust Leo to have noticed that.

"Sweetheart, we don't have to play with the whip if you don't want to," Wolf assured her. "But you should know that what you hear, that cracking sound is something Julian controls with the flick of his wrist. Really look at Finn's back. Julian is in complete control. That whip can be horrible if he handles it wrong. Or it can whisper across Finn's skin. It can bite on the right side of pain. It can be what Finn needs it to be. Do you see any blood?"

She didn't. There were several pink lines on Finn's flesh, and now she could see the way he'd relaxed, his shoulders slumping and head lolling back. Finn seemed to be getting what he needed.

"He feels like you did when I spanked you." Wolf's voice was a deep rumble over her skin.

"You spanked her?" Leo sounded like Wolf had said he'd beaten the crap out of her.

Julian turned and stared back because Leo's voice had carried through the dungeon.

"Sorry," Leo said, holding a hand up.

She felt Wolf move behind her as Julian turned back to his task. That crack split the air again, but she saw it differently now. The spanking Wolf had given her had been so different. It had changed her world.

Wolf leaned over behind her, speaking to Leo. "She ignored certain key parts of our contract. She was assaulted, and she didn't call me. I went to her place, and she was there with some fucking former SEAL mercenary shit."

"Holder?" Leo asked the one-word question with a sort of hushed awe.

106

"Yeah, how did you know?" Wolf asked. "Wait. He called you, right?"

"Yes," Leo replied. "Did you say she was assaulted? Get back here. We can't talk up here."

She was pulled back, two arms on either of hers. She almost stumbled, but Wolf held her up. He finally cursed and shoved a bulky arm under her knees, hauling her against his chest. He followed his brother as Leo made his way through to the back of the crowd. She could hear the whip crack again and again, Finn's soft moans filling the air, making her believe he was enjoying the experience.

What would it be like to trust someone the way Finn trusted Julian?

"Explain." One word, but Leo made it sound like a long Shakespearian speech.

"She had her laptop stolen on the train," Wolf replied before she could get the words out. She was rapidly figuring out her response was not required.

"She was robbed?" Leo asked like he gave a damn. Logan had followed him, staying behind Leo like a properly trained lackey.

"Yes, I was," she managed, keeping her voice down because even she knew not to disrupt a scene. "Though the thief was an idiot because I bought that laptop bag at Target, and he had full access to a handmade Versace. I know which one I would have stolen."

Wolf turned her toward him. "Are you sure about that? He could see it? He had obvious access to something that was more valuable?"

She nodded. "Yes, he stared at it. There's no way he could mistake my bag as the more expensive one. That Versace was beautiful. Mine was beaten up. I shoved it on the floor. The leather is warped. It got wet. I was stupid and set it down in the rain when I was trying to unlock my car. I can't replace it so it looks like hell."

"So the only thing valuable was the laptop, and it was visible?" Leo asked.

"No," Shelley said quietly, well aware she was still in the middle of a scene. This couldn't wait until later? "My laptop bag was big enough that I could close it."

Wolf and Leo shared a long look.

"I'll check into it," Wolf said, his words sounding like a promise.

"Have you read her file?" Leo asked.

"I have a file?" She wasn't aware of it. Crap. She should have been. Julian Lodge looked like the kind of man who kept a lot of files.

"Of course," Wolf replied. He turned back to Leo. "You think this is about her ex? I can go talk to Tag right now."

Shelley's skin went cold. What about her ex?

"No idea," Leo answered. "But if someone is coming after her, I want to know what it's about."

"I'll look into it," Wolf promised.

Leo nodded. "I'll let Tag know, but he's the one who trained Ben and Chase. They're specifically here to handle things like this. We'll meet tomorrow at noon. Chase is one of the best hackers in the world. If someone has said anything about her on the net, Chase can find it. If some asshole wrote an e-mail about her, Chase can give it to you."

"We'll be there," Wolf promised.

"I will?" Shelley asked.

"You will." Wolf and Leo said the words at the same time, with the same deep inflection.

"Fine." She couldn't fight both of them.

There was a long pause. She stared at the scene in front of her. She thought they were being overly protective, but then she hadn't had anyone who was protective of her besides her brother in years. Maybe never since her father died. Bryce had married her for specific reasons, and when those dried up, he'd ignored her.

"Did he hurt you?" Leo asked, putting his hands on her shoulders and turning her around.

"No." She looked into his face, stark and lovely. God, he was a beautiful man. "He didn't touch me. He just took my bag."

The whip cracked again. She turned her face back, but now she was flustered. Her heart was racing. Why had that man taken her bag when there was something much more valuable in his grasp?

Had it been random? Why wouldn't it be random? What could she have that someone really wanted? She was living hand to mouth. She'd lost all of the property she'd owned with Bryce.

"Hey, calm down," Wolf ordered, his voice commanding her. "We're going to handle it."

Leo watched her for a moment. "She sometimes has anxiety

attacks, nothing serious, but she can get herself worked up. If you don't talk her down, she'll be anxious for hours. Shelley, why don't we all go up to my office and we can talk about what's making you nervous?"

Now Leo was making her nervous. God, the last thing she wanted was to become one of Leo's patients.

"I think I can handle this, brother," Wolf said, taking her hands in his.

Leo's eyes narrowed. "And I think I'm the one with the degree in psychology. If she doesn't want to talk to me, I'll go get Janine. Honestly, I should have thought about putting her in Janine's group in the first place."

Wolf squared off with his brother. "She's my sub, Leo. I have zero problem with her getting into Janine's group, but for now let me handle her in the way I see fit."

She wasn't sure what group they were talking about, but it didn't seem like the time to argue. Leo stood, his arms across his chest, and she worried for a moment that he was going to argue with Wolf.

"I want to stay with Wolf." She looked up at Leo. This was the longest conversation they'd had in fifteen months, and instead of being her friend, he wanted to be her shrink. She didn't want that. She wanted what Wolf could give her.

Leo took a step back, his disengagement clear. "Of course. Come along, Logan. We still have work to do."

The two men walked away, losing themselves in the crowd.

"Come on." Wolf pulled her back toward a corner of the room. She could still see the stage, but it was slightly darker away from the lights. Wolf settled his big body on a chair that had been shoved into the corner. "Sit down. We're going to talk for a minute. What's your safe word?"

She needed a safe word to talk? "Gucci. I have to find a chair. Hold on."

His hand came out to tug her to him, settling her on his lap. She was surrounded by him, his arms encircling her waist, the warmth of his chest touching her skin. "Did you do as I asked?"

"What did you ask?" She had to put her arms around his neck for balance.

Wolf's hand was on her knee. "I gave you some specific grooming instructions."

Oh, god. She shivered. He was talking about her pussy. She'd thought about him the whole time she'd been in the shower. She hadn't been able to think about anything else. She'd carefully shaved her mound, pulling the lips of her pussy apart and gingerly running the razor over her flesh. Every stroke of the razor had sensitized her skin. "Yes, Sir."

"Let me feel. Spread your legs."

She swallowed, hesitating. "But there are people here."

The Dawson twins were close, Kitten at their side. And Ian and Charlotte Taggart were cuddled together, not far away. She could see the big, sarcastic dude whispering to his wife.

Wolf's voice came out in a hard grind. "I don't care. And neither will they. Now spread your legs and let me feel your pussy or use your safe word."

It didn't exactly seem fair, but she'd known it would be this way going in. She could choose to obey or this particular portion of her evening would be over. And she wasn't sure she wanted it to be over.

Shelley took a deep breath. She was either in and willing to explore or she should walk away. She'd been so passive when it came to Bryce because she hadn't been willing to fight. She wanted to be done with waiting for something to happen to her. Wolf was giving her a choice. This wasn't some passive activity. She had to make the decision.

She spread her knees. She looked around, trying to see if anyone was watching.

"Stop it," Wolf said, his hands tightening. "You're not to worry about them. You're going to focus on me. Now, I gave you instructions, and I intend to find out if you followed them or if you're going to get another spanking."

She wouldn't mind the spanking, but in this case, she'd been a good girl. And despite the fact that it had made her uncomfortable, she'd only put on the clothes Wolf had given her. And he hadn't given her a pair of underwear.

He kept one arm wrapped around her waist, and the other found her knee. He forced her to open further. She could feel the cool air on her flesh. A thrill went through her. She'd never done anything like this, but she'd dreamed of it. In her darker fantasies, she'd been placed on display and touched and admired. Bryce had told her she was a freak when she'd mentioned her desires to him.

But she didn't want to think about Bryce. She wanted to think about Wolf's hand on her thigh.

"Tell me something, sweetheart." Wolf's voice was thick and dark, his lips tickling her ear. "Are you thinking about what happened on the train now?"

So this was Wolf's version of therapy. She had to admit, she preferred Wolf's hands on her to sitting in Leo's office. "Not anymore."

And she was calmer. Oh, her heart was racing, but her mind wasn't now. Her mind was on one thing—the hand that was doing a slow slide up her leg. He'd started at her knee, his fingers skimming the soft flesh of her inner thigh.

"Good. I don't want you to worry about it. If you're still scared, I'll sleep on your couch or I'll talk to Julian and get you a room here for the night."

"I'm fine." She sighed as his hand reached the top of her thigh, pushing back the tiny skirt, leaving her pussy on full display. From Wolf's vantage point, he couldn't see it, but other people could. "He took my laptop. He was an asshole criminal. I was due a new laptop anyway."

And now, with Wolf's fingers starting to tease their way toward her pussy, it didn't seem so ominous. Not everything was about Bryce Hughes and his crimes. Sometimes bad crap happened because it happened. She'd done what she needed to do. She'd called the police and filed the proper reports. Worrying about it now would do nothing but bring her misery.

And she had better things to do.

"Do you want me to stop?" Wolf's voice was low and teasing, as though he knew what her answer would be.

"No." She shifted her legs wider apart. That damn skirt was in the way.

He taunted her, brushing his fingers against her pussy. Soft, tantalizing, tormenting. He made small circles with his fingers. "I'm glad. One of the fantasies you indicated on your contract was public exhibition."

"I said I was curious." And now she was pretty sure she was curious.

"Someone's watching."

Her heart skipped a beat.

"Tell me if you want me to stop."

She felt eyes on her. She lifted her face and saw who was watching her.

Leo.

Leo stood at the edge of the crowd, his back to the stage. Julian was working Finn over. No one else was paying a bit of attention to her, but Leo seemed laser focused in.

"Don't stop." If Leo wanted to watch her, then she would let him. He'd proven he could compartmentalize. So could she. In the dim light of the dungeon, she could still see the way his eyes latched on to her.

"Tell me something, love," Wolf said, his fingers finally parting her labia. "In all those weeks we talked, did you ever touch yourself while you were thinking about me?"

She sighed and relaxed in Wolf's arms, her eyes never leaving Leo's. She felt like there was an odd connection to him in that moment, like an invisible rope crossed the space between them. "Yes. Wolf, you know my past. I've had two lovers in my life. My high school boyfriend and my husband. And I hadn't slept with Bryce in over a year before he died. I'm afraid I touch myself a lot." She frowned. "Well, I did until some bossy man told me I couldn't anymore."

He chuckled behind her, and she gasped when he stroked her clit. His fingers moved easily against the flesh of her pussy. She was so wet. She'd gotten soft and moist as she stood there watching Finn Taylor take his Master's whip.

"Well, now you don't have to touch yourself. I'll do it for you." Wolf slipped a single finger into her pussy, rotating and stretching her.

Her eyes met Leo's. There was no way to mistake the erection he was sporting. Leo's leathers had tented, but he didn't make a single move to cover himself up. He merely watched, his gorgeous face stony.

"So you never slept with my brother?"

The question brought her out of the sensual haze Wolf was weaving. "No. I never slept with Leo."

Just that one perfect kiss when she almost forgot all of her pure reasons for walking away from him. When Leo had kissed her, she'd nearly sunken into him, as though she could bind their flesh together. One perfect kiss and then it was all over.

"Because the way he's looking at you makes me think he wants you badly." Wolf's voice had turned serious, but he never let up on the slow slide of his fingers.

It was getting harder and harder to think. Leo was watching while his brother finger-fucked her. God, Leo could see her pussy. What was she doing? Why was she doing it?

"Do you want to come?" Wolf asked.

How long had it been since she'd come? Had she ever really? Her sexual life had consisted of a "too green to know what to do" boyfriend and her husband, who hadn't cared whether she'd enjoyed the experience or not. For the longest time, she'd decided that sex was a lie perpetrated by men. It was severely overrated, and then Leo had kissed her.

And she'd wanted. Truly wanted. She'd felt like a hormonally crazed teenager—the way she had before life and all its mundane miseries had beaten her down. She'd wanted, and she'd known that she might get what she'd wanted.

Wolf was offering her that. Weeks of talking to him had given her a sense of intimacy. The contract they'd signed gave her both peace that everything was out in the open and confidence that Wolf wanted this, too.

"Make me come," she said. She wanted. She wanted to want.

There was a hard pinch to her clit, and she nearly screamed at the sensation. It wasn't pain exactly. It sparked from her pussy and sizzled out across her flesh.

"Do you talk to your Dom that way?" The question was whispered into her ear, but there was no way the volume of his voice softened the words. They were harsh, a nasty, dirty, sexy threat.

Oh, yeah. She was beginning to understand how much of a freak she could be, and the crazy thing was, she was perfectly fine with it. For the first time in years, it felt like her eyes were open wide and the world was hers for the taking.

"No."

He slapped her pussy, an open-handed smack that had her yelping even as her pussy became drenched with juice. "What do you call me? You're going to have to learn some manners, love. What do you call me when my fingers are in your pussy? What do you call me when my hand is smacking your ass? What are you going to call me when my cock is halfway up that pretty asshole you have?"

"Sir." She couldn't get the word out fast enough. "Sir. I call you Sir. Please forgive me."

As much as she'd like the spanking, she wanted to come. She wanted those big fingers deep inside her.

And she wanted Leo to watch. God, his eyes on her were making her crazy. She looked up.

Wolf chuckled. "Yes, love, he's still watching. If he doesn't come in his leathers, I'll let you spank me."

She laughed at the thought of big, strong Wolf taking his pants down and offering up his ass.

Wolf's hand pulled the skirt up roughly, forcing it around her waist. No question now. She was on display. Her current Dom was displaying her to the man she'd loved. Wolf was showing off her pussy, his fingers gliding in and out, wet with her cream. Leo was watching unabashedly, his cock straining against his leathers. And she was writhing in pleasure, her legs spread, giving Wolf access and Leo a better view. It was decadent. It was perverted. It was the single most erotic experience of her life.

"Come on," Wolf commanded. "If big brother wants a show, we can give him one."

She gasped as he impaled her on two big fingers. He slid his thumb over her clit, making tight circles as he scissored his fingers open and closed deep inside her pussy. Her heart raced. She could feel the blood pumping through her body, a pounding rhythm that was leading to one and only one conclusion.

"Pretend that's my cock deep inside you. I'm fucking you so hard you can't tell where you stop and I start. You can't get your legs open far enough because you want to take all of me. And I want to give it to you. I want to feel the hot clasp of that pussy milking my cock. Fuck, baby, I won't ever have felt anything as hot as your pussy. You're going to rock my damn world. I won't ever want to stop fucking you."

His words dripped like honey over her, getting her as hot as his fingers working her flesh did.

"You're fucking gorgeous, little sub of mine. I'm going to train you to come for me. I'll be able to look at you and your pussy will flutter because you'll know how long and hard I can fuck you. I'm going to be the man who gives you what you need. You come for me. I want to feel your pussy clamping down on my fingers. I want to feel it all the way in my cock."

His fingers curved up, and his thumb rubbed in perfect time. Shelley exploded in a beautiful song of pleasure. His fingers made the music, his voice the words that sent her over the edge. She shook, quaking in his arms, his hands the only real thing in the whole world.

Wolf's hands and Leo's eyes. Through her pleasure she could see Leo still watched, his fists clenched at his sides, his jaw a strong, firm line.

"Perfect, love."

Her skin tingled. She could feel Wolf's lips nuzzling the back of her neck as he petted her pussy, bringing her down slowly and with a piercing sweetness. She'd promised herself she would take it slow with Wolf, but now she couldn't help the fact that she felt so close to him. She leaned back, reveling in his gentle care. It was as nice as the orgasm, this touching and his light kisses.

"What do you say now, love?"

She knew what he wanted and was more than willing to give it to him. "Thank you, Sir."

"You're welcome. And I think big brother definitely ruined those leathers of his, though I'm sure he'll keep a stoic look on his face and politely excuse himself. See, I'm different. I'm going to tell you and anyone else who asks that I came like a fucking teenager. You were so hot, my cock couldn't handle it."

She stifled a laugh. He was so ridiculously open that it made her comfortable with everything happening between them. "You're so different than what I expected."

He stopped, his hands stilling on her flesh. "You expected someone like Leo."

Fuck. She didn't want to open that can of worms. But honesty was the best policy. And who did he think his brother was anyway? "Wolf, you remind me of Leo, of the Leo I first met. He was funny and sweet and he made me laugh. He could laugh at himself. I turned him into this cold man. I didn't mean to, but I did and I can't fix it." She sat up, regretting the loss of intimacy, although this talk was close to her heart. She'd spent weeks pouring out her fantasies to this man and listening to his in return. She wasn't going to lose him over a love affair that had never gotten off the ground.

She wanted a relationship with Wolf. God, that was a relief. She felt a smile cross her face.

"What?" Wolf asked.

"Kiss me. Yes, I'm being aggressive, and you can spank me later, but it occurs to me that you've spanked my ass and had your hand up my pussy, but you've never kissed me. I want you to kiss me, Sir."

His lips curved up. "Maybe I want you to kiss me."

He was so stinking gorgeous. What the hell was she doing here sitting on his lap with her skirt around her waist? Her pussy was sopping wet, but he didn't seem to care. He was a huge hunk of man with no sexual inhibitions and a seeming desire to be with her and her alone. She wasn't a fool. Leo, for all the longing glances, had still kept his distance.

She leaned forward and pressed her lips to his. She felt him tremble before she touched him and realized that despite the fact that he'd put her on display, this small intimacy meant something to him. He was serious. At least that was how it felt.

She kissed his lips, softly molding hers along the seam. She reached up and cupped Wolf's face with her hands, feeling the bristles of his five-o'clock shadow. She kissed his mouth, thrilled with the fact that he was letting her explore. He would almost always take the lead, she knew that, but she thought he needed this. He needed to be the one being worshipped. And maybe he would like a few words, too. He had the filthiest, sexiest mouth she'd ever had the pleasure of listening to.

"This is my mouth on yours, but when you command it, Sir, I'll put my mouth on your cock."

"Are you trying to make a man crazy?"

The fact that she could feel his cock twitching against her thigh sent a thrill through her. How many times had she wondered if she wasn't a sexual creature? That she lacked what other women had? But the Meyer brothers had shown her differently.

She brought her tongue out, licking across his plump bottom lip, his every shudder making her bolder than she'd ever dreamed of being. "I'll lick it, Sir. I'll start at the tip and then make my way to the base of your cock before starting back up. I'll make sure to not miss an inch. And I'll lick your balls, sucking them in my mouth."

His tongue surged in, and he took over the kiss. He sank his hand into her hair, and the kiss went from sweet to carnal.

His tongue dominated, sliding against hers. His arms wrapped around her, pulling her into the cradle of his body. She felt cool air on the flesh of her ass. Her skirt was still around her waist, but she didn't care. Nothing mattered in that moment except the feel of Wolf's lips against hers and the wild caress of his tongue. She was ready to take him then and there, but he finally pushed her gently back, his kisses going soft and sweet once again.

"Thank you, love. I needed that." He sighed and pulled her close, cuddling her against him. "So can we safely move this from a test drive to an actual training relationship? I know we signed the contract, but it feels more real now, doesn't it?"

Her heart skittered. It would mean a collar and a commitment. It wasn't a commitment to love and honor forever, though "obey" would definitely be in the wording. It was a commitment to try. It was serious. It was what all those late-night conversations and flirty texts had been leading to. There was a two-week trial written into their contract, but Wolf seemed impatient.

It meant accepting a collar from him.

It meant giving up on Leo forever.

But maybe it meant betting on herself this time. Wolf Meyer was everything she could want in a man. Their chemistry was sizzling. Leo had been a dream, but Wolf was a stunning reality that might be great if she took the chance.

"Yes, Sir."

She was rewarded with a brilliant smile that made him look years younger. "I'm glad. That's awesome. I mean it. I knew it would work out." He kissed her again, a hard, affectionate peck, and then she squealed as he playfully smacked her ass. "On your feet, love. I need to go change."

She stood on her wobbly feet, pushing her skirt back down. Now she noticed that Julian was tending to his partner, his hands rubbing their way across Finn's back. Several people seemed to have realized there was more than one scene being played out in the dungeon. Yep. Strangers had watched her getting off on her boyfriend's lap.

Wolf was her boyfriend. *God.* She had a boyfriend. She hadn't had a boyfriend in ten years. She'd had a piece-of-crap husband, but no relationship she would even vaguely call affectionate.

Except her friendship with Leo. She looked across the room, and he still stood watching. She gave him a smile. He would always have a place in her heart. He'd given her the strength to break free. He'd been the thing she was striving for as she'd fought her way back to life. And he'd given her the keys to find what she needed.

His face changed, going from stony to sad in an instant, as though he recognized that what they had was now irrevocably changed.

"Hey, babe," Wolf said, getting her attention. "Great scene. Let's go get cleaned up and grab a beer." He held his hand up.

And her boyfriend proved he was a very silly man. She gave him what he wanted. A damn high five. He'd high-fived her in appreciation of her sexual services.

She caught sight of Leo, smacking his forehead with his hand and shaking his head.

She couldn't help but smile. At least Wolf Meyer wasn't perfect. He grabbed her hand and with a wink led her out of the dungeon.

* * * *

"I want the bitch dead," a feminine voice said, pulling him away from his thoughts.

Mitchell Cross sighed as his wife walked in the room. He leaned back over and finished the line he'd started, the cocaine beginning to work in his system. "I'm handling it, Brenda."

Brenda had started losing her looks years before, but she'd fought it with every dime Cross had. God, her fucking plastic surgeon was one of the reasons he'd been forced to make deals with men like Steve Holder.

Brenda huffed. "You're not doing anything. You're pathetic. It's exactly like everything else. I end up having to do it all myself. Did you use it all? Or do you have a stash for that whore you call an intern?"

He sighed. He actually was keeping some for Stephanie. She was so much more willing to go down on him when she'd had a snort. But between his dick getting some happy action and being forced to listen to his wife harp on him, his dick always lost. "It's in my desk."

Brenda's expression never changed. That wasn't surprising. She had enough Botox running through her system that Cross was pretty sure he could stab her and she would still have that blank, wide-eyed look on her face as she went down, her trout lips still in a slight smile because they didn't move anymore, either. She pulled out the small plastic bag quick enough.

"What are you waiting for? If you kill that bitch decorator, everything will be over. We won't have to worry about that damn tape coming out."

He wasn't even sure there was a fucking tape. But the timing was right. If there was even the possibility that the tape could get leaked, he had to take the chance and eliminate the threat. "I told you I'll handle it. It's been over a year. If she was going to come after us, she probably would have already."

Brenda snorted the cocaine, the nasal sound turning Cross's stomach. When she came back up, she sniffled and massaged her nose. The nose had work done on it, too. One of these damn days it was going to fall off, and he'd be charged with buying her another one. "I wouldn't have come after you."

"Why do you say that, dear?" God, he wanted to be alone. Her voice had started to haunt his dreams, and he couldn't get rid of her. She still played well to his constituency.

"I would have waited. Look, Mitchell, if you think about it for two seconds, it makes sense. She had a lot of heat on her after that drug lord took her husband out. She was lucky someone was willing to pay for a lawyer because the way I understand it, the feds came in and froze all of her assets. She still hasn't gotten most of it back."

"Yes, so the bitch needs money." And it would make sense to come after his since he'd paid her husband so quickly to stop the release of his sex tape. "She would have come after us."

Brenda shook her perfectly coiffed head. "With all those agents still looking at her? I don't think so. I would have waited until some of the heat died down. That woman had the press all over her. When was she supposed to set up a new blackmailing circle? Not if she has a brain in her head. She got off. She was probably nervous, but I doubt she'll stay that way for long. When everything calms down, we'll get one of those nasty e-mails."

God, he hoped she was wrong, but she made sense. "We don't even know the tape exists."

"And we don't know it doesn't. Obviously the feds don't have it or you would be in jail, dear. They might not give a damn about your two-inch cock, but they would care about the fact that you accepted a half a million dollars to push a contract for security through the committee. They would damn straight care that those men are using their role in security to run drugs and blood diamonds out of Africa."

Nausea rolled in his stomach. He could see the tabloid headlines. He could see the arrest warrants. How was he going to pay the blackmail on this? He was rapidly running out of money and there wasn't an upcoming election where he could milk his constituents for funds. That was a year away. He was fucked.

He was fucked. *God.* He was going to go to prison.

"You're going to prison." Brenda sounded almost excited at the prospect. There was still a line of white powder on the desk. She scraped it up with her manicured finger and indelicately spread it on her gums.

"Well, maybe you should switch to the cheap stuff, darling," he said, venom dripping from his tongue. "Because if I end up in jail, you won't have a dime to your name."

"Daddy's company pays me well," she said with a sigh. "Still, I wouldn't like to think about what this scandal would do to the family name. We have children, you know."

They had two piece-of-shit boys who could barely spell their own names, much less keep out of trouble. They were utterly worthless, but they were somewhat attractive and looked good on the yearly Christmas photo. He had his family-friendly photo op with them once a year and then he was able to happily send their asses back to boarding school.

Which he also wouldn't be able to pay for if this decorator bitch decided to milk him for cash he didn't have.

"I'm taking care of it." Brenda's words dropped like a ticking bomb.

"What have you done?" Cross asked, considering for the first time if he wouldn't be better off without her. Sometimes accidents happened, after all. Sometimes a poor woman with a hidden addiction got some bad coke and overdosed. A grieving husband made for good news.

"I handled it," she repeated.

Fuck a god damn duck. He stood and took her by both shoulders, shaking her. Even through the Botox, he was able to see some small amount of fear in her eyes. "You tell me what you did."

She pulled away, trying to straighten her designer dress. "I hired someone to take care of it. That bitch is going to meet a few nice men tonight. I've had them tracking her for a couple of days. The minute she leaves that building she works in, she's not going to be a problem anymore."

She was going to fuck everything up. "I already put someone on this."

"And he's taking too long. You talked to that asshole days ago and she's still out there. My guys are going to move fast. They are being paid to go through her apartment and find what we need, then they're going to kill her and the problem will be solved and we don't have to worry about it ever again." She reached for a cigarette, lighting it with some designer lighter that had probably cost him more than a fucking car. "Now run along, Mitchell. I've handled it. I think if you hurry, you can catch Stephanie before she finishes for the day."

He stared at her. God, he hated her. She'd taken his balls long ago, and he couldn't fucking look at himself in the mirror because all he could see was the man she'd made of him.

And yet, if Shelley McNamara Hughes really was dead, maybe it would be the end of the problem and then he wouldn't need Steve Holder anymore.

He turned away from his wife with a sigh. Maybe sweet twenty-one-year-old Stephanie could take his mind off his troubles.

Chapter Eight

Wolf felt magnificent despite the fact that his dick was languishing in hell. He walked into the men's locker room with a huge grin on his face. He'd kissed Shelley, those gorgeous, sensual lips pressing against his, and dropped her off at the women's dressing room with strict instructions on how to dress and where to wait for him.

She'd smiled and called him bossy and agreed.

She was fucking perfect.

He glanced around the locker room. It wasn't some cruddy, poorly lit gym locker room. Oh, no. Everything at The Club was first-rate. Gleaming hardwood floor at his feet, and the lockers were engraved with the name of the member. Locker wasn't the word for it. His storage space was more like a small closet.

This place was unlike any club he'd been in before, and he got to work here. He'd spent months trying to get back on the Teams, and he'd worked on a ranch, but when he'd walked into this club, he'd had the oddest feeling that he was coming home.

"You high-fived her? What? Are you still in fifth grade?"

He grinned as Leo marched into the locker room followed by Logan. Yes, his brother was bitching at him. It truly did feel like home. "Hey, I thought Shelley and I made a great team. And she totally deserved that high five. I would have patted her on the ass, but I'd already spanked it earlier."

Leo kicked off his boots. Naturally, he'd been given the locker right next to his brother's.

"Yeah. I'm not sure you should be spanking her when she doesn't have a collar on yet, but that's beside the point. Nowhere in all of the clubs I have been in have I ever seen a Dom high-five his sub after a scene," Leo complained.

Wolf wasn't stupid. Shelley might never have slept with Leo, but they'd had something serious going on. He'd spent the whole afternoon thinking about the problem. The minute he'd figured out that Shelley had something to do with Leo's yearlong crappy mood, he'd wondered if he hadn't made an enormous mistake.

And then he'd realized he had a choice. He could walk away and hope that Shelley and Leo found what they needed. Or he could be what they needed and bring them together. And all the while he could make a place for himself.

A family. That was what he wanted, and he couldn't think of anyone he'd trust more to share a family with than his brother.

It worked for his friends. Hell, he'd seen men who hated each other bond over a shared woman. Why couldn't it work for him?

"Hey, she was hot, man. I would have high-fived her, too," Logan said, giving Wolf a thumbs-up.

Leo turned back to his charge. "I told you to watch Julian's form. You were supposed to be studying the scene."

Logan shrugged. "When some hot chick has her cootch on display, I'm not going to be capable of studying two dudes. It ain't happening."

"I am surrounded by twelve-year-olds," Leo said.

Leo had never been huggy, but god, he hadn't been this dried-up prune. Leo's sarcastic, snarky self seemed to have been replaced with someone Wolf didn't understand.

"Well, it worked. It took her mind off what happened this afternoon." But his brain was working overtime. He couldn't help but follow his instincts. And he didn't like the fact that Steve Holder had been in the exact right place at the right time to rescue Shelley. It felt wrong. "I don't want her in that apartment alone."

Leo untied his leathers. "You know about the trouble she had during her marriage?"

Wolf shoved his leathers into his gym bag and pulled out a pair of jeans. He would need to buy another couple of pairs of leathers if he was going to be in The Club every night. And he needed to find a dry cleaner who wouldn't mind some unsavory stain removal. "I read the file Julian sent me. Her husband seems like he was an asshole."

"He put her through hell."

Yes, he understood that. If he could, he would love to have a long talk with Bryce Hughes. A single bullet to the head hadn't been painful enough. "You're worried that someone's going to try to take revenge on her?"

"I don't know." Leo shoved his legs into a pair of boxers and sat down on the bench in front of his locker. "The feds cleared her, but that doesn't mean there aren't a lot of people out there who would love to get some revenge on someone, and Bryce is no longer available. It won't work. She doesn't know anything."

"I believe you. You were around this guy. Why the hell did she marry him?" It surprised him that she would stay in a bad marriage. Shelley seemed so smart, so capable. Yes, she was submissive, but she knew what she wanted. He couldn't see her wanting this Bryce guy.

Leo sighed and leaned back against his locker. "Go away, Logan."

Logan's eyes lit up like a prisoner who'd realized he might get parole.

Leo frowned. "I find you in the bar and we're going to have trouble. Go join Ben and Chase. Follow them around for a while."

"Cool. That Kitten chick seems like a trip." Logan was out of the locker room in a flash.

Leo looked up at him, his eyes narrowing. "He doesn't seem as broken as you said he was. I actually thought he would be unsettled by the scene, but he simply watched you get your sub off, paying no attention at all to the intense punishment going on onstage. I thought I would use it as a talking point, but I guess I'll have to find another way."

Wolf shook his head. Leo was barking up the wrong tree. "Logan isn't going to be disturbed by a lot of this stuff. He grew up in Bliss. I've heard that most of the men of the town have visited Stef Talbot's playroom. I spent the last summer with Logan and his best friend, James. Logan's into some kinky shit, but don't think for a minute that he's not troubled. You haven't found his pressure point yet. Now, tell me about my sub."

He was satisfied with the way Leo's eyes tightened at the word "my." Leo wasn't as remote as he liked to pretend. "I met her when I started treating Trev."

"Yeah, I knew who her brother was. I probably should have put two and two together, but math was never my strong suit."

Leo's eyes rolled. "God, I wish you would stop the 'I'm dumb' shit. Anyway, I liked her. It was obvious that she loved her brother and that her marriage sucked. You know me. I like to flirt."

Wolf liked to flirt, too. Though unlike his brother, he preferred to flirt with women who he could actually have a relationship with. But then Leo wasn't big on relationships. He'd had a few girlfriends in high school, and he'd married Janine, but other than that, as far as Wolf knew, he hadn't even had a permanent sub. Having spent the day talking to the other Doms and some of the subs who worked at The Club, he knew that Leo was a bit of an enigma. The Doms respected him, and the subs fought for his attention, each one desperate to be the one sub who finally caught him. But Leo was a hard case. "So you fell for her?"

Leo closed his eyes, his head against the door. "I guess so. I only know that I felt more for her than I've felt for anyone in a long time. I might flirt with my friends' wives, but I wouldn't touch them. They're safe. So are the subs I work with."

Yes, Leo had been running from the whole idea of commitment for a long time. "So after years of anonymous sex and flirting with no real intent, you meet Shelley and suddenly you can't help yourself. I can see it. She's amazing. She's gorgeous. She's funny. So why didn't you try to get her away from that asshole?"

Leo's eyes flew open, and his face hardened. "You think I didn't? Goddamn it, Wolf, I offered to take her away. I told her I loved her. She told me to stay out of her marriage."

He could guess what had happened next. Leo would have stepped back and walked away. "Why did she do that?"

"Because she didn't want me," Leo replied stubbornly.

"Bullshit. Why did she do it? I've known her a month and I would bet my life she did it because she thought she was protecting you. But your pride got hurt and you walked away when you should have tied her ass up and shoved her in your truck."

Leo leaned forward. "It's nice to know you would have done it differently. It's over now."

"Is it? Does it have to be? Do you want it to be?"

Leo laughed, but there wasn't a damn thing humorous about it. "You're going to give her up?"

"Why should I have to?" There, he'd put it out as flatly as he could.

Leo stood and slammed open his locker. "You've spent too much time in Bliss. It wouldn't work. I'm too possessive. I can't share."

"Bullshit. You aren't possessive enough." Maybe it had been too soon to bring that up. Wolf grabbed his jeans and started to get dressed. "You can use a word like possessive all day long, brother, but you let Janine walk out on you. Now you're letting Shelley walk away." He shoved his feet into his boots. "But I'm not going to make the same mistake. She's the one. I'm crazy about her, and I think I can get her to love me."

Leo sighed, the sound making him feel like he was five years old again. "You've known her for a fucking month. You just met her in person. You have always jumped in with both feet, never bothering to look and see what you're jumping into."

He wasn't about to argue with that assessment. "I go with my gut. My gut tells me she's special. My gut tells me to go for what I want. And my gut tells me to share her with you because we could give her what she needs. But I'll handle it by myself if I have to. She has ménage fantasies. I thought you could help with that. But I have friends who won't mind."

"Don't you fucking dare."

That was what he wanted to hear. His brother was actually quite possessive, though he had spent the last several years hiding it well. Or he simply hadn't cared enough about anyone to be possessive. Wolf knew the feeling well. "It's my job to give her what she needs. If I decide that she needs a ménage, then I'll make it happen."

He wouldn't. He wouldn't share her with anyone except Leo, but

Leo didn't have to know it. Wolf had known the minute he'd laid eyes on Shelley that he wouldn't share her. He'd enjoyed the temporary ménages he'd been a part of, but she was serious and only a seriously committed ménage would work. If Leo wouldn't go along with it, then she would have to be satisfied with toys and fantasy.

Wolf had needs, too, and in this case, they trumped hers. He needed her for himself—and his brother.

Leo's fists tightened at his sides. "I swear to god if you hurt her, I'll kill you myself."

"Yeah, that should be a pleasant conversation with Ma." He felt unaccountably better. If Leo had shrugged and said go for it, he would have known it was all over. But he hadn't, and seeing that Wolf intended to put his sub on display as often as possible, Leo wouldn't stand a chance. He would come after Shelley.

The only question was, would Leo accept him as his partner?

It was a dangerous game he was playing, but he didn't have another choice. The minute he'd figured out Shelley and Leo's deep connection, he'd known it was only a matter of time. He was crazy about Shelley. He loved his brother. He wanted the best for both of them.

And he wanted the best for himself.

"I'll stay at Shelley's tonight. I don't like the idea of her being alone until we figure out if the robbery was random." He glanced at himself in the mirror. He didn't look terrible, but he could use a good night's sleep. He probably wouldn't get it on Shelley's couch, but he also wasn't going to press his luck.

She was probably in some serious sub drop. She'd been caught up in the adrenaline of the scene, and now she would be thinking about the fact that she'd been naked. He would have to calm her fears by taking it slow.

But he didn't want to. He wanted to take her back to her place and shove his cock deep inside her.

"Dear god, Wolf, can't you control that thing?" Leo asked, his eyes rolling.

Yep, he had an erection again. "Nope. Little Wolf is very upset, but there ain't a damn thing happening to you tonight, buddy."

A smile finally broke over Leo's face. "It's good to know you still talk to your cock."

"Hey, sometimes it's been my best friend." It was an old joke between them. One they had started when Wolf was twelve and had gotten caught in the middle of math class with an erection because Penny Wells had worn a V-neck for the first time and she'd magically grown breasts over the Christmas break.

"Go and take care of her." Leo looked weary. "Call me if you need me."

Wolf started out the door.

"And Wolf?"

He turned. His brother's eyes opened and a sad smile crossed his face. "I'm glad you're here. We'll work this out. And god, don't bring Ma down on me."

"I promise nothing." He walked out the door, pleased with the way the evening had gone.

* * * *

Shelley stood right outside the women's dressing room. She practically cringed every time someone walked in or out and gave her a smile.

Were they smiling because they were friendly or laughing because they'd seen her ass? It had seemed so hot at the time, but now she was thinking about the fact that her ass wasn't as perky as it had been. And she'd never actually gotten a mirror out and looked at her pussy. It could be hideous.

And Leo had seen her. *God*. She'd spread her legs in front of Leo Meyer and writhed on his brother's lap. When she went wild, she really went wild.

"Hi, Shelley. Great scene. Very hot." Marcy, a sub who also worked at the bar, said as she walked up. "My Master was impressed. He shoved me onto a sawhorse and, wow. That was some of the best quickie sex I've ever had."

She felt her cheeks go up in flames. "Glad I could help."

Marcy had a pixie-like bob that shook slightly as she spoke. "I always thought you would end up breaking Leo's self-imposed exile, but, hey, his brother is even hotter. Although he's a little informal for my tastes."

Yeah, high-fiving her after a scene wouldn't make people take Wolf seriously. "He's different."

"Oh, yeah. I'll say." Tara, a regular who attended with her husband, agreed. She was a cute redhead who had patiently answered many of Shelley's questions when she'd first been interested in the lifestyle. "I just wish he'd managed to get his leathers off."

"I heard that, sub. That's ten," her husband called out. But he was wearing a grin on his face as he slapped her ass. "Come on, baby, give me another ten."

"Wolf Meyer is hot."

"Oh, yeah. Now I'm getting the crop out." Tara's husband kissed her cheek and strode into the men's locker room.

It was that sort of easy relationship she wanted. Tara didn't look like she would be sitting around terrified someone was making fun of her cellulite. Tara seemed secure in her relationship, and Marcy looked perfectly happy to have had some amazing sex.

"I hear you're getting all the subs in trouble, love."

God, he was so damn sexy. Wolf stood in the entryway to the locker room wearing a perfectly respectable pair of jeans, a T-shirt, and a light leather jacket that he somehow turned into something ultra sexy. His broad shoulders filled the entryway, but she was caught on his male-model-worthy smile. She sighed.

And so did Tara and Marcy.

Tara leaned over and gave her a hug. "I'm going to change before I really get in trouble. I'm into Darin for double digits with a crop already. If he catches me mooning over the new Dom, he might attach a TENS unit to my pink parts."

"God, and you're running from that?" Marcy asked, giving Shelley a wink before she followed her friend.

"I'm glad to see you're getting along with the other subs."

He looked so self-satisfied that she had to wonder how much he'd overheard. "They were sympathizing with me because my Dom is so sadly unattractive."

His grin grew. "Is that right? Poor Shelley. Well, I'm the lucky one because all anyone can talk about is how hot my sub is."

How did he do that? One minute she was vowing to never be

naked again and the next she was perfectly willing to throw off her clothes as long as he took her. What had Charlotte told her to do? Listen to the man. Judge him by his actions. He truly thought she was gorgeous.

"Come on, sweetheart. I'm going to take you home."

The evening was ending already? "I thought we were going to have a drink?"

"Fet wear only in the bar. I thought we could stop somewhere vanilla. If we stay here, we'll have to talk to other people, and I would like to focus on you. And then I can get you drunk enough that you don't fight me when I tell you I'm sleeping on your couch tonight."

He was what? "Why would you sleep on my couch?"

"Because you got mugged and you might have nightmares?"

The truth hit her with all the subtlety of a runaway train. "You think it was a setup. You think he knew who I was. Why would he steal my laptop? Oh, god, he was looking for information."

It was happening again.

"Hey." He reached out and grabbed her hand. "I'm probably being paranoid. As a man who used to fight some of the worst human beings and terrorists in the world, you have to understand that I sometimes see the glass as half empty, and maybe there's a bomb at the bottom of it."

But what if he was right? It had always been there in the back of her mind. The press had reviled her for months. It didn't matter that she'd been cleared. She'd been the one who had unwittingly placed the cameras that had caught the blackmail material Bryce had used on her clients. For months, she'd received nasty phone calls and e-mails calling her every bad name in the world. After a year, it had quieted down, and she'd hoped it was over.

What if it wasn't over? Her son-of-a-bitch husband was never going to let her go. He still had a hold on her, even from beyond the grave. She was going to have to give up another man she cared about.

She shook her head. "No. You should stay here. You shouldn't get involved in this."

Wolf took a step forward, his lips curving into a snarl. "What did you say?"

"She said you should leave her alone, Wolf. She obviously wants to be assaulted." Leo was suddenly beside him, the Meyer brothers taking up all the available space.

She found herself pressed against the wall. "I'm trying to protect him."

Leo snorted and slapped his brother on the back. "Protect him? This two hundred and twenty pounds of pure Navy SEAL?"

"He isn't a SEAL anymore," she pointed out. He could be out of practice.

"Once a SEAL, always a SEAL, love." Wolf's tight smile seemed predatory.

And Leo's matched him. "So you think you're going to be able to handle a potentially dangerous situation better than Wolf?"

He was willfully misunderstanding her. "I think Wolf shouldn't have to handle this."

Leo's head shook. "I disagree, and I damn sure think he disagrees. I watched him bring you to orgasm not half an hour ago. You had your legs spread wide for him, and you gave him everything he asked for. He owes you his protection."

"He doesn't owe me anything." The last thing she wanted to do was to bring Wolf into her nightmare. It wasn't fair. He hadn't done anything wrong, and he could get seriously hurt if he got involved. She couldn't live with Wolf getting hurt any more than she'd been able to handle the thought of Bryce hurting Leo.

"Then you were using me?" Wolf asked, his eyes stony.

"I told you," Leo said to his brother in his first sign of sibling solidarity. Naturally it was against her. "She did the same thing to me. When she no longer needed me, she told me to get out of her life. At least she gave you some sort of excuse. She told me to leave. No reason."

He hadn't been willing to discuss this for almost a year and a half, but he brought it up now? Frustration threatened to overtake her. "I had a reason. I tried to explain that to you. I didn't want Bryce to hurt you."

Leo's eyes rolled. "Yes, Bryce Hughes, who I outweigh by forty pounds of muscle. Bryce Hughes, who ran away from a bar fight. Yes, he was going to take me out. Bullshit. It's a ridiculous argument, and it won't fly."

"He had guns. I found them that day." She could remember how terrified she'd been when she'd opened the drawer to Bryce's desk and found his gun. All she'd been able to think about was Leo taking one of those shiny bullets.

"Yes, dear, because no SEAL ever had to deal with guns." Sarcasm dripped from Leo's voice.

Wolf pulled at the side of his jacket, and sure enough, there was a gun in a shoulder holster. "I have a permit to carry concealed. Julian made sure of it before he hired me. Besides being one of his resident Doms, I'm also considered a trained bodyguard. Finn has worked some controversial cases in the last few years and a rich man's wife is always a target."

She turned to Leo. She'd never imagined that he would be walking around Dallas with a gun. "And you?"

Leo stood, his legs apart in a stance she was sure had once terrorized new recruits. "I don't carry in The Club, but when I escort Dani or Finn or even Julian himself somewhere, I carry. And, sweetheart, that day you dumped me, I had two SIG Sauers and a sniper rifle in my truck. I also do some training work with Dallas SWAT."

Wolf turned to his brother. "Are you seriously telling me that you don't have a weapon on you?"

"Well, I don't have a gun on me right this second."

"And if I checked your boot?" Wolf asked.

"You might get your hand sliced up," Leo admitted.

Shelley stared for a moment. The world seemed to have tilted slightly. "You have a knife?"

Leo tapped his boot against the floor. "More than one, if you have to know. And I had more than one on me the day you dumped my ass. It was only my remarkable patience that kept me from killing your asshole husband the night before in a bar fight. I thought you might have been angry."

Had she made a terrible mistake? Was she making one by trying to protect Wolf?

"I'm going to make this easy on you, sweetheart." Wolf crossed his arms over his chest in a show of mulish stubbornness. "You don't get a choice in this. I am going to take you home. I am going to stay on your couch. And I am going to bring you back here tomorrow. If you want to safe word on me, go on. I won't be your Dom anymore, but until I'm certain that you're okay, you won't be able to get rid of me unless you call the cops and have my ass hauled to jail."

"I'm not calling the cops." Tears blurred her vision. She'd given up so damn much, and now Leo was standing here telling her it had all been for nothing. If she'd gone with Leo that day, would things have turned out the same way? Or would Beth and Bo have been in an even worse position?

Misery washed over her. Regret.

"I'm glad to hear that," Wolf said, his voice softening. He reached out for her, his big hands enveloping hers. "Shelley, this is what I want. This is who I am. I want to protect you. I want to be the big badass who stands in front of you. It's all I'm fucking good at."

"You're going to have to work on his self-esteem," Leo said. "But he's right, and if you try to get away from him, I'll call your brother in. How do you think Trev will handle this? He's trying to settle in and now Beth is having a baby. Do you want him to have to leave his new ranch and his pregnant wife because you're too stubborn to accept protection?"

"Damn it, stop being so hard on her," Wolf complained, pulling her close. "She's had a rough day. She's not going to call the cops."

But Leo's words had formed a hard knot of guilt in her belly. Wolf hugged her, but she simply stood there in his arms. She'd been happy when she'd heard Beth was pregnant, but there was a nasty kernel of envy in there, too. Trev had done everything wrong and still managed to build an amazing life for himself. She'd sacrificed everything for the people she loved and she was alone, and it seemed she always would be.

"I'd like to go home now." The words came out in a flat monotone. "I think I need some rest. Wolf can stay on my couch."

"Baby, don't be so glum," Wolf cajoled. "I really can protect you."

Leo took a step back. "And tomorrow we'll all sit down and discuss it. It's Saturday. We all have to have breakfast with the boss to discuss the weekend's parties and scenes. We'll talk about your situation. And we'll put Ben and Chase on the case. It's been forever since Chase got to hack something. He'll be thrilled. I think I saw Tag in the locker room. I'll let him know we might need extra help. I won't let anything happen to you. I didn't before, and I won't now."

"What is that supposed to mean?" She looked up at Leo. "You haven't talked to me for over a year."

Leo frowned and looked like he wished he hadn't said anything, but Wolf's face lit up.

"Julian didn't pay Finn, did he? You did. Finn was her lawyer."

Shelley thought her heart might break. Leo had paid Finn? "I thought he was doing it pro bono. Trev told me he was."

Leo wouldn't quite look her in the eyes. "Finn would have done it, but I knew damn well that he wouldn't be able to give it his full attention if he was still working on his other stuff. So I paid him to get you to the top of the list. Finn didn't actually make the money. He used it to bring in the consultants we needed to hurry things along. I also had Alex McKay put a good word in for you with the feds. He used to work for the FBI and he still has good contacts there. Money and power were the only way to solve the problem. If I hadn't given Finn money to grease a few wheels, you would still be under a cloud of suspicion."

"Why would you do that?" He'd acted like he couldn't care less whether she lived or died. He'd utterly ignored her, refusing to take her calls and making up excuses to not see her.

"It doesn't matter now. It didn't matter then. I spent a lot of money making sure you were okay. I would prefer you didn't blow it all by not allowing Wolf to protect you. And he can handle a few bullets. Half of him has been replaced by titanium rods and his skull is far too thick to ever let a bullet pass through it." Leo turned and began to walk back into the locker room, retreating. "I'll speak to you both in the morning."

Wolf grinned down at her. "Wow, he is such a coward. He ran back to the men's locker room because he doesn't think you'll walk in there with half the Doms in The Club down to their bare asses."

"He's right." Her mind was reeling. What did any of it mean?

Wolf kissed the top of her head. "Well, it's progress all the same. Now, let's go get that drink. I could use a beer. There's a store across the street. We'll grab a six-pack and head back to your place."

She stared at him. It seemed to her it was time to start training her Dom.

He stopped, and she could see him thinking. "Or we could get a bottle of wine."

He waited as if hoping against hope he'd penciled in the right answer.

"I would love a white, thank you."

"And a six-pack of beer." He was back to grinning as he led her down the hall.

Shelley looked back at the door Leo had disappeared behind. It seemed one of them was always closing the door on the other.

* * * *

Wolf took Shelley's hand as he walked past the security guard.

"Mr. Meyer? Do you want me to bring your truck around?"

He wasn't sure why this guy needed to bring his truck around when he himself had two legs, but he figured it was a "Julian Lodge" thing and he should get used to it. The same young man had insisted on parking the truck when he'd driven in, so he guessed this was the new norm.

He was going to have to start watching Leo and taking his cues. Wolf had been either in the Navy or on a ranch most of his life. He sure as hell wasn't used to wealth and people doing stuff for him, but it seemed to be the way The Club ran.

"Thanks, Nelson. We're going to run to the store across the street. Just have it ready when we get back. Give us ten minutes or so." It seemed silly to get into the truck, drive across the street, and then look for parking when they could dash over there and avoid the headache.

But maybe Shelley didn't want to walk. God, he was so out of practice. He'd spent the last freaking year of his life trying to get back into the Navy, fighting his discharge. He'd forgotten how to treat a lady.

He'd high-fived her. He felt a flush go through him. "I'm sorry about the high five. I was feeling pretty good. I'll be more formal next time."

"Don't you dare." She stepped out of the garage onto the sidewalk. The streets were quiet at this time of the night, but there were a couple of restaurants and a bar that still seemed to be hopping. She turned her face up to his, her skin luminous in the moonlight. "Wolf, I want you the way you are. I really do. I get that you were in the Navy for a long time, but the man I've been talking to through e-mail and on the phone is one of the nicest, most charming men I've ever met. I can handle the occasional high five. And you're obviously very smart, so I wish you would stop talking about yourself like that."

He growled, but it was definitely not at her. "I get this way around my brother. I've kind of been in his shadow for a long time. Our dad left when we were young, and he took care of me. He became the man of the house. Leo went into the Navy because he didn't have the money for college. When he got out he whizzed through his undergrad and straight through to his PhD. He's the smartest guy I know."

They walked down the street toward the corner. "Well, you're no slouch."

"I read a lot." He'd gotten ribbed for his reading tastes by his teammates. He'd read in his downtime. Pretty much anything his mom or brother would send him. Thrillers. Mysteries. History books. Books on psychology and sociology. But he didn't have a formal education.

"You can learn a lot from books. College is nothing but having a guide to reading the right books." Her hand in his felt so damn right. She took a long breath. "Mexican food smells good."

Well, he could fix that. "Come on. I'll get you some enchiladas. And a margarita. You'll see. This whole thing is probably nothing, but it's best to be safe."

A cloud of worry passed over her face, but he could see plainly that she had accepted the inevitable. "I will feel safer if you sleep over. But maybe we can talk about the couch thing. It's small and probably uncomfortable."

And the only way he didn't end up burying himself in her before the end of the night. "I've slept in worse places."

And then he felt it. It was a little thing, but he'd learned to trust it. A prickle ran up his spine as though his body could process his surroundings faster than his brain could, and it sent a warning. He stopped in the middle of the street.

The night was quiet, only the muted sound of mariachi music coming from the restaurant down the street. He looked up and down but there was no one out. Just him and Shelley.

But he knew they weren't alone.

"Hey, did you change your mind? We could get some wine and go back to my place." Shelley looked up at him.

He held a hand up, his fingers in a tight fist.

"You want to punch something?" Shelley asked, her mouth hanging open.

Of course. It was a habit. That fist would have told anyone in the military to go silent, but she hadn't served for years and didn't have the same instincts he had. "Hush, love. Stay still. If I tell you to run, you run."

Up ahead there was a long line of bushes that garnished a small store. The store's lights were out, but the streetlight glowed through the leaves. Except in one place. There was a man-size dark spot. Wolf looked down. Shoes.

Fuck.

Adrenaline, his old friend, began to pump through his body. He loved the fight. God, he'd missed the fight. Even now his muscles were loosening and his mind sharpening as he got ready to fight for his life.

But he had Shelley.

Double fuck.

His need to kill would have to wait. He pulled his SIG and grabbed his cell, pressing a single button. "We're heading back to the garage, love. You stay behind me."

Those feet were starting to move.

"What's up?" Leo asked over the line.

"Trouble. Grab Taggart and come now. I'm taking her to the garage." He slid his cell back in his pocket, certain Leo was on his way.

The streetlight above the shrubs flickered, and Wolf could see that whoever had been waiting there was moving a bit faster now, hugging the brick of the wall. Wolf gave the guy thirty seconds before he hit the end of the shrubs, and then he would be out in the open. There would be no more play. There would be a bullet.

It was the lightest of sounds that had him turning, realizing that Shrub Guy wasn't alone. Someone was coming up from behind him, and it sure as hell wasn't his brother. Leo wouldn't have made that mistake. Leo wouldn't have made a sound. The only way Wolf would have known Leo was there would have been when Leo wanted him to know. It would be the same with Ben and Chase, who had also put in their time with the Teams.

So it was an easy thing to turn and, in the blink of an eye, the scene played out in front of him. A single tango coming in at a run. The infiltrator held a gun in his right hand. He wore all black, and he'd covered his face with a balaclava.

Yeah, he knew how to handle that. Wolf aimed and squeezed twice, moving his hand not more than an inch. The sound broke up the night. The minute he squeezed the trigger, he turned, absolutely certain that asshole wouldn't get off a shot of his own. His aim would be true. There would be two holes, one in each lung. Wolf grabbed Shelley around the waist with one hand as he heard Shrub Guy's shot. Wolf dove, curving his body around hers and trying to take the brunt of the roll he had them in. He heard Shelley's gasp as they hit the street, but he protected her head.

"Stay down."

Another bullet whipped by, but this guy wasn't a pro. His shots were going wild.

Wolf's didn't.

Two final shots rang through the night, and the man who had been running at them stopped, went still, and then fell to the sidewalk, his lungs both useless now that Wolf's bullets had lodged there. He wished he could do what he knew he needed to. He'd prefer to leave nothing to chance. Two to the chest, one to the head. But Shelley was here. He had to take care of her first.

Wolf kept a hand on Shelley's head, his eyes searching the night.

"Goddamn it, Wolf. You couldn't have left one of them alive?"

Yep. He only knew Leo was around when Leo was ready to start bitching at him. With a long breath, he reached for Shelley. "Hey, sweetheart, are you all right?"

Her whole body was shaking. Her eyes were wide. Wolf's blood was still pumping hard through his system, but his heart softened. Shelley had been here before. She'd had someone—her husband—shot dead right in front of her. What if she was scared of him now?

She nodded, but her eyes were on the second dead man.

"I'm sorry. I acted on instinct." He'd killed two guys on their first date. He was glad he hadn't taken the head shots.

"Sorry?" She sounded like she was in shock. "You're sorry?"

"I should have gotten you away."

She threw her arms around his neck and held on for dear life. "You saved me. Don't you dare feel bad for killing them. You saved me."

She sobbed against his neck, but he relaxed. It was natural that she would cry, but he was so damn grateful she understood that he felt a smile cross his face.

"This one's dead, too, Leo," one of the twins said. Wolf thought it was Chase. The big Dom had a gun in his hand as he examined the body.

"Yeah, he's gone soft." Big Tag was shaking his head, staring down at one of the dead guys. "He forgot the head shot."

Charlotte Taggart was standing beside her husband. There was a gun in her hand and she looked like a woman who knew how to use it. "I think it's very romantic."

Taggart smiled his wife's way. "It is, baby. You remember that time we were in Paris and the dude from the rival Russian syndicate tried to murder us?"

She was all up in her husband's business, her body plastered to his. "Yeah, I do, babe."

"We have privacy rooms," Ben huffed. "Unlike Sanctum, which is rubble."

The Taggarts did not seem to mind making out over a corpse or two.

"Oh, excellent." Julian Lodge stood over the scene with his arms crossed. A tall, well-built man stood beside him wearing slacks and a dress shirt. He knotted his silk tie as he said something quiet to Julian and then pulled out his phone and walked away from the crowd.

Wolf pulled Shelley closer. He was going to get fired. He'd killed two people on Lodge's property. He would do it again, but, fuck, he was getting tired of having to find new jobs. He was running out of places to work. Taggart didn't seem to mind the corpses.

Julian walked over to the first dead guy, staring down with unabashed fascination. "Do you know how long it's been since I had to deal with corpses? It's been ages. I almost felt…legitimate." He said the word with a shudder. "You never kill anyone anymore, Leo. Ian always kills people in exotic places where I can't be involved. And Ben and Chase are far too lazy. Wolf, you're my new favorite. You get an extra waffle tomorrow morning." He sighed and straightened his shirt. "Well, I should get inside. The police chief is calling this in. It will be handled with discretion, but I think we want this on the record. Ian, Charlotte, privacy room, please. We have to explain the violence. Let's not explain public sex. Wolf, don't incriminate yourself."

"I'll make sure he doesn't," Leo said with a frown.

Taggart groaned and kissed his wife one last time. "I'll stay and talk with the cops. Chief, can you send in Brighton? He knows how to handle this particular situation. Ben, Chase, it's going to be a late night. We need to ID these guys, and I'm not willing to wait for DPD to do it. We'll send Brighton everything we find."

Chase huffed. "Someone has to make sure Kitten isn't humping some random Dom. I'll get her and take her back to our place. Send me whatever you can get and I'll get Chelsea on the line. Charlotte, is your baby sister still single? Because I would love to get some of that."

Taggart laughed but Charlotte turned to Chase, her hands on her hips. "I know a British guy who might have some trouble with that."

Chase shrugged. "I think I can handle some Brit."

"He will snipe you, Chase," Tag promised.

Chase frowned. "Fine. That's pretty rude though."

Ben slapped his brother on the arm. "Come on. Let's save some poor Dom from Kitten's affection and then you can hack a bunch of systems. Let us know if you need us down here. We're good at hiding bodies if you change your mind. Big Tag teaches a class."

Shelley ignored all the sarcasm. She simply shook and held on to him. He tightened his arms around her. He'd almost lost her. Damn it.

Someone was coming after her, and it pissed him off. Two assholes had hidden in the dark with the intent of taking her out. He didn't believe for one stinking second that this was random, and that meant that this afternoon hadn't been random, either. Someone wanted his girl, and they would have to get through him.

And his brother. Leo stood over the man who had tried to kill Shelley, and Wolf saw his intent. Leo would kill anything that came her way. Leo's eyes came up, and they were dark and hard, his brother every bit the SEAL he'd been trained to be, only this time he wasn't protecting his country. He was protecting the other half of his soul.

While Shelley wept out all her anxiety, Wolf and Leo made a silent promise.

They would take out anything that came her way.

Chapter Nine

Shelley walked into Leo's condo feeling distinctly zombie-like. Her feet shuffled in, but it was an instinctive thing with no real purpose behind it. Since that moment when she'd realized someone was after her, she'd simply followed Wolf's instructions. Wolf had been something real and tangible to hold on to. His big hands had gripped her, holding her to reality. His strong arms had protected her. He'd covered her with his body, willing to take any bullet that came her way.

He'd killed two men for her.

She couldn't help it. She was in love with Wolf Meyer. And yet Leo still held a piece of her heart.

Wolf turned, smiling. He'd been a rock for the last several hours. He'd been the rock she'd clung to. He'd never faltered. He'd simply held her and patiently dealt with her, never once making her feel weird for her anxiety. He'd handled his interview with the police with charm and aplomb. She was pretty sure the officers who had taken his statement either wanted to be him or do him. They'd stated plainly that they admired him.

Wolf could take care of himself. He could take care of her.

"You can take my room, sweetheart. I'll be right out here all night long." He gestured toward the couch.

"Ben and Chase should be here soon," Leo said as he shut the door behind him. "Big Tag is still with the police handling the clean-up and he's got someone working on IDs. I sent Ben and Chase to check out your place and bring you back some clothes."

She was pretty sure they wouldn't bring back underwear. She would be lucky to get a bra when two Doms were packing for her.

She looked around. She'd never once been invited into Leo's condo, but it was everything she'd expected. Cool, lovely, a bit Spartan. It reminded her of the man himself. The whole condo had been done in neutral shades. She would have liked a pop of color herself, but it was nice.

And the sofa wouldn't hold Wolf. His knees would be drawn up all night long.

What was she waiting for? She wanted to sleep with Wolf. The only thing that was holding her back was the fact that Leo was in the room.

"How about a Scotch? I could use one." Leo strode to the kitchen.

"Are you okay?" Wolf looked down at her, his sensual mouth so close it had her heart pounding.

She let her hands drift to his waist. "Someone wants to kill me."

Saying it helped. It made it real. It made it something she could look at and fight. She wasn't going to lie down. She wasn't going to accept this fate.

"We're going to take care of it, sweetheart," Wolf promised. "Me and Leo. We won't let you down. We fight a lot, but when we want to, we make a good team. I promise I won't let them near you."

He wouldn't. He would fight, and from what she'd seen tonight, he would win. He'd been miraculous. His body had moved like that gun was a part of it. One moment he'd been smiling and happy and talking about margaritas, and the next he'd been a killing machine with one thought—to protect her.

And she found that infinitely sexy.

She was well aware that her sudden sex drive had a lot to do with adrenaline and emotion. She shouldn't push it. She should let everything settle. It's what Leo would tell her to do. He would tell her to take a step back because she could be making a horrible mistake by rushing in when she should take it slow.

"I don't want you to sleep on the couch." She'd spent her whole damn life doing the "right" thing. Or maybe that was the wrong way of thinking about it. She'd done the most acceptable thing, the logical thing. But this, being here with Wolf, this felt like the right thing.

The only thing that would be missing was Leo, but she'd given that up.

Wolf's face went blank. "Sweetheart, if you climb in bed with me…" He stopped and took a long breath, obviously coming to some sort of decision. "All right. If this will make you feel better, I can do it. Why don't you go and take a shower? I'll find you something to wear. And me. Crap. I don't exactly do pajamas."

He turned away from her, his shoulders squared as he looked out the window. The lights from the Omni Hotel sparkled, changing from blue to red and green. "It'll be fine."

He thought he wasn't getting any. God, he was so damn sweet. Under that big, badass exterior there was the heart of a teddy bear. Granted, he was a teddy bear with some nasty teeth, but he was so tender with her that she couldn't hold herself back. Leo had called to her in a different way. Her attraction to Leo had been immediate and visceral, but with Wolf it had been a long, slow dance of words and distance that led to a sweet lust.

And her new man had some very specific kinks. In for a penny, in for a pound.

Shelley fell to her knees, her head down in the submissive position she'd seen Dani and the other subs in so often. She spread her knees, wincing at the scrapes on her legs. Leo had insisted on calling paramedics to make sure she hadn't been brain damaged by Wolf's protective roll. The paramedic had cleaned and bandaged a couple of places and made some statement about how lucky she had been to not get torn up more given her lack of clothing.

Wolf kept talking about all the things he would need to do before he was ready for bed.

"I should wait up for Ben and Chase. We were lucky the police chief was here or we probably would have spent the whole damn night at the station. And it was lucky there were so many witnesses."

She kept her head down but smiled. Did he really think she hadn't noticed that several upstanding members of The Club had managed to *see* the whole incident when she was damn sure no one had been outside? Julian was excellent at creating a perfect case for self-defense.

She wouldn't want to be on Julian's bad side.

"Of course, we'll still have to do some follow-up with the police."

She wasn't sure who Wolf was talking to anymore. And the position wasn't one she was used to. When was he going to turn back and look at her?

"Your back isn't straight enough. Bring your spine up. Like there's an invisible string pulling you toward the ceiling."

God, she'd dreamed of that voice. Leo. Leo was telling her what to do. She glanced up and saw him in the reflection of the glass in his windows. He stood behind her, his eyes focused on her back. Wolf turned suddenly, and he stared for a moment.

Shelley straightened her spine.

"Eyes down, love," Wolf said, his voice going dark. Gone was the nervous chat of before, and in its place was a deep command.

"She needs to spread her legs." Leo's voice was tense.

She kept her head down but couldn't help but glance up to see Wolf's lips curve in a small smile.

"You should tell her that," Wolf said. "I'm sure you can explain it well. You always have had a way with words."

"She's not my sub. Damn it, Wolf."

She could hear the tension in Leo's voice. What exactly was Wolf doing?

"You're a trainer. We're a new D/s couple. This is what you do," Wolf stated with a calm his brother didn't possess right now.

Her heart was starting to race. If she wasn't so damn sure of Wolf's innate kindness, she would wonder if he was trying to torture his brother. But Wolf wouldn't do that. She knew it deep down. Was he inviting Leo in?

Was he asking Leo to join them? And what would she do if Leo said yes?

Leo walked forward. "You've been doing this for years. You know what to do. I should leave the two of you alone."

Wolf chuckled. "After tonight, I'm pretty sure all the rules I understood are moot. I need to learn all of The Club's rules. And you're my brother. You've taught me all my life. Who better to instruct us both?"

"You're a fucker, Wolfgang."

"Back at you, Leonardo."

Shelley couldn't help it. Her head came up in a heartbeat. "Wolfgang? Leonardo? Seriously?"

Leo frowned her way. "Eyes down, pet, or I will spank you despite the fact that my brother covered you in bruises tonight. We have to talk about your protection methods, Wolf."

She looked back down, but she couldn't control her heartbeat. Leo didn't sound like a man who was about to walk away. He sounded more comfortable. More in control.

"Well, she isn't dead. I was calling it a win," Wolf shot back.

She felt a hand reach for hers. Leo brought her arm up, and he showed off a tiny cut she'd received as Wolf had rolled her onto the street in his successful attempt to keep her away from a bullet. "What do you call this?"

Shelley called it a teeny tiny wound that had already scabbed over.

"Collateral damage," Wolf replied.

"You have to be more careful with her," Leo insisted.

"He was dodging a couple of bullets at the time." She felt a need to defend her savior. "But, you know, the whole 'getting saved' thing would have been easier if I was allowed to wear panties."

Leo looked down at her, his blue eyes icy. His Dom look. That look went straight to her pussy. "Your response is not required, pet. And panties would not have helped you. Now, get yourself back in the proper position, or I will tie your hands behind your back, put a spreader bar between your knees, and clamp those lovely tits. And then Wolf and I will have a long conversation."

Nope. Her response was not required. She put her head back down. She caught sight of Wolf's grin before he took on his steely look again.

"Leo, I promise next time I'll be more careful."

She winced. There probably would be a next time. *Damn it.* Someone wanted her dead. She had no idea who it was or when they would try again. It struck her forcefully that this moment was all she could count on. Her father had died suddenly, her mother a long, slow slide. And Bryce. Bryce hadn't known what was coming for him. He'd been alive one minute and a corpse the next, his expression barely changing as he moved from the living to the dead.

She wanted to live and not merely to move through what some people would call a life. She wanted to really be alive. And she wanted the Meyer brothers. She might not be able to keep them for long, but she would take whatever small moments she could get. She would take them and hold them close and dive into each memory when she was alone again.

And she would always know that for a brief time, she had been alive.

"Sweetheart?" Wolf got to one knee, his hand coming out to tilt her chin up. His face showed his deep concern. He brushed away tears she hadn't known she was shedding. "Come on. I'll put you in bed. You've had a rough day."

She looked up at him and glanced back at Leo. Leo had his arms crossed over his chest.

"Go on, Shelley. Get some rest." No more "pet" from Leo.

They didn't understand. "No. I don't want rest. I need this. I need you. Both of you."

The room went super still.

"I don't think this is a good idea," Leo said, making her heart ache.

"You do what you have to, brother. But if she needs something, I'll find a way to give it to her eventually," Wolf said, leaning over to brush his lips against hers. His eyes focused on her. "You're sure? I'll wait."

"I don't want to wait. I've waited forever, Wolf. If Leo won't play with us, then I'll be fine. I'm sure you can find a way to fill me up, Sir."

His smile illuminated the room. "I can, love. Now take off your clothes and resume your proper position. I want to play."

She got to her feet, shaking but not with fear. Desire coursed through her body. And Leo hadn't left the room. She was deeply aware of his presence, like a reluctant lion who hadn't decided whether or not to pounce yet. She pulled her top over her head, her nipples immediately puckering as the cool air hit her skin. Wolf held a hand out, taking her shirt and placing it aside.

Leo huffed and then grabbed the shirt, neatly folding it.

Wolf grinned. "He's a total anal-retentive neat freak, love."

"I don't want to live in squalor. And your room always smelled like a locker room," Leo complained.

If she didn't get control again, the Meyer brothers would be doing a weird form of family therapy, and she wasn't interested in that type of therapy. She pushed her tiny skirt off her hips and prayed the sight of her naked body would bring them back in line.

Silence reigned. She felt their eyes on her, and for the first time since she'd started this play, she felt a bit of trepidation. She wasn't perfect. She wasn't a woman who worked out, and she tried to diet, but she really liked Mexican food and margaritas. Leo and Wolf were perfect specimens. What if they had only thought they wanted her?

Wolf moved forward, his mouth a hard, sensual line. "You're lovely, Shelley. Fucking gorgeous. Turn."

She followed his instructions, giving him her backside with only the slightest hesitation. Turning put her straight into Leo's line of sight. He stared at her, his blue eyes drinking her in. She couldn't mistake the hard line of Leo's erection. He might not want a relationship with her, but he seemed to want her.

She gasped as she felt a hand on her backside. Wolf's big, warm palms cupped her cheeks.

"Have you taken a cock up this ass, love?" Wolf's words came out in a low rumble.

"I doubt it," Leo replied. "She's actually quite innocent."

But she didn't want to be. And she didn't see why it was dirty. Having vanilla sex with Bryce had made her feel dirty because there hadn't been a drop of love between them, but standing in front of the Meyer brothers, her every girl part on display, didn't feel dirty. It felt right.

"No, Sir. I haven't. But I'm willing to try," Shelley replied.

Wolf let his hands curve around, skimming over her hips and stomach, pulling her back against him. She felt his cock rubbing against her ass. "I'm glad to hear that, love."

He worked his hands up to cup her breasts. Every inch of her flesh was coming alive under his hands. And Leo's eyes watched every moment. Wolf buried his face in her hair as though he wanted to inhale her.

"God, she smells so good."

Leo's eyes tightened. "Jasmine. She smells like jasmine."

"I don't know what it is, but I fucking love it."

Her shampoo was jasmine and so was her body lotion. She loved the smell. And Leo knew it? Her heart was pierced by the sweetness of it, and their distance made her ache. She wanted to reach out to him, but he was so wary she feared he would walk away.

Wolf stepped back. "What did I tell you to do? I'm still the Dom here."

He'd told her to find her position. She got back down, her knees sinking into the thick rug that covered this portion of the immaculate living room.

"You're going to have to work on her form," Leo said, his voice a mere whisper.

Wolf put his hands on her shoulders, squaring them. "Yes, but she's still lovely like this. I know some knotty time will get her in shape. Perhaps tomorrow I'll tie her up and keep her at my feet for a while." He stroked her hair. "I'll need that from time to time. I'll need you to simply kneel at my feet after I've properly bound you. I'll talk to friends or watch a game on TV, and I'll feed you and stroke you. I'll find it calming."

God, she would be his pet in those moments. She wouldn't have to think about anything except how much her Master cared about her, how much they could bring each other joy.

"She would look lovely in suspension," Leo offered.

"Yes, I believe we'll get to that, too. But tonight I have something else in mind. I got to play with this pussy earlier, but I neglected a few things." Wolf knelt behind her. "Spread those legs further. I want access to my pussy."

His pussy. The words crept sensually along her skin. She forced her knees open.

"Do you have a safe word?" Leo asked. "I want to make sure you're okay before I leave you to your Master."

He was leaving? She forced back her tears. She couldn't make him stay. And begging wouldn't help.

"I have a safe word," she admitted. Only the feeling of Wolf's hands on her seemed real.

"I need to hear it. I need to know you negotiated this with Wolf," Leo said.

"Gucci." It seemed silly now, but that was the word she'd chosen.

Leo's face softened. "Not Prada?"

He remembered that her dream bag had been a Prada. How could he remember everything she'd ever told him, spend thousands of dollars to make sure she was safe, and still walk away? She didn't understand him. "I never say no to Prada."

Leo nodded and turned away.

Wolf's hand slid down her body. "It's okay, sweetheart. I don't intend to give you a single reason to say no." His voice got low, whispering in her ear. "Baby, I can take care of you."

She nodded. He could. He would do everything he could to make sure she was happy. She couldn't ever let him know how much she would miss Leo.

She would just have to sink herself into Wolf. She would have to make sure he was as happy as he would try to make her.

She leaned back against him, his chest offering her strength. His fingers slipped all around her pussy as he eased her back. Before she knew what was happening, Wolf had her up and on the couch, cradling her between his thighs. She could feel the rough rub of his jeans against her hips.

"Relax, sweetheart," Wolf commanded. His feet caught hers, spreading her wide. There was something deliciously decadent about being completely naked while he was fully dressed.

She closed her eyes, letting Wolf surround her. She wouldn't watch Leo walk away. If she kept her eyes closed, maybe she could pretend Leo was still here, that he wanted to be with her. It was a harmless fantasy. She would get over it. She would be happy with Wolf.

"Tell me you don't want a taste of this," Wolf said.

Shelley felt his cock against the cheeks of her ass. It pressed against her flesh, promising all manner of pleasure. He was a big man, far larger than she'd ever had before. She could only imagine how that enormous cock would fill her mouth. "Yes, Sir. I want a taste."

His voice tickled her ear. "I wasn't talking to you, love."

Her eyes flew open. Leo stood at the end of the couch. He'd had every chance to walk out of the room, but he stood there watching her, his fists clenched as though he didn't quite trust himself to not reach out and touch her.

"Tell me you don't want a taste of this pussy, Leo. You never tried it, did you?"

There was a short pause before Leo answered. "She was married."

"She was married to a douchebag." Wolf's hands stayed right where they were, rubbing her pussy.

"The vows are the same. I haven't touched her. Not like that. I've only kissed her."

"Then you have to be starving for it," Wolf said. "I've only known her for a month, and I'm dying to get my mouth on her pussy."

His fingers slid through the petals of her pussy. She felt herself softening and getting wet all over again. She wanted to writhe under his fingers, but she held herself still, waiting for whatever Leo was going to do. The wait was killing her, but she didn't even breathe for fear that she could scare him away.

"She's going to taste so good. I can already smell her," Wolf said on a sexy groan.

"God, you're an asshole, Wolf." Leo bit the words out.

"Maybe," Wolf replied. "But I'm an asshole who knows how to share. I'm an asshole who knows what we all need."

"What if she doesn't want to be shared?" The question came from Leo's lips with no small amount of challenge.

Wolf's breath was warm on her ear. "Tell him, sweetheart. He won't believe it until he hears it. Tell him you want him to join us. Tell him how much you want his mouth on your pussy."

She knew exactly what she wanted. "I want you, Leo."

A hand came up and pinched at her nipple. "That wasn't what I said."

God, he was going to make her say it. Every second she hesitated, he tightened his grip on her nipple. The pain bloomed, stinging and making her restless. "I want your mouth on me."

"Harder, Wolf. The sub doesn't seem to understand what you want." Leo leaned over, his face a hard mask. His hair had come out of the queue he usually kept it in. The thick brown locks hit his shoulders and made him look the slightest bit savage.

Wolf gripped her other nipple, both hands on her breasts, twisting to the point of pain—and bursts of aching pleasure. "You're not listening, love."

"Pussy." She got the word out as fast as she could. "Leo, I want your mouth on my pussy."

Wolf didn't let up. "Tell him how much you want him to eat your pussy, like a nice ripe and juicy peach. You want him to eat it and suck down all that juice you're making. Tell him. I want to hear you say it in that oh so sweet and polite tone you use. Politely ask Leo to eat your pussy and then maybe, just maybe, he'll give you some cock, too."

If he didn't stop talking, Wolf was going to make her freaking come with nothing but his words. She felt every dirty phrase low in her womb. And she couldn't deny him. She knew that in the light of day she might be horrified, but here and now, she simply obeyed.

"Please eat my pussy, Leo. I want you to suck and love my pussy, and I want you to prepare me to take your cock. I want your cock so badly. I've wanted it since the minute I met you."

The vise on her nipples released, and she could breathe again.

"Very nice, love," Wolf whispered. "So, Leo, are you going to help me reward this sweet sub, or am I the only one getting a little pussy tonight?"

"Fuck you, Wolf." But Leo tossed his shirt aside. He didn't take the time to fold it as he had with her clothes. He climbed on the couch between her legs.

Shelley leaned back and gave everything over to her men.

* * * *

Her scent assailed him. God, she'd shaved her pussy. It was right there, a ripe testament to feminine perfection. Leo breathed, letting the scent wash over him, memorizing it for later. He would dream about how fucking good she smelled.

He leaned over and rubbed his nose across her labia, delving lightly inside. He wanted that smell all over him. If she was his sub, this was how he would start every day. He would shove his nose in her pussy so her scent would stay with him all day.

Shelley moved restlessly, and he heard Wolf growl.

"You stay still," his brother said. "Do you want him to eat your pussy, or do you want another spanking? I was easy the first time. I won't be again, love. I'll spank that round ass of yours until you can't sit, and then you'll suck my cock and get nothing for yourself."

"No." Her whimper went straight to his cock. Fuck, he was so hard. His cock was pulsing against his jeans, but he didn't dare let the greedy bastard out. If there hadn't been the discomfort of clothes between them, he would already have shoved his cock deep inside. He would be riding that pussy, and he didn't want this to be over so quickly.

It might be the only time he ever got to have her. It might be the only time he ever gave in to temptation. It had to last.

"I can see we have a lot of work to do, love. You have to be still when we're fucking you," Wolf ordered.

"He's going too slow," Shelley complained.

Oh, she hadn't seen slow yet. "I'll go however fast or slow pleases me. I'm in charge here. And Wolf left out the part where I tie you up so you can't touch yourself. Think about that when you try to take control. You'll be tied up and spanked and forced to take both of our cocks down your throat. And then we'll leave you like that."

He heard her sniffle, and he softened slightly. He leaned down and placed a delicate kiss on her clit. Plump and swollen, the jewel practically pulsed under his attention. "Or you can be a good sub and let your Doms have their way with you. Now beg me."

How long had he waited for her to beg? He'd dreamed about cries and pleas coming from that succulent mouth since the day he'd met her. He'd gone to talk to her about her brother's condition. He'd said all the right words that day, but all he could think about was getting her to kneel at his feet, placing a collar around that graceful neck, and making her his.

"Please, Leo."

Normally he would insist on Sir, but he loved the way she said his name. He knew he should correct her. He should keep that small but necessary distance, but instead of what he should have said, he teased her pussy with the tips of his fingers. "Again."

"Please, Leo. Leo, I need it. Please."

He couldn't wait a minute longer. He dropped to his belly and settled in. He pressed her legs wider and pulled the petals of her sex apart, revealing glorious pink and coral and red flesh, all of it painted with the pearly juice of her arousal.

With a long, slow lick of his tongue, he tasted her for the first time. Tangy and sweet, the flavor exploded on his tongue, penetrating his senses. He was filled with her. She invaded his every sense. He ate at her pussy, reveling in her taste. He breathed in her scent until it was the only thing he could smell. Her skin was soft beneath his hands, and he couldn't help but stare at her pussy. It was a work of art. The more he licked and suckled and gently bit, the more it bloomed for him like a flower that had needed light for so long and had finally found the sun.

Her whole body quivered. Leo looked up and saw that Wolf was holding her down, his big hands acting as bondage, keeping her still. Wolf was whispering to her, his tongue coming out to lick along the shell of her ear. His brother kept her spread for his pleasure, a living, breathing, sentient bond. But unlike the thin jute rope Leo preferred, his brother wasn't a simple tool. Wolf had made an active choice to share his sub, and now he chose to allow Leo to go first.

What the hell was wrong with his brother? Did Wolf want to force her to choose between them? Was he trying to compete?

Or was he trying to bring them all together and form the odd family he'd been looking for since the day he'd been old enough to know what he wanted?

Leo kissed her thighs and gently worked his finger into her pussy. Her tissues were swollen with blood and slick with juice, every inch begging for a cock. His mind whirled. This was more than a fun fuck. Would he be able to walk away?

He couldn't share. Not long term. Hell, he wasn't even sure he could commit long term. His marriage had been a mess. He'd distanced early on. What if this was all he could offer a woman?

The muscles of her pussy quivered around his finger. What if Wolf was offering him the best of both worlds? A sub he could sink into again and again and walk away from when he needed to. Wolf would take care of her. Wolf would love her. Wolf would offer up his enormous heart on a platter. He probably crapped hearts and rainbows. Wolf would be her everything if she let him.

And he could be that guy who gave her a quick fuck. Yeah, that was what he was good for. So why couldn't he walk away? Because if that was all he could get, he would take it as often as he could. She never had to know that he thought about her every minute of the day. She never had to know how she'd taken a stranglehold on his heart and soul to the point that he hadn't fucked another woman in almost two goddamn years because all he could see was her face.

Wolf was offering him the only piece of heaven he would ever have, and damn if he wasn't going to take it.

And he wasn't about to be a selfish prick.

He pushed himself up. "Come on, pet. Your Dom has been incredibly patient. I'd like to see how you suck a cock. Start with Wolf's." He turned to his brother. "If you high-five her, I swear I'll punch you."

Wolf grinned as he helped her sit up. Shelley's chocolate brown eyes were dazed, and Wolf passed her off to him, settling her naked body in his lap. He wrapped his arms around her.

"But I was so close," she whispered. "It was right there."

Bryce Hughes was a motherfucker, and if he'd been alive, Leo would have killed him. "Baby, he never made you come, did he?"

She shook her head. "I didn't even think I could until tonight."

When his brother had gotten her off in front of a dungeon full of people. Wolf had given her her first real taste of pleasure. The least he could do was give her the second. "Get on your knees, baby. You're going to suck Wolf off while I finish the job."

"I like the way big brother thinks, sweetheart." Wolf had tossed off his T-shirt, and his hands were on his jeans. He shoved them down and proved he still enjoyed the term "commando."

Shelley sat up. Leo couldn't help but sigh. It was obvious she was impressed with little brother's package.

"Well, pet, go on. It's obvious you would like to inspect that monster more closely." He patted her ass as she got up, then shot his brother a look. "Now I understand why you act the way you do. You don't have any blood in your brain, do you? It's all in your cock."

His brother grinned, palming himself. His cock stood straight up, practically pointing where it wanted to go. "Who needs a brain right now? But you could probably use some of this." Wolf tossed him a blue container.

Lube. Damn, Wolf was going to kill him. He wanted Leo to start stretching her ass so one day she could take a cock up it. Wolf's cock, most likely. The idea of his brother taking Shelley's ass didn't piss him off the way it should. Wolf would be gentle with her. Wolf would rather cut his cock off than hurt her, but Leo wouldn't be there. The thought made him ache.

Leo lubed up his hand. He had some work to do. He wouldn't think about the future. He wouldn't think about anything except how good it felt to finally have his hands on her. He got down on his back and slid between her legs. Fuck. This was his favorite place in the world to be, staring up at her pussy. He let his hands find her ass, cupping the round cheeks and getting a nice firm grip. "Take him in your mouth, pet. See how much of that monster you can handle."

"How am I supposed to concentrate when you're doing that?" Shelley whimpered as he pulled her down so she was almost sitting on his face. He pulled her cheeks apart and started to rim her asshole. He couldn't see it, but he knew it would be tight and rosy pink. He worked his pinky finger over and around and around, pressing in lightly as he tongued her pussy.

He smacked her ass with his free hand. "You will if you want me to continue, pet. You'll make Wolf howl."

"Yes, Leo." She breathed the words out. She leaned over, bringing her pussy onto his mouth.

He latched on, suckling her clit, letting her taste fill his mouth once more. He had to concentrate. It would be so easy to lose himself in her, his tongue thrusting up, fucking her like his cock would take her. He could suspend himself in the moment, never needing to leave. But he needed to get her ready.

He nosed her clit.

"Don't you stop sucking me." Wolf had lost any semblance of

playful lover. His brother's voice had gone to that hard Dom place he knew so well. "I'll pull you off him if you stop."

He sort of wished he could see her. God, when had that happened? He actually wanted to watch her suck his brother's cock. She would be beautiful, her tongue lavishing affection. He could sit back and enjoy the view and know it would be his turn next.

He pressed his finger in, the tight ring of her asshole finally giving way. He stretched her, massaging the hole until he got in to his first knuckle. Shelley's body moved in a staccato rhythm as his brother seemed to get damn serious about fucking her mouth. He rode the wave, his tongue worrying her clit, his finger fucking her ass in earnest now.

Her whimpers and moans let him know he was hitting all the right spots. He sucked her clit between his teeth as he heard Wolf hiss and groan.

"Fuck, baby, take it all. Swallow it all down. Oh, god, Leo, whatever the fuck you're doing, don't stop. She's killing me," Wolf said, his pace becoming ragged.

Arousal coated Leo's tongue. Shelley's hips pumped, thrashing against his tongue, shoving back as though she wanted way more than a finger in her ass. She was going wild and he liked it. Later, he would bind her so fully that she couldn't move, couldn't fight anything they wanted to do to her. She would be trussed up and waiting for his pleasure. She would be gorgeous with her hands and legs tied, her ankles in a spreader and her breasts bound, forced to stand up and wait for her Masters' torture. He and Wolf could clamp those tits and get her ass rosy and ready for a long, hard fuck.

Shelley moaned. Wolf must have freed her because her groan filled the room. Leo pressed his finger in and circled her ass as he gently bit her clit, and she went off, wailing and pleading.

His cock felt like it was going to explode for the second time that night. He'd come in his leathers like an untried boy when he'd watched Wolf get her off earlier. It was about to happen again, but she softened, coming down from the high of the orgasm.

Leo pulled his finger out. She'd need a plug. He would find one in The Club's treasure trove of sex toys. He would select a brand new one from the stores and prepare it and...hand it over to Wolf because she was Wolf's sub.

He nearly protested when Wolf lifted her off his face. He licked his lips, wanting to get every bit of her.

"Hey, brother, grab some condoms, will you? Let's take this to an actual bed. I think she'll be more comfortable." Wolf held her in his arms. She looked sweet and so damn submissive against Wolf's massive chest.

He pushed himself up off the floor. She was so fucking beautiful with her dark hair hanging in a waterfall, brushing the tops of her flushed breasts.

He was a total fool. He'd had all he was going to get, and he didn't blame Wolf for carrying off the prize. Wolf turned and headed for the guest bedroom.

It rankled a bit that his brother had asked him to play the sexual equivalent of a water boy, but after everything Wolf had given him, he would honor his brother's request. He reached into Wolf's leather bag and searched for the condoms he was sure to find there.

His brother hadn't brought much with him. A couple pairs of jeans and some shirts. Socks. A tablet reader. And a picture. He felt his heart clench. It was a picture of him and Wolf, but not as anyone would know them today. They had been kids. He had been twelve and his brother seven. They stood in front of their ramshackle cabin, the mountains in the background. It had been high summer, and Leo could still feel the sunshine on his face. He stared at the camera, his arm around his brother, but Wolf looked up at him. He stared up at his big brother, adoration plain on his face.

He'd pushed Wolf away for years, and yet his brother still came looking for him.

He shoved the feelings down and grabbed the box of condoms. He walked into the room. He would stay and watch. He would work with his brother to bring Shelley as much pleasure as possible. He swore he would stand by and watch with a smile on his fucking face because he wanted more than anything in the world for these two people to be happy.

They were his family, and just because there was something broken inside him didn't mean he didn't love them.

He would watch as Wolf made Shelley his. Maybe it would help him accept the fact that Wolf was better for her.

Wolf kissed her, his body covering hers, his hands everywhere. He rolled off and glanced up, palming a gorgeous breast. His brother gave him a smile. "Well, are you ready?"

Wolf wasn't going to let up. *Fucker*. Wolf was going to try to pull him in. Wolf spread her legs, and Shelley looked up at him, her eyes dreamy. She was laid out like a feast.

And Leo didn't turn down a feast.

Chapter Ten

Shelley looked up at Leo from the safety of Wolf's arms. She could still taste him on her lips. Her tongue had tasted every inch of his dick. Wolf's cock was a thing of beauty. Big and outrageously thick, it had taken work to get it in her mouth. She could still feel his hips pumping against her cheeks, the firm muscles of his ass under her fingers. She'd loved the way his ass had flexed as he'd pumped into her mouth. She'd had to relax, and that had been a hard thing to do when Leo had tortured her with his tongue and his fingers.

Her asshole still burned a bit, but she welcomed the sensation. The rest of her body felt drugged with pleasure. The orgasm had been stronger this time, as though her body was learning to accept more and more ecstasy. Wolf kissed her, his mouth covering hers. He kissed like a Master, giving her everything he had, taking more than she could have imagined.

She felt small and submissive and more powerful than ever before.

Wolf winked down at her before looking back toward the door. "Well, are you ready?"

She forced her brain to work, trying to shove the cobwebs of desire aside. Leo stood in the doorway. This time he didn't hesitate. He tossed a small packet at Wolf. Condoms. Oh, god. They were really going to do it. She was going to spread her legs and take their cocks into her pussy. Her heart skittered, and her pussy swelled. Though she was sure she couldn't come again, she wanted the feel of holding Leo and Wolf deep inside her body. She wanted to look up at their gorgeous faces and see the pleasure she brought them. After all, they had shown her pleasure she'd never dreamed of.

And she felt so close to them. That she felt close to Leo wasn't a surprise. She'd felt that way always. Leo had been her rock during those years when Trev had battled his addictions. Leo had talked to her on the phone and come to her mother's funeral. If only she'd met Leo before she'd married Bryce, maybe her life would have been different. Feeling connected to Leo was just normal, but the deep comfort she found in Wolf was a revelation.

Wolf felt right. His arms around her. His cock in her mouth. They felt real and lovely. Wolf's huge body housed an unbelievably warm heart. In a single day, he'd saved her life and showed her how sexy she could be. He'd forced her to really look at him and see past his gorgeous good looks to the sweet, affectionate man inside.

And he'd welcomed Leo. No matter what came after, she would always have had this one night with Leo, and Wolf had made that happen.

Leo's hands went to the fly of his pants, and he made quick work of them, shoving them off his lean, muscled hips. She felt her lethargy dissipate. She watched as Leo's ripped, hard body was revealed. She stared at the tattoo on his upper left pectoral muscle. It was small, not anything large and showy. It was the only ink she could see.

"You like his tat, sweetheart?" Wolf asked, a smile on his impossibly handsome face.

"I can't really see it," she admitted. But she could see the rest of Leo. So beautiful. He was all lean, hard, and masculine. And he'd commented on Wolf's big cock, but now he proved himself to be a total hypocrite. Leo's cock was every bit as thick and long as his brother's, standing straight up almost to his navel. His heavy balls were drawn up close to his body. She wanted to taste him, too. She wanted to get them to stand together, and then she could suck and lick them in turn.

"I'll show you," Leo said, walking forward.

But Wolf turned her forehead toward him and twisted his

shoulder a bit. "It's the same as mine."

Sure enough, there was an intricate tattoo on Wolf's left shoulder blade. There was a trident, an anchor, and a rifle all neatly enfolded in the arms of a righteous eagle.

"You got it?" Leo asked, looking shocked. He stared at the tattoo on his brother's back, and Shelley got the feeling it meant more than either was saying.

Wolf turned back and nodded. "I went in after I made the decision to take the job from Julian."

"Good," Leo said, climbing onto the bed.

"I know I'm not going back now. That's why I came here," Wolf said, almost as though he was admitting something.

"Is it a SEAL thing?" The tat did look very military. She reached up, trying to touch Leo's, and then thought better of it. She pulled her hand away. She wasn't sure how much leeway she had. There were rules, and she wasn't sure she knew all of them.

"Hey," Leo said, reaching for her hand. He brought it up to his chest, touching her fingers to his skin. "There's no high protocol here. You can touch me. I want you to touch me."

She smiled, letting her fingers play over the fierce-looking ink. She was fascinated by the way it looked on his skin. "I didn't know. I'm new to this."

She really was, and she wasn't only talking about the BDSM. She was new to lying in bed, her whole system suffused with pleasure and reveling in her lovers' bodies.

"It's the SEAL symbol," Wolf explained. "But you won't catch an active SEAL who has it. We don't wear insignia. Nothing that would let the enemy know who we are."

Because SEALs performed the most dangerous of missions. Because SEALs were targets. Both Wolf and Leo had been in very dangerous situations, fighting for their country. They'd had to be smart and skilled to have gotten out alive.

"You get the tat when you get out," Leo explained. "Wolf's been trying to get back in despite the fact that his last mission nearly took his leg and now he has parts of his body that are made of metal. The fact that he has that ink on his body means he's let it go. He's ready to move on. I'm glad. It was time."

Wolf nodded and then seemed to shake off a bit of sadness. His hands cupped her breasts. "I have new things to obsess about now. Like making this sub come a couple dozen times."

Wolf leaned over and sucked her nipple into his mouth. She gasped. Wolf's tongue and mouth surrounded her with heat, sending sizzling pleasure across her body. Leo leaned over and took the other nipple in his mouth. Her heart thudded in her chest. She sank her hands into their hair, holding them to her breasts. Leo's hair was thick and lush, soft to the touch. Wolf's bristled, short and dense. So different and yet both wonderful.

She writhed under their mouths. She squirmed when she felt their hands wandering over her body.

"Spread your legs," Leo ordered, the words humming against her skin.

She did as he ordered, spreading her legs wide, and she immediately felt a hand claim her pussy.

"Someone liked her orgasm," Wolf whispered. He bit gently at her nipple. "You're wet, sweetheart. So fucking wet. God, Leo, what the hell did you do to her?"

She didn't have to talk. They were doing all the talking for her. There was something sexy about lying back and letting them have her. There was something erotic about listening to them talk about her like she was a sex toy they could share.

Leo licked at her nipple before answering. "I did what she asked. I ate that pussy. She was sweet as any pie. How well did she suck your cock?"

"Best head I've ever had." Wolf chuckled. "She sucked me hard. She took everything I had. I'm already hard again. I already want her again. This time I want to come in her pussy."

Leo groaned. "God, man, I don't think I can wait."

She couldn't either. She wanted someone to make love to her. "Please. Please."

"She's begging for it. That's was what you wanted, right, Leo? You wanted her to beg for your cock." Wolf's fingers fluttered over her clit, torturing her with his light caresses. Now that she'd had a real orgasm, she wanted more. She craved it. She wanted a cock deep inside her pussy.

"She's your sub," Leo said, sitting up.

"Yes, and I had her mouth already. She's been a good girl, now give her what she needs." Wolf tossed him a condom. "Leo, this is about Shelley. I want to make the night special. We nearly lost her."

"Don't remind me," Leo said on a groan. "You did good. Though next time, try to leave one of the fuckers alive. I'd like to have had some words with one of them."

Shelley shuddered. "You think it's going to happen again?"

Wolf kissed her shoulder. "If it does, the end will be the same, sweetheart. I'll take them out. Well, I'll make sure one of them can answer all of big brother's questions. I don't think Leo there will be following Geneva Convention rules. Those two assholes are lucky they died. Now calm down. We'll talk about this in the morning. Tonight is all about pleasure."

She pushed her fears to the back of her head. She didn't want her anxiety to ruin this one perfect night.

Leo rolled the condom on his cock and forced her legs apart, his face hard with desire. "Wrap your legs around me. You answer 'yes, Leo.'"

He liked to hear his name. He couldn't know how often she said it in her head. A hundred times a day. It was an easy thing to follow his command. She'd fantasized about it for years. She wrapped her legs around his hips, feeling that big dick right at the edge of her pussy. "Yes, Leo."

"Such a good sub," Wolf murmured, settling in beside her. "Do you know how amazing you are, baby? You're everything I wanted in a sub. I can't go back to the Navy, but I can make a whole fucking career out of making you happy."

Tears pricked her eyes. He was the perfect one. It was perfect that he was beside her. Never once in her fantasies about making love with Leo had another man been whispering sweet words to her, but now she couldn't imagine not having Wolf with her and Leo.

What if she could keep them both? Leo hadn't mentioned anything about this going beyond a single night, but why should she let him walk out? Wolf seemed perfectly happy with his brother joining them. Why should she lie down? Why the hell shouldn't she fight for exactly what she wanted?

"Please, Leo," she whispered, her hands finding his shoulders. "Please. I need you so badly."

A fire seemed to light in those deep blue eyes. Her soft words seemed to get to him in a way yelling never would have.

"Then I'll give you what you need." His face hardened as he pushed his hips up and started to work that huge cock into her pussy.

Wolf kissed her, sweet butterflies across her face and hair that reminded her he was still here with her.

Leo groaned, moving tentatively. "You're so fucking small."

And he was damn big. He stretched her pussy, but the burn felt good.

Leo glanced at his brother, a desperate look on his face. "She feels too good. God, Wolf, I haven't done this in a while. I'm not going to last. Help me. You're the expert at this."

Wolf grinned, his perfect lips lifting in what looked like pure happiness. "Finally something I'm better at. Kiss me, sweetheart, and let us make you come."

She didn't feel even close to coming, but it was all right. Her body still hummed with everything they had already given her. It didn't matter. She just wanted to feel Leo as he worked over her. She wanted to feel his body stiffen as she brought him to climax. But if Wolf wanted to kiss her while it was happening, she was more than fine with that.

She had a sudden vision of being between them. One on top and one behind her, both of her men using her body, both of her men giving theirs to her.

Wolf kissed her, his tongue surging inside as Leo groaned and finally slid in, his heavy balls caressing the cheeks of her ass. She moaned at the exquisite feeling of being utterly filled with Leo's cock.

Wolf broke off the kiss and winked down at her before letting his hand slide down her torso.

"What are you doing?" Leo asked, never letting up on the slow slide of his cock.

"Helping," Wolf replied. "You can pick up the pace. She'll come in less than sixty seconds. Try to find her G-spot. Twenty bucks says we can make her scream."

"You don't have a serious bone in your body. And of course I can find her G-spot." Leo growled and twisted his hips, proving that she did indeed have a spot deep inside her that felt amazing.

"Oh my god," Shelley gasped, the sweet pressure beginning to build as Wolf's hands reached their destination, her clit. Wolf began to rub her clit, matching Leo's thrusts as though they had played this particular symphony a hundred times together.

"Come for me, baby. Oh, come all over my cock. I want to feel it," Leo said.

"Clench down, sweetheart. Milk his cock," Wolf cajoled as he pinched her clit.

Leo thrust up, hitting that magical spot as Wolf pressed down, and she screamed for them. She clutched at Leo's shoulders, feeling her nails digging into his flesh. She pressed her hips up, trying to keep that cock inside. Wild pleasure thrashed through her system as they kept up the unrelenting pace. She couldn't breathe, but it didn't matter because she could feel. She gave up thinking about the uncertainty of the future or the sorrow of the past. She simply was. She was a ball of pleasure, giving and taking.

Leo's whole body tightened, and he fucked into her harder and faster, not giving her a moment's rest before the next wave hit her. He stiffened above her, growling and pressing in, grinding out his orgasm.

A sense of peace drifted over her as Leo collapsed. Wolf's hand came out from between them, and he leaned back as though giving the moment to them.

She was covered in a fine sheen of sweat, and she couldn't tell if it was hers or his. It didn't matter. His cock was still inside her. He hadn't pulled away. He wrapped his arms around her and, with a lazy, satiated look in his blue eyes, took the time to kiss her. Their bodies mingled, arms and legs entangled, his chest on her breasts, his belly nestled sweetly against hers. His tongue slid around hers, but it was a long, slow slide.

Afterglow made her feel languid and happy.

Leo came up for air. He put his forehead against hers. "Thank you, baby. I waited a long time for that."

He kissed her again and then rolled off. She looked over at him, a bit of her glow fading. Was he going to leave? He rolled to his side and got off the bed, his hand dealing with the condom, covering it in a tissue and tossing it into the trash can. She swallowed and forced herself not to beg him to stay.

Instead of walking out, he climbed back on the bed and lay down on his side, propping his head up in one hand.

"Staying to watch, brother?" Wolf asked.

She turned to see Wolf slipping a condom over his ridiculously hard cock. Her breath caught. Again? How could she possibly come again?

"I've been a voyeur in my time. Never with a woman I really cared about, but I'd like to see how I handle it. You've been pushing my boundaries all night long. Let's see where this one goes. Fuck her hard. She feels so damn good," Leo said, his words a delicious thrill to her.

And then Wolf was on top of her. "You're going to be sore tomorrow, sweetheart, but don't worry about it. We'll take care of you."

Wolf worked his cock in and proved he was a man of his word.

* * * *

Steve Holder took a long breath and prayed he hadn't heard what he thought he'd heard.

"What did you say?" He was well aware that the question came out of his mouth like a cobra ready to strike. If he'd been in the same room with Mitchell Cross, he would have struck. He would have reached out and broken the imbecile's neck in a heartbeat.

"I said we took care of it."

Cross's words were slightly slurred. Drunken cokehead idiot. Holder looked over at Kyle, who was sitting at his computer. Holder was pretty sure the kid slept at the computer. Kyle's head came up.

He put a hand over the phone. "Check police activity on Shelley McNamara Hughes from tonight."

Kyle's fingers started flying across the keys. He hoped he was wrong, but he doubted it. If that dumbass had tried something, it had more than likely failed.

"Explain to me exactly what you took care of, Senator." Holder had a bad feeling that he knew what it was, but he needed to hear it from the man's own mouth.

There was a hesitance as though the senator finally understood Holder wasn't thrilled with his late-night phone call. He cleared his throat, the sound jarring. "I thought you should know that the blackmail situation has been handled. The woman won't give us any more trouble."

Holder felt his stomach turn. "You're going to have to be more specific. Did you kill the target or talk to her and decide to form a partnership?"

"She's dead."

Holder turned to Kyle, who looked up from his monitor. He nodded, mouthing the words, "Got a hit."

"Give me a minute, Senator. Don't you dare hang up on me." He covered the mouthpiece and looked back at Kyle. "Give me some good news. Tell me she's alive. If she isn't, then we're never going to find that fucking file, and we're always going to be looking over our backs."

"I can help you out there, sir. I pulled up a police report involving your girl," Kyle said. Holder could hear the printer starting to warm up. "It looks like she was attacked outside that club she's working in. She's alive. Two attackers are dead. The police are calling it an attempted mugging. You can read it for yourself."

Rage threatened to choke him. Stupid man. He gripped the cell, surprised he didn't break it. "You fucker, she's alive. Your men, if I can even call them men, are the dead ones."

"No. That's not possible." There was a shuffling sound as though he was walking around, ambling. "She was so sure. She paid the money."

"Who the fuck is 'she'?"

There was a whine in the senator's voice. "My wife. I didn't do this. I trust you, but she doesn't. She's a manipulative bitch, and now she's fucked everything up. I was told she hired two men, killers. How did that tramp get away? How did she take them out?"

"She didn't, you idiot. I'm sure she had an escort. The last time I saw her she was with one of the Meyer brothers. Do you have any idea what kind of a reputation those brothers have? They're legends in the SEALs. They're known for being able to kill without really thinking about it."

God, this stupid fuck had placed him in an awkward position. If he was Leo Meyer and he gave a damn about Shelley McNamara Hughes, he would wonder why the fuck an old teammate had shown up at the same time his girl was threatened. He knew exactly what Meyer would think. He would think that the old teammate had something to do with it.

Senator Mitchell Cross had fucked him.

"It wasn't me," Cross said, his voice low, as though he didn't want someone to hear him. "I didn't even know about it. I didn't plan it. My wife is a bitch. She's a loose fucking cannon. I can't control her. I can't make her get into line."

He didn't give a shit about Cross's wife. If Cross didn't have scene control, then Cross didn't fucking deserve to live. God, did that fucker have any idea how hard he'd made this job? He wasn't sure which of the Meyer brothers had been with her at the time, but it didn't matter. Brothers were brothers, and it was worse when they were all former SEALs. That connection bled through anything he could throw at them.

He wouldn't be able to turn them against each other. So he would have to find another way in. He would have to give one of them something he wanted.

Luckily, he had something Leo Meyer wanted very badly.

"If this gets traced back to you, you better keep your fucking mouth shut." He was well aware that his words dripped ice. Cross should be damn happy they weren't in the same room. Money meant something to him. The fact that Cross was a senator would make it more fun to murder his ass once he became a liability. And there was no doubt Cross was a damn liability. He was a drug addict, and he couldn't control his idiot wife.

Cross huffed. "It won't get traced back to me. Damn it. I didn't do this."

How quickly he forgot. He'd called all happy and righteous, arguing that he'd managed something Holder couldn't. "I doubt that. But if you think you can bring me into this, you're wrong. I'll get to you long before you can say my name to the cops."

He had a lot of people on his payroll. He would make sure Cross never testified against him. He might make sure Cross never fucking breathed again. Just because he was pissed as shit. Politicians were useless.

"Damn it, don't try to intimidate me." Cross's statement would have been more effective if his voice hadn't broken in a sad whimper. He lowered his voice suddenly. "It's my wife. It's all her. You should take her out. Do me a favor. She's going to screw us all."

"Keep your wife in line, Cross. If we have to have this conversation again, it will be in person, and you won't like the outcome." Holder hung up the phone and turned it off. He wouldn't answer the senator's calls for a day or two. The politician was scheduled to go to The Club in a couple of days, and then Holder would be forced to deal with him, but until then, he wouldn't give him the fucking time of day.

"Lieutenant?" Kyle said, his voice polite.

Holder took a long breath. At least Kyle had a damn brain in his head. "Yes? Who was with her? Leo or Wolf?"

"It was Wolf, sir. He apparently took both men out, easy peasy. Two bullets each. Two to the chest. I bet if he'd been alone, he would have put one more to the head, but she was with him. I know if I was on a date, I wouldn't blow some guy's head off. Girls don't like that. Well, some do, but I find those chicks disturbing."

Holder tossed the cell aside. He didn't need to hear about Kyle's dating requirements. "I need you to print out that file I gave you yesterday."

Kyle's eyes went wide. "The super-creepy dead chick file?"

Holder shrugged. It was a pretty accurate description. It was an old file, but he'd learned that information was power. He never got rid of files. He couldn't guess when he would need the information. It was precisely why he didn't trust Shelley Hughes. If he was in her position, he would have kept that tape. "Yeah. Print it all out, complete with an address that makes it look like it came from someone other than me. And get me the plans for that club. I'm going to have to go in myself."

If Leo Meyer wouldn't come to him, then he could damn sure go to Leo. A little theatrical flair was all he needed to get Meyer's mind off the fact that Holder was a possible suspect. Leo wouldn't be able to resist trying to find out who had killed his Afghan girl.

And Holder would explain that he was here to help.

Meyer never needed to know that he was the one who had killed his lover. Or that he fully intended to kill his new lover.

Chapter Eleven

Wolf rolled over, well aware that his brother had left minutes before. Wolf had been awake for over an hour, the years of ranch life and military life ingrained on his body's rhythms. He'd lain in bed, listening to the sounds of Shelley's breathing. He'd felt at peace. He stretched, feeling better than he had in months.

Everything was falling into place.

He didn't think for a minute that Leo wouldn't pull back and do his dumb-shit, this-is-only-for-sex routine, but Wolf knew better. Leo could fight it all he wanted, but six months from now, he and Shelley would still be right here in this condo and Leo wouldn't know exactly what had hit him. Sometime after that, he would find his ass standing in front of a group of their friends putting his own collar around Shelley's neck and a ring on her finger. And sometime after that, he would wonder where the hell those kids had come from.

Yeah, his brother would wake up and find himself settled down and happy. Wolf was going to make sure of it.

Shelley sighed against him. When Leo had left the bed, she'd turned, cuddling up to him.

His cock got hard in an instant. He felt a grin split his face. He'd fucked her twice the night before, but he was so ready for more. He couldn't get enough of her. He'd dreamed about her as he slept, as though he hadn't wanted to leave her side even in his own brain. He reached over and grabbed a condom, rolling it over his dick. He palmed some lube and greased up his cock, anticipation making him focus.

He loved morning fucking. He loved waking up in a warm, sleepy haze and rolling onto his sub's soft body. He hadn't had a steady girl in a long time, and never one he cared about the way he did Shelley.

"Baby? You want to wake up, right?" He kissed her cheek, moving his lips along her jawline.

She sighed, and her lips spread in a sweet smile. "Absolutely. I want you to always wake me up right."

He had her legs spread and her pussy penetrated before she could open her eyes.

He stroked into her. Despite last night's exercise, she was still so tight he had to be careful with her. But he believed in starting as he meant to go. She was his. He would protect her with his life, coddle her, indulge her whenever he could. He would be her champion and her worshipper, but she was his. She would be his to fuck and love any way he wanted. He would wake her up with his cock and put her to sleep the same way, with his dick deep inside her pussy.

She sighed again, her arms wrapping around him.

"Good morning," she said, those gorgeous kick-him-in-the-gut brown eyes fluttering open. God, Julian had been a smart man. He'd insisted on a month of contact between the two of them without any exchange of pictures or in-person meetings. If Wolf had seen her, he would have been all over her curvy ass without ever having said a word. She was even more beautiful because he really knew her. He'd spent a month getting to know her hopes and fears and fantasies.

He leaned down and kissed her, never letting up on the slow drag of his cock. He loved her lips. They were plump and soft. "Morning, sweetheart. I think Leo's making coffee."

Her eyes darkened, but she let her hands drift up around his shoulders, and her legs gripped his waist. "It's okay. I know it was only for the night."

And she had such little faith. Wolf pumped into her, enjoying the penetration. Last night had been a whirlwind of lust, but this morning was a slow, languid dance. She didn't need the lube now. Her pussy had slicked up nicely. She was so fucking responsive. He cuddled his chest to hers. He loved the feel of her nipples poking up at him.

"He'll walk through those doors in a few minutes, and he'll start bitching at me because we're all going to be late to this breakfast thing. And then he'll bitch about me being on top of you. Really, sweetheart, his bitching is the way he shows affection." He twisted his hips, satisfied with the way her mouth came open and she gasped. Yeah. That was her sweet spot. That was the spot that got her motor running and fast. He felt her nails start to bite into his shoulders. He liked the fact that his kitten had some claws on her. He didn't mind the marks.

He intended to leave a few marks of his own.

"Goddamn it, Wolf," his brother said from the doorway. Sure enough, Wolf could smell coffee. "Do you know how sore she must be? We weren't easy on her last night. Did you even wake her up before you started fucking her?"

The light came back in Shelley's eyes, making them sparkle with mirth. "I gave him permission to wake me up every morning just like this. Oh, oh, oh."

He winked down as she started to come. He felt the sleek muscles of her pussy milking his cock, and he gave over. He would love to fuck her for another couple of hours, but they really would be late for Julian's meeting. He picked up the pace, grinding down on her clit as he felt his balls draw up.

Blessed relief. One day he wouldn't wear the condom, but it wasn't time yet. He pumped himself into her, wishing he was shooting it into her womb.

He collapsed on top of her, thoroughly satisfied with how his morning was going. He breathed in her scent. She smelled like sex. It was good. He nuzzled her neck, kissing and showing his deep affection.

His brother's voice broke through his happy lethargy. "Seriously, you have like twenty minutes before we're supposed to be there."

Wolf groaned. They were back to his preteen years when Leo would wake him long before he needed to be at school. "I only need like two minutes. I can get dressed fast."

And then he could spend the other eighteen minutes in bed with his sub. It was a good plan.

But like he'd been when they were kids, Leo was relentless. "And Shelley? Have you thought about what she needs? The subs are having a breakfast gathering as well. Do you think she's going to be happy walking into her breakfast without having taken a shower?"

"Oh, god," Shelley said, pushing at Wolf. "I'm supposed to be at Dani's this morning. I'm going to be late. I have to wash my hair. Do I even have any clothes?"

"Ben and Chase dropped off your bag late last night," Leo explained. "I put it in the guest bathroom, where your shower should already be nice and hot."

Shelley looked up at Leo with an expectant look on her face.

"No panties," Leo said with a frown. "Ben and Chase know the drill."

She huffed and tried to sit up. "Panties are perfectly nice. I don't know what you guys have against them."

Wolf gave up. He rolled off her, and she was out of bed in a shot, clutching her sheet and running for the bathroom. He grabbed the coffee Leo was holding and shot his brother a look. "Spoilsport."

There was a high shriek. Wolf started, but Leo held a hand out. "I think she just figured out Logan is here. He was in the kitchen when I left him."

He hoped Logan hadn't gotten an eyeful. "We're a busy household, aren't we?"

"That was supposed to be for Shelley," Leo pointed out, staring at the mug in Wolf's hands.

He shrugged, taking a long sip. "I'll share."

A tight look came over Leo's face. Here it came. The denial. "Yes, I can tell you're all about the sharing. What the hell was last night about?"

He often envied his brother's brilliant mind. This was not one of those times. Leo couldn't simply allow things to happen. He had to question everything. "It was about her. She'd been through a lot, and she needed something special."

"Don't you try to tell me it was all about sex. I know you. You care about her."

Damn straight he did. He was in love with her. He'd fallen for her over their weeks of conversation, and being close to her physically had done nothing but make that bond stronger. "She's mine. I'm trying to give her what she needs."

Leo looked back at the open door, gesturing outward. "Don't you fucking think for one minute that you can share her with your friends because you think she needs it."

Ah, there was that jealousy he'd been waiting for. Leo could lie to himself, but Wolf saw right through him. "She only wants you, man. I wouldn't have done that with anyone else. If you walk away from her, then we'll be exclusive. I threatened to use someone else because I wanted you to get off your ass."

There was a long pause as Leo considered him. "I don't like being manipulated."

"And I don't like being ignored. I guess we can't always get what we want." He sat up, looking for his clothes. It was time to retreat or he was going to get pissed off, and that wouldn't help his cause. They needed to concentrate on Shelley, not have a family therapy session.

The room was quiet for a moment. Wolf grabbed his jeans and pulled them on. He really did need a shower. He'd had sex a bunch of times and killed two dudes. Some serious grooming was required.

"I didn't intend to ignore you," Leo said, his shoulders deflating. He sat down on the bed, his eyes straying to where Shelley had lain. "I guess time got away from me. You're seeing something that isn't there."

He doubted it. His brother had been out of touch for a long time. But if Leo didn't want to go into it, he was fine. "No problem. What am I supposed to wear to this thing?"

Leo's fists clenched. "Don't change the subject. Wolf, you're my brother. I love you. I know I don't always show it, but I do. I just...I know what you want, and I don't think I can do it."

"Because of me?" If his brother had that big a problem with him, then this couldn't work, and he would need to rethink his whole plan to live here.

Leo shook his head. "No. It's a lot of things, but mostly it's because of her. I don't think I would be good for her in the long run. I can't do what you're doing. I can't open up and offer her everything on a silver platter."

Wolf knew that. He wasn't an idiot. "Then join us for the fun stuff until Shelley doesn't need it anymore. But you need to understand that I am serious about her. She's not going anywhere."

"See, you met her yesterday. How can you possibly say that?" Leo threw his hands up as he asked the question.

Logan had asked him the same question on the long drive from Bliss. "I've been talking to her for over a month, but I won't lie. I knew it was serious about two conversations in. I can't help it. I follow my instincts. My instincts tell me she's the one."

Leo's fists clenched. "I envy you that. I've known her for years, wanted her for years, but I couldn't act on it and now I won't. I can't have the relationship you want. Hell, I'm not even sure I could have a relationship with her. I think Janine is right. I prefer to deal with patients. I don't want the responsibility of a relationship. I tried it with her, and I was terrible. I guess I have more of our dad in us than I would like to think."

"Is that what this is about? You think you're going to bug out like our dad? That's ridiculous, Leo. You never walked out on one thing in your life." Leo had stepped up at a young age.

"I walked out on you."

Wolf felt his eyes roll. He had no idea his brother had been carrying around this much guilt. "You didn't walk out. You were eighteen. You joined the Navy."

Leo's eyes narrowed. "You honestly think I didn't want out of that cabin? You think it was all self-sacrifice so I could help out with money? I could have gotten a job and stayed in Del Norte. But no, I had to get as far from Colorado as I could. I wasn't being selfless."

"I'm not stupid. Damn, man, I wanted out, too. It was hard. We were dirt poor, and Ma was overworked. You sent every bit of cash you could back. Me and Ma were fine. It's normal that you would want out. You basically had to raise me. You were a kid and you had to raise me. It's normal that you would want some freedom, but you've had years now, and it's time to think about the future. Are you telling me you don't want a family?"

Leo's face closed off, and his eyes seemed to focus on something far away. "What if I don't? What if I'm living exactly the life I want to live?"

Wolf didn't believe him for a second, but now wasn't the time to fight. He was starting to understand what Leo's real problem was, and he wasn't going to push him now. "Then you won't mind helping me with Shelley. I'm offering you the best of both worlds. I'll take responsibility for her. You can have fun."

"Why?" Leo seemed to have a need to harp on that one question.

He wasn't sure how many times he would have to answer it. "Because I think she needs this. She talked about a man she cared about. She never mentioned his name, but I think it was you. I know it wasn't her husband. One of two things is going to happen. You'll either come around or she'll screw you out of her system and we can move on."

That was as plainly as he could put it.

Leo shook his head. "It won't work."

It had to work. He was betting everything on the fact that this was going to work. "Then you will have lost nothing. Now, tell me what I should wear to this thing."

Leo sighed. "It's casual. Well, Julian will show up in a suit, but I swear he would wear one to hike through a swamp. The rest of the Doms usually wear jeans and T-shirts. It's freaking Saturday after all."

Good. He could do jeans.

Leo started out the door and then turned back. "But, brother, we're going to have to find you some clothes if all you brought is that one bag. You can have Shelley take you to the mall or I will."

He kind of wanted to barf at the whole idea of shopping. There had been plenty of shitty things about the Navy, but one of the good things had been the fact that he didn't have to shop. His clothes had been provided for him. Uniforms. He liked uniforms.

Leo had a shit-eating grin on his face. "A good black T-shirt with jeans or slacks. Consider that your uniform."

Yeah, his brother knew him. "I'll let Shelley buy some stuff. She seems to like clothes."

He would wear whatever she picked out for him.

Leo's smile became a sad thing. "She does." He sighed and looked at his watch. "You now have ten minutes. Please take a shower. I think Jack Barnes is in town. He's not terribly fond of me. I

179

would prefer his first impression of my only brother be a good one, not that you have hygiene problems."

"What did you do? Hit on his wife?"

A devilish light hit Leo's eyes. "As often as possible. His sub is a lovely woman. Trust me, if you didn't have Shelley, you would hit on her, too. Make a good impression, brother. It might keep the man from killing me."

Leo turned and walked out of the room.

It wasn't perfect, but it would have to do. Time. That was what Leo needed. He needed time and patience. Their father had done a number on everyone in their little family. His mother had finally moved on. Of course, she'd moved on with one of the craziest people Wolf had ever met, but she was in love and happy. Wolf knew what he wanted.

Leo was floundering.

For all his brilliance and perfection, Leo was struggling in a way Wolf wasn't.

Leo had spent half his life taking care of him. It was Wolf's turn to look out for his big brother. Whether Leo wanted it or not.

Wolf grabbed his bag on the way out of the bedroom. Shelley might not know it, but her training didn't end because they left the dungeon.

Logan looked up from the kitchen table. "Dude, your girl's hot."

"I can still kill you, Logan," Leo shouted from the back of the condo.

Wolf gave Logan a thumbs-up. Logan really seemed happier since they had left Bliss, but Wolf wasn't buying the act entirely. He'd let Logan be for the time being. It was another problem for another day. Shelley was his concern now. It was time to see how his hot girl liked having a plug worked up her ass.

Wolf had a grin on his face as he walked toward the guest bathroom. He would sneak into Shelley's shower and show his sub a good time.

Because the good times never had to end when a man loved his family.

* * * *

Leo took a deep breath before opening the door. The events of the night before weighed on him.

He'd watched Shelley come in his brother's arms. He'd nearly lost her to a goddamn assassin's bullet. He'd finally gotten inside her, and now he felt closer to her and his brother than he could have imagined.

The night before had been the best fucking night of his life. Why was he pulling away now?

"Leo," Julian said with a broad smile. He pushed back his chair and stood. A long, dark wooden table dominated the elegant dining room. It was covered in a crisp, white tablecloth and some lovely china. Leo would have preferred paper plates because he was always worried he would break that damn dainty stuff, but he'd learned to deal with it. He'd become somewhat comfortable in Julian's super-wealthy world.

Wolf, on the other hand, looked terrified at the ritzy spread in front of him.

Yeah, he was happy about that. His brother seemed to take almost everything with an annoying aplomb.

"Julian," Leo acknowledged. "Nice spread."

"Always," Julian nodded, gesturing around the room. There were several men standing around the room talking as they drank coffee or orange juice. Well-dressed servers filtered through the room, offering drinks. "You know everyone. Jack, you remember Leo."

Jack Barnes turned, his big body encased in a snowy white dress shirt and slacks that Leo was damn sure his lovely wife had picked out. Jack used to wear jeans and Western shirts to everything. Jack was another of Julian's projects. Julian had an instinct about talented, intelligent people who could make something of themselves.

Jack reminded him of his brother. He had chosen well when it came to wives, and he was crap at dressing himself. Jack worked hard and had a positive attitude despite the crap life had thrown at him. Leo kind of admired both men.

"Oh, I can hardly forget Leo," Jack said in his long, slow drawl. "And who's the new guy?"

Julian looked thrilled to be able to answer. "That's Wolfgang

Meyer."

Jack's eyes went wide. "Wolfgang? Seriously?"

Wolf sighed beside him. "Our mom liked artists. She liked painters and composers. I was named after Mozart. Leonardo there was named after da Vinci. If she'd gotten knocked up again, we would have had a Giuseppe because she loved Verdi. I am grateful she didn't. We would have been defending that kid every day on the playground. Ma didn't get that names are important when it comes to avoiding an ass kicking. Though I would probably be less tough if she'd named me Nick or Jake."

Jack Barnes laughed out loud. "I like it. So this is Leo's brother? The one who's now screwing Leo's girl? I like him. I don't know him, but I seriously like him."

Yeah, Jack Barnes wasn't his biggest fan. "She isn't my girl."

Jack's face went chilly. "No, of course she isn't. She's your brother's." He turned to Wolf, a broad smile on his face. "It's nice to meet you. You've been working with Jamie Glen out on the G. Nice ranch. I like having another cowboy around here. I heard you took care of some problems last night. I heard you did a real fine job. Big Tag was impressed and that means I am, too. I like a man who can take care of business. Tell me how Jamie and Trev are doing."

Leo watched as Wolf stepped up and started talking to the rancher. In mere seconds, Wolf had Jack Barnes laughing out loud and talking about everything having to do with cows.

Leo took a step back. Jack had never responded to him like that.

"It looks like your brother is fitting in," Julian said, slapping him on the back. "And your charge is doing well, too."

Leo followed Julian's line of sight. Logan stood in front of the big windows that overlooked the city skyline. He had a grin on his face as he talked to Dane Hawthorne. Dane was a Dom who worked at the same law firm as Finn and Lucas O'Malley. He was a big, all-American looking guy who had a real light touch with the neediest of subs. Logan was laughing as he talked to the Dom.

"Yes, I think my charge might have been less traumatized than advertised." Leo stopped. Crap. Was he actually upset that this guy wasn't as fucked up as he'd been told? He really did hide behind his patients.

A vision of Shelley's lovely face assaulted him. She'd been perfect. She'd opened herself body and soul to him and Wolf, not holding a single thing back.

He'd almost lost her. His heart still seized at the thought. He could still hear Wolf's monotone as he'd called and said flatly, "Trouble. Grab Taggart and come now."

That was all. A couple of sentences and he'd come running. Wolf hadn't thought to explain. He'd called and known that his big brother would move heaven and earth to help him.

Maybe he wasn't as far from his brother as he thought.

One of the servers offered Leo a cup of coffee. He took it as Julian talked about something that was going on with Finn. He nodded, but his brain was on his earlier talk with Wolf.

Maybe he should take his brother up on his offer. If Wolf and Shelley were cool with it, why should he hesitate? Why shouldn't he take everything they were offering? He could have Shelley and not have to worry about it ending because she would be fine. She would have Wolf. Wolf wouldn't leave her. Wolf would make her the center of his whole fucking world. He would build a life around her.

And Leo would show up for some nice long fucks.

Wasn't that what he wanted?

"And then I gave away everything to charity. This is our last day in The Club. It's being taken over by the Society for Smarter Butterflies."

He shook his head. "What?"

Julian frowned, his face a mask of disapproval. "Well, it was obvious you weren't listening to me."

"Sorry, boss." He had to get it together. He didn't have to make any decisions today. He needed to think. He never acted on his instincts the way Wolf did.

Except that once when he'd tried to get Shelley to run away with him. And he'd seen where that got him.

"Do I need to get Wolf his own condo?" Julian asked, his eyes looking to Wolf. "There's an open spot on the tenth floor."

Two days ago he would have jumped at the offer. "No. That unit is a one bedroom. Mine is a three. We're fine."

He was surprised at how fast the denial came out of his mouth.

He didn't want Wolf to move. He didn't want Shelley to leave. There had been an oddly comfortable domesticity to the morning. It had been nice to not be alone. He'd woken up with Shelley's head on his chest, his arms wrapped around her.

Of course, he'd also woken up clinging to the edge of the bed because his brother was so oversized he took up most of the queen-size mattress. Leo and Shelley had barely been left with enough room for one person, much less two. He hadn't minded snuggling, but he'd almost ended up on his ass.

They needed to move into his room. He had a king.

"So you're comfortable with your brother and his sub staying with you?" Julian's eyes pinned him as though he couldn't quite believe that was possible. "It's necessary that they stay close, but they don't have to stay with you. I don't believe Shelley should be on her own right now, but I understand it could be difficult for you. Should I move Logan out? You only have the three bedrooms. I seriously doubt Wolf was comfortable on your couch."

"He was comfortable enough, Julian. He didn't sleep on the couch."

Julian nodded. "Well, that was inevitable. He seems to work fast."

Julian didn't know the half of it. Leo stared out over the Dallas skyline. "And he talks in his sleep. And he hogs the damn covers."

Julian Lodge was a man of perfect manners. It gave Leo a lift of joy that Julian spit his coffee out, sputtering as the words hit him.

With an elegant twist of his hand, his boss put the coffee down and wiped off his suit. "So I am to assume that the adrenaline of the night before led to some physical interaction?"

Leo felt a grin cross his face. He hadn't fucked with his boss in over a year. How much of himself had he cut off after Shelley had denied him? He'd gone into his shell, and he was only now coming out of it. Screwing with Julian had been his favorite pastime. "If you're talking some serious playtime, then yes. My brother is open-minded."

And generous. And might know him better than Leo thought.

The door to the dining hall came open, and Ben and Chase walked through, their gaits in perfect time. He and Wolf might not be in such perfect synchronicity, but they had been able to please their sub anyway.

Leo winced inwardly. There it was. Possessive words. Shelley wasn't his.

Julian watched the twins walk in. "I'm going to talk to Ben and Chase for a moment. We'll start breakfast in ten minutes. We need to discuss the scenes for tonight and tomorrow night. We have some VIP politicians coming in, and they need some unique setups."

Leo stifled his groan. He hated politicians, and they tended to be tourists. But still, he had a job to do. "All right. I can accommodate them. When are we going to talk about the situation with Shelley?"

"Ian and I talked to the police chief last night. I'm sure Ben and Chase found something as well. When we're done here, we can all go up to the penthouse and discuss it. Be right back."

Leo watched Julian walk away with a growing impatience. It had been easy to forget about the assassins after Shelley when he'd had his face in her pussy. Now, in the light of day, the enormity of the situation hit him squarely in the chest.

Someone tried to kill her. They'd messed with her twice already. The incident on the train hadn't been a mugging. They'd been after her.

Leo walked to the balcony and slipped outside. The early-morning air had the slightest chill, but he welcomed it.

No way was he going to let Wolf move even to another floor. He couldn't stand the thought of not knowing where Shelley was. And more than that, he didn't particularly want to lose track of his brother.

He could still remember how angry he'd been when Wolf had given him the news that he was joining up. Wolf hadn't exactly discussed the situation with him or their mother. He'd been on his way to Great Lakes when Leo got the news.

And then years of not knowing where he was. Years where his brother's location on the planet Earth had been a state secret. He was well aware that he'd put Wolf and his mother through the same thing, but damn it, he'd had a plan. He'd been doing it for them.

"I hear you've come to the dark side."

Leo closed his eyes briefly. Jack Barnes. Well, he did flirt outrageously with the man's wife. "Dark side?"

"I heard you finally got into Shelley McNamara's bed."

God, Julian had become a gossipy old man. "It's really not your business."

"I don't know about that," Jack said in his Texas accent. "I like the hell out of her brother. Trev spent some time with Barnes-Fleetwood a couple of years back. I enjoyed working with him. I wonder what he would think about you playing around with his sister. Julian might think this is funny, but that girl is going to get hurt."

"Don't be a hypocrite, Jack. You share your wife."

"Yes, I share my wife with my partner," Jack replied. "We're all committed to our lives together and the family we're raising. You're playing around."

Leo felt his eyes narrow. "You don't know anything about this situation."

Jack stared out over the city. "I know the way she's looked at you for years and the fact that since she walked into this club, you haven't spoken to her. She was lost and broken and you didn't reach out. You reach out to every goddamn person in this club, but she gets nothing. If she meant a thing to you, I can't tell."

Anger rolled in his gut. "I asked her to marry me, Jack. She turned me down. So now who's the asshole in this situation?"

Jack turned to him and raised a single brow, and Leo had the sudden fear he'd been manipulated to the exact position Jack wanted him in. "I would say it's you since she doesn't have a ring on her finger or your protection."

Leo took a deep breath to keep from shouting. His words came out quietly, but with pointed sarcasm. "Do you not understand the words 'she turned me down'? I offered to save her from that hellacious marriage, and she told me to leave."

"Yeah, I get what she told you to do. I don't understand why the hell you did it."

Leo frowned, staring at the cowboy. "She didn't want me."

But those words were starting to sound like an excuse.

"Bullshit." Jack leaned against the elegant railing. "I don't claim to know exactly why she did it, but I would make a bet that she got it into her head that she was protecting you. Women do that with men they love. Don't think for a minute that because they're soft and submissive in bed that they don't know how to protect what they love. I've never seen anything more ferocious than my Abigail when she thinks me or Sam or one of the kids could get hurt."

How many times was he going to have to hear this argument? "That's ridiculous. I've gone over this with her. I'm a freaking former SEAL. I can handle myself."

"But she doesn't want you to have to handle yourself. You spend all your time psychoanalyzing people but you're playing blind when it comes to her."

His head was starting to pound. None of this shit mattered. Jack was pushing him. "No matter her reason for doing it, she was right to reject me. I was a crappy husband the first time around. I'm glad Janine and I didn't have kids or they would have to grow up the same way we did. Without a dad."

Jack stopped and stared for a moment, and Leo wished he hadn't opened his damn mouth. "I didn't have a dad, either. It's hard. I watched how hard it was on my momma. She struggled. And then she died and I didn't have anyone. Tell me, Leo, do you think that affected the way I view marriage?"

Leo snorted. "Of course. Look, I know where you're going."

"No, son, I don't think you do. I don't know that I would have married Abigail if Sam hadn't been around. I wouldn't have touched her because I would always have worried about what would become of her if something happened to me. I spent years having sex that didn't mean anything, but Sam freed me. Sam would kill or die for our wife and our kids. If I left this earth tomorrow, Sam would be there. I don't have to worry about Abby because we have Sam."

It was a beautiful thought, but he wasn't sure it applied to his situation. "I don't know if that can work for me. Your wife never tried to push you away."

Jack leaned over and laughed. "Think you know everything, do you? Abigail kicked me out of her life before we got married. Abigail, sweet, loving Abigail, told me she didn't love me. She told me I was only good for sex."

Abby had done that? He couldn't imagine it. Abby worshipped her husband. She looked at Jack like he was the sun in the sky. "Why would she say that?"

Jack's eyes moved away, his mind obviously lost in memory. "She thought a little old lady was going to ruin my life and that I wouldn't be able to stop it."

Leo had to laugh. Jack Barnes was a ruthless son of a bitch. He'd built his ranch on hard work and by taking what he was owed. The thought of one small redhead trying to protect him seemed silly.

And yet hadn't the fierce love Shelley had shown for her mother and brother been one of the very things he'd been attracted to?

An idea played at the back of his mind. A question he'd always wondered about.

Why had Shelley—beautiful, vivacious, smart Shelley—why had she married someone like Bryce Hughes?

He'd never asked, a bit afraid of finding out she'd been madly in love. What if she'd had different reasons?

Emotion, regret, and no small amount of fear threatened to well up inside. "What did you do? What did you do when Abby told you to leave?"

He was pretty damn sure Jack Barnes hadn't turned away.

"I didn't even think about it. I knew that woman. That woman has held a piece of my soul since the day she was born. I told her if she left that I would follow her. I told her that if she didn't love me, then that was okay because I would love her until the day I died. I would love her enough for both of us. You're a smart man, Leo. You're probably the smartest man I know, but you haven't figured this out. It isn't about how much she loves you. It's not about how much she can give or withhold from you. It's about what you feel. If you had really loved her, you wouldn't have been able to walk away, not knowing her circumstances. You would have stood by her. You would have protected her even when she didn't return your feelings. You would have done it because you couldn't do anything else." Jack sighed and patted Leo on the shoulder. "So don't worry about it. It wasn't love. Hopefully it's going to be different for your brother."

Jack Barnes walked back into the condo. Leo stared after him.

He'd made a horrible mistake.

He had to force himself to breathe. He'd shoved Shelley away because she hadn't answered correctly. He'd been like a child with a toy that hadn't worked exactly how he'd wanted it.

And he couldn't take it back.

The French doors flew open and Wolf stood there. "Waffles are going to have to wait, brother. We have trouble."

"Shelley?" Why hadn't he put on his shoulder holster? He needed to carry all the fucking time now. He'd been out of the game for far too long.

"No. It's Kitten. She's got a package for you in your office." Wolf's face was a blank slate. It terrified Leo. It meant that whatever Wolf had seen had affected him. So deeply he had to hide it.

"What is it?" He had the sudden urge to run to Julian's condo and make sure Shelley was safe. He wanted to see her, hold her. "Where's Shelley?"

Wolf held out a hand. "She's with Dani, and apparently there are a bunch of men at this breakfast for the subs. Sam and Finn are with her. She's fine. This isn't about Shelley." Wolf swallowed and took a minute as though he couldn't figure out how to say what he needed to say.

Leo took a step forward, unable to stand the waiting. "Goddamn it, Wolf, just tell me."

"It's about Ada."

He felt the whole world tip, and he didn't like where he landed.

Ada. The woman he'd cared for in Afghanistan. Ada. The woman he'd killed.

Chapter Twelve

Shelley thought about sitting down. She thought about walking around. She thought about killing Wolf Meyer.

But mostly she thought about the plug in her ass.

"First time, huh?"

Shelley turned, startled. She'd been trying to blend into the wallpaper. Dani's apartment was full of lovely women and a few truly gorgeous men. They all seemed to know the others. Their easy manner with each other made Shelley realize how long she'd been without a social network. Bryce had cut her off from her friends, insisting that she spend time with his business acquaintances. She'd gotten used to "friendship" being an exchange of pleasantries that went no further than commenting on clothes and shoes.

She missed Beth. Her brother's wife had been the first person she had been able to talk to in years, but she'd moved away. Now, she felt odd in a room full of women and men who seemed to be friends.

The redhead in the truly stunning white, surplice-cut dress looked at her expectantly. There was a mimosa in each hand and a smile on her face.

It was as good a time as any to jump back into the pool. She wasn't going to make friends by standing in the corner. *Damn it.* She'd been good at this once. She could be good at it again. "Yes, it's my first time. I've been in the penthouse before but not for Saturday-morning brunches. It's all so lovely."

The redhead laughed. "That wasn't what I meant, hon. I was asking if it was the first time your Dom forced you to walk around with a damn piece of plastic up your butt."

She felt her face go up in flames.

The woman pressed her extra mimosa into her hand. "Drink up, honey. It really does get better. I'm Abby Barnes, by the way."

Shelley drank the whole damn glass in a single gulp.

A gorgeous blond man in jeans, a Western shirt, and a cowboy hat stepped up, his arm going around Abby's waist. He held out another mimosa. "We were right, weren't we, baby? You'll feel better after three or four of these."

She took the proffered glass but sipped it at a more sedate pace. "Can everyone tell? How can everyone tell? Oh, my god."

Abby patted her shoulder encouragingly. "It's a little thing, hon. Sam caught it when you walked in."

The man named Sam tipped his hat her way in a sweetly old-fashioned gesture. "I sure did, ma'am."

"There's a tightness around your eyes, and you're walking a bit carefully." Abby took a sip of her drink. "It's nothing the vanilla world would catch on to, but we've all been there. Poor Sam here didn't sit down for hours."

"Jack was kind, baby. He sent me out to get my tat. It's on the back of my neck. I had to lie on my stomach in that chair for about six hours. It was perfect." Sam's hand went to the back of his neck. Shelley could see the tendrils of a well-done tattoo coming around the place where his shoulders met his neck. "I think Jack was way nicer than this poor lady's Dom. He didn't send me to a party the first time he shoved a plug up my butt."

Shelley couldn't help but grin. It actually was kind of funny. "At least he sent me to a party where everyone's in the lifestyle. I think Wolf would find it highly amusing. He's got a bent sense of humor."

And the most amazing tongue. He'd joined her in the shower and gotten on his knees, telling her he needed his breakfast. He'd eaten her pussy right there in the shower. He'd shoved his tongue up her pussy until she'd cried out, and then he'd soaped her whole body, washing her with a tenderness that made his rough use of her in bed

191

even hotter.

And then he'd dried her off and forced her to bend over and accept a plug up her ass.

It felt weird.

Sam's blue eyes had gone wide. "Wolf? As in Leo's brother Wolf?"

"You know Leo?" The question came out of her mouth, and then she realized how stupid it was. Of course they knew Leo. Everyone at The Club knew the resident Dom.

Abby put her drink on a passing waiter's tray and turned, revelation in her eyes. "You're Shelley McNamara. Sam, she's Trev's sister."

Something passed between the two and then Sam nodded slightly, a bit more sober than before. "We've never been introduced, but you've met our Dom, Jack Barnes."

Now that was a name she did know. Jack Barnes had been deeply helpful with her brother, teaching him new methods of ranching. "Of course. Jack is such a nice man."

Abby grinned. "He is, indeed. And yet he still made us walk around with that damn plug. Can we help you sit down? It can be awkward until you get used to it."

She had a sudden vision of herself being lowered into a chair with a crane. Nope. She would stand. Maybe forever. "I'm fine."

Abby nodded. "I did the same thing. It was a long time before I could sit with one of those damn things." Her eyes lit up. "Oh, my baby girl is here. Sam, you didn't tell me Lexi was coming up."

Shelley looked over and Lexi O'Malley was walking into the room with Lucas on her arm. She waved toward her mother and stepfather. Abby and Sam rushed off to greet her. Shelley gave her a nod. They knew each other in passing, having lived in the same small town for a while.

Shelley sipped her drink and looked around. She knew she was probably being paranoid, but it felt like everyone was watching her, whispering behind their hands. She'd come because Dani had invited her, but now she wondered when she could leave. Maybe she could sneak out.

And Wolf would be pissed since he'd told her he would come by and pick her up himself.

Not being able to walk around without an armed escort was going to get damn annoying. She looked up and saw a lovely blonde woman coming her way and then realized she shouldn't walk out of here. She needed to run.

Janine. Leo's ex-wife was walking up to her, a look of purpose in her eyes. "Hey, Shelley. How's it going?"

She decided that if she was in for a penny, she might as well be in for a pound. Maybe some humor was needed when dealing with her pseudo ex's ex. "I have a plug up my ass. How about you?"

"Oh, we're going to get along nicely." Janine smiled and seemed friendly, but she'd been around small-town sharks long enough to know that a smile was merely a way of baring teeth. "I love the sarcastic ones."

Shelley was confused. She remembered that Janine had talked about topping her husband the night before. "I thought this brunch-thing was for subs."

Janine nodded. "Yes, and we lucky switches get to pick. You'll note that almost all the switches come to the sub events. Lucas O'Malley over there could go to either, but he prefers the ladies. I do, too, though for different reasons. Lucas is bi. I just can't stand all the testosterone at Julian's gatherings. So much chest-thumping alphaness, and that includes the Dommes. It's way more fun here. Besides, Big Tag eats all the lemon donuts on the buffet. I don't know where he puts them all, but he downs those suckers as fast as he can. Here I know I can get one. So how is Wolf these days?"

It occurred to Shelley that this woman had known both the brothers for a long time. She wanted to talk about them, to ask about what they were like when they were younger, what kinds of trouble they'd caused. Janine had known Wolf as a very young man. But she was wary. "He's great. We're getting along nicely."

"Yeah, I could tell from that scene last night."

She choked on her mimosa.

Janine laughed. "Get used to it. It's an open lifestyle. There isn't a single person in this room whose private parts haven't been on full display. And seriously, I will cheer the first time Wolf gets naked. I will bless you as a goddess among women if you get that man out of his leathers in a public place."

"I thought you were married to Leo." Shelley was a bit confused.

"A girl can dream, right? I met Wolf when he was a kid. He was like twenty-one. He was six foot five and a slab of pure muscle. I can't imagine what it would have been like to have him in a high school class. He was a goddamn *Lifetime* cautionary tale on two legs. Leo had already introduced me to the lifestyle by the time we met, and the first thing that went through my head was we should have a ménage."

Again, she felt her face heat.

Janine's eyes narrowed. "A girl would be damn lucky to be in between those two."

She had the distinct feeling Leo's ex-wife had a point. "I suppose so."

Janine frowned. "Are you using Wolf to get to Leo?"

Ah. There was the point. "Not at all. I didn't even know Wolf was Leo's brother when we started talking. He was supposed to be the Dom who trained me, but then, well, he's Wolf."

"I understand that," Janine began, "but I talk to Leo a lot. I know it's unusual for exes to be friendly, but we're not ordinary. I still love Leo. Always will. I know how he felt about you. I even encouraged him to go after you despite the fact that you were married."

"It wasn't much of a marriage."

Janine shrugged casually. "Yet you picked your marriage over Leo."

Shelley rolled her eyes. God, she was so tired of this. "Yes, I chose my drug-dealing, blackmailing, cheating husband over Leo. You know why? Because I loved it so much when he fucked every meth head in town, and I was thrilled when he used my business as a front for his crimes. Oh, and I couldn't resist the way he'd blackmailed me into our marriage. All of that was too much to walk away from."

Janine nodded sagely. "Ah. So he threatened Leo, and you were protecting him."

Well, at least Janine got it. "Yes."

The blonde woman sighed. "And then Leo did his whole overanalyzing intellectual thing. I can see how that went. He couldn't believe you would think he needed protection so he decided you had used and discarded him. God, he can be such a drama queen. See, this is why Wolf is easier. Wolf would have simply grunted and not stopped following you around. So, has he totally screwed this thing up with you, or does he still have a shot?"

"Wolf? Well, I'm not happy about the plug, but I have to admit, I'm crazy about him."

Janine shook her head. "No, honey. I was talking about Leo. Has Leo completely screwed this up or can I talk you into giving him another chance?"

Shelley had to take a breath and another sip of her drink. God, hadn't she spent every moment of every day for the last year wishing that Leo wanted another chance? But he'd shut that down. "He doesn't want a second chance."

"He can say that all he wants, but I watched him last night. I've talked to him. He's never gotten over you. When I left him, he barely skipped a smile. He was joking with my new boyfriend at the lawyer's as we filed for divorce."

She wondered how much that had hurt. "Leo's pretty resilient."

"Not for the last fifteen months," Janine pointed out. "He's changed. He's been quiet and withdrawn. He hasn't spent time with friends. He's stopped flirting. Do you understand how worried that makes me? Leo loves to flirt. And he hasn't flirted. Not since the day he met you." Janine leaned against the wall, her arms crossing. "He knew he'd found the one. And now you're with Wolf, and I worry that if you sleep with Wolf, you won't ever give Leo another chance. And Wolf works fast."

"Yes, yes, he does." He'd worked fast, and he hadn't been alone.

Janine's face fell. "Well, then, I guess that's that. I can't see Leo breaking up something good for his brother. You're going to laugh at this, but I was actually going to try to convince you to tempt Leo into a ménage. I really think he would thrive in that type of relationship. But he would have to be there in the beginning. I don't think his pride would allow anything less."

Shelley stared down at the floor. She wasn't sure she should say a thing. It hadn't meant anything. Leo had said it himself. It had been sex and adrenaline. When she'd woken up, he'd been gone, and he'd seemed a bit distant all morning long.

Janine reached out, taking her hand. "I wish you all the best with Wolf. He really is a great guy."

"How would I do it?"

Janine stopped. "What do you mean?"

"How would I convince him to stay?" She had to try.

"I don't think it will work now." Janine's words had taken on a sympathetic tone. "He's possessive, and he has his own odd code. If you're sleeping with his brother, he won't break up that relationship, and I doubt even if you walked out on Wolf that he would consider it. Certainly not anytime soon. And Wolf seems to really like you."

She was going to have to say it. "Let me make this plain. I have absolutely no desire to walk out on Wolf. And Leo might not work as fast as his brother, but they have their timing down, if you know what I mean."

A blank face stared back at her. "I do not."

How did she put this? There was no Miss Manners for conversation openers about ménage relationships. She stuttered, the words dropping from her mouth in a staccato. "Leo and Wolf and I, well, there was an incident. Some men tried to hurt me. Wolf took care of it, but we were all emotional."

Janine's eyes widened. "Oh, you slept with them both. Together?"

She nodded. "I did. But this morning, Leo was a little distant. I don't think he's ever going to forgive me for sending him away. I think he's trying to work me out of his system. I've thought about this all morning. I'm crazy about Wolf. I think I'm falling for that man, but can I have a relationship with him if Leo walks away? I've tried to cut Leo out of my heart, but it doesn't work. How am I going to go to Christmas dinner and look across the table at Leo's new girlfriend?"

Janine relaxed a bit, her shoulders coming down and a satisfied smile crossing her face. "Honey, that's not going to be a problem. He hasn't even had a collared sub in years. Leo's been solitary, even when he was married. You're the first woman I've seen him get animated about. If you want Leo, you have to have a soft touch. Let Wolf work on him. Be the woman he fell in love with. He'll come back. Hell, if he's shared a woman with his brother, he's much further down the road than I would have imagined. Be patient with him. And I know I'm the ex, but you can always call me. I know what it's like to love Leo."

A kernel of hope kindled in her chest. What if she didn't have to let Leo go? What if she could have them both?

"And if you ever want to tell me exactly how big Wolf is, I will listen. I really will. God, that man is hot."

Finn Taylor walked up. Shelley had seen him with Dani earlier, laughing and caressing her big belly. His humor was gone now, replaced with a grim fierceness. Lucas O'Malley was at his side, the downturn of his lips telling Shelley that something terrible had happened.

A million horrible scenarios played through her brain. "What's happened? Leo? Wolf?"

God, someone was trying to kill her. What if they'd gotten her men instead? Her heart threatened to crack.

"They're fine," Finn said. "But they want you back up in Leo's condo. We're going to take you there and stay until they can come up."

"What's going on?"

Lucas sighed, a low, tired sound. "Leo's past is catching up to him. And it looks like you're in the line of fire."

Shelley thought about those enigmatic words as she walked out of the penthouse.

* * * *

Wolf felt the tension in the room, and he couldn't blame the sub for cowering a bit. The room was thick with testosterone, and she was the only sub there, surrounded by six big Doms, all of whom stared straight down at her.

Kitten's eyes were wide. Her mouth was open. But Wolf wasn't sure anyone was home.

Of course, after seeing those damn pictures, Wolf had lost his appetite, if not the actual power of speech.

"Tell us what happened, Kitten," Julian said, his voice a flat monotone. He leaned against the desk Kitten used. The folder with the photographs was right there by Julian's fingertips, but they had been turned over.

Not that Wolf needed to see them again. He doubted he would ever get the images out of his mind.

A lovely woman with skin the color of rich sand, tied up in a beautiful, masterful tortoiseshell pattern of Shibari bondage. Her dark hair was spread on the mattress she'd been laid out on. A lovely scene, except for the blood and her unseeing eyes. His stomach turned. Someone had brutalized the woman. Leo's woman.

Leo stood away from the pack, his face a careful blank. Ada had died years before, but Wolf could plainly see those pictures had brought it all back for Leo.

"Kitten, speak." Ben got to one knee, using his most forceful voice. "Now."

Chase sighed. "Damn it. Kitten, come on. This is ridiculous. You have to talk."

"I think she's broken," Ben said with a shrug, his eyes sliding away from the photos. His voice was even, but Leo knew those photos upset him. "I mean, obviously, but I think she's even more broken than before."

"What is wrong with that girl?" Jack Barnes asked.

"She's Finn's cousin. She's a little odd," Julian said, stating the obvious.

She sniffled, her mouth opening as though she wanted to speak. All six Doms leaned forward expectantly, and Kitten's mouth closed again.

A collective groan went through the room.

"Someone tie her up," Leo said. "She finds it comforting. It's Saturday. She gets tied up on Saturdays. Kitten is a creature of routine. If you tie her up, she might be comfortable enough to talk."

Wolf started for the door to Leo's office, but Chase pulled out a length of rope from his pocket.

The big Dom shrugged. "What? Don't we all have some?"

"Proceed, Mr. Dawson," Julian said with a long sigh.

Chase began an elaborate pattern, binding Kitten's wrists behind her back and then winding the rope all around her torso. The Dom moved with an economical grace that bespoke of his long practice.

While Kitten was being tied, Wolf moved toward his brother.

Leo was closed off, unapproachable. Luckily, Wolf was stubborn. "Why didn't you tell me?"

"You knew Ada was dead and that I was involved with her before her death," Leo replied, his tone bland.

He'd known that but only because there'd been an inquiry by JAG. Leo had been cleared of suspicion. The time of death had been calculated as the same time in which Leo had been on a weapons raid on a Taliban stronghold. As alibis went, it was a pretty good one.

What Leo hadn't told him was the manner of Ada's death.

"You wouldn't have left her bound like that," Wolf said with utter certainty.

A single eyebrow arched. "Of course not. When I left Ada, she was perfectly fine. We'd played all afternoon and then I got called back to base. I would never leave a sub unattended. But that was my rope the killer used."

"Shit, Leo. This was about you."

"You think I don't know that? You think I haven't had to live with this every day since?"

The weight of guilt must be oppressive, and Leo hadn't bothered to share it. With anyone, he would bet.

"Is that better, Kitten?" Chase asked.

"A spanking would help, Sir," Kitten said, her voice magically reappearing now that she was tightly embraced by rope.

Chase growled in her direction. "You get nothing until you talk, Kitten. And if you don't tell us everything, you'll be vanilla for a week. No spankings. No bondage. No dungeon."

Her lower lip quivered. "But tomorrow is Suspension Sunday."

"It won't be if you don't start talking. This is not a game. This is important to Master Leo," Julian explained.

She sniffled and nodded, seemingly much more in control now that she was bound. "Kitten understands. Kitten is sorry. Those pictures were left on Kitten's desk. Kitten opened them. The envelope said Master Leo's name on the front. It's Kitten's job to open his mail. But Kitten was very disturbed by those photos. Kitten likes bondage for fun. That poor woman."

Tears leaked from Kitten's eyes.

Julian placed a hand on her head. "I am sorry you had to see those. Do you remember anything else? Was anything out of place?"

"The door was unlocked," Kitten said.

Julian's eyes went past Wolf's to Leo's.

"I always lock it. I have patient files in here. I lock the inner and outer doors." Leo's eyes strayed to the folder with the photos.

Wolf tried the door that led to Leo's office. Locked up tight. He crossed the outer room in three long strides and dropped to one knee. If Leo said he'd locked it, then Leo had locked the door. The mechanism was a simple bolt lock, and sure enough, he only had to glance at it to see the telltale signs. A few scratches on the metal casing of the lock told him that someone knew how to use a torque wrench and a pick.

"Someone picked it," Wolf announced.

Julian cursed under his breath. "How the hell did he get past the front desk? I'll have security see if they can find anything on the cameras. Damn it. I need more cameras."

"They might help, but I still would have gotten around them. They're all on a set pattern on this floor."

Wolf didn't even think about it. He reacted. He was up and off his feet before the man had finished the word *floor*. Wolf had his SIG out and at the man's throat before anyone could breathe.

"Holder?" What the hell was he doing here? And how had Holder gotten the jump on him? Damn, he was out of practice. He needed to get back into the sweet paranoia of his former Navy days.

Holder's hands came up, showing he didn't have a weapon. "You're still fast, Meyer. I thought you would lose your mobility after that IED damn near took your leg."

Wolf shrugged. He'd lost a lot of things after that damn mine had gone off, but months and months of painful therapy had brought back his mobility. It hadn't saved his career. "Navy thought so, too. It's why I'm here instead of the Middle East. Now you better talk and you better talk fast or you're going to find out that my trigger finger still works, too."

"Mr. Meyer, would you like to introduce us?" Julian asked. "Perhaps you could bring the intruder into the office before you kill him? It's so much more private in here, and Leo's office is due for a remodel anyway."

"I'm unarmed," Holder said.

But a SEAL was never without a weapon. A SEAL was a weapon. Holder didn't need a gun to cause damage, and he seriously doubted the man was truly unarmed. He let go and nodded toward the room. Holder straightened his dark shirt. He was pushing fifty but there was no middle-aged spread on the man. Holder's hair had gone a stately silver, but his body was trim and fit, his face hawklike, and his gray eyes bespoke a sharp intelligence. He was dressed all in black.

He was dressed like a man on a mission.

"Holder. I should have known you were in on this the minute I heard you had called," Leo said. His mouth was a flat line. "Julian, this is Steve Holder. Former Lieutenant. We were on the same team in the SEALs, though not the same squad. Now he's one of the founders of a mercenary group."

"I prefer to call it a security firm," Holder said laconically in his deep Georgia accent.

"You say potato," Leo replied with a humorless grin.

"I'm not sure why I'm a mercenary but you work with Ian Taggart," Holder pointed out. "What exactly would you call him?"

"Well, I'm going to call him any number of names since you managed to get through his security," Julian replied. "He's certainly going to be working this weekend, if you take my meaning."

Yeah, he bet Taggart would have the whole crew refitting the building with every bit of crazy security equipment money could buy. Wolf could have told him no matter how secure a place was, there was always a way for a man like Holder to find his way in.

"Hello, Holder."

Holder nodded to Ben. "Dawson. Nice to see you and your brother are still close. You get out at the same time?"

Chase nodded. "Ben left. There wasn't any reason for me to stay in."

Holder turned to Julian. "And you must be Julian Lodge. I find it interesting that an investment manager needs four former Navy SEALs as bodyguards. You must have a lot to protect, Mr. Lodge."

Wolf watched as Julian's eyes became sharp. He could see the

201

exact moment that Julian began to see Holder as a true threat.

"Would you like to explain why you broke into my building, Mr. Holder? You have exactly three minutes before I have you hauled bodily out of here by several members of the Dallas police department. I assure you, I can get enough of them in here that you won't be able to take them all out."

Holder's face softened slightly. "I would rather you didn't do that. I broke in because I was worried that Leo here wouldn't see me until it was too late."

"Too late for what?" Wolf asked, his every instinct on high alert. Something bad was happening. Those pictures had sent Leo to a dark place. How much had Leo hidden from him?

Holder stared at Leo. "He's back. I don't know why he came to me instead of you, but he's back."

"Does someone want to bring me up to speed?" Wolf asked. Something was happening between his brother and Holder, some communication only the two of them understood.

"Yes, I would like to know as well," Julian said, his eyes darkening. "Is this about what happened in Afghanistan?"

The room got deathly quiet. Jack Barnes studied the crowd, leaning against the wall as though he was perfectly happy to merely observe. Chase stroked Kitten's hair, but in an almost absentminded fashion. Ben was the only one in motion. He paced, his fists clenching at his sides. Ben had been on Leo's squad. Ben knew something, and it didn't seem to be good.

"Why you and not Ben?" Leo asked, suspicion plain in his voice. "I'm much closer to Ben than anyone from our old team."

"I don't have an address," Ben said with a frown. "Chase is completely paranoid. He's taken us off the grid. Even our money is registered to several holding companies. If you want to find us, you would have to dig for a long time, and even then, Chase would know someone was coming."

Leo's eyes rolled. "God, Chase, please climb on my couch and never get up again. You're so wrong."

Chase shrugged, an elegant movement of his shoulders. He never let up on his petting of Kitten, whose eyes had closed in seeming happiness. "I'm perfectly satisfied with every one of my psychological disorders. So the guy who killed Ada is back. Why now? Holder is fairly high profile. He would be easy to track. You've gotten careless, Steve."

Holder flashed a sneer Chase's way. "I've gotten into business. People in the real world don't hide, Dawson."

"Yes, that's why they often get screwed." Chase made his pronouncement with a look of sympathy for all those who didn't agree with him.

"I want to know what's going on with my brother." If someone didn't talk soon, he was going to fucking explode.

"Would it do me a bit of good if I told you it isn't your business?" Leo asked.

There it was. That ache in his chest that bloomed every time his brother shut him out. Why was he even bothering to try? He should go and pick up Shelley and shove her in his truck and take her right back to Bliss. She would love Bliss. His designer sweetheart would adore being married to a cowboy and living in a ranch hand's house.

Leo moved in his space, his hand on his brother's shoulder. "Forgive me. It's a force of habit. I'll get used to this." He turned to Ben. "We can talk. No one in this room is going to let the story leave here."

Ben's face flushed. He looked back at his own brother, who gave him an encouraging smile.

"You can pet Kitten while you talk if you like," Chase offered.

"God, you're a pervert," Ben said, before turning back and addressing the room. "Ada was a translator in Kabul. She was American, but of Iranian descent. She was excellent with languages. And she rather liked bondage."

Leo took up the story. "I met her when she came into camp. I knew a sub when I saw one. Ben and I had talked about the fact that we'd frequented clubs in the States. You have to understand what it's like over there, Julian, Jack."

Jack held up a hand as if to stop Leo. "Son, you don't have to make a single explanation to me. You took your comfort where you could. No one is going to blame you for that."

"I didn't love her," Leo said, his lips turning down. "She was pretty and submissive, and I needed someone to spend time with. I liked her, but I didn't love her."

"I did." Ben's words were quiet, a confession. "But she would never have accepted what Chase and I need. She saw Leo and me separately. Never together."

Holder stared openly at Ben. "I had no idea you were involved with her."

Ben took a deep breath, old pain obviously surfacing. "She was crazy about Leo. I was secondary. She let me in when she couldn't have Leo and when she died, Leo made sure no one knew about my relationship with her."

"I'm sorry, Ben. I thought you were having fun," Leo said, his eyes grave.

Ben shook his head. "I don't blame you, man. I never told you. I wanted to die when I found out she was gone and how it had happened. But I never blamed you. And I never once believed you would have left her tied up."

Leo's jaw was a hard line, his words precise and controlled. "During the inquiry into Ada's murder, it was brought up that I might have left her tied up as a punishment. The rope was mine. I had left it there. The JAG prosecutor knew he couldn't get me for the murder, since I was literally on a mission when she died, but he did accuse me of leaving her alone and vulnerable."

"You wouldn't. I would never believe that." Wolf vehemently denied it. He knew his brother. Leo could be hard on subs, but he took their safety seriously. He wouldn't turn his back on a bound sub, much less leave one to go on a mission.

"They tried to say Leo was punishing her," Ben offered. "I shouldn't have stayed in. I should have stood up beside you. I should have spoken up for you."

Leo studied Wolf for a moment. "You believe me?"

How could Leo think for a single second that he didn't? "Yes. I believe you."

Leo nodded as though something had settled in his gut. He seemed more comfortable, his words coming easily. "It wouldn't have helped, Ben. I could have stayed in, too. Our CO was adamant. But I was ready to leave. I was ready to start over. But if I had known you loved her, I wouldn't have kept certain things from you. You have to understand, man, I was trying to protect you."

"Tell me now." Ben's legs were in a hard military stance, his body rigid.

"Whoever killed Ada left a note," Holder said. "The asshole who sent me the pictures also sent the file. Damn, Leo. Am I the only one who knows this?"

"Outside of the closed hearings, yes. It said *Whore*. Written in blood. Hers." Leo shoved his hair back. "It's why JAG decided it was some Taliban asshole. Ada looked Afghan. We were off base. It would have been easy. I left her there. I should have walked her back, but I got the call and she didn't want to leave."

Ben's face had gone stark white. "Fuckers. They killed her because she had sex. Hypocrites."

"I think JAG got it wrong," Holder said, pulling an envelope out of his jacket pocket. "I got this note along with those photos and the file."

Wolf grabbed it. He was closest to Holder. He had a moment to look at the note, handwritten in an almost childish script.

He's found another whore. This one will go just like the last.

And there was another photo. One that hadn't been included in the package Holder had left. It was a picture of Shelley getting off the train right in front of the building that housed The Club. Her face was turned up to the sun, her ivory skin practically glowing, her dark hair a waterfall of ebony.

Wolf felt sick.

Leo snatched it, and his skin paled as he read the words. He passed it to Ben, who sent it to Chase and Julian.

"I'm so sorry," Holder said, his voice a rumble of Southern sympathy. "I don't know why he picked me to send it to. I only know that I'll help you any way I can. I have a whole company that stands ready to help you. We were SEALs together. That's a brotherhood, man. I couldn't let you ignore this."

But he and Leo had blood. Thicker than service. And they had a shared risk. Shelley. The woman they both loved. He stared at his brother, their eyes locking.

He wouldn't let Leo down.

Chapter Thirteen

"Please tell me what's going on." Shelley looked around Leo's apartment. Finn and Lucas were sitting on the couch.

"Wolf should be here soon," Lucas explained in his smoothest tone. "He'll know more than we do."

"It's going to be okay," Finn assured her.

But it didn't feel that way. She'd been hustled out of the breakfast by Finn and Lucas as though she was under some sort of immediate threat. Her stomach turned.

"Is this about Bryce? Has something else come up? Did the feds find something new?" It was her greatest fear. Bryce had used her in a myriad of ways to cover his crimes. She'd been too trusting. She'd signed documents she hadn't really understood, giving Bryce a place to hide his money. She'd unwittingly given him a vehicle for his blackmail operation. He'd hidden spy cameras in the various lamps and vases she'd used in her designs. He'd gotten her the clients, wealthy, powerful men. She hadn't known a damn thing. She'd been stupid. She'd always known it would catch up to her.

"I don't know, Shelley," Finn said. He seemed to be trying to soothe her. "I only know that Julian asked that we escort you down here and we don't let you out of our sight until Wolf and Leo get here or someone from McKay-Taggart. Julian's put a call in and Big Tag's on his way. He wasn't here this morning or I'm sure he would be downstairs with the others. From what I understand, Aidan is handling the weekly meeting because everyone else is dealing with this situation."

That meant it was damn serious. There was a hierarchy at The Club. If Julian couldn't handle something then Leo would. Ben and Chase were next in line. Aidan wasn't even a full timer here. If Aidan was talking to the employees about the Saturday-night scenes, then every Dom on the payroll was in this emergency meeting.

It was serious. And it was about her.

Tears threatened.

"Would you like some tea?" Lucas asked. "Or coffee? Have you eaten anything?"

Shelley shook her head. The last thing she could think about was her stomach. "I'm fine. I think I'll freshen up."

She started down the hallway to the bathroom. She needed a minute. She could hear Finn and Lucas talking.

"Should we let her go?" Finn asked.

"We're sixteen stories up. There's no back way out, and we swept the place when we came in. She's fine. Give her a minute," Lucas replied.

Fine? Not anywhere close. Fine was a state she'd moved away from a long time before.

She closed the bathroom door behind her. But she'd been more than fine the night before. She'd been perfect. She'd been held between Leo and Wolf. She hadn't had to think. She'd simply felt the press of their bodies against hers, into hers. She'd been surrounded by them, safe and protected.

God, she wanted to be between them now, and not for sex. She wanted them to hold her, to promise her it would be all right.

She walked to the sink and turned on the cold water, splashing it on her face. To hell with her makeup. She couldn't breathe.

The phone in her pocket trilled.

Leo? Wolf? She scrambled, her fingers fluttering as she pulled the phone from her pocket. It was a text, and she didn't know the number.

I know what you did. If you want to leave the men out of it, meet me in five minutes. The Mexican place down the street. If not, I can kill those two and then we'll still talk. You have five minutes.

She dropped the phone as though it had burned her flesh.

All of her nightmares were real. Someone knew and they wanted revenge. The question was, would she let her men stand in the way of it?

Hell, no. She'd hidden for too long. The thought of Leo taking a bullet was worse than her own death. An image of Wolf's big strong body forever silent threatened to wreck her.

She couldn't let it happen. She needed to call the police, but what would this person do if she didn't show up in the requisite five minutes she'd been given? How vulnerable were Leo and Wolf?

Or was the text referring to Lucas and Finn? They had wives who depended on them. They weren't security professionals, precisely the reason she was waiting on Taggart. But he wasn't going to be here in five minutes, and she didn't think those law degrees of theirs would protect Lucas and Finn from a couple of bullets.

She took a deep breath. She needed a few things. She winced. The first thing she needed to do was get the damn plug out of her ass. She couldn't run with it. Wolf would be pissed, but she might not see him again.

She got it done, anger coursing through her veins. She should be exploring, having fun with her new Dom and trying to bring Leo in, but no, she was still dealing with Bryce's shit. He would never let her go. He was dead and gone and still screwing with her life.

One mistake. That was all it had taken. One mistake she'd made when she was too young to know better and her life was over. It had been the day she'd said yes to Bryce.

She smoothed her hair back. She couldn't look like a woman who was about to make a break for it. Damn it. She missed the stupid plug. It had been a reminder of Wolf, as though he was there with her. Now she was alone.

And she had a job to do.

As quietly as she could, she slipped out of the bathroom and down the hall. Wolf had talked about carrying a gun. She wondered if he had more than one. She went into the small bedroom she'd shared with the men the night before. Wolf's duffel bag was on the bed. Guilt knifed through her. Wolf trusted her, but she wasn't sure what else to do.

Lucas had a son. Finn had a baby on the way. She couldn't risk them. She'd gotten herself into this position. She was going to get herself out.

There it was, right past his spare pair of jeans. She had no idea what the make was or the name. It was a gun. It was big and shiny and metallic, and it would kill people.

She grabbed Wolf's hoodie. It was enormous. It would hide the fact that she had a gun in the pocket of her jeans. Her hands shaking, she carefully placed the gun, muzzle down, handle up. She wasn't going out without a fight.

She walked back out. Finn sat beside Lucas, both men watching their phones as if waiting for some message they were sure would come.

"Lucas, I changed my mind. I am hungry," she said, trying to give him a wan smile. She clutched at the cotton of the jacket as though cold.

Lucas stood up. "Of course. I'll go see what Leo has. I'm sure I can make you an omelet."

He walked back to the kitchen and Finn got up as well. He sighed and held out a hand, finding hers and squeezing it. "It's going to be okay. I promise. Wolf can handle this. If you're worried about him leaving, I wouldn't. And Leo will come around. Trust me. This is all some horrifically convoluted plan of my Master's to bring everyone together. Julian tends to get what he wants, and he wants all three of you happy."

She nodded and brought a hand to her temple. She wasn't worried about Wolf leaving. She was worried about Wolf staying and taking a bullet. "I know. I'll be all right. I just have a horrible headache."

"Stress. Of course. I'll go see if I can find you something." Finn turned and walked toward the bathroom.

She had so little time. Grabbing her purse, she moved as quickly as she could. She opened the door and slipped out. The moment she had the door closed again, she sprinted.

The carpet beneath her masked the sound of her feet pounding against the floor. She ran as silently as she could toward the elevator. She would use the stairs but she was all the way up on the sixteenth floor. But, perhaps…

She broke for the stairs. Finn would figure it out pretty quickly, and then he and Lucas would look for her. They would check through the apartment first, but then they would look in the hall. They would find her standing by the elevators.

If she ran hard, she could make it down a couple of flights of stairs and then catch the service elevator at the back of the building. She'd used it many times while working on the penthouse. It was large and utilitarian, unlike the elegant main elevator. It was big enough to hold furniture and appliances. It ran down to the garage.

From the garage she could make it to the street very quickly. She would be gone before Wolf or Leo was even told she'd left the apartment.

Her steps echoed through the stairwell, every single one making her wince, but she didn't hear another set. Her breath sawed in and out of her chest. If she survived, she was joining a gym. Her muscles burned, but she didn't stop. She had so little time.

She burst through the door on the fourteenth floor and made for the left hall. *Fuck.* She turned. It was on the right. She passed the main elevator, rushing past doors that led to suites. This was the part of the hotel Julian ran for his guests and club members.

There it was. The service elevator. Thank god.

She could catch her breath while she waited.

She pressed the door to call the elevator. Her hands were shaking. She looked up and down the hall. Tears threatened.

She didn't want to do this. God, she didn't want any of this. She wanted to be back in that too-small bed, pressed between Leo and Wolf. She wanted to be back there, and she wouldn't leave. She would stay in that bed, in that moment when everything seemed possible. It had been a nice dream. She'd been loved and cared for. She'd been what they needed. She hadn't needed to pretend or be someone she wasn't. She'd just been Shelley.

And that was over. Even if she survived this encounter, she doubted Wolf would forgive her. She knew Leo wouldn't. It would be more direct proof that she couldn't trust.

Trust. What the hell was that supposed to mean? How did wanting him to stay alive mean she didn't trust him?

Where was the damn elevator? Panic threatened to swamp her. Time was running out. She pressed the button again, but it was finally opening. The doors split apart, and she started forward.

Only to stop in an instant because the elevator wasn't empty.

Leo Meyer stood in the center, his face a mask of cold fury.

Her breath hitched. Her heart raced. If she hadn't had such good control of herself, she might have peed a little because Leo looked ready to kill. His normally warm blue eyes had gone an arctic shade— the color of water right before it froze. He turned those dark eyes on her, his mouth a flat line. He held a cell phone in one hand.

"Fourteen," he said simply before shoving it into his pocket.

No hellos. No questions about what had happened. Just a number spoken to whoever was on the other line.

He took a single step forward, and Shelley gave in to her instincts.

She turned and ran.

She wasn't even sure why she was running except for the fact that Leo scared the crap out of her. The man in the elevator was a predator, and she felt like prey. She ran almost mindlessly, not really knowing where she was going. She headed back toward the door to the stairs. Her chest felt like it would burst.

If she could make it to the stairs, maybe she could salvage this.

The door to the stairs swung open, and her nightmare was complete.

Wolf stalked out of the door. She had no idea how many flights of stairs he'd run up. She'd been pretty sure he'd been on the tenth floor. But he didn't show it. His breath was perfectly normal, as though he'd gotten out of his easy chair instead of run full tilt up a bunch of flights of stairs.

She faltered as she tried to stop. She fell, her ass hitting the ground. She tried to get back up, managed to get to her knees, but got hit by a Mack truck from behind. She fell forward, her chest hitting the carpet and the breath whooshing out of her lungs.

"Not on your life," Leo whispered in her ear. She could feel the heat of his body holding her down. "You try to run again and you will regret it. I swear to god I won't hold back, and no safe word in the world will be able to fucking save you. Do you understand me? If you move one inch that I don't tell you to, I will give up all my rights in the club, all my rights as a Dom, for the simple joy of beating your ass until I'm satisfied you can't run again."

"Maybe we should find out why she ran in the first place, brother," Wolf said.

Shelley could see his boots in front of her face. She struggled to breathe, but there was a part of her that was happy to be on the floor. If she was here, she didn't have to look into Leo's eyes and see the rage there. She put her face down on the floor, submitting completely. Tears leaked out of her eyes. She couldn't fight them.

She couldn't fight anyone.

Leo cursed, the sound a low growl in her ear. "Don't you fucking cry. You don't get to cry."

"Leo, come on," Wolf said. "Can we figure out what the hell is going on?"

Leo pushed off her, his weight leaving, and she could finally catch a real breath. She was shaking. Her time was up. It had to be. She'd failed. Leo turned her over, and her own anger bubbled to the surface.

"You have no right to do that. Let me up and let me go." At the very least she could distance herself. It probably wouldn't work, but she could try. Maybe if she could get to the restaurant, whoever this asshole was would at least see she'd tried.

She started to roll up, but Leo straddled her hips, pinning her arms with his hands. His chest hovered over hers. "No."

"You can't tell me no. You have to let me go." She tried to fight, but he was too strong. He was so strong. She struggled, but it was a weak, ineffectual thing.

Leo's icy-cold eyes stared down at her. She could feel his cock. His eyes might be cool, but there was a part of him that was heating up. His cock thickened against her pussy, but there wasn't a lick of desire in those eyes. "I don't have to do anything. It's been recently pointed out to me that I have allowed you to manipulate me over and over again. I'm done with allowing you to do that."

"Manipulate you? Are you kidding me?" What the hell was he

talking about?

"I think we should go back to the condo and sit down and talk this out." Wolf was the calm voice of reason. "We have no idea that she was planning on doing anything dangerous."

Thank god one of them had patience.

"Really, brother," Leo said. "Can you think of a good reason for her to have run away from the men we asked to watch out for her?"

Wolf shrugged, those big shoulders moving up and down. "Maybe she was scared. Maybe she was looking for one of us."

Leo laughed, but it was a bitter sound. "She ran the minute she saw me."

"Dude, you looked kind of psychotic. You still do. Maybe you should try a sympathetic smile." Wolf looked down at her. His handsome face was upside down, but she found comfort in it. His lips had curved slightly, his eyes warm. "Want to explain this whole thing, baby? We weren't trying to scare you. We need to tighten up security when it comes to you. We were going to come up to explain it to you. Finn and Lucas were only watching out for you until we could do it ourselves."

Leo got up, his muscular body moving with grace. He ran a hand through his hair, shoving it back. "She wasn't looking for us. And she wasn't hungry and trying to find a goddamn vending machine. If she had been doing either of those things, she wouldn't have felt the need to steal your extra gun."

"What?"

Wolf didn't look quite so reasonable when he reached down and hauled her up.

"It's in her right-hand pocket. At least I assume she stole it from you. Maybe she has a whole bunch of guns I don't know about. I wouldn't put anything past her at this point." Leo's fists were clenched as he pulled his cell out. "We have her. Tell the others they can stand down. No. We can handle it. We'll be back down in my office in five minutes. Yeah, she'll be with us. No. She'll be in one piece, boss." There was a long pause as Julian obviously made a request. Leo shook his head before replying. "I told you she'll be in one piece. I promise nothing more than that."

Wolf had her up and on her feet. His hands ran down her torso, stopping when he got to the gun.

"Wolf," Shelley began. She couldn't quite find the words. She thought she could handle Leo's anger more than Wolf's disappointment.

Wolf reached under the cotton front of the jacket and pulled the gun free. His eyes closed briefly, and his mouth firmed into a grim line. "The safety isn't on. I left the fucking safety on. I know I did."

She looked down at the gun. It was a foreign, dangerous thing, and now she was starting to realize she didn't know much about it. "I might have fumbled with it. I might have accidently pushed it off. I don't know. I didn't know it had a safety."

She'd never worked with handguns. Her father and brother had used shotguns and rifles on the ranch. How was she supposed to know?

There was a loud crack. Shelley started. Wolf wrapped an arm around her middle and hauled her back.

Leo had put his fist through the wall.

"What are you doing?" Shelley asked, shocked. Leo was always calm.

"Hush or I'll start your punishment here and now," Wolf promised. "I'm only calm because my brother isn't. You're going to keep your mouth shut unless you want to apologize sweetly and beg for some forgiveness."

"I am sorry, but you don't understand what you've done," she said, trying to wiggle away. Tears coursed freely now. There was a huge part of her that wanted to do exactly what Wolf had said. She wanted to get down on her knees and ask them to forgive her. She wanted to calm Leo down. She didn't like seeing him on the edge of his control.

Leo pulled his fist free of the wall. Miraculously, he hadn't broken anything but the wall. There were scrapes, but he managed to flex his hand.

"Are you done taking it out on the walls or should we move on to other inanimate objects?" Wolf asked. He didn't let up on his hold.

Leo's face was a blank as he turned back to them. "Better the wall than her ass. I can't touch her right now. Set the punishment for later. Neither one of us is in any headspace to lay a hand on her." Leo took a deep breath. He closed his eyes, and when he opened them, he seemed to have more control. "Why?"

"It's none of your business. I would like to go now." They couldn't hold her. They couldn't force her to stay here. She would get her things and leave. She would try to text this guy back and figure out another meeting. She would find another gun.

"Try her phone, Wolf."

Sneaky, too-smart-for-his-own-good son of a bitch. "Hey, that's mine."

Leo was too smart, and Wolf was too fast. He had the phone out of her pocket and tossed it to his brother.

"Damn it," she cursed.

Wolf's arm tightened around her waist. "I have a good memory, love. Every time you curse me or Leo, you're doing nothing but adding to your punishment. And it's bad right now. I can't begin to tell you how bad it is. Do you see how that vein over his right eye is throbbing?"

Sure enough, Leo's eye twitched. He didn't seem to mind. He didn't look up, merely began going over the contents of her phone. His mouth tightened.

"That's his tell. You think you've seen him mad before, but you haven't until you've seen that tic. You pushed him too far."

"I was only trying to protect you." There was nothing left to do. Leo had read the text.

"Mother fucker." Leo read the text out loud. "Bring her along, Wolf. I don't dare lay a hand on her. We'll deal with her when we get her down to my office. I want to see if Ben and Chase can do anything with this. And I want a full workup on Holder, man. I don't like the fact that he showed up just as someone is after Shelley."

Shelley dug her heels in. "No. You guys have to let me go."

Wolf simply lifted her up, and in a show of pure power, turned her in the air until she was over his shoulder and her stomach was flattened against him.

"Damn it, Wolf, you do not have to obey him."

Wolf started to follow Leo back to the elevator. "That's not what our momma said."

He was frustrating. And it was very difficult to talk to his ass.

Even though it was a spectacular ass.

"Besides, if I hadn't listened to Leo, you probably would have gotten away. I was going to take the main elevator," Wolf admitted. "But Leo said that you would probably run either down or up and try to get to the service elevator because you would think we would go up to the condo."

Leo pressed the button to the very service elevator in question. "And I had men in the garage and at all the exits. The minute Finn called me, there was no way out of this building, Shelley. I had everyone in place before you could even make it to the elevator. Remember that the next time you decide to take things into your own hands."

The only thing she could take into her own hands now was Wolf's ass, and she thought that might be pushing things. "Please let me take care of this. It's my problem. Did you not read that text? Don't you get it?"

The elevator doors closed behind her, and Leo gently lifted her head up. "Do you know what they would call you in writing circles? I know about this. I've thought often of writing a novel of my own. You wouldn't be the heroine because anyone who read it would say you're too stupid to live."

She felt herself flush. "Screw you, Leo. I was trying to protect you."

Wolf put her down, her feet hitting the floor as the elevator shuddered to a stop. Wolf stared down at her. She barely reached the top of his shoulders. He outweighed her by a hundred pounds. He knew that guns had safeties.

Yeah, maybe she was too stupid to live, but she'd only been trying to make sure they didn't die.

"I'm sorry." She couldn't look at him. "I didn't want to drag you into this."

Leo put a hand on his brother's arm. "Don't. The elevator will be infinitely harder to fix than the wall."

"You got to punch something," Wolf said with a frown.

"I'll let you punch the hell out of the condo later. Or maybe Chase. He annoys me at times. Yes, punch Chase." Leo actually smiled at his brother. "It's all right. This is what she does. I let her get away with it once. Don't make the same mistake I did."

The doors opened.

She took a deep breath, still trying to find a way out of this. "Guys, I know you're mad. I know you think I'm stupid, but I had my reasons. This isn't your fight."

Wolf's fists clenched. "She's pushing me, Leo."

"Yep," Leo agreed. "It's what she does. Of course, you're her Dom. You know she's going to require a bit of training. Come on, Shelley. Don't give me any more trouble. You've already made us both look like idiots."

She found herself following Leo down the hall, Wolf hard on her heels. "I didn't mean to. And I don't see how me trying to handle a situation makes the two of you look bad."

Frustration was starting to crowd out her panic. There was nothing left to do now except convince them to let her go. Except they didn't seem to want to listen to her.

Leo stopped, turning on his heels. It threw her off balance and sent her stepping back, where she ran straight into Wolf. Wolf didn't seem to feel the same need for personal space that she did. He was a brick wall.

"Wolf is your Dom," Leo pointed out. "You signed a contract to obey him. Everyone in this club knows we slept together last night."

"Everyone?"

Leo's eyes rolled. "Yes, everyone. It's a small club, and I have a housekeeper. She comes in early on Saturdays. She caught me coming out of Wolf's room this morning. If Kristina knows, then everyone knows. And if everyone knows that I slept with you, then everyone will know that you're a disobedient brat who can't mind her Dom or her lover. Every goddamn Dom in this place is questioning us right now. You reflect on your Master."

Wolf's voice was a low rumble. "And if I hear one more time that this isn't my fight, I won't care about the damage. I'll punch my way through something."

She felt her fists clench. "I don't understand."

"Then let me explain it to you," Wolf began. "I enjoyed your body last night. I took it over and over. I take that seriously. We have a contract. You aren't letting me do my job. I don't have anything else. I can't be a SEAL anymore. There wasn't a place left for me in Bliss. For the last month, all I've thought about is you. I got that tat two days after we talked for the first time. You told me about growing up with Trev and how you weren't sure of your place in the world anymore. I was in the same boat. I thought maybe we could find it together, and I made a choice. I gave up trying to fight my way back in. I was done because I had something else I wanted. You. So I want you to tell me here and now if you're using me for sex or fun or whatever the hell a woman like you wants from a man like me."

Oh, god, what had she done to Wolf? Her heart ached. He stood there, a big, glorious piece of masculinity. She'd been so stupid. She hadn't seen past his good looks and grace. He was a man, a man who could be hurt. She gave up fighting. She walked up to him and put her arms around his waist, placing her head over his heart. "A woman like me is crazy about a man like you. A woman like me can't stand the thought of a man like you getting hurt."

His hands came up, stroking her hair. "I would rather take a bullet than have you rip my heart out, baby. Leo made a huge mistake when he let you kick him out of your life. He won't make it again. And I won't make it at all. I don't care how mad you get at me. I'm not allowing you to make this decision. I'm never going to let you walk into a dangerous situation alone. If that means that you won't be with me anymore, then that's what happens. But I won't let you go until this situation is settled."

She'd thought she was doing the right thing, but as she stood there hearing the beat of Wolf's heart, she realized that maybe she'd been wrong. She'd spent so much time in a relationship that didn't work that she no longer really knew what did work. Her parents had been in love and not once during their years together had one of them pushed the other away in the name of protection. They had been bound together, their troubles and their joys shared. The risk was shared, too.

It was what people in love did. Good. Bad. Life. Death. All shared.

She'd done this to Leo.

"I'm so sorry," she whispered. If the positions had been reversed, she wouldn't have wanted Leo to push her away. She would have wanted to stand by him. She would have demanded her place, as Wolf had. "I won't do it again. I am sorry."

Wolf's arms tightened around her. "I'm glad to hear it, sweetheart. I don't want to go through this again. We're either in this together or we're not."

"Together." She wanted them all together, but she might have burned that bridge with Leo. He was proud, and he might never again open his heart. Time. She needed a bit of time to show him that she understood now. Wolf had opened that door. It was up to her to make sure it didn't shut. She sniffled and turned out of Wolf's arms, looking to Leo. He stood, staring at her, his expression closed. She wanted to turn back to Wolf. He was safe and warm and secure, but she was done playing it safe. "I'm sorry, Sir."

One of Leo's brows lifted. "Are you? You might be more than sorry when you realize what Wolf is going to do to you."

She'd known this was coming. "Only Wolf? I lied to you, too. I'll take my punishment."

"Both of us, Shelley. I think a breach of trust this big requires more than one Master's hands. If you're up for it," Wolf offered.

Leo nodded slowly. "I will help you. I think she won't like some of my suggestions, however. She's going to get a rapid-fire education in what happens when a sub breaks her word."

She took a deep breath, dread coming from more than one side now. She was absolutely certain that neither man would really hurt her, but Leo had a diabolical mind. She was in for some extreme discomfort.

And she would handle it. "I'll be good."

"Excellent," Leo said. "And you'll start in just a moment. You will be polite and obedient while we're in my office. You will accept your bindings."

"Bindings?" Was her punishment starting early?

"Yes." Wolf put a hand on her shoulder. "I'm going to show you what happens to subs who run from their Masters." His lips cracked a bit, a smile appearing. "But I will say that I'm surprised you managed to run as fast as you did. A lot of subs struggle with the plug in the beginning."

Leo sighed. "You're kidding right?"

Shelley chewed on her bottom lip, trying to look as sweet and vulnerable as possible because Wolf was going to be upset.

Wolf's eyes narrowed. "You took out my plug?"

"I couldn't run with it. I could barely walk with it. I'm sorry."

"Now you've done it," Leo murmured. "He doesn't explode when you nearly get yourself killed, but watch what happens when you take that plug out."

Wolf's face flushed, even white teeth flashing. "Move. Leo's office—now. Go into the bathroom and pull those pants down and spread your cheeks. I'll make sure you remember to leave my plug where I put it."

"Wolf, let's talk about this," she stuttered.

Wolf wasn't in the mood to talk. He picked her up, flipping her over his shoulder again.

"Damn it, Wolf. You have to stop treating me like a sack of flour." She squealed as he slapped her ass. It wasn't a pansy-ass slap. It stung.

"No cussing. And I'm done talking."

She caught a glimpse of Leo's smile as Wolf stalked past. She was once again staring at Wolf's perfectly perfect ass. This time she was wondering exactly what he was going to do to hers.

Chapter Fourteen

"He bribed a security guard. I've fired the security guard and let him know he will never work security again." Taggart looked positively enraged and Leo was happy he hadn't been the dumbass security guard who'd probably thought Holder just wanted to check out the building.

"That doesn't explain how he managed to evade our security cameras, Ian," Julian pointed out.

Tag had his hands on his hips. "You went with the lowest bidder on the contract to put the system in. That's what happened. It's a state-of-the-art system, but if it's not properly installed it won't work the way it should. Alex and Jake are looking into the problem right now." His gaze went to Holder. "And Adam is pulling up everything he can on our intruder."

"I know our intruder," Leo said. "I'll fill you in on everything."

Tag still had those icy blue eyes on Holder. "I know him, too. I don't particularly like some of the work he does."

"Hey, you're the one who worked for the Agency," Holder shot back. It was obvious these two didn't get along.

Julian stepped in. "How about we all calm down. Ian, I appreciate you getting out here so quickly."

Tag nodded and then his whole demeanor changed. "I wish I'd been here earlier. I heard the new sub got herself in trouble. Looks like Wolf can handle it."

Leo had to stop himself from smiling as Shelley reappeared from
the bathroom. She had tears in her eyes and that gorgeous bottom lip
of hers quivered. Wolf had obviously chosen to forgo taking her
clothing the way he would have, but now that he thought about it, he
was actually happy with that decision. She could be naked in The
Club, but in the confines of his office with so many men around, it
seemed too intimate a thing to share.

But Wolf hadn't been too kind. She walked in a stilted pattern
that made him wonder how pissed off baby brother had been.

"Did you shove an elephant plug up her rectum?" Leo asked, well
aware that everyone was looking at their sub. *Fuck*. His brother's sub.

Shelley nodded, but Wolf shook his head.

Again, the laughter bubbled up.

"He requested a plug that was slightly larger than a starter,"
Julian explained. "She's fine, Leo. It's a perfectly appropriate
punishment, and I asked her what her safe word was before Wolf shut
the door. I believe what Miss McNamara is protesting is the lubricant
your brother chose."

He felt his jaw drop. His little brother was far more of a sadist
than he'd believed. He felt almost paternalistically proud. "You used
the ginger lube?"

Big Tag offered Wolf a high five. He would have to keep those
two apart.

"It didn't sound so bad at first," she admitted, her breath puffing
from her mouth. "It sounded exotic. It kind of sucks, Leo. It really
sucks."

It burned was what it did. And it appeared that Wolf wasn't
finished. Jack Barnes handed his brother a length of jute. The thin
rope was around Shelley's arms before she could move.

His brother was damn good with rope.

"I don't get you people." Holder looked on with a frown on his
face. Leo could easily read the man's disdain. "First that one and now
this one."

Kitten was still tied up. She'd been sitting serenely until the shit
had hit the fan. The minute they got the news that Shelley was on the
run the tears had started, and Jack had been forced to pet her while

Ben and Chase had hightailed it to get to their positions, one in the garage and the other on the bottom floor. He'd enjoyed the big cowboy's obvious discomfort with being left to babysit a twenty-five-year-old woman.

Ben and Chase walked back into the room. Ben still looked a bit ashen, though he had control of himself again. Chase was silent, walking slightly behind his brother. Chase hadn't known Ada. Was this a part of his brother's life he couldn't understand? It would be difficult. The two men now worked together with flawless precision. Any breach between them would be felt deeply.

Unlike his own brother. Wolf had been gone for years, and Leo was only now feeling the true distance.

He'd missed his brother. He'd missed the loyal child Wolf had been and the steadfast man he'd become. He could never have handled Shelley the way Wolf had. They would have fought, and she would have walked away again. Of course, Wolf was also far too soft until certain things were pointed out. If Leo hadn't been there, Wolf might likely have ended up a pool of goo at her feet, believing every stupid excuse she gave him. And that would be dangerous for her.

Without the two of them, she might have been in real trouble.

"You don't have to understand it, Mr. Holder. You merely have to tell us everything you know," Julian said, his eyes on the mercenary. When Finn had called down, it had been Julian who had kept his head long enough to realize that no one wanted to leave Holder in the office by himself.

Holder was the wild card.

"Ah, so the little sub gets what she deserves," Chase said, watching as Wolf began winding the rope around Shelley's body.

Wolf seemed infinitely calmer now that he'd begun his discipline. He worked slowly, as though finding comfort from the intricate bindings he created. Leo understood. There was an elegant dance to Shibari. He found it soothing. How much more meaningful would it be to share it with someone he genuinely cared about? How long had it been since he'd been in love? He wondered now if what he'd had with Janine was even love. He'd let her go so easily. Of course, he'd let Shelley go as well, but he'd felt it like a kick in the gut every day he was away from her.

He approved of the pattern Wolf had chosen. His brother's fingers moved in a nimble dance. Shelley's arms were in front of her body, palms together, elbows touching. Maete Hiji Shibari. It would be fairly comfortable for Shelley, with no real worries about nerve damage. But she would have no illusions that she wasn't caught. Her eyes found his. He expected to find pleading in them, a request for clemency.

Instead, she winked at him.

Adorable brat.

"She's lucky," Leo said, watching Wolf. "I wouldn't have left her with the comfort of clothes."

Shelley's eyes got wide. Leo felt his cock jump at the thought. He rather liked being the bad cop when it came to her.

Wolf finished his pattern and tied it off. "I didn't feel like showing her off today. Knees, love, now."

"Are you kidding me? Wolf, I can't walk much less get to my knees."

No matter how adorable she was, she was going to get spanked. Leo decided to back up his brother. "Wolf, if you don't I will."

He was taking liberties with his brother's submissive, but he couldn't seem to help himself. Wolf might have opened a door the night before that he wouldn't be able to close.

Wolf pressed her back, leaning her forward, and gave her five hard smacks right on her ass. Shelley squealed, letting Leo know that his brother hadn't really hurt her, but the plug was most likely burning. Every swat of Wolf's hand would have jarred the plug, making her pretty asshole light up.

When Wolf brought her back up, she awkwardly fell to her knees. "This part sucks, Wolf. It really, really sucks. I liked the last-night part, but I am officially protesting this part."

God, she was so sexy. He would spank her just to see her pout. He wanted nothing more than to walk right over and kiss those luscious lips until she couldn't breathe. He wanted to fuck her while she was tied up, while she was utterly open and helpless to him.

But it was Wolf who leaned over and pressed his lips to hers. "Are you going to run again, love?"

She smiled. "Certainly not when I know you have access to a

plug and kitchen herbs."

Wolf smiled, kissing her forehead. "I always have access, so my job is done. You won't run again. Hush, now, love. Or I'll have to gag you."

Kitten pouted. "Kitten doesn't understand, Masters. Kitten was very good and did her job and behaved perfectly, but Shelley gets all the treats. No one has plugged Kitten. And no one ever figs poor Kitten. It's not fair."

Chase pulled a ball gag out of his pants pocket and shoved it in Kitten's mouth. Kitten enthusiastically worked her mouth around it. "Can we get down to business now that all the subs are accounted for and properly punished or rewarded?"

Shelley opened her mouth, most likely to say something bratty.

Leo stared her down. Those beautiful eyes slid away and suddenly seemed to find the floor endlessly fascinating. At least he could still do one thing right. Wolf's hand came out to pet her head.

Leo passed Shelley's cell phone to Tag. "She got this text. It's what sent her running."

Tag read the text and then passed it to Chase. "You can try to trace the number back, but you know what I'm thinking."

Chase nodded before passing it to Ben. "If this guy has half a brain, it's a burner. So she thought she would be safer someplace other than here?"

Leo continued to stare at her, his anger rising all over again. God, he'd been terrified at first, and then rage had taken over. She'd done it again, and this time she'd done it to both him and Wolf. "She thought it would be a good idea to go and meet the guy and apparently shoot his ass with Wolf's spare piece."

Every eye in the room went to the sub on the floor.

"Oh, you are lucky that Wolf here has a soft heart," Julian said, his voice cold.

She smartly kept her eyes to the floor.

"Do you want me to call in the police?" Jack asked, breaking up the tension.

"I've already alerted Lieutenant Brighton. I've made sure he's our DPD liaison," Tag said. "He's making a record of it."

Leo nodded. "Thank you. I don't want cops swarming The Club.

It tends to be bad for business. Besides, this is a family affair, apparently. But when I inevitably have to kill someone, I would like to have justifiable cause."

Julian shrugged. "If you kill someone, simply call and give me adequate preparation time. I have several suitably horrible people I've been trying to find something to pin on. Mr. Taggart keeps files."

Tag smiled, a predatory look. "We're totally ready."

That was his boss. Always a giver.

Chase was sitting at Kitten's laptop, his hands flying across the keys. He looked up with a frown. "I got the cell number. You're right, Tag. Untraceable. Paid in cash. Disposable. He obviously knows we would be after him. He's not an idiot."

Wolf looked up. "You got all of that in two minutes?"

"Why? Should it take longer?" Chase looked around. He wasn't the most aware person in the world. He pretty much thought everything that was obvious to him would be the same to everyone.

Leo turned to Holder. He was the key. "When did you get the message? Did it come by courier or through the mail?"

"Three days ago," Holder explained. He didn't flinch, didn't seem uncomfortable. "I had some of my in-house guys go over it, but it came through the mail. We found some prints, but they were postal employees. No return address. I tried calling you, but you didn't answer. I don't have your cell so all I had was your office number, and even that was hard to find. I couldn't get past security. Well, not in any legal fashion. I'm sorry I had to do it this way, but I needed your attention. I didn't think leaving another message was a good idea."

"But breaking into my office was?" Leo wasn't at all happy about that.

Holder shrugged. "I thought about waiting around, but I figured I would freak the girl out. I left the envelope and waited for you. Sure enough, you showed up." Holder took a deep breath. "I was pissed that you wouldn't talk to me."

"It was a busy day." Leo eyed Kitten. "And that one doesn't take the best of messages. I blew you off because I know you've been recruiting, and I didn't want to deal with it. I honestly thought you might be looking for my brother. The last thing I wanted was for Wolf to end up as a mercenary."

"Yeah, I moved way too slow," Tag said under his breath.

Julian gave him a shit-eating grin. "I didn't have to pay you to train this one."

Holder's mouth firmed to a flat line. "I did want to talk to Wolf, actually, but I can see he has a job tying up girls."

"Best job ever," Wolf said.

Holder shook his head. "Nevertheless, I was an asshole, but I had good intentions."

Leo wasn't so sure about that, but it did no good to press. He had other matters to get to. "And you're telling me you had no idea who Shelley was when you talked to her on the train?"

Holder shrugged. "I tried to make an appointment with you. Check the lobby records. I walked out and hopped on the train which takes me straight to the place I'm staying. She's a lovely woman. I was trying to hit on her. Then I was trying to help her. She had a bad day. Though it looks like today has been rougher on her."

All perfectly logical. Every question he asked, Holder had an answer for. Leo didn't like it, but he also didn't have anywhere else to go. "Can you send us everything you have?"

Holder nodded. "Of course. I'll have them send you all the reports, but we're still looking into it. I also think it might help to get back into Ada's case."

Leo's stomach turned. That was the last thing he wanted to do.

"I have the case files. Don't ask me how, but I got them yesterday. I thought you would need them. Whoever took those photos probably killed Ada. It's got to be someone on our team." His eyes trailed toward Ben.

Fuck. The last thing he needed was a new inquest. He was in a corner. If Holder took this shit back to the Navy, they might reopen the case with a new suspect. Ben. Ben had been on base at the time of her death, but Leo had no idea who would remember him. He needed to placate the bastard and fast.

Leo looked over at Julian, who nodded shortly. He and Julian had worked together long enough to know what the other was thinking most of the time. Julian was giving him permission to bring his troubles into The Club. "Steve, I would appreciate any help you could give us. Please, bring in the files, and we can go over them."

And it would be a great way to keep watch on Holder.

Holder agreed and got on his cell, talking to an assistant.

Ben stepped forward, his voice low. "We can't trust him."

"Leo doesn't trust him." Tag followed Ben's lead, whispering. "He's keeping that asshole close because it's obvious Holder knows more than he's telling. I don't like any of this."

Neither did Leo, but he wasn't sure what else to do. Something was going on, and until he knew what it was, he didn't want to let Holder out of his sight. The morning had been utter chaos. He still hadn't spoken to Ben and Chase about what he'd wanted to. He turned to Ben. "Did you and Chase check out her place when you picked up the clothes?"

He looked over at Shelley. She seemed calmer as Wolf stroked her. She leaned into him, her head resting against his thigh. Jack Barnes was talking on the phone. Julian was speaking quietly to Chase.

Neither of those men were worried about their women because they knew Abby and Dani were safe. Sam and Finn would lay down their lives. It allowed Jack and Julian some freedom. It allowed Leo some freedom. He could talk to Ben without worrying about Shelley's welfare because Wolf was taking care of her.

Fuck. He didn't want to think about that. Could he do it? Could he really share long term?

Ben scrubbed a hand through his hair. "It looked fine at first, but I would bet a lot that someone's gone through it."

Leo let his eyes close. That wasn't what he'd wanted to hear. Everything was going to hell, and he could only thank god that he wasn't alone. His brother had impeccable timing. "Anything taken?"

When he opened his eyes again, Ben was shaking his head. "Nope. Just an immaculately done search. I would have said no on the search, but her underwear was moved around. Her clothes are all almost compulsively sorted, but someone had moved her underwear around. It was pushed to the front, as though someone was searching through her drawers. I talked to her neighbors, but no one remembered much. The security there is complete crap."

Leo nodded. "She won't go back there. I get the feeling if my brother has his way, she won't ever leave this club again. Let's keep a close eye on Holder. If he's here, then we know he's not somewhere else plotting. Tag, I need to know where he's been and what he's been doing for the last several years."

He nodded. "I'll get on it now. I get that this is about a translator's death. Leo, you have to let me look into this. There is no judgment here, man."

It made his gut twist, but Ian was more trustworthy. "I'll send the file to you."

Ben's face tightened. "I did a lot of research into Ada's death, and I believe it was a SEAL. I hate saying that, but everything points to someone on the team. I think Ada knew something. I don't know if it was about a mission or something criminal, but someone silenced her. I don't buy that this whole thing is strictly about you. If all this guy wants is revenge, why wait this long?"

"Maybe because I haven't had anyone serious in my life."

"Leo, you were married and divorced since then," Ben pointed out. "And you hadn't touched Shelley when this guy sent this stuff out. It doesn't make sense."

But he had to go with it. "We need to look at everything with a fresh eye. That's where Tag can help us."

Ben sighed, a weariness settling over him. "I'll send you both everything I've pulled together over the years. I truly believe Ada died because of something she knew or saw. The only man who could have been pissed at you was me, and I didn't kill her. I think I could solve this damn thing, but I haven't been able to get back over there to talk to witnesses."

No. It would be hard to get into the middle of a war zone. But Big Tag could probably make it happen. He had Agency connections. Between Tag's connections and Chase's ruthless will, they could move mountains.

Leo looked over, and Chase was watching them. Leo could see it there in Chase's eyes. He'd been trying to protect his brother, and now it was going to hell.

Leo knew the feeling. Holder got off the phone and started talking about logistics.

Leo listened, but his mind was on something else. His past was catching up to him, and Shelley was caught in the cross fire.

Coincidence? It seemed odd that she would be caught in her husband's shit storm only to walk straight into Leo's.

Perhaps Shelley was simply unfortunate. Or perhaps Leo wasn't seeing the whole picture.

One way or another, he would protect her.

* * * *

Holder almost couldn't hold back his glee as he left the building.

It had gone even better than he'd hoped. He wasn't happy with the addition of Taggart, but he could handle that asshole. It didn't matter because he had something amazing. Not once had he expected that Leo Meyer would simply open up and hand him the keys to the kingdom, but damn, he'd found a way in.

Ben Dawson.

God, he'd known Meyer was a freak, and now it looked like Dawson was one, too. He'd had no fucking idea that Dawson had been screwing the girl, too. What a bit of luck.

He made sure there was plenty of space between him and the building before he ducked into a busy coffee shop. He bought a cup of decaf and waited. Ten minutes. Fifteen. Twenty.

If he'd been followed, they weren't close. Still. He was a cautious man. He slipped into the bathroom and locked the door. Alone at last. He dialed Kyle's cell phone and got an immediate answer.

"Did it work, boss?" Kyle asked.

"Beautifully." Holder was perfectly happy with the geek. He was never going anywhere without one again. "She caused some nice chaos. And they take it seriously now. I'm in. I'm supposed to come back tomorrow. We can make plans on when to take the girl then. The security's good, but not perfect. I doubt Lodge will have time to upgrade before we can nab her."

"I have confirmation that Jagger, Klein, and Shaver are en route. They'll get here and obtain a nice quiet place to have our talk with the target." Kyle hesitated for a moment. "She's bad, right?"

Holder felt his eyes roll. His geek needed to toughen up. "She's really fucking bad for us. Do you want to go to jail?"

Kyle huffed. "Of course not. Look, this list of stuff you had me buy creeps me out. Are you planning on torturing her?"

"I might have to rethink that. She might actually like it." Freaks. "Listen, you won't be there. Do your job. Now, did you get the intel I sent you?"

After he'd broken into the office, he'd spent some time making sure he knew all about the security system. It was good, but there were always ways around it, and now he knew Taggart was in charge. He would have to deal with the security cameras. He would study the other buildings that McKay-Taggart had serviced. He'd found several ways in. There were too many people who lived there for it to be truly closed down. The building itself was large, but once he'd gotten past the few residential floors, the office space had been quiet since it was the weekend. It would be the perfect time to take her, and now that he knew she would run, he had a plausible reason for her disappearance.

He would be there, standing right next to Leo, when Shelley McNamara disappeared.

And he knew who to pin it on.

"I need you to pull up everything you can on Ben Dawson and, Kyle, you better be careful. His brother is a paranoid freak with computer skills to rival your own. He claims he's taken them off the grid."

"No one is good enough to really be off the grid, sir. And I doubt he's as good as me. I'll dig up the dirt."

And then Holder would have everything he needed for a successful op. He would have his target and a patsy to blame the whole thing on.

Chapter Fifteen

Leo stared out of the window. The sun was starting to go down. It had been a ridiculously long day, and it wasn't over yet. He felt old and tired. Seeing those photos of Ada had brought back guilt and horror. Realizing Ben had been in love with her had opened up a whole new door of regret.

And then Shelley had proven that nothing had changed.

She'd run again. And his first thought had been to run himself. He'd thought about letting Wolf deal with her.

"You still with me, Doc?"

He shook his head and looked back at Logan. "I'm sorry. I drifted away. It was a long day."

The deputy's shoulders moved up and down in a negligent shrug. "It's not a problem. Look, I don't think I need this. I'm not saying anything bad about therapy, but I actually feel fine. I feel better than I have in over a year. When Trev's sister ran earlier and you had me guarding the exit, I wasn't even thinking about killing anyone. I was absolutely going to incapacitate the bad guys, and I wasn't even going to enjoy it. I think I'm good."

Leo sighed and turned back to the young man. They'd spent the last hour talking about his youth. He'd had a rough start in life, but he'd been a baby. Logan understood on a logical level that his father had been abusive and his mother had run away. He'd read the police reports on how his mother's friend had been forced to kill his father when the man had tried to kill Logan's mother and take him away. It was a horror story, but Logan had been nine months old at the time. When he talked about his childhood, Logan's face lit up. He'd listened to Logan's numerous happy childhood stories about growing up in Bliss with his moms and his friends.

Leo had found himself slightly jealous. He'd grown up one town away, but it had been different. His mother was odd, and she hadn't been accepted as easily as Logan's moms had been. Until Cassidy Meyer had met a man named Mel who lived in Bliss, she'd been alone and raising two boys.

And yet his own childhood had been good. Despite the fact that he'd wanted to see the world, he remembered being loved. He remembered good times with his brother, running through the forests, feeling free.

When had he lost that? And how did he get it back?

"I needed to get out of Bliss," Logan said with a long sigh.

Leo turned to him, staring at the young man, his attention finally pulled from his reverie. "You said you loved Bliss. And yet you believe you would be happy not going back?"

Logan shrugged. "Well, I guess it's time for me to leave home. Not everyone stays in their hometown."

No. Not everyone stayed in their hometown. And sometimes they could check out even when they stayed in one place. Leo had checked out the year before. He'd drawn in on himself after Shelley had turned him down.

He really was a pussy. One rejection from the woman he loved and he'd walked away.

Because he'd been walking away for a very long time. Because deep down, he was worried he would leave the woman he loved alone like his mother had been. Like he and Wolf had been. Because he'd never gotten over his guilt concerning Ada's death. Because he'd married a woman he hadn't loved and failed her in so many ways.

Fuck. Goddamn it to hell. He was twelve kinds of screwed up.

And yet he knew what to say to Logan. "You're telling me you're willing to give up your home rather than working through the problem?"

Was he willing to give up Shelley, his chance at a family, because it was more comfortable to not face his own issues? And Wolf. If he turned away from the gift his brother was trying to give him, he doubted he would ever really get close to Wolf again. Wolf wouldn't turn his back, but he would close off that piece of himself that had deep down longed for this kind of family. Leo had no illusions. Wolf would take Shelley, and he would do his best to make her happy. Wolf would give her his all. His brother was tenacious. Wolf might worry about his place in the world, but Leo thought he might have already found it. Wolf would be Shelley's husband, her loving Master, her best friend.

And he was willing to make a place for Leo if only Leo was brave enough to take it.

Logan's face had gone grave. "I can visit. Later on."

"You have a job, friends, family back in Bliss."

"I can make new friends." He shook off his gloom and pasted a sunny smile on his face. "Now that I think about it, it's a good thing. I have a friend in New York who I can go see."

"I don't think that's a good idea." Distancing himself wouldn't make the problem go away.

Logan stood, pacing a bit. "Doc, I appreciate everything you're trying to do for me, but I'm fine. I feel better, like a weight has been lifted. I'll stay for a week or so if that's okay, but then I'll make arrangements to get out of your hair. You can help someone who really needs it."

Leo kept his mouth closed. He was starting to see through the deputy. Perhaps because the deputy had shown him so much of himself.

Logan Green was scared. Angry, perhaps. He was stuck in a corner, but he'd decided he could pretend that corner was the world.

Leo could tell him where that would end. It would end in loneliness and broken promises. He'd promised so much to himself and his family and allowed fear and pain to lead him to a place where no one could touch him. If he continued down this path, Logan could smile and joke and laugh. He could even feel for his friends. He could give to the people around him. And he would have nothing for himself.

"Perhaps you'll change your mind. Come to the dungeon tonight. Continue the BDSM training. We don't have to have sessions like this." Of course, the BDSM training was simply another session, but most of his patients didn't see it that way. He'd gotten good at being sneaky. Tag didn't realize their weekly two on twos was a way to make sure Tag understood how to support his wife. Charlotte Taggart was in Janine's domestic abuse support group. He intended to get Shelley into it, too.

Logan stood. He shook his lanky body as though he'd expected more of a fight but was happy to have gotten off easily. "Sure, Doc. I have to admit, I'm intrigued by the whole Dom thing. I don't mind that part."

Then that was where Leo would attack. Most therapists would smack him for putting it that way, but he'd spent enough time in the military that violent metaphors were definitely in his repertoire. And so was subterfuge. With Trev McNamara, he'd used sports and working out to get him talking. Logan would take something different.

Logan walked out, promising to see Leo in the dungeon that night, and he was left alone again.

He tried to breathe, lowering himself to the floor, legs folded. He placed an open palm on each knee and allowed his breath to become very deliberate. He tried to release his issues, to allow his mind to become a peaceful blank. When his mind was empty, perhaps he would find some peace.

When he found some peace, perhaps he would find some clarity.

Could he share with his brother? Long term?

He let the question flow out of his mind. He needed a blank mind. He needed peace.

A vision of Shelley, her brown eyes filled with need, her mouth open and gasping out the pleasure he brought her, assaulted him.

Damn it. He couldn't stop thinking about it.

It teased at the edge of his consciousness. Shelley in his arms. Shelley with his collar around her throat and his ring on her finger. Shelley in his bed every night.

And Wolf.

It wasn't how he'd envisioned his life.

There was a knock on his door. *Thank god.*

Leo got up from his place and called out. "Come in."

Wolf opened the door. "Got a minute?"

He nodded. He was actually getting used to Wolf walking in at any given time. And he rather liked being called "brother." And he definitely liked what Wolf hauled in after him. Shelley held his brother's hand. She'd been untied, but her eyes were submissively on the floor as Wolf led her in.

"I need to go out for a while and pick up a few things for tonight." Wolf brought Shelley into the office. He kissed the top of her head and settled her onto the sofa. "You be good or I can put that plug back in, and I will be overly generous with the lube."

She shuddered. "That's not nice, Wolf."

His brother winked down. "That's why I'm the Dom, baby. And your punishment isn't over yet. Wait 'til you see what I have for you tonight."

"I don't know if I want to," she admitted.

Wolf touched his nose to hers in a sweetly affectionate gesture. "Trust me, baby."

She nodded, their connection evident. How had his brother managed that in so short an amount of time? Leo could remember the first time he'd seen her. She'd been sitting next to her mother's hospital bed. She'd been tired and haggard and so damn beautiful his heart had skipped a beat.

But he'd held back. Even before he'd known she was married. Wolf had jumped in with both feet.

"Can you watch her while I'm out?" Wolf asked, his face open.

Shelley rolled her eyes, brattiness in her every move. "I told you, I won't go anywhere. I'll sit and watch Kitten. Even though it's weird. She's still tied up. Chase is hauling her around like a piece of luggage. He sets her at his feet wherever he goes, and every now and then, he'll take the ball gag out of her mouth and pass her some Skittles. But like I should talk. I spent most of the day with ginger up my rectum."

"Poor baby," Wolf said, and then his voice got hard. "Are you going to take out my plug again?"

"No." The word was sweet, but those lips told a different tale.

They were bratty and pouty.

"You're going to kill me, baby. Now, mind Leo. I'll be back, and I'll bring you some food. We're all going to need some energy for later. Well, me and Leo will. You'll just have to lie there and maybe whimper some. I'm totally looking forward to it." Wolf got all the way to the door before looking back. "You okay with watching her? I don't want to disrupt any, like, patient stuff you have."

"My patient list is growing smaller by the day," Leo admitted. "Your friend has decided to leave my care."

Wolf's face fell. "Damn it. He's wrong. Whatever he's thinking, he's wrong. I know he thinks he's better, but it's right there under the surface."

An idea played on the edges of his brain. He needed to draw Logan out. He'd read his file a million times. He thought he was fine having left Bliss? How would he handle being confronted by his fears? "I'll try, Wolf."

It surprised Leo that he was going to try for more reasons than simple professional pride. He would try because Wolf wanted him to. He would try because he wanted to help Wolf's friend.

"Thanks," Wolf said, and then a slow smile crossed his face. "So, take care of our girl. And if you can think of a way to occupy her time, you should go for it. She's been quite good since the incident. Be back in an hour or so."

The door closed, and he was left alone with the only woman he'd ever really loved. And his brother had given him permission to fuck her. Damn him.

She stood up. "Look, Wolf is paranoid. I'm fine. I'll go up to the condo and wait for him there. You don't need to babysit me."

"Sit down."

Apparently he'd put enough force into his voice that she obeyed.

"Do you believe me to be easier to deal with than my brother? What have you been smoking?" Wolf was practically a teddy bear compared to him. At least when it came to being a hard-ass with a sub.

"I believe you to be busy. Busy enough that you don't need some chick hanging out in your office."

"It's Saturday. Despite the earlier chaos, I really didn't have many plans." He'd planned to watch some football with Ben and Chase before the evening's play. He'd planned to walk his new charge through a few scenes. He hadn't planned to spend the whole day thinking about Shelley McNamara.

Hell, he hadn't planned it, but he would have done it anyway. And now he had her all alone for an hour.

"Tell me why you married Bryce."

Her eyes widened. "What?"

He sat back, trying to look like the pro he was, but there was nothing professional about his curiosity. "Tell me about your marriage. I never asked before. I'd like to know now."

She sat up, her hands in her lap. "Why?"

One question. One minefield. He could shrug and reply that he was curious. Or he could be as honest with her as he wanted her to be with him. "Because I've asked myself the question every day since the day I found out you were married. Because there's a hole inside me that I can't fill until I understand."

Shelley was silent for a moment, but then began to speak, her voice steady but quiet. "My mother worked for him. Briefly, but long enough. After Trev moved out, we had to sell the ranch, but the market was bad, and the ranch hadn't paid in a long time. We'd taken out a second mortgage a couple of years before my father died." She turned toward the window. Her hands fisted, her voice shaking a bit.

He couldn't take it. He got out of his chair and sat down beside her. He pulled her into his lap. She was stiff for a moment, but then she sighed, and her body sagged into his.

He felt the deep connection immediately, his own body relaxing. This was where he wanted to be. "It's okay. Please tell me the story."

She was quiet for a moment. "Bryce came into town a few years after I finished college. We had money then. Trev would send us some. It would be huge checks when he was sober enough to think about it. But we still had bills. Mom had fought off cancer while I was in school. She seemed healthy, and she got the job as Bryce's office manager. He asked me out a few times, but I said no. I was going to move to Houston. I had a friend there, and we were going to set up an interior design business. I didn't want to get involved with any man."

He felt his stomach turn. This wasn't going to go well. He knew for a fact that once she'd returned to Deer Run, she hadn't left it again until she'd moved to Dallas. "Why didn't you go?"

She sniffled. "You have to promise me you won't ever tell Trev. I told him this was all my fault. I didn't want him to feel guilty about it so I lied. Trev has enough guilt and Mom is gone now, so it seemed the kindest thing to do."

Trev's guilt could fill a lake. He could understand why she would protect her brother. "I won't ever say a word, sweetheart."

She nodded and continued her story. "My mom was accused of stealing some money. Quite a bit, actually. She was going to be fired and prosecuted. Bryce gave me one way out."

God, if Bryce Hughes had been standing in front of him, Leo would have choked the life out of him. "You have to know that Trev could have hired a lawyer."

"Did I? I could barely get him on the phone at that point in time. He was so far gone. He'd stopped sending money. He needed it for drugs and those parties he would throw. You can't ever tell him this story. Let him think I was a wide-eyed idiot. He can't know. It would kill him."

She sounded panicked. He forced her head back down on his shoulder. He stroked her hair until she calmed down. "There's no need to tell Trev anything. It would only hurt him at this point."

She'd tried to protect her mother. She was still protecting Trev. His heart hurt. No one had protected her. Not even him. Jack had been right. If he'd been the man he claimed to be, he wouldn't have left. He would have watched over her from afar if he needed to.

"I married Bryce. I think he thought having a connection to Trev would help him. At the time, I thought he wanted to be able to put Trev's face on his billboards, but now I think he believed that Trev could help him make connections so he could become, I don't know, drug dealer to the stars or something. You can imagine that he was upset when Trev walked away from football. But even though he was mad about Trev, Bryce was okay with me. In the beginning I actually thought it might work out. He seemed to genuinely care about me. He helped me set up my business. He helped get me clients. He told everyone how smart and talented I was. Of course, he had his reasons for doing that."

"Was he violent?" He wasn't sure he could handle it if she'd been brutalized. Guilt was gnawing at him. He'd left her.

She shook her head. "He hit me, but it was only once, and it was right before he died. I walked out after that. He threatened to kill you if I left with you. I told him I would come home and be a good girl, but I didn't. I talked to Trev after you left, and he wouldn't let me go home."

At least Trev had some sense. Leo had left her alone. He'd known Bryce was bad for her, but he'd left her alone. The same day he'd driven away from her had been the day Bryce's crimes had come to light. She, her sister-in-law, and Bo O'Malley had been taken hostage by a man Bryce owed drugs to. She'd barely survived, and she'd been forced to watch as Bryce was killed. "You were in that house with a gun to your head while I was driving back to Dallas like a toddler who'd had a fit."

She sighed, seemingly more relaxed after she'd told him the worst of it. At least he hoped that had been the worst. "I made it through. I had nightmares. Sometimes I still do, but I didn't believe for one second that I was going to die."

"Really?"

"No. The drug cartel guy assured me that he was taking me with him because I would make an excellent addition to a brothel."

"What?" He fairly screamed the word, the picture assaulting his mind.

She put a hand over his. "Stop. It's over, and I'm fine. I survived. I knew I would."

He'd dealt with so many people with PTSD. How was she so calm? It seemed like he had been more traumatized than she'd been. "Why? How did you know you would survive? Did you honestly have that much faith in the universe?"

"No, I had faith in you."

He stilled and then forced himself to move. He gently pushed her off and brought her chin up so she looked him in the eyes. She'd been crying, crystal tears streaming down her face. "I walked away."

"And when you found out I was gone? Would you have looked for me? I thought so then. I knew it deep in my heart." Her eyes turned down. "I was sure of it at the time. I probably wouldn't be now."

He needed to make one thing plain to her. "I would have moved heaven and earth to find you."

She nodded, but he could see she didn't really believe. "Because you're a good man. Leo, I have something I want to say to you. I want to thank you. I know I screwed everything up, but you can't imagine what you've meant to me. You saved Trev. He would be dead if you hadn't taken him in hand. I believe that deep in my soul. My brother would be in the ground. When my mother died, she believed he was changing because of the things you said to her. My mother died a peaceful death because of you. And me. I can't tell you what you've meant to me. You were the dream I had for so many years and then, when you tried to get me to go away with you, then you were this beautiful reality. I know I ruined it, but I think about that moment every day. I think that if I could change one thing in my life, it would be to take your hand and walk away."

"Shelley," he began, his heart aching.

She put a single finger to his lips, silencing him. "Don't. I want to have my say, just once, and then never again. I love you. I love the man you are. I love the funny, stalwart, infinitely compassionate man who lives deep inside you, and I am begging for that man to come back to life. I know I should be the bigger person and walk away and let you find someone else to make you happy, but damn it, I'm the one, Leo. I'm the one for you and I'm the one for Wolf, and that's the way it is. I will screw up. I'll do it a lot, and you know what, I'll happily let you beat my ass when I do. But I won't let you walk away, and I won't let you go into your shell. I screwed up. Mea culpa, but I'm done with hiding in a corner and loving you from afar. You can tell me no, but I'll say this over and over again. I love you. I love you. You can send me off, but I'm keeping your brother, and you're going to have to watch us, and every time I feel your eyes on me, I'll say I love you. So you better get ready."

He had the choice. He could embrace the future and try or he could fight it. Why would he fight it? Yes, he was afraid he couldn't share her long term. Yes, he was terrified it would all end the way it had with Janine. He was worried that he would screw up somehow, someway, and leave her alone.

He stared at her. "I don't know if I want kids."

She stared right back. "You don't like them?"

"I should rephrase that. I'm scared of having kids. I don't know how good I'll be at raising them." He hadn't had a dad. He'd only known how wonderful and loving and alone his mother had been. Life was so fragile. He would never leave his children, but anything could happen.

"You'll be amazing."

"Shelley, are you listening to me?"

"I think I'm done listening to you. When you can say something to me that doesn't have its roots in some fear, then I'll listen. You're the big, bad Dom, but your sub is laying out some rules of her own. I love you. I want to have your kids. I can't promise you that everything will work out. I can pretty much promise you that it won't. What I can promise is that I'll love you through all of it. I'll love you for the rest of my life and through whatever comes after. That's the only sure thing here. It's either enough for you or it isn't."

Forever. He wasn't sure if he believed in it, but she did. She believed with all her heart, and she was offering it to him.

"I don't know if I can share you long term. What are we going to do about Wolf?" He was a possessive man. He knew it, and yet somehow it had felt right to share her with Wolf the night before, as though she was more woman than either could handle. She was a woman with a huge heart who deserved as much love as she could take.

"What was that?" Shelley asked, turning toward the door. She stared for a moment and then shook her head. "I thought I heard something. I'm paranoid now."

She had every right to be. "We're safe here." His cock was aching. God, he wanted her.

She straddled him, her curvy body positioned over his. His cock jumped. If he'd stripped her down, he would have been able to play with her pussy. "You asked what to do about Wolf."

He flushed. It was an excuse, and he hated that he kept making them. "He's huge, baby. Seriously. I don't know what's wrong with him. I think it's the amount of beets he ate as a small child. We need a bigger bed."

Chocolate brown eyes rolled. "Bigger bed, check. I'm glad you said that. And about the sharing long term thing…I know you're worried, but don't be because you can do it. I have faith."

Bossy, bratty thing. He put his hands on that ass he firmly intended to get his dick in very soon. Not now. Wolf should be around to hear her squeals and watch her squirm the first time her pretty asshole got invaded by one of her Masters' cocks. "You've been laying down a lot of rules, pet. I think it's about time to get this relationship on the right footing. You have a choice. You get out of those clothes now or I can rip them off you."

Her lips curved up in that oh-so-sultry smile that made his heart skip like some fucking fifteen-year-old kid with his first crush. "What is it with you Meyer men? Yesterday Wolf cut me out of my undies."

Yeah, his brother was good with a knife. "If I know my brother, you're no longer allowed to wear undies. Get up, pet. Take those clothes off and understand that if you've disobeyed Wolf, I'll take it out on your sweet ass. You want two Masters? You better get ready because we won't let you play us off each other."

She pouted sweetly. "Why does everyone believe the worst of me?" She shrugged out of her shirt and bra. Her nipples were already puckered, begging for him to bite and lick them. She pushed at the waist of her jeans. "And I'm a deeply obedient girl."

Leo snorted. "And I believe in unicorns."

Her voice got husky as she dragged the denim down to her thighs. "I'm obedient when it comes to this."

Fuck. There it was. Her pussy all perfectly shaved and ripe. "Stop right there. Turn."

Her eyes flared. Finally she was the slightest bit nervous. She'd called the shots up until now. Every goddamn one of them. It was way past time for him to take his place as her Master. "Okay."

"Hush. From now on, the only words I want to hear from those lips are 'yes, Leo,' and all the pleas that you can think of to make me stop torturing you." He pushed gently at her spine, leaning her forward. "Grab your ankles."

"Why don't you let me get out of these jeans?"

He smacked her ass in a short, sharp arc. She squealed, but her hands were on her ankles, her breath already ragged. "Those jeans are right where I want them. They're holding your legs together as well as any rope. Now grab on to your ankles. I want to inspect my pussy."

"God, Leo." She groaned the words.

He slapped her ass again. "You aren't listening to me."

"Yes, Leo," she corrected herself quickly. She held fast to her ankles, finally getting into the position he wanted her in.

Her ass was in the air, her cheeks already turning a lovely pink. And her pussy pouted out from between her legs, a pink, juicy flower. He could smell her arousal. Pearly dew coated the petals of her pussy. He ran a finger through her labia, coating his skin with her arousal. "Do you feel vulnerable like this, baby?"

"Yes, Leo." The words were shaky, with not a drop of her previous confidence. He loved her faith in herself and in him. He loved the fact that she'd been strong enough to stand up to him. In some ways, she was even stronger than him. But he wanted her off-kilter here. He wanted her soft and submissive here. She would get her way in their normal life, but here he was the Master.

"Good, because we have a few things to work out. You'll be punished tonight. Do you understand?"

"Yes, Leo. You and Master Wolf are going to punish me because I ran."

"Because you almost took something precious from us," he explained, running his hand over her ass, loving the way she trembled. "Do you understand what you almost took?"

"Trust," she said. "I broke trust."

A good answer, but not the one he wanted. "No, Shelley. It was you. Trust doesn't mean shit to me if you're dead. Trust is meaningless to Wolf if you're not here for him to hold. You're the important thing. And it is utterly unacceptable for you to put yourself in the line of fire."

He slapped at her ass. Five quick, easy smacks. He had to save up the rough stuff for later, when his brother was here to help. "This is a warm-up. Tonight, you're going to feel my crop on your ass."

And tonight, he would lay aside the past and finally look toward the future.

Chapter Sixteen

Shelley felt her whole body trembling. She ached in more ways than one. Her legs were starting to hurt, but the hollow feeling in her pussy was worse. She was ready to take Leo's crop if it meant he would do something, but the sadistic bastard stood there, his hands caressing her gently.

His gentleness was starting to get to her.

"You look so lovely like this. I can see your pretty pussy. Do you know how wet you are? All that cream is coating your flesh. It's like you're begging for me to taste it. Do you want that, baby? Do you want my tongue in your pussy? Do you want me to shove my face right between these legs and eat your pussy until I've had my fill?"

That was the easiest question he'd asked all day. "Yes, Sir."

His hands, so close before, moved up, stopping on her lower back. She nearly moaned with frustration. Leo chuckled. "Or I could sit back and watch you. I can see your pouting pussy and I can see something else."

He pulled apart the cheeks of her ass.

"I can see your asshole."

She closed her eyes, forcing herself not to move. God, she wanted to move away from him.

"It's so tight, baby. No one's ever fucked this asshole, have they?"

"No, Sir." God, they were really going to do it. They were going to fuck her ass. She was scared and aroused all at the same time.

"Excellent." He pulled her cheeks even further apart, and she would have sworn she could feel his eyes on her. "Did Wolf brutalize your asshole, baby? Did he stretch it and make it burn? Did he fuck you with his fingers first? Tell me how my brother plugged this ass."

His words were seduction in and of themselves. Holding the position was making her shake, but he'd given her a task. She would focus on it. She would think about the task ahead of her and ignore the way her limbs ached. "He was rough at first."

"He was rather angry at the time." Leo stepped away. "Keep talking. I'll be right back."

He was going somewhere? Damn him. She heard the drawer to his desk open and close. He placed something on the top, and then she could have sworn she heard him unzip and the sound of something crinkling. Talking. She had to keep talking. "He made me undress. He inspected my body."

"Was he pleased with your body?"

She could still remember the way Wolf had stared at her. He'd reached out and tweaked her nipples in turn. He'd plucked at them until they had been hard berries, begging for his affection. She'd been forced to turn and look at her naked body in the mirror. "He made me watch as he played with my breasts. He made me spread my legs and watch as he dipped his fingers in."

There was a low growl from behind her. Leo was back. "In where? Don't you leave anything out."

"My pussy, Leo. He sank his fingers in my pussy." Wolf had played with her, those big, long fingers fucking in and out of her pussy. "He used one, and then two on me."

She felt something cool and wet dribble on the crack of her ass. She stiffened, praying he wasn't doing what she thought he was doing.

She heard a deep chuckle. "No ginger, baby. Just lube. I want to play. Wolf got to play with this asshole. Now I want the same chance. Tell me more."

Her jaw clenched. She knew what she'd heard. She'd heard him lower his zipper, and she'd heard the very distinct unwrapping of a condom. What was he waiting for? He was making her crazy. And he was also a brick wall. He wasn't going to give her what she wanted until she'd obeyed him. "He played with my pussy for a long time. He made me watch in the mirror. He made me watch as his fingers got coated in my arousal. He made me watch as he licked his fingers clean. He told me how good I tasted."

Talking about the way Wolf had tortured her made her hot all over again.

"I know how good you taste."

Pressure. Erotic pressure made her spine tingle as Leo started to work her asshole. He rimmed it, working the lube in and all around.

"Did Wolf get you off, baby?" Leo asked. "Did he make you come?"

She sniffled a little. "No. He wouldn't let me come."

Wolf had played for what felt like forever, those big fingers teasing her until he had her shaking and begging. He'd made sure to stay away from her clit. He'd skimmed and taunted that bit of flesh, but he wouldn't press down in any meaningful way.

"He was angry, baby." Leo growled, the sound sparking across her skin. "He was mad that you had disobeyed. Little brats don't get orgasms. Little brats get crops and whips across their ass. Little brats get to please their Masters and take nothing for themselves."

Tears nearly blurred her vision. He was going to punish her. Damn it. If she survived the day, she would be surprised.

Leo's finger penetrated her ass, making her squirm. She was so open, so vulnerable in the position he'd put her in. She felt stretched and shaky, totally bent to his will.

This was what he wanted. It finally kicked in. He wanted her to let go, to be totally focused on the moment and not thinking about anything except pleasing him. He wouldn't demand it in their daily life, but he was giving her a place to go when the world became too much. She relaxed and let go of her frustration. She breathed in and found an odd place of peace.

Leo's finger sank into her ass. "What just happened, baby?"

She felt herself smile, a lazy, relaxed expression. Even her legs felt softer now. "I gave in."

Leo's finger rimmed her ass while his free hand ran down her spine. "You won't regret it. Shelley, this is a good place. Find your subspace. It's safe to do it with me. Wolf, too. Neither one of us will ever hurt you. We'd rather cut off our dicks than cause you a real moment of pain. Pain can enhance pleasure, and that's all we're trying to do."

But she wasn't so afraid of the pain. She knew neither Leo nor Wolf would really hurt her physically. Her heart was another matter. But Leo was here. Leo wouldn't be standing here with her if he wasn't serious. He might play around with her when Wolf was there to take care of her, but this felt different. This felt like commitment.

"Are you going to stay with me?" Shelley asked, knowing the answer. Leo Meyer might be a tough nut to crack, but he was loyal and stalwart. She'd said she loved him. If he was going to walk away, he would have done it. As his fingers were currently deep inside her rectum, she had a feeling he was planning on staying.

"Say you love me." He didn't sound like a Dom. He sounded like a man. A man she'd burned before.

"I love you." They were the easiest three words she'd ever said. She'd loved Leo for years.

"I love you, too, baby. And it will work out with Wolf. It will. He's my brother. If I don't share with him, my mother will show up on our doorstep, and I would like to avoid that. She's a bit crazy. But she's very sweet. She just thinks aliens impregnated her and that everything is made better with beets. I hate beets."

She groaned as he added another finger. God, he was stretching her.

"So you're going to have to deal with my family, and I'll deal with your lamentable lack of discipline." The Dom was back, that hard edge in his voice making her heart flutter. "Now, tell me what I want to hear. Tell me how my brother tortured this asshole."

Rather like Leo was doing. "He stretched me. He used the lube on me. At first it was warm, but then it burned, and I squirmed a lot and I pleaded with him."

Leo's voice was warm, as though he'd found his own happy place. Dom space. She had subspace, and he had Dom space. "I bet he liked that."

Wolf had liked her pleas. She'd also known all along that he would respect her safe word. She could have used her slow-down word or her stop word, and Wolf would have obeyed. He would have slowed and talked to her or stopped all together. Despite her precarious position, she was really in charge. She was giving her Doms what they needed and taking what she needed.

"He was very hard, Leo, but he wouldn't give me his cock."

"No, cock is for good subs. Cock isn't for brats who give their Masters heart attacks." He fucked into her ass with his fingers. "I've never seen a man move as fast as Wolf. If you try anything like that again, it won't merely be ginger lube on a plug. I'll buy the largest piece of ginger root I can find, and I'll carve a massive dildo and that will be your plug. Don't think I can't do it. I'm actually quite the artist."

Yes, he was a perverted artist. She was getting used to the burn of his fingers in her ass, beginning to feel the first stirrings of pleasure from the way he stretched and fucked her.

"Let go of your ankles and grab the desk. I think Wolf tortured you enough, and given what he's probably planning to do tonight, I think a little respite is called for."

Very carefully, she released her ankles. Blessed relief flooded her. She sighed at the feeling that wouldn't have been possible without the previous discomfort. And she felt an odd pride. She'd taken what he'd dished out, and now she was ready for her reward. She softened her knees and reached for the edge of Leo's elegantly appointed desk.

"Master Wolf did say you were in charge of me," she said, tilting her head to look back. Leo's hair was down, falling around his shoulders. There was a decadent look on his face.

"Yes. Don't you forget that. Eyes front or you won't get your treat." He barked the order in that low voice she would bet he'd used to get many a sub to do his will. But she was his sub. As far as Club gossip went, he'd never collared anyone outside of his wife.

His fingers kept up the slow fuck on her ass.

"Do you know how much I want to fuck your ass? It's going to feel so good. But this will have to do for now." He pressed in, and she suddenly felt something large forage between her legs. "Think about this. Is this what you want? Do you want to be full? Do you want to be packed full of cock? Because that's what's going to happen. Your pussy and your ass will get stretched and filled with your Masters' cocks. The next time someone plays with this asshole, it won't be fingers. It's going to be that monster of my brother's fucking you. Think about that while I play. But you can't make an informed decision without a test drive. I won't leave your pussy lonely."

The head of his dick moved around her pussy, pausing at the entrance. She stopped breathing. God, she wanted him so much. She held still. He hadn't given her permission to move. She wanted to be so good for him. Everything else fell away. Her self-consciousness floated away as she simply allowed herself to be in the moment.

She bit back a groan as Leo's enormous cock began to invade. He pushed his fingers into her ass as his dick began to work its way into her pussy.

"Oh, you feel it now, don't you? You feel stretched out and invaded."

"Yes, Leo." And it felt magnificent. It was the right side of pain, and she closed her eyes, imagining that Wolf was here with them, his big hands on her flesh, his cock moving in time with Leo's. Leo worked her masterfully. He fucked in and out, finding a rhythm that had her panting and moaning.

"Come for me, baby. Come for me. I'm not going to last long. I can't. You're too fucking hot. You're so goddamn tight. I love you, baby. I love you so much."

The words worked magic on her, filling her heart and soul as Leo filled her body. She was off the leash. She moved against him, pressing back to take him as far as she could. His cock hit a perfect spot inside of her, and the orgasm blasted through her system, making the world seem hazy and everything unreal except for the man behind her.

Leo's fingers came out of her ass, and she felt both of his hands on her hips, gripping her as he shoved in one last time and shouted as he came. He pressed in as though grinding out everything he had.

A sweet, heavy languor swept through her system. She could feel the blood pounding through her veins. Leo swept her up in his arms. She looked into seriously blue eyes. His sensual lips were turned up in a smile.

"You said it," she said on a breathy sigh. He'd said it.

Those frequently chilly eyes were warm on her now. "I said it. I meant it. And I mean it when I promise you that Wolf and I will work something out. When I get overly possessive or obnoxious, he can just try to hit me. He's bigger anyway."

She laughed at the thought of having to play referee to her men. "I'm not going to let him hit you."

A superior look crossed Leo's face. "I said he could try. He's bigger, but I'm way more flexible, and despite allowing him to do the majority of the running today, I'm actually faster than him. Remember that the next time you try to run."

No more running for her. Leo set her gently down on his sofa.

"I'm not going to run again." She stared up at one half of her world. He was so beautiful, and he was finally hers. "I promise the next time someone tries to kill me to let you or Wolf take the bullet."

"Damn straight," he replied, winking. "And again, Wolf is half metal. He's like the bionic man. We should let him take the bullets." He kissed her lightly. "Let me go clean up. Actually, we should both clean up. Come on. There's a shower in the bathroom."

"I saw that. Why do you need a shower in your office?" Shelley asked, getting back on her feet. She knew she should be self-conscious, but that seemed to have fled with those three words from his lips. He loved her. He loved her. That meant he had to love her cellulite, too.

Leo shrugged. "I've had to listen to some weird shit. Listening to some of Kitten's fantasies made me want to take a shower. There's a reason I shipped her over to my ex-wife."

She laughed. She had the feeling she was going to have to get used to the oddities of her boyfriend's secretary.

"Come on, baby. Let's get washed up. I haven't even kissed you properly."

Leo opened the door to the bathroom, and she walked through with a serenity in her heart that had been missing for years.

* * * *

Wolf stared down at the delicate choker he'd ordered the day before. It was lovely, something Shelley could wear all day and no one in the vanilla world would see it for what it was—a commitment, a promise, a future.

Of course, none of those things belonged to him. Not when it came to Shelley.

His mind leapt back to an hour before. Standing outside the door to his brother's office. He'd opened it a crack, and then he'd heard her passionate words.

I'll love you for the rest of my life and through whatever comes after. That's the only sure thing here. It's either enough for you or it isn't.

Wolf had stopped. She'd made her play for Leo. He'd known it would happen. He'd wanted it to happen, and still, hearing those words struck through him. She hadn't said them to him. She hadn't said them in front of him. She'd said them from the comfort of Leo's arms. He'd been able to see her gorgeous face shining up at his brother, her love for him plain for anyone to see. She loved Leo.

That was okay. He wanted her to love Leo. The whole ménage thing wouldn't work if she didn't love them both. He'd stood there and forced himself to concede that Leo had known her longer. He could have the first *I love you.*

He'd been about to walk in when he'd heard Leo's response.

I don't know if I can share you long term. What are we going to do about Wolf?

With those low words, Wolf had felt everything fall apart like a house of cards imploding under the smallest of winds.

He'd shut the door and walked from the office, his feet feeling leaden.

"Sir? Is it what you wanted?" the immaculately dressed clerk asked.

"Dude? Are we going to stand in Tiffany's all day?" Logan asked, giving him a light punch. Logan looked at the clerk as though realizing something was wrong. "Could you give us a minute? I think he's figuring out if it's the right one."

The well-trained clerk nodded. "Of course. Sometimes these things look different in person than they did on the website. Please let me know if you would like to look at something different."

The clerk walked away.

"What the hell is going on?" Logan asked. "Don't shrug me off again. I'm not stupid. You were fine and then you turned into a morose ball of goo. What the hell happened when you went to tell Leo how long you would be?"

Wolf tried to focus on the small necklace. There was a circlet of white gold and through it came two tails, each with another circlet. Three circles connected. He'd seen it and thought about how he and Leo wouldn't be getting close again without Shelley. Three circles, the two lower ones flowing from the one in the middle. She was the sun, and he and Leo were the planets that worshipped and orbited around her.

He sighed and placed it back on the velvet display case. He couldn't waste that much money on something that wouldn't mean a thing after tonight.

"She's in love with Leo."

Logan's brows came together. "Okay. I thought we knew that. I don't see the problem."

Of course Logan didn't see the problem. In Bliss, it would be a simple thing. Wolf would simply go after her until she loved him, too. Hell, it was practically expected in Bliss. If someone told a Bliss woman she had to pick between two men she wanted, she might start shooting. But he wasn't in Bliss.

"Leo won't share."

Logan gasped. "Shit. Wow. Does your mom know?"

Crap. He missed Jamie sometimes. James was the more mature of Wolf's best friends. "I'm not calling my mom in. She loves him. Leo loves her. There's no place for me. I'm going to do the only thing I can do. I'm going to hand her over to my brother and wish them well."

It made his heart ache. He'd fallen for her completely. She was the sunshine he'd been missing for most of his life. He even loved the bratty way she tried to manipulate him. He didn't want perfection from her. He wanted her beautiful body and the sassy, loving soul that went with it.

But those belonged to his brother, and he owed Leo a lot, too. He couldn't take away a woman his brother loved. He'd made his play, and he'd lost.

"Fuck, man. I don't like the sound of that." Logan crossed his arms over his chest. "Shouldn't you, like, beat the shit out of him until he sees things your way?"

"That wouldn't work with Leo. He's smaller than me, but he's mean in a fight. And he's a stubborn asshole. And he's my brother. I don't think he's ever really been in love before. I can't take it away from him. I love her. I do, but it can't work like this. If I press my claim, it's only going to make her miserable. And in the end, she'll pick him and then I won't have a relationship with either of them. I need to bow out gracefully. I need to make a good show."

"That sucks, man."

Yep. Logan was succinct. Wolf raised a hand, and the clerk came over quickly. "I need to see something different. Do you have something more like a lock with one key?"

"Absolutely, sir. I'll bring you several to choose from." He swept away the necklace Wolf had chosen. It was gone like the future he'd briefly had.

"You're going to hand her over tonight, aren't you?" Logan asked.

He nodded. "I'm going to pretend like it was my plan all along. Like this was my gift."

Logan looked at the tags on the jewelry surrounding them. "It's a pretty fucking expensive gift."

Yes, it was. In more terms than money. It was going to cost him a piece of his soul. And he would pay it. He would pay it because his brother had never faltered. Leo had been the one to make sure he'd eaten breakfast and gotten to school. Leo had sat up with him explaining homework and reading to him when their mother had to work late. It was a debt Wolf could never really repay.

He selected a pretty lock with a small key. It was gold and would look lovely against Shelley's skin. Leo would hold the key. Wolf would be the kinky brother who'd once played into his sister-in-law's fantasy. After a while, they wouldn't think about him at all. He would merely be part of the family. Neither one would know that he would love her until the day he died.

"I'll take this one," Wolf said.

"You're a better man than me," Logan said as the clerk placed his selection in its blue box and got it ready to go.

"I don't know about that. I'm doing what I have to do."

Logan looked at him seriously. "Come to New York with me. I have a friend I'm going to see. He's kind of a crazy billionaire. You know that search engine everyone uses? Yeah, he invented that. His granddad kept a summer cabin in Bliss, and he came up every year from June to late August. We called ourselves summer brothers. Come with me, man. His place is incredible from what I hear."

"You're leaving The Club?" He handed his bank card to the clerk. "You've only had two sessions with Leo."

Logan shrugged. "He's good. I'm totally fixed. I haven't tried to kill anyone in like a week. Haven't even wanted to. I just needed to be away from Bliss. I'm staying for another day or two and then I'm headed to Manhattan. Seth can get me a job. He can get you a job, too. Come on, man. Let's try the city out."

He was pretty sure that was a bad idea. No matter how calm Logan seemed now, it was still there, simmering under the surface. But he hadn't shown a single crack last night during the scenes. Wolf knew Leo had been watching Logan for a reaction.

But no one had set up a scene that played on Logan's trauma.

It was a horrible thing to do, but if Logan was really fine, then what Wolf had in mind wouldn't faze him.

"I'll think about it," he told Logan. "Hell, I don't have anywhere else to go."

But if he had his way, Logan wasn't going to New York. He would stay and let Leo help him. All Wolf needed was help from some new friends. When he had a chance, he called Jack Barnes and gave the cowboy the game plan.

Tonight he would help all the people he cared about. And then he would talk to Taggart about a job because he couldn't stay here and watch his brother and the love of his life settle down. He'd heard Taggart was talking about starting up a London office.

And then he could walk away with a clear conscience and a heavy heart.

Chapter Seventeen

Leo looked out over the dungeon. A sense of peace had settled over him. He could do it. He could share Shelley with his brother because it was what she needed.

And also because she'd threatened to kick his ass if he didn't. It totally made his decision easier.

"Is he here yet?" Shelley asked, her eyes trailing around the large space.

"I don't see him. Don't worry, baby, he'll be here. He's not going to miss a chance to beat your ass after the stunt you pulled today." He felt unreasonably cheerful. He still had a whole fuckload of problems to deal with. Someone was trying to kill his girl. Holder was hiding something. Logan was going to walk. Tomorrow the entire building was getting a security upgrade, and he'd have to deal with the most sarcastic group in the history of time. Yeah, his life was complicated, but he was getting some tonight.

"That is so comforting, Leo." Shelley frowned up at him. She was dressed in exactly what Wolf had left for her—very little. Her breasts were pressed together in a black leather corset that offered them up like tempting fruit. Her hot ass was covered in a barely there thong, and those curvy legs flowed down into a pair of four-inch stilettos she hadn't stopped complaining about since the minute she'd forced her feet into them.

Yes. Despite the shit storm they were in, his world felt pretty fucking perfect. Even his sense of humor was coming back. "It wasn't meant to be comforting. It was meant to remind you how much trouble that hot ass is in. Damn, you look fine tonight. Did I mention how fine you look?"

She bit back a smile and went up on her tiptoes. Those ridiculously high heels put her closer to his height. "You might have mentioned it a time or two." She pouted and batted those lashes at him. "Do we really have to do this public punishment thing? Wouldn't it be more intimate to go back to our place and make love? I can make both my Masters very happy. I can prove what a sweet sub I can be."

Brat thought she could get out of her punishment? He brushed his lips to hers, reveling in the fact that he could fucking kiss her all he wanted. "Oh, baby, that sounds perfect. You can prove to me what a sweet sub you are right after you prove to me how red your ass can get."

She pulled back, but there was a laugh on her lips. "Fine. I suppose I deserve it."

"Richly," Leo replied.

His brother walked through the doors, his massive shoulders barely clearing the frame. California-king bed. That was what he was going to have to order.

Shelley's face lit up as she noticed Wolf. She waved a hand. "Wolf!"

His brother looked up, but the grim expression on his face didn't change. Logan walked behind him. Both men had changed into leathers, but neither looked particularly happy to be in the dungeon. Shelley tottered over to Wolf and tried to throw herself into his arms. Wolf caught her, but there wasn't passion in his hold.

What the fuck was going on?

If Shelley noticed, she didn't give it away. She was chattering happily about the fact that she'd forced Leo to sit through two hours of HGTV while Wolf had been gone.

Wolf's eyes grew round as he looked at Leo. "Dude, why were you getting punished?"

"Next time it's your turn," he said with a shake of his head.

Shelley's nose wrinkled sweetly. "It wasn't so bad. And I'm going to completely redo the condo. I have swatches coming on

Monday."

"Don't ask. I think it's the decorating equivalent of a crop. It's meant to beat us into submission." Leo watched Wolf carefully. Something was going on. He hadn't suspected anything when Wolf had called earlier and told him he would be longer than he'd expected. He'd claimed traffic and that he was putting together a surprise for tonight. He'd expected that his brother was buying toys for their sub.

Now he was wondering.

He put a hand on Shelley's gloriously round backside that was going to be horrifically abused in oh so many ways in a mere half an hour. "Baby, give me a minute with Wolf, okay?"

"So you two can talk about how to torture me?" she asked. Both he and Wolf stared at her. She finally sighed. "Fine. But only because you gave me Dom eyes."

Wolf glanced at Logan, who he seemed to have some sort of silent shorthand with.

"I'll make sure she doesn't get in trouble." Logan walked after her.

Leo wasted no time. "Is there something you need to tell me?"

Wolf's normally open face was a closed and locked book. "No. Everything is fine. Look, I got you and Shelley a gift is all. I think you'll both like it a lot."

"Do you want to tell me what it is?" He wasn't convinced.

Wolf shook his head. "It's a surprise, but one I've been planning for a while. Just go with it, brother. Now, there is something else I need to talk to you about. It's about Logan. He's planning on leaving for New York."

"I know." Responsibility weighed on him. He owed it to his brother. "I'm going to do everything I can to keep him here. I have a few days."

He wasn't sure what he would do if Logan couldn't see he had a problem, but he was going to try.

"I set something up for tonight. Look, I know you're the shrink, but I know Logan. He thinks because he's out of the situation that he's fine, but he's wrong. Jack Barnes and his partner are setting up a scene that is similar to what happened to Logan. If he can stand there and be fine, then I'll eat my words, but I don't think so."

Leo took a long breath. Wolf was playing a dangerous game.

"You know this could blow up in your face."

Wolf's shoulders moved up and down in a negligent shrug. "I know. But it's important. Sometimes we do things simply because they're the right things to do. I think you should be with him, though." He glanced down at his watch. "I think Jack and Sam are going to start in a couple of minutes. I thought it was best to get this out of the way early in the night. I know you and Shelley will want some time after her punishment."

"Yes, I'm sure Shelley will need some attention after what we do to her. I would rather not have to play shrink when I could be playing Dom." He glanced over to where Shelley was talking to Logan. She kept her backside to the wall as though trying to make sure no one could see it. He was going to have to work on that. He was proud of that ass. He wanted to show it off.

"Come on then," Wolf said.

Leo put a hand out to stop him. He still didn't like the look on his brother's face. "Is there something else? Talk to me. You know Big Tag has a whole team working late all weekend looking into this. The big bastard is working around the clock, and his sister-in-law is calling in favors to dig up whatever she can. If you found out something about this situation with Holder, I want to know. They need to know."

"I told you what I was doing," Wolf replied. He put a hand on Leo's shoulder. "We will figure this out. Tomorrow I'm going to help install the security system and I'll work with the team all week. You have to know that whatever happens, I'll protect her. I'll help you in any way I can." Wolf stared over at her. "I'll be here for you."

Leo stopped, his brother's words snagging him. "You better fucking help. You got me in this situation. Do you have any idea how much trouble she's going to be?"

He meant it as a friendly jab, a way to point out their camaraderie. He'd thought about nothing else during the whole torturous time Shelley had forced him to sit through endless shows about people buying homes and installing toilets. And they said he was a sadist. But while he'd sat there, he'd thought about what it meant to be in this sort of relationship. It meant he was never alone. It meant no matter what happened, his brother would be around to take care of Shelley. It meant there was another human being in the world who knew what it meant to love her. It suddenly didn't sound so terrible.

"You can handle her, brother." Wolf glanced down at his phone. "Jack's ready. Let's move."

Leo put a hand out. "I don't think we're done here. Do you want to explain why you keep using singular nouns? For two days, all I've heard is how we're going to take care of her and now you keep using the word 'you.' I'm not an idiot, Wolf. If you have something to say, say it."

"I will. And you aren't going to be upset. It's fine. It's all part of the plan, but if we don't get moving, we'll miss this scene and then Logan is going to have to wait until I can set up another one."

Leo wasn't anywhere close to satisfied with that, but Wolf was right. He was interested to see what his brother had cooked up. He walked behind Wolf, noting that while Wolf smiled down at Shelley and acknowledged her, he didn't reach for her hand. He said something to Logan and then moved forward with his friend.

Shelley stared at his back. "What's wrong? Did I do something?"

"No, baby. He's in his Dom space. He's getting ready for the scene, and he has something he needs to do with Logan." He kissed her, trying to reassure her. It was all a lie. He was pretty sure his brother was twelve kinds of fucked up, but now wasn't the time to push him. They would get through Logan's shit, punish their sub, and then he would kick Wolf's ass if he needed to.

"I don't like his Dom space." Shelley held his hand as she walked along beside him.

"We'll work on him." He squeezed her hand as they began to walk up the stairs that would take them to the playroom. What was this scene Wolf had planned out with Jack and Sam?

He had a sinking feeling in the pit of his stomach as they rounded the corner. They walked past the gyno lab where Kitten was being rewarded for her earlier good deeds by having a TENS unit attached to her pink parts. Chase worked over the sub. Ben was nowhere to be seen.

"Eight o'clock tomorrow?" Chase asked as he dialed the unit up to a place that had Kitten purring.

Leo stopped briefly. "Yes. In the conference room. Did Holder send the files he has?"

Chase nodded. "Ben is poring over them now. He wasn't in a place to be here tonight."

"I'm sorry, man. I didn't know he had real feelings for her." That guilt weighed heavily. Shelley leaned into him as though offering him support. Sweet sub. He put an arm around her to let her know he would take whatever comfort she had to give.

Chase's face was grave even as he attached electrodes to Kitten's nipples. A Dom's work was never done. "He didn't want you to know. He didn't tell you. He knew you would have walked away from her, but he also knew she was more into you. This is why I stay free of the whole commitment thing. But I would appreciate your help with him. This has stirred the whole mess up, and Ben needs some fucking closure."

"I promise," Leo said. "We'll find out what happened. It's past time."

Ada had been a shadow over his life for far too long. But now, with Shelley here, he felt ready to face the situation. Chase gave him a salute, and Leo turned to the crowd that was gathering at the office space.

Damn it. Of course. Logan had been taken into his boss's office and held there for hours. He'd been beaten to a bloody pulp, tied down, and forced to endure anything they gave him. He'd been made to feel small and helpless, and it had changed his worldview.

And Wolf was going to force him to watch it happen to someone else.

This was possibly going to be a huge mistake.

But Jack was already at work. His male sub, Sam, was tied down to the top of the desk. They used the office play space to enact fantasies about bosses and secretaries, but this was something different. Though the crowd didn't find anything wrong with it, Logan Green would think of it as his own personal nightmare.

Sam was dressed in khaki pants and no shirt. Jack was in black. He had a crop in his hand and, at first glance, it appeared he was brutally beating his sub. Anyone with a skilled eye could see that Jack was pulling his strikes, and some of them actually landed on the desk behind Sam. Sam covered the sound of the crop hitting wood by screaming. Another tell. Sam never screamed. Sam was a bit of a pain slut. He genuinely enjoyed being spanked and whipped by an experienced hand. But now Sam seemed to be in agony.

"Tell me what I want to know!" Jack screamed at the blond man on the desk.

"I don't know anything," Sam cried. "Please. Please. I don't know anything."

"Are they doing some sort of spy torture scene?" Shelley asked.

Leo looked over the tops of the heads in front of him, searching for Logan. One of two things was going to happen, both of them potentially harmful. Logan would crack or his protective shell would harden further. His brother needed to leave the fucking therapy to him. Janine slid in behind Shelley.

"Do you know what's going on, Leo? This is an odd scene. There should have been an announcement that an intense scene was being played out. I would ask Julian to stop it, but Jack isn't actually hitting him most of the time. Is this for Sam's benefit?" Janine asked.

And then he heard it. A roar filled the playroom. It was a sound of primal rage that nearly shook the walls. Logan charged the small play area, ignoring the boundaries, pushing past everyone in front of him.

"Leave him alone!" Logan screamed, his face a mottled red. He leapt, trying to get his hands on Jack, but at least Wolf had done one thing right. He'd stayed close enough to catch Logan before he killed someone. Wolf's arm went around Logan's waist, and he hauled him back. Jack dropped the crop and held his hands up.

"It's all right, Deputy. My sub is fine. It was nothing more than a scene." Jack's hands worked on the bindings that held Sam down.

"You're a fucking asshole. Let him go!" Logan didn't seem to know where he was.

Leo pressed through the crowd, pulling Shelley in his wake. He wasn't about to leave his own uncollared sub walking around unattended, but he had a job to do. When they reached the front of the crowd, he ordered her to stay right there and climbed up on the slightly raised area.

Sam was sitting up. "It didn't hurt. Jack was playing. We were playing. I wasn't even thinking my safe word."

But Logan was far gone. Wolf had a brutal hold on him, but he was still fighting, still trying to get at some assailant who now only existed in his mind.

"Logan!" Leo stood right in front of the deputy. His tone was calm but loud and firm. "Logan, you're in Dallas, Texas, in a club called…The Club." Why had Julian been so lazy when naming his freaking club? "You're safe. Sam is safe. This was a scene. This has nothing to do with what happened to you."

Logan stopped and seemed to focus on Leo. He stilled. "What?"

"You're in Texas." He kept his tone calm and cool. "Not Bliss. This is a scene, not reality. Jack barely hit his sub. What you saw was a bunch of smoke and mirrors."

Logan looked over to where Sam stood holding up his hands. "He barely hit me, man. And he would never hit me enough to do anything more than redden up my skin. The one time he cut me when he was using a whip, he felt so guilty I had to force him back into play. I trust that man with my everything. He's goddamn half of my soul."

Logan went still, and then he slumped forward. If it hadn't been for Wolf's arms around him, he would have fallen to the ground. A low wail came from the young man's throat, and he wept openly.

Wolf went to the ground with him. "It's okay, man. It's okay. You're safe."

"Janine? Please?" Leo looked to his ex-wife.

Janine started moving the crowd away. "Please, follow me to the doctor's office. I hear a very naughty kitten might finally be forced to use her safe word."

The crowd shuffled off, and Leo was left with Wolf and Logan and Shelley, who was crying, too, now. He knew her heart wouldn't allow her anything less. And she could help.

"Come here, baby." Despite Logan's happy-go-lucky demeanor, Leo felt the young man had the core of a Dom. He'd tried to protect the people around him. He'd looked out for those weaker than him. And he'd been surrounded by women growing up. When he needed comfort, he would look for a female. He nodded toward Logan, and Shelley seemed to understand. She dropped to her knees and offered the crying man a hug.

Logan pulled away from Wolf as fast as he could. What he couldn't take from Wolf, he had no problem accepting from someone soft and sweet. Logan held her, but the way he would hold a mother or a sister. He buried his face in her shoulder and sobbed. Shelley played her part beautifully because it was natural for her to reach out and comfort someone in pain, even someone she didn't know well. She smoothed back Logan's hair and promised him it would all be okay.

Wolf got to his feet. Leo pulled him out of hearing reach.

"That could have gone very badly," Leo scolded.

Wolf's eyes turned down. "I didn't know what else to do. He was leaving for New York in a few days."

"And he still might. He might not trust anyone in this club ever again."

Wolf turned to Logan, who was starting to calm. "Logan, I did this. I set it up. I knew what it would do to you. I did it. I did it behind Leo's back because I knew he wouldn't agree with me. And I timed it so Leo couldn't stop it. Leo didn't do this. I did this. So if you hate someone, hate me."

Logan looked up, his head still resting on Shelley's breasts. "How about I hate that fucker who did this to me instead? I'm not stupid. And I may be stubborn, but I'm not an asshole. You wouldn't have done this if you didn't care. And it wouldn't have worked if I wasn't in trouble."

"You need to stay here. You need to work this out," Wolf said, practically pleading.

Logan nodded. "I know I do. I wanted to kill that man. I don't really know him, but I was going to kill him. I could feel my hands wrapping around his throat. I wanted to watch as I squeezed the life out of him. God, Leo, can you fix me? Can you make the images go away? I can't not think about it. I can't meet a new person and not wonder if they would hurt me if they could. I don't want to live like this. Can you fix me?"

"He fixed me." A quiet, deeply authoritative voice broke through the quiet. Julian Lodge was still in his business suit. He hadn't changed for the evening, which told Leo that he'd had a busy

Saturday. Julian got to one knee in front of Logan. "I know where you are. I've been held down and tortured against my will. I was forced to watch as someone hurt the woman I loved. It was only through my partner's quick thinking that Danielle and I survived. And for almost a year after, I sat in Leo's office once a week and we talked. And eventually it went away. I still think about it, but I'm in control now. Leo can help you take back that power if you allow him to. It's your choice."

Julian stood back up and held a hand out. Logan couldn't possibly know how far Julian had come that he would reach out, telling his own story. The deeply guarded man now knew when to open the gates to his soul.

Logan took his hand, and Julian helped him up. "I want to stay, Mr. Lodge."

"Then you are welcome. Men like you are always welcome at The Club. Shelley, dear, thank you for being the sweet soul you are. Perhaps your Masters will take that into account this evening. Logan, let's have a drink. One or two should do. We can talk a bit."

Logan nodded back at Wolf. "I'll see you later, man. Guess we won't be headed to New York."

Julian turned back. "Everything is set for your scene with Shelley. Hurry along, you two. You don't want to keep that crowd waiting."

Wolf helped Shelley to her feet. He seemed to be ready to take a step back, but he suddenly hauled her into his arms and wrapped himself around her.

"You were great with him. Thank you." Wolf breathed her in, seeming to try to lose himself in her scent.

"You're welcome, but all I did was hold him." She held Wolf, too. She went on her tiptoes and pressed kisses along his shoulder.

"Sometimes that's all you need, love." Wolf stepped back with an audible breath. He calmed himself and looked to Leo. "Shall we begin?"

Leo eyed his brother. He had the worst feeling that Wolf wasn't done with pulling crazy stunts. "Sure."

He took Shelley's hand and followed his brother out of the playroom and down to the dungeon.

* * * *

Shelley took a deep breath as Leo helped her on to the dungeon's raised stage. She loved the heels. They were gorgeous. They were also torture devices. They were part of her punishment, and like everything in BDSM, there were good and bad points. Good point—they were stunning and designer and she kind of wanted to kiss them. Bad point—they made her never want to walk again.

She rather thought her men were about to make her never want to sit again.

There was a spanking bench in the center of the stage and a plethora of devices meant to beat on a poor, did-it-all-for-love sub's ass. All of it would have been perfectly doable, except for one thing.

Wolf had barely looked at her. She wasn't sure what was going on with him, but she was starting to feel brutally self-conscious. Leo kept eating her up with his eyes, and the man had his hands on her all the time. It made it easy to forget that she was half naked. But Wolf was making her remember. He wasn't the same man who had awakened her this morning by rolling her over and fucking into her before her eyes were even opened.

He was distant and that hurt.

"Find your position, baby," Leo whispered in her ear. "You'll get through this, and then we'll figure out what's got baby brother's panties in a wad."

She couldn't help but smile. There was her Leo. The man she'd fallen in love with was funny and sarcastic and always had a quip. His blue eyes stared down, promising he would take care of it. How much easier this was than her marriage, where she had felt so alone. Even though Wolf seemed far away, Leo was close, promising to bring his brother back to her.

Yes, this was what she wanted, and she was willing to fight for it.

She dropped to her knees and spread her legs wide, her palms up on her thighs. She lowered her head submissively, and suddenly she wasn't afraid of that spanking bench. Neither man had brought her anything but pleasure. The bites of pain had merely enhanced her sexual fulfillment. She enjoyed the feel of their hands on her ass, the rope around her flesh. It meant she was performing for her men, bringing them what they needed.

Her pussy got soft and warm at the thought of the spanking that was coming. And the sex. She doubted they would deny her cock, and if they tried, she intended to beg sweetly until they gave in. For the first time in her life, she felt powerful. She made the choices. She decided her fate, and it was to be their woman.

"Sub, do you understand the violation you're being punished for?" Wolf asked, his voice ringing out.

"Yes, Sir." She gave him the words Leo had taught her to use.

"And do you cede control here and now to your Masters?" Leo asked.

"I do. I cede control to my Masters." She kept her head down. They would call for public punishment, and Julian was supposed to agree. She didn't know who would give the go-ahead now, though she'd seen Chase hauling a happy Kitten with him toward the front of the stage. With Julian out and Leo involved in the scene, it was probably up to Chase to speak for The Club.

"Do you cede control to your true Master?" Wolf asked.

That was off script. And she'd already answered the question. "Yes, Sir. I do."

Wolf wasn't done. "I have a gift for this submissive and for her true Master. Leo, will you accept this in the spirit in which it is given?"

She brought her head up. No one had said anything about gifts, and Wolf's voice had taken on a grave tone that worried her. He was trying to hand Leo a box. It was a brilliant blue that would typically have her jumping up and down, but now she wanted to know what the hell was happening.

Leo took the box, his eyes wary. "That depends on what spirit we're talking about, brother."

"In a spirit of brotherly consideration," Wolf replied.

Leo opened the box, pushing aside the white bow and opening the lid. His brows lifted. "It's a collar. It's quite nice. There's only one problem."

He turned the box to her. In it was a lovely, heart-shaped silver locket. There was a space for a single key. That key lay next to the locket.

"Leo, she's meant for you," Wolf said, his voice heavy. "You've loved her for years. I would never take her from my brother. I came to Dallas to bring you together. My work here is done. I wish you both all the happiness in the world."

"I am begging you to rethink this right fucking now, Wolf," Leo said, but the words seemed far away.

He'd come to Dallas to bring her together with Leo? He'd written to her for a month, sending her his secret fantasies and making her fall in love with him so she could be with Leo? Her heart started pounding. Vaguely she heard them talking.

"Leo, I did this for you."

"Well, unfucking do it because she's about to blow, and you do not want to see that. I have no idea what caused this, but she's about to make us both look like idiots, and I don't know how to stop it because if what you're saying is true, she has every right to be pissed as shit with you."

Wolf had courted her, made her believe in him, made her love him, and all he'd wanted from her was to pass her off to his brother? No wonder he didn't want to touch her.

But it didn't make a lick of sense. When he'd made love to her, he'd been all in. He'd been there with her. Had that been a lie, too? Tears pricked at her eyes. Had she been played? She loved Leo, but damn, she loved Wolf, too. She needed them both, and one of them was either lying to her for god only knew what reason or he'd played her for a fool. Wolf had seemed surprised when he'd found out about her prior relationship with Leo. Had that been spectacular acting on his part?

She knew what she should do. She should simply nod and take what they gave her and get through the next few moments with the dignity of a lady.

Being a lady had gotten her nothing. It had gotten her a marriage to fucking Bryce drug-dealing son-of-a-bitch Hughes. Being a woman had gotten her Leo. She'd thought it had gotten her Wolf. If she was wrong, then she would go out as she'd begun.

She'd been through one hellacious marriage where she'd been ruled by fear. She wouldn't live her life like that again. Not for one second.

She pushed herself off the ground, forcing her legs to hold her.

"Shelley?" Wolf sounded utterly shocked. "Find your position!"

But she wasn't listening to his orders anymore. She wanted answers, and she didn't care if she had to get them in front of an audience. She grabbed the package out of Leo's hands. "What does this mean?"

Wolf looked at Leo. "Are you going to control your sub?"

Leo, it seemed, really did have all the brains in the family. He took a step back. "I am going to take cover. Would you like to explain what this is about? Maybe we should go back to my office and talk about this."

Maybe he wasn't so damn smart. "I'm not having a session with him. I want to know why there's only one key. Is he planning on being a brilliant lock picker for the rest of our lives?"

Wolf's jaw squared. "You know you belong with Leo."

She did. And she knew she belonged with him, too. "You tell me something, Wolf Meyer. Did you sign a contract to top me with the sole purpose of passing me off to someone else?"

He paled a bit. "That makes it sound worse than it is. I know you love Leo."

"I love you, too. You made me love you. You wrote me letters. You spent hours on the phone with me. You told me you wanted me."

Wolf's face fell. "I did this for you."

What the hell was going on? She felt a sob building in her chest. She knew she should be happy she still had Leo, but damn she wanted more. She wanted it all, and she'd thought for a moment that she'd had it. She'd thought when Leo had made love to her this afternoon that everything was settled, but now half of her heart was walking away.

She threw the beautiful, gorgeous, would-have-been-perfect-if-it-had-two-keys necklace at Wolf. "You can go to hell. You say you did this for me? For me? I love you." She hated the fact that she sniffled and that tears were starting to course down her cheeks. "I love you. I wanted a life with you and Leo and you promised me that last night. But it was a fucking lie. You're just like all the rest. You can say you're different, but you lie with the best of them, Wolf Meyer."

"I didn't lie." He tried to take a step forward, but she discovered she could move in those heels when she wanted to.

"You did. You made love to me. You shared me with Leo and promised with your body that you would be there. You signed a fucking contract!" That was the worst bit of all. She'd played by his rules, and he'd still burned her. Rage flowed. "You sat down and negotiated that contract with me and I thought you meant it."

"I did." The words puffed from his mouth, and his eyes tilted up in horror.

"No. That fucking necklace tells me you didn't. It tells me you were pimping for your brother. Did you think I would accept this? Did you think I would shrug and walk away and the next goddamn family reunion you could bring your girlfriend and I would be okay?"

Leo shook his head. "I take no responsibility for this."

"You stay out of it, Leo. I love you. I'm still talking to you. Keep it that way." She turned back to Wolf. "I know I'm being a brat. I know I'm being a bad sub, but damn it, you told me that discipline meant getting what I wanted. This is not what I want. I won't accept less. If you think you can have some happy family after this, you're wrong. So here's my advice to you, Wolf Meyer. You better fucking choose again. I don't know what happened between this morning and tonight, but you better forget it and you better take that necklace back and get something more suitable or the rest of your life is going to be hell. I do not accept this. Gucci, Wolf."

Her safe word seemed to hit him with the force of a Mack truck. "I haven't even touched you. How can you say your safe word when I haven't hurt you?"

"Haven't hurt me? You hurt my soul, Wolf." She deflated like a balloon that had lost its air. Her heart ached. She was standing in front of a dungeon full of people who probably thought she was the biggest brat in the world. She'd wanted to belong here, and now she'd more than likely ruined all of her chances.

And Leo. Leo probably thought she was a horrible sub. Tears blurred the whole word. She cried and turned away. Leo caught her.

"It's all right, Shell. It's all right, baby. No matter what happens, we're fine. I love you. That's all that matters." He kissed her forehead. "Go on. Go back to the condo. Chase will escort you up there. I'll figure this out."

He was her whole world in that moment. He held her and balanced her and gave her strength. Protocol didn't matter. The Master-sub relationship didn't matter. He was her man. He was going to take care of her.

"I love you, Leo," she whispered.

"I love you, too. It's going to be all right," he promised.

Chase was at the edge of the stage, clearly ready to take her in hand. Chase helped her off the stage. She could feel a hundred eyes on her.

"Shelley," Wolf said.

But she turned because she was done with him. For now. She walked away as fast as her heels would take her.

Chapter Eighteen

Wolf watched her walk away, his whole world tilting and moving and shifting.

What the fuck had happened?

"Are you happy with yourself?" Leo's voice grated on his every nerve.

Leo was the one with the girl. Leo was the one with a life. "I was trying to help you. Can't you get that? I was trying to make this easy."

Why was Leo fighting him? He'd been doing it all fucking night long. He'd fought him about Logan, and now he was pushing back about Shelley, and this was all about him. Wolf was giving him what he wanted. Couldn't Leo see how this was tearing his fucking heart out?

Leo got in his face. "Easy? Do you know how much you're going to have to grovel? Do you know what Julian's going to do when he finds out how fucked this scene was?"

Wolf was aware of how many people were watching. He felt every eye on him. "I was trying to do something good for you."

"By pissing off our wife?" Leo shook his head. "I know she isn't, but damn, Wolf, she practically is. She signed a contract with you. She has a verbal agreement with me. What the hell more do you want?"

"I want my brother to not hate me!" Wolf yelled, his frustration flowing.

Leo stopped. "What does that mean? Damn it, Wolf, I don't hate you. I never could. You're my brother. I spent most of my life making sure you were all right. I went into the damn Navy because we couldn't send you to college."

"I showed you," Wolf said bitterly. He hadn't thought about it at the time. He'd merely wanted to follow in his brother's footsteps. He'd thought Leo would be happy, proud that he was joining the Navy.

"You did, man." Leo put a hand on his shoulder. "You were twice the SEAL I was. You were it, Wolf. You were everything they wanted you to be. Still are. I was always too much in my head. I loved the missions, loved protecting my country, but I didn't live the life the way you did. I was pissed you didn't take what I offered, but don't you think for a second I was ever ashamed of your service. Not once."

Kind words, and they meant something to Wolf, but they didn't fix the situation at hand. He needed to get out of here with some modicum of dignity. If he had any left. He picked up the really expensive collar and put it back in its box. He wasn't sure what had gone so wrong with Shelley, but his brother had to see reason. "Take it, please. She doesn't want it now, but she will later."

He wanted to know she wore something he'd bought her. Even if she was Leo's wife.

"Why are you being such a dumb fuck?" Leo asked. "She will never wear this. If you walk out on her tonight, she won't even hold it in her hand. Why are you doing this to her?"

"I'm doing this for you, asshole."

Leo threw his hands up. "Why? So I have to comfort her? So I can sit and watch hours of mind-numbing shows about people cooking things I can't eat and installing tile? You need to talk, now. And do it fast, because the longer she stews, the worse this is going to get. She could lock us both out of the bedroom, and if that happens, it's your ass on the couch, understand?"

Leo stalked off the stage toward a more private part of the dungeon. His boots rang out over the silent space. The minute he walked away, the chatter began. Gossip. They were talking about how the Dom in residence had gotten his ass handed to him by a sub, and

273

his brother had not done a thing right all evening.

He'd fucked Leo over, and he hadn't meant to. His stomach turned. Everything had gone wrong. He could still see the betrayal in Shelley's eyes. He'd been so sure she would pick Leo. He'd been sure there would be a part of her that would welcome not being forced to make a decision between them.

She hadn't looked happy at having the decision taken away from her. She'd seemed downright pissed that there was a decision to be made at all.

He'd wanted to find a way to live with them in some form of harmony, and now they were both so angry at him that neither one wanted to look him in the face.

But Leo had said it. Damn it. He'd heard it.

He stalked off after his brother, determined to figure this thing out. He hadn't done everything he'd done only to lose his relationship with both of them.

"You said you couldn't share her long term," Wolf accused.

Leo turned, his brows up in that fashion that always let Wolf know what a dumbass he was being. "I said that when?"

He felt himself flush, but this wasn't the time to turn back. "I heard you say it to Shelley. You told her you couldn't share her, and you asked what the two of you were going to do with me. I made it easy on you."

Leo's eyes narrowed. "Well, baby brother, the next time you decide to eavesdrop, maybe you should hang around and hear the whole conversation. Shelley told me flat out she wouldn't take me without you. Apparently, she's got it in her head that she can have us both. I wonder who gave her that idea?"

Wolf felt the bottom drop out of his stomach. Had he missed something? He'd heard Leo's words, and he'd wanted to find a corner and lick his wounds. Should he have stormed into the room and demanded that they all talk?

Leo pointed an accusatory finger his way. "The answer is you did it. You walked into this club with a plan, and don't you dare try to tell me that the plan was to walk in and hand Shelley off to me. What the hell? That is the single dumbest thing I've ever heard, and I've had therapeutic sessions with Kitten. You didn't make love to Shelley because you were trying to push her off on me. You've done everything you could since the minute you walked in here to throw the three of us together."

"I didn't know she was the girl you were crazy about until after I fell for her."

Leo scrubbed a hand through his hair. "And then you decided to be a self-sacrificial idiot?"

God, no one on earth could make him feel as dumb as his brother could. "I couldn't take her away from you."

A slow smirk crossed his brother's face. "As if you could."

Asshole. But his arrogance was starting to spark Wolf's own. "You didn't get into bed with her until I came along. If I hadn't come to town, you would still be yanking your own dick."

"Would I? I don't know about that. I do know that we're both going to be out in the fucking cold if you don't find a way to suitably grovel. You hurt her."

Shame coursed through his system. He hadn't had faith. "Why did you say it? I heard you. I get that I misunderstood and I'm a dumb shit, but I don't understand why you would say it if you didn't mean it."

Leo sobered, his shoulders slumping slightly. "The relationships I've had before were disastrous. I can counsel people all day long, and I can make sense. I haven't been good at following my own advice. I made Janine miserable."

According to Janine, he simply hadn't loved her the way she'd loved him. His brother had been faithful. Wolf would have bet that if Janine hadn't left, Leo would still be married to her, still clinging to his vow, though he felt more friendly toward her than passionate. "Janine still loves you."

"But I didn't love her very well." Leo's eyes found the ground. "I think I have a lot of our dad in me."

His jaw nearly dropped open. "Are you fucking kidding me? We're back to this again?"

Leo shrugged. "I probably should have stayed and taken care of Ma. I couldn't wait to leave."

"You wanted your own life. Kids are supposed to leave their homes. Ma is proud of you. You should hear the way she talks about you. You would think you walk on water. She wanted us to find our places. She never wanted us to stay and take care of her. She's really happy with Mel. They would get married, but they're worried about aliens tracking the paper trail. You're under some mistaken impressions, and there's nothing of our dad in you."

Leo sighed, the sound a heavy weight. "I don't know if I can do the kid thing. It scares me. I want them. I really do. I can't tell you how much I envy Jack and Julian and Aidan. But I have no idea how to be a father. I didn't have a dad."

Wolf felt his heart squeeze in his chest. "But I did. I had a great one."

Leo's eyes came up. "I was a dumb kid who was trying to help our mom out."

"And yet you raised me. Why the hell do you think I was willing to give her up? I love her. I can't tell you how much I love Shelley. I fell for her before I even laid eyes on her. Choosing to honor you by giving her up was the hardest thing I've ever done. I did it because I owe you."

"Stop owing me anything. Be my brother. Damn it, Wolf, that's part of the problem between us. I don't want to be this man you look up to. I only want to be your brother."

Being with Shelley had pointed a few things out to him. Part of his problems with Leo were just that—*his* problems. If he wanted this ménage to work long term, he had to move forward and find himself. "I want that, too. I love her. I want to marry her. I want a family with her. I can't think of anyone I would rather have for a partner, man. But you should know that I won't be bringing a ton of cash into this relationship. Not for a while. I want to go back to school. I don't know what I want to do, but I can go to college and figure it out."

He might be one of the oldest freshmen around, but it was past time to make a choice about his future, and he wasn't going to merely be a guy who stood in the way of bullets. He was going to push himself, be better, for his wife, his brother, his future family.

"I think I can handle you sponging off me for a while," Leo said, his smile wide. "Besides, you'll find that Julian blows up from time to time and then he cools down and passes out the bonuses. I've saved a lot of money over the years. And Shelley is serious about her business. Julian is going to give her a sterling recommendation. She might be the primary breadwinner. You could get that degree and find yourself playing Mr. Mom."

He would do it with joy in his heart. And then he remembered what he'd done. "I think it could be a while before she talks to me again."

"I doubt it. I think she's waiting somewhere to yell at you right now."

Julian Lodge stalked through the crowd, his face a mask of frustration. He walked right up to Wolf and Leo and pointed a single finger. "Do you understand the wretched evening I've had? First that fucking senator shows up with four—count them—four bodyguards. I had to let in four extra men because Senator Cross is a paranoid idiot, and if I didn't owe his father a favor, I would have told him to go to hell. I didn't want to pull Ian off the work he's doing so I have four men in my club who I don't know. I'm down a guard because of the trick Holder pulled. I swear I'm never letting Senator Cross in here again. I've paid his father back."

Wolf wasn't sure what this had to do with him. He sent his brother a questioning look.

"Julian hates politicians for the most part, and he really hates surprises." Leo stood watching his boss like this was a normal part of the day.

Julian's eyes narrowed. "And then someone decides to explode a ticking time bomb in our midst. I don't know if I like this new therapy via scene approach, Leo. But worst of all, I heard a ridiculous tale of a sub gone wild. Tell me what I heard is a ridiculously overblown rumor."

Leo looked over at Wolf. "This would be one of those times I told you about."

Julian turned on Wolf. He could feel a definite chill coming off his boss. "You are an idiot and you're fired."

Wolf opened his mouth to protest. He needed the job, at least part time. Leo held out a hand.

"Let him throw his fit."

Julian's face turned a nice shade of red. "Fit? Fit, Leo? You were supposed to publicly punish your submissive who created complete chaos with her disobedience. You were not supposed to allow her to turn into the BDSM version of Spartacus. And you." Those silver eyes turned back to Wolf. "You signed a contract with her. I set this up. I paired you off. Do you think you know better than me? Have you been doing this longer than me? You're a fucking embryo, Wolf. Did you think you could pass around your submissive? Do you think you can make a gift of her?"

"No, sir." Wolf simply was going to agree with everything Julian said. Julian Lodge in a rage was truly something to see. And Leo didn't seem to think anyone was going to actually die. Wolf knew he'd fucked up. He could take his medicine, and if that meant he got fired, he'd take a cab to the MT building, sit down at an empty desk, and ask where his paycheck was a week from now. According to Tag, that's how most of his employees started out. It wouldn't be perfect, but he would be close.

Julian was continuing his tirade. "She's a human being. You understand that, right? We use the term 'slave' in a nonliteral fashion. Should I give you a history lesson?"

"No, sir. I understand. No passing off my sub. If it helps at all, my brother's already kicked my ass, and I get the feeling Shelley is going to want a piece of me, too."

Julian stopped. "Then you've sorted this out? You're staying with her?"

Wolf smiled slightly. "I intend to grovel, Mr. Lodge."

Julian made a gagging sound. "Well, if you must, but not in public. And you two better get her on that stage and soon. Tomorrow night at the very latest. I expect a red ass on that sub. Otherwise all of the subs will decide to throw a temper tantrum every time they don't get what they want."

Wolf thought Shelley had thrown more than a temper tantrum. She'd fought for what she needed. It made him proud of the woman he loved.

Julian took a deep breath. "I'll allow it since this was what I had planned all along."

"Manipulative son of a bitch," Leo said, but there was affection in the words.

"Yes, that is on my resume." Julian straightened his suit. "Well, my work here is done. I will get back to Logan."

Leo cleared his throat as Julian turned.

"Damn it, Leo, I didn't fire you," Julian complained, never once turning around.

Leo shook his head. "No, you manipulated me into a position where I have a sub, a brother to put through school, and more than likely, a few babies in the next couple of years, which was your long-term goal. You just can't go into the whole 'dad thing' all alone, can you? You have to pull the rest of us in with you. Tell me something, Julian, who's next?"

Julian sighed. "Ben and Chase. I found a lovely sub for them. She works out at Danielle's spa. I'm going to bring her to The Club in a few months. My child is going to need peers. I will import some if I have to, but I would rather keep it in the family, so to speak."

Julian started to walk away again, and Leo once more cleared his throat.

"Damn it, Leo. Fine. Five percent."

"Ten percent, and I don't mention this to Ben and Chase."

Julian's shoulders slumped in defeat. "Ten percent. And you're a bastard. See that your brother behaves from now on. Wolf, you're rehired. No raise for you until you prove you can handle your sub. Come along now and join Logan and myself. Shelley needs time to cool off or I fear she will potentially take your brother's balls, and that would cut my chances in half. I expect children, Leo, and soon."

Julian walked away. Leo smiled over at Wolf. "That's how you handle the boss."

Julian wasn't his main problem. "Tell me how to handle our woman instead."

Leo frowned. "That could be much trickier. Let's grab a beer and talk about this. First off, we need better jewelry."

Wolf frowned, but he could handle it now. And he wouldn't be alone. He had his brother as backup. He followed Leo up to the bar where Julian and Logan were waiting. And somewhere upstairs was his wife. Oh, she might fight him on it now, but he would win.

He settled into the well-appointed booth beside Leo, and for the first time in a long time, he felt like he belonged.

* * * *

Shelley forced her feet to move toward the condo. Kitten walked beside her, a blankly serene look on her face. She appeared to be somewhere in her mid-twenties. She didn't seem to be madly in love with the Dom who'd held her leash most of the evening. She seemed more comfortable with Chase Dawson than anything else.

The big Dom walked behind her and Kitten. He'd unhooked the leash from her collar the minute they'd exited the club portion of the building. He'd been nice enough to grab a robe for Shelley to wear, but he hadn't said much, his mind seemingly somewhere else.

They reached the door to the condo, and Chase swiped a card through the keycard lock.

She walked in with Kitten and wondered if she shouldn't pack.

No, damn it. She wasn't going to run away without a fight.

"Why don't you go and get changed, Shelley," Chase offered. "I don't know what's going on with your Masters, but they could be a while."

They were fighting. She hated that. The last thing she'd wanted to do was come between them—well, in a nonphysical way. "You can go ahead and leave, Chase. I'll lock the doors."

Chase stood there in the middle of the living room looking at her like she'd said something stupid.

She shrugged. "Okay. Stay, then. But I'm going to change and then I'm making hot chocolate. I need comfort food."

"I'll take one, too," Chase said, settling onto the couch and turning on the TV. He propped his long legs on the coffee table and appeared perfectly comfortable taking over Leo's living room. The man wasn't going anywhere. "Kitten will, too."

Kitten smiled brightly. "Kitten likes chocolate."

Chase looked around the place. "And you're lucky Julian has Big Tag working on those files Holder brought in or I would have him send over a bodyguard or two. I'm going to enjoy the quiet tonight because tomorrow the whole place will be crawling with contractors and I'll have to deal with Julian and Big Tag's nasty moods. I prefer being the brooding one."

Kitten was still dressed for play in a minidress that appeared to be made entirely of leather belts. How she managed to keep it on was a total mystery to Shelley.

"All right." She wanted to lie down on the bed and cry, but maybe company would keep her from falling apart. Anger. She needed to hang on to rage. That way when Wolf Meyer showed his face again, she would be ready to smack him. "I'm changing into pj's."

"Kitten likes pj's, too. Warm, soft pajamas."

It was all Shelley could do to not laugh. Well, at least she didn't sleep in her PVC. "I can find you a pair."

Kitten looked to the Dom, who sat watching some form of sports. He waved at her, giving his assent.

Shelley moved toward the guest room where her suitcase was. She would move it into the master bedroom. Yes. That was exactly what she would do. She wasn't going to be waiting for Wolf when he came back. She would do what he'd wanted. She would move in with Leo, and he could screw himself.

Kitten threw herself on the bed. "Kitten likes to jump."

Shelley wasn't going to waste a lot of time. She had a point to make. "We're not staying in here. Grab that bag. We're moving all of my stuff into Leo's room."

Kitten picked up the smaller of the two bags. "Do you have permission?"

She didn't give a damn about permission at this point. She stepped around Wolf's duffel bag. It lay near the closet. This morning she'd promised herself that when she had a chance, she would unpack for him. Wolf was one of those guys who would live out of his suitcase because he would never think to unpack. Earlier she'd wanted to make sure he felt at home. Now she was worried that if she looked into that bag, she might be tempted to take one of his guns again.

She was so mad at him.

"He's not my Master. Didn't you watch that scene, Kitten? Didn't you see him give me away?"

Kitten followed after her. "I saw the scene, but perhaps I saw it differently than you. I saw a Master who thought he wasn't wanted. By you or maybe his brother. I saw a Master who was trying to keep some sort of place for himself, even if it meant giving up his precious sub."

Shelley stopped. "I think you've got a vivid imagination."

Kitten shrugged, her nipples peeking out of the belts that covered her torso. "Everyone thinks Kitten is crazy, but Kitten sees more than you would think. Kitten sees lots of things. Master Wolf is unsure of his place with his brother. That makes him unsure of his place with you."

Could Kitten be right? Was she overreacting when she should be asking questions?

"Where are you two going?" Chase asked as they crossed to the back of the condo. He didn't glance back but kept his eyes on the screen.

"Shelley is moving into Master Leo's room because she wants Master Wolf to spank her," Kitten said cheerfully.

Yep. Kitten wasn't the visionary she thought she was. At least Kitten didn't know what was going on in her mind. "I'm going where I'm wanted."

She huffed a bit as she carried the bag past the kitchen and into Leo's austere bedroom.

"You're right, Kitty Cat. She's going to get her ass spanked," Chase called out as she shut the door.

"You're going to have so much fun," Kitten said with a smile.

Shelley pulled out a couple of T-shirts and pajama pants. Kitten proved she could change clothes really fast. She looked incredibly odd in flannel pants, a tank top with tiny hearts all over it, and her thick leather collar with its ring and the small charm that hung from it.

Shelley changed, feeling strangely comfortable around the sub. For all Kitten's oddities, she seemed rather nice. Shelley pulled the T-shirt over her head when she heard an odd sound, like electricity sparking. She looked around but the lights seemed fine.

Kitten, however, was not fine. Her eyes went round. Her mouth opened and closed. She looked at the door like it was a monster waiting to attack.

"What?" Shelley asked.

Kitten was suddenly in her space, pressing a hand over her mouth and hauling her back toward the private bathroom. She pulled Shelley through, her hand over her mouth.

"That sound was a Taser," Kitten whispered. "Kitten knows that sound too well. Be very quiet. Kitten doesn't think Master Chase intended to be hit with a Taser. And he wasn't carrying one. He refuses to use it on Kitten no matter how good Kitten is. Master Chase doesn't like the Taser."

Shelley's whole body went cold. She could hear people moving in the condo. They were quiet. Leo and Wolf wouldn't be quiet. They would be yelling for her. Who the hell was out there?

Kitten's fingers threaded through hers and pulled her back. She slid open the door to the massive closet and jerked her inside.

"You're in trouble. Kitten heard the men talk about it." Her hand was on her collar, pulling at it. "That's why they're putting in the new security system tomorrow. No one expected them to come after you again so quickly."

She wanted her collar off? Now? Shelley's heart was pounding. Who was out there? What the hell did they want with her? Why had she left Leo's side? Her hands were shaking. She had to hide. God, had they killed Chase? Had she gotten Chase killed? How would she live with herself?

Kitten twisted her hand, and the charm attached to her collar popped off. Kitten held it out. "You should swallow it. Kitten doesn't think they're here for her."

Kitten was bent. Shelley pushed her toward the back of the closet. There was soft light coming from the fixture above. Shelley looked around, but the switch was outside the door. *Damn it. Damn it.* Leo's closet was pin perfect and spacious. Beautifully appointed. He used the space with a neat perfection that left no place to hide.

Kitten got up close. She pressed the charm to Shelley's lips. "Swallow it."

Shelley took a step back. They had seconds before those assholes found them. They needed to look for weapons. Wolf's guns were back in his room, but surely Leo had a few.

"Swallow it." Kitten was stronger than she looked. She forced the charm past Shelley's lips. "GPS. Kitten gets lost. Master Julian put GPS on Kitten's collar because Finn gets upset when Kitten is lost."

GPS. It wouldn't matter if they killed her, but at least someone could find her body. At least her brother would be able to bury her.

But if she managed to stay alive, Leo and Wolf would come for her. They wouldn't stop. And they would have the element of surprise because no one would dream that she had a damn GPS locator in her stomach. Though it wasn't easy, she managed to swallow the charm.

"Miss McNamara, we have your friend out here."

Shelley could hear the low voice as someone entered the bedroom.

"How long he stays alive is up to you."

They had Chase. They could be lying, but if they weren't, then she couldn't take the chance. And Kitten. They probably didn't know about Kitten.

Shelley put a hand on Kitten's shoulder. The crazy, whack-job, smarter-than-she-looked sub had tears in her eyes.

"Do you think they will kill Kitten?" Kitten asked, her voice so soft she could barely hear her.

Not if she could help it. "You stay here. Hide. Don't make a sound no matter what you hear. When you think they're gone, count to one hundred and then go and find Master Leo and Master Wolf. Tell them what happened. Tell them how to find me."

Kitten nodded and moved her body to a corner, making herself as small as possible.

Shelley had no choice.

"It's not looking good for Ben Dawson, Miss McNamara."

They thought they had Ben? The fact that they knew names told her someone had planned this operation. Maybe that meant someone wanted more than just her head. *Stay alive. Stay alive.*

She opened the door and stepped out, holding her hands up. "I'm here. Don't kill Ben."

She wasn't going to correct them. She wasn't sure why they thought Chase was Ben, other than the fact that they were identical twins.

An enormous man dressed all in black stepped into the bathroom. "Guess you want him to live after all."

Shelley nodded. He was so big, and there was something in his hand. She couldn't quite see it.

He moved faster than she could breathe, and she felt the heat of his body and then the sting of something pressing into her neck. The world got foggy.

"Time to take a nap. When you wake up, we're going to have a long talk."

She slumped in his arms, reality receding. Before the whole world went black she held on to one thought.

Leo, Wolf, find me.

Chapter Nineteen

Leo sat back, looking around the bar, feeling a sense of contentment he hadn't felt in a long time, perhaps ever. Wolf was talking to Logan, the deputy nursing his beer and looking a bit more settled than before.

Logan was staying. Logan was dedicated to getting better.

Wolf was staying. Wolf was dedicated to Shelley. Oh, he was going to have to grovel and make Shelley accept that he was a dumbass, but a dumbass who loved her. It would be kind of fun to watch, and even more fun to spank Shelley's ass when she inevitably took the argument way too far and turned that bratty mouth on him. He hadn't forgotten that she'd told him to shut up. He mentally added it to her punishment list. There was a whole lot of gingerroot in that girl's future.

Ben walked into the bar. He looked completely out of place. He was in sweats and a T-shirt, his dark hair ruffled. There was a stack of papers in his hands. He glanced around the bar and then made his way to the table Leo shared with Julian, Logan, and Wolf.

"I thought you were over at McKay-Taggart." The whole group had been working on the plans for tomorrow's security upgrade and looking into the situation with Ada.

"I've been on the phone with Charlotte's sister and Adam, but I wanted to be alone." Ben was frowning. "Has anyone seen Chase?"

"I sent him upstairs with Shelley about an hour ago. Why?

What's up?" Leo asked.

"I need Chase to run through some things, but I found something disturbing. Adam Miles sent us a bunch of info on Holder's company, White Acres. Some of his financials are a bit odd. And this afternoon Chase managed to find several large transfers to his accounts during the time he was on the Teams. How the hell did he manage to make a million dollars while he was active duty?"

Leo felt the room go cold.

"Investments, perhaps?" Julian asked.

"He wasn't a trust-fund kid," Leo replied. Holder had been one of the guys. He'd talked about his rough-and-tumble childhood. He'd grown up the hard way. There was no way he'd had the type of money he would have needed to make it to a million dollars.

Wolf's face went dark. "There was a rumor a couple of years back that someone was aiding drug runners in Kabul. No one believed it."

"No one wanted to believe it." Ben frowned. "Most of Holder's squad now works for White Acres."

A whole unit involved in something criminal? God, the thought turned Leo's stomach. "Ada had some sort of meeting the afternoon she died. She mentioned it to me."

"She was meeting with her CO," Ben said. "Ada spent a lot of time talking to locals. If anyone would have heard something, it would have been her. The translators often found things out the soldiers couldn't."

"But why now? If Holder killed Ada, why would he bring it up now? He's gotten away with it for a very long time. Why would he deliberately reopen old wounds?" Wolf asked.

Julian sat forward. "Leo, would you have made plans to see this man?"

"Probably not. We weren't close at all, and I dislike his business. He preys on former special ops, turning them into mercenaries, and from what I've heard not particularly scrupulous ones. White Acres isn't like McKay-Taggart. They provide ground security for some of the world's worst dictators. Big Tag wouldn't do that. Holder's men train their armies."

Julian shuffled through the papers Ben had brought down. "He

287

wanted to talk to you. He needed to either see you specifically, Leo, or he wanted access to the building. He tried to call. You didn't return it. He forced the issue with the only thing he knew would get you talking. Ada."

Wolf paled. "Someone tried to kill Shelley the night before he showed up."

"Tried to kill or wanted to take her?" Julian asked.

Wolf's head shook. "No idea. Maybe. If they were trying to take her, they damn straight changed their mind. Why would anyone want to kill Shelley? The feds cleared her. Do you think this is someone her husband screwed? Do you think Holder's become an assassin?"

Julian's eyes closed briefly, but not before Leo saw a flare of guilt.

"Julian, what did you do?" Leo's mind practically exploded with possibilities, catching on one. His boss had a brutally wicked brain, and there was nothing the man liked more than information. "I called you the minute I found out about Bryce."

"Trev called me sooner," Julian admitted. "Ben and Chase were already on their way to Deer Run by the time you called."

"The minute we found out about the blackmail op Bryce Hughes was running, we knew we had to make sure nothing could be traced back to Shelley," Ben explained.

"But nothing was found on her computer. Nothing in her office." She'd been perfectly clean despite the fact that her husband had used her business to get his dirt.

Ben frowned. "Nothing was found at all after Chase got through."

Leo felt his blood pressure jump. "You didn't bother to tell me?"

Julian held his hands up in apology. "You were in a bad place at the time. You didn't even want to talk about her. You simply gave Finn a ridiculously large check and told him to handle it. I was rather worried you would take it poorly."

It took him a second for those words to sink in. Wolf understood before Leo did.

"I don't care what was on that computer," Wolf said. "Shelley didn't know. She would never do anything like that. If she had known what was going on, she would have told someone. Leo, you can't think she had anything to do with this."

288

Shelley? Truly involved in Bryce's schemes? Fuck no. She was sweet and honest. She had a bratty mouth and a soft heart. She would never be able to sit around while her husband was hurting people. "I know that. But I will admit at the time I was upset with her. I think Julian was worried that I would take it as evidence against her."

Julian looked tired all of the sudden. How much had his boss tried to shield him from? How much did Julian think he was risking? He could fix that last question right away. He wasn't mad at Julian. Julian had done what he thought was right for both him and Shelley. Julian was a manipulative bastard, but he gave a damn.

"Julian, I am grateful for everything you've done for all of us, but the time to protect me is over. What did you find?"

Ben sighed. "A bunch of stuff. There were hours of footage buried in her system. Her asshole husband had set it up for her to take the fall if anyone found out. Luckily, Chase turned all of that around. We managed to load some of the information on to Bryce's system. Enough to make the feds happy they had the right guy. The rest of the stuff we downloaded to a hard drive."

Oh, there was a bad feeling in the pit of his stomach. "Where is this hard drive?"

"It's being stored at McKay-Taggart," Julian admitted. "I didn't look at it. I simply had Ian put it in a safe place for me. I have to admit, I didn't have the stomach for it at the time. Kitten had just shown up on our doorstep. You were in a depression. Danielle was trying to get pregnant. It kind of slipped away, and then it seemed like a bad idea to get into it."

Wolf stood. "We need to look at those files. We need to figure out who's after Shelley. This is about her, and Holder is involved."

"If I find out he's the one who killed Ada…" Ben began.

"Do what you need to do," Julian said. "Just be smart and let me know what the alibi is. I'll make sure it holds water."

That was Julian. He was a law in and of himself.

"I want to talk to Shelley," Wolf said. There was a deep crease between his brows. Leo understood what was going on in his brain. He wanted to find her, hold her, make sure she was safe.

Leo wanted it, too. "She's in complete lockdown. She doesn't go outside of this building." He pulled out his cell to call Chase. Then he would call Big Tag and get a team over here.

No signal.

What the hell?

"Wolf? You have your cell?"

One of the bouncers called out for Julian as Wolf pulled his cell. He held it up as though trying to find a signal. Julian waved the bouncer over.

"I have nothing," Wolf said.

Ben was the same.

"Mr. Lodge, we're having a problem in security. Everything went black. Harry is working on it, but the cameras went out ten minutes ago, and we can't get them back on. Does this have something to do with the install tomorrow? We tried to call you, but the cells don't work."

Fuck. Fuck. Fuck. Leo got to his feet, adrenaline pumping through his system. This was how he'd felt when he was going into a mission. "Someone is jamming the whole building."

Wolf was right behind him. "Shelley."

Julian began barking orders. "Get everyone you can here now. Find that goddamn jammer and turn it off. I want to know where everyone is. I mean everyone. Every member, every employee, every guest. And have someone find a landline and call Ian."

Leo ran, praying the elevators still worked. He was in luck. Ben followed Wolf. Not a one of them had a gun. They weren't allowed in the dungeon. Wolf's SIG was in his locker. Wolf reached into his boot and came up with a wicked-looking pitch-black knife. Leo had a similar one in his own boot. He felt naked without some form of weapon on him.

He prayed it would be enough.

The doors opened to the sixteenth floor, and Leo saw it. The door to the condo was wide open. Chase would have secured the door.

"Fuck," Ben breathed. "They've got Chase. I didn't feel it. How could I not feel that? We're connected. How could he be gone?"

Chase wouldn't have hidden. If someone had come for Shelley, they would have had to get through Chase. Though it gave Leo a sick feeling, he had to agree that something bad had happened to Chase Dawson.

Wolf moved forward, sinking into a standard stance. He kept near the wall, moving with a silent, deadly grace. For the first time, he had to admit that he was willing to follow his brother's lead. Leo had joined up because he'd wanted out of Colorado, and he'd wanted to help his mother.

Wolf had joined up because he truly believed. Wolf was a soldier, deep down to his soul. Leo followed him, though his first instinct was to run screaming into the room. Wolf was right. Leo had been out of the game for far too long.

Wolf entered the condo, his face completely blank. It was only after he realized no one was there that he broke down. The living room was in shambles. The couch had been knocked over, and there was a streak of blood on the coffee table. Two of his lamps had been broken.

"She's gone." Leo felt his fists clench. Helpless. He was totally helpless. Shelley was gone. She was out there somewhere. He didn't know if she was dead or alive or being hurt. His heart clenched.

He'd wasted time. He'd wasted so much fucking time. He loved her. He'd never loved another woman the way he loved Shelley McNamara. She was in his heart, and if she was dead, it wouldn't matter if his body walked the earth, he would bury himself with her.

"Leo." Wolf's calm voice cut through Leo's panic. "They took her. They want her for something or we would have found a body. Chase, too."

Ben had made a sweep of the whole condo. "I can't find any of them. Kitten isn't here. The living room is the only place that shows signs of a struggle. They took Chase down in here."

Wolf pointed to a bloody handprint about halfway up the door frame. The fingers trailed as though someone was pulled out of the doorway. "They carried Chase out."

Leo walked to the master bedroom. He had some guns in a case in his closet. Having his SIG Sauer in his hand might make him feel less helpless. He needed to think. He had to get into those files that Ben and Chase had taken off her computer. The key was buried somewhere in there. Holder had her. With his connections, Holder could get out of the country and disappear quickly. He could change identities and never miss a paycheck.

But Holder obviously wanted something, and Leo would bet his life that whatever he wanted or his client wanted was in those files Julian had taken.

Bet his life? Fuck all. He was being forced to bet hers.

Wolf walked in, a grim look on his face. He held his spare gun, the one Shelley had stolen earlier in the day. It looked like the third time had been the charm for those bastards.

"Come on. We're not going to get anything here. We need to track Holder down." Wolf checked his piece and slid it into the holster he'd put on.

Finding Holder was their only shot. She was out there in the city somewhere.

"All right." Leo went to open the closet door, and he heard a soft sound.

Wolf went silent.

"Seventy-two. Seventy-three. Seventy-four." The sound was so quiet he'd almost missed it, but it was soft and feminine. And not Shelley. He opened the door and found Kitten, her arms wrapped around her knees. She held herself in a tight ball, her eyes closed and her mouth moving in her almost silent count.

"Kitten?" Leo felt Wolf move in behind him. Felt his deep disappointment that she wasn't Shelley. But if Kitten had survived, she might be able to tell them something, anything.

Her eyes flew open, and her lips trembled. "You made Kitten lose count."

Oh, god. Kitten could be fragile at the best of times. "It's all right. You don't have to count."

Tears squeezed from her eyes. "Shelley told Kitten to. Shelley saved Kitten, and Kitten will do as Shelley asked. She told Kitten to count to one hundred after the bad men were gone. But Kitten lost count. Three times. Kitten was never good at math."

Leo got to one knee in front of her. "Bad men? Do you know how many there were?" Any information would help.

She sniffled. "I think there were four."

It was the first time since he'd known her that she'd referred to herself in anything but the third person.

"I heard steps, lots of steps, but only four voices. They were

292

calm. They weren't angry. They had Tasers. They Tasered Kitten's keeper." Fat tears rolled down her cheeks. She was so young, and Leo knew how hard this must be for her, yet she was trying.

Wolf got to one knee, his deep voice gentle. "Kitten's keeper is in danger. Shelley is in danger. Is there anything else you can remember, sweetheart, anything at all? You would make everyone so happy if you could recall even the smallest detail."

"Did they say anything?" Leo asked, holding his hand out.

Kitten sniffled again and took it. "They told Shelley they would kill Kitten's keeper if she didn't show herself. But they were not smart. They thought Master Chase was Master Ben. How could they make that mistake? Master Chase is much different than Master Ben."

Not physically he wasn't. It was interesting.

"Shelley asked them not to kill him, and then she was silent. One of the bad men told another that he had both targets and to fall back to the meeting point."

Targets. They were organized. Most likely they were all White Acres employees. But both targets?

"Why would they want Ben?" Wolf asked.

Leo shook his head, and then it hit him. "Fucker. Ben is the perfect patsy. He had a relationship with Ada. Holder didn't know about it. The Navy didn't know about it. I'm sure somewhere out there Holder has a hacker making sure those photographs look as though Ben had them stashed somewhere. That way if all goes bad, he sets up Ben to be the killer."

Wolf growled a little. "And then Ben would either kill himself or have a convenient accident. Son of a bitch. We handed that to him. We have to find her. They think Shelley has those files that Bryce stored on her computer. When they realize she doesn't, they'll kill her."

Kitten nodded, her hand going to her collar. "Yes, find Shelley."

Leo squeezed her hand in what he hoped was a reassuring manner. "Let's get you to Finn. You can stay with Finn and Dani tonight. You did very well, Kitten. If you think of anything else, let Finn know, and he'll tell us."

"You'll find Shelley?" Kitten asked.

"I'm going to find her. I'm going to bring her home." He had to.

There was no other acceptable outcome.

Kitten smiled. "Good. Because Kitten's collar is naked without its charm."

Leo's eyes flew to the ring where one of the staff attached a leash on Kitten the nights she was in the dungeon. His heart nearly stopped. Two months before, she'd wandered off while her Dom for the night was dealing with a scene gone bad. She'd gotten lost and nearly allowed herself to be taken home by a man she didn't know. Finn had been worried. Kitten didn't have limits. It was one of the things they were working on with her. If a true sadist with bad intentions picked her up, it could go poorly. Her past proved what trouble she could get into.

So Chase had fitted her collar with a GPS tracking system.

Kitten was far smarter than anyone gave her credit for, and in that moment, Leo vowed to figure the young woman out. He would work with Janine. He would find a way to give Kitten the life she deserved. Because if he was right, Kitten had saved his life. He couldn't live without Shelley.

"Does Shelley have the charm?"

"What's the charm got to do with anything?" Wolf asked. "We're wasting time."

"Kitten made Shelley swallow the charm so the bad men wouldn't know she had it." Kitten smiled.

Leo turned to his brother. "The charm is a GPS tracker. We just have to put in the code and we'll know where she is."

Wolf's jaw dropped. He pulled Kitten into a bear hug. "Thank you. Thank you. Thank you."

Kitten was blushing as he put her back on the floor. Her eyes slid away, and she sounded more stable than Leo had ever heard her. "I know the difference between BDSM and real pain, Master Leo. I'm not as crazy as I sound. She was willing to save me. I couldn't do any less for her."

"I am very certain Master Julian will have a very nice reward for you."

"Kitten has been eyeing an overly large anal plug," she said, following them as they strode out of the closet.

Leo got them to the elevator.

"We'll find her," he promised Wolf.

Wolf nodded. They would find her. And then they would never let her go.

* * * *

Shelley's head was pounding as she came to consciousness. She tried to move her hands, to ease the ache in her temples, but her wrists held fast. She felt heavy and groggy. Had she overslept? What had happened? Where was Leo? Why wasn't Wolf close to her? She was cold, and she shouldn't be cold in between her men.

She forced her eyes to open. She wasn't in bed. She could make out low florescent lights.

"Welcome to our nightmare, princess," a deeply sarcastic voice said quietly.

Chase. She remembered. Chase had been taken with her. Where were they? Her eyes wouldn't seem to focus.

"If you want to pretend to be out for longer, I think we can put off the moment when they decide to cut my balls off and stuff them down my throat."

"Where are we?" Shelley asked, keeping her voice as quiet as possible. It still seemed like she was screaming.

"Hell," Chase replied. "Either that or it's a warehouse somewhere near downtown. That would be my guess. I would say we're roughly three miles from The Club. I was a little out of it, but I think we went north and then west. If by some miracle you get a chance to run, run toward the freeway. Someone will see you. They can't take you back if there are witnesses."

Her stomach rolled. She seemed to be duct-taped to a chair. She tried to move her feet. At least she could kick if she had to. She glanced around the large room. She didn't see anyone but Chase. They were in a huge, industrial-looking space. She tried to find the exits. There were several large windows overhead, but she couldn't see a door.

"I don't know if I could run. I feel terrible."

"It's from the drugs they used to knock you out. Probably ketamine," Chase explained. He was taped down in a similar fashion.

The big Dom looked worse for the wear. His left eye was swollen shut, and he had a fat lip. Silvery tape wrapped around his torso, holding him upright. "It's a tranquilizer. Veterinary. Easier to get than the human stuff, but it works."

"It made me sick."

"Again, it is supposed to be used on horses. And I wouldn't mind a dose of it right about now. I think one of those fuckers didn't expect much of a fight. Holder seemed pissed as shit that I was damaged goods."

Her brain was still a foggy mess. She tried to clear it. Holder was the man who had helped her with the robber, and then he'd shown up at Leo's office with the pictures of Ada. Shelley put two and two together and came up with the fact that Holder was an asshole. "He arranged for my laptop to be stolen. Jerk. What does he want?"

There was an echo of footsteps. She forced her head to turn.

"I want a certain tape that your husband made." Holder frowned down at her. Any vestige of charm was gone. Holder was dressed in black, the stark color a contrast to his silver-white hair. Icy-gray eyes pinned her. "You can tell me where that tape is and make it easy on yourself, or we can do this the hard way. I'm prepared for either."

He flicked a hand and another man in black walked up, carrying a small metal tray.

"Is that what I think it is?" Chase asked.

"It's sodium amytal." He picked up the hypodermic needle.

"I don't know anything." They could give her all the drugs in the world, and she wouldn't be able to help them.

"You should tell them. The jig is up, sweetheart. Holder knows." Chase's voice was gravely. "Time isn't on our side here."

He emphasized the word "time."

He wanted her to stall. God. She had to buy them some time. If Holder decided that she didn't know anything, there would be zero reason to keep them alive.

"Tell me something, Holder," Chase was saying. "Why did you kill Ada? Don't pretend you didn't. You wouldn't have had those pictures if you didn't. I assume you're planning to pin this whole thing on me."

A cold smile curved up Holder's lips. "You've been out of the game too long, Ben. You should never have revealed that emotional shit to a roomful of people. I was worried about how I would handle getting rid of Miss McNamara here. I thought I might have to cover it all up, but this is so much easier."

"You won't be able to cover anything up," Shelley said. "Leo and Wolf will look for me. They'll find me."

Her stomach rumbled again. The charm. By now, Kitten would have finished up her count and gone to find Leo and Wolf. They would turn on the GPS, and they would come for her.

Despite the fact that she was pissed at Wolf, she knew he would come in with guns blazing. She needed to give him time.

Holder seemed willing to talk. "And now, thanks to Ben here, they can find a corpse because Ben has an axe to grind with your pervert boyfriend, Leo. Leo was fucking his girl. Leo was the one she wanted. It's funny how plans come together, isn't it? I tried to pin Ada's murder on Leo. I even studied that damn Shibari crap so the bondage would look right. I've been careful, and though I didn't manage to pin it on Leo back then, I can sure as hell pin this on you now." Holder got close to Chase.

"So I get pissed off after all these years and decide to take it out on Leo's sub?" Chase asked. "Why now?"

Holder shrugged as if it didn't matter to him. "Maybe you like brunettes. Maybe you waited until Meyer found one he truly loved. I don't know. It doesn't matter. After the cops hear about all the weird shit you guys pull on women, they won't be surprised you decided to rape this one and kill her and then yourself."

Rape? She felt her strength return on a tidal wave of anger. "I'm not telling you anything. I hope that file gets out."

She had no idea what file he was talking about, but she bet it was criminal and could cost whoever was on it some jail time.

Holder was perfectly calm, as though the outcome had already been decided. "You will talk. You'll talk, and then you're going to make this all look good for the papers. Meyer will be caught in a shit storm after Ben here writes a long letter detailing how Meyer was involved in a drug-running deal that Ada caught wind of. Ben will say he found out about how Meyer paid to have his bondage girl killed."

"An interesting story," Chase said with an uptick of his lips. "But

I do see a few problems with it. First of all, how are you going to get me to do anything with only you and the Hulk there? It took four of your assholes to take me down the first time. And a Taser."

Holder squeezed the syringe until a bit of the drug squirted out. "I don't need all my men now that I have you two properly secured. Besides, I needed them back at that club. I got them in as bodyguards. I think Lodge might notice if the senator's bodyguards disappeared. They're back with the senator now. I doubt anyone noticed them at all."

"I don't think I'll cooperate, Holder," Chase said.

Holder laughed, the sound grating on Shelley's nerves. "Your cooperation isn't necessary. My teammate here will simply use your dead hand to fire a bullet from the gun that will take Miss McNamara's life, and then you'll be covered in gunpowder residue. Don't worry too much about it, Ben. I'm good at covering up my crimes. I don't make mistakes."

He pulled up the sleeve of her T-shirt, the needle in his hand. She shrank back as much as she could. That needle terrified her. She was still shaky from the last drug he'd pumped through her body. She wasn't focused. How would she handle something else? Would her heart simply slow and stop? Would she die without ever seeing them again?

She wished she'd never walked off that stage. She should have stayed and fought it out with Wolf.

She braced herself for the strike, but Chase's voice stopped Holder's hand.

"You made a huge mistake, Holder. I'm not Ben."

Holder's eyes went wide, and he turned to the big guy standing next to him.

"Don't look at me, boss. I wasn't there." The big guy got on his phone.

Holder took a step back. "You're lying."

Chase grinned. "Why don't you pump me full of that shit and we'll see who's lying? I'm Chase, not Ben, dumbass. I never met Ada. I wasn't even in the same country when she was killed. I was in Iraq. And I have zero reason to hate Leo Meyer. Good luck with that."

Holder's face got red, and she worried that Chase had made a horrible mistake. And then Chase nodded, turning his chin up, and she saw him. A shadowy figure moved across the window. Chase started to shout at Holder, giving the man on the fire escape the ability to step up. He went to one knee, a rifle in his hand.

Leo or Wolf? It didn't matter. They were here. They had come for her. She loved them so much. If they all survived, she wasn't going to be apart from them again.

Holder sneered down at Chase, waving at him dismissively. "Joe, kill this asshole. If he isn't Ben Dawson, then he's useless to me. We'll have to figure something out, but we can't let him live."

Joe pulled his handgun and, with a smile on his face, started toward Chase.

"No," she yelled, trying to move.

Holder turned back to her. He pulled at her hair, jerking her head to one side. "You're going to tell me what I want to know. I want those files or I swear to god whatever those perverts did to you will seem like heaven. You'll beg me to let you die. Do I make myself clear?"

She winced, her scalp stinging. She tried to pull away, but there was nowhere to go. She turned her eyes to Chase, who had tried so hard to keep them both alive. He'd bought them time. He couldn't die now.

Joe held up his gun, but Chase merely smiled at the man.

There was a loud crack, the sound ringing through the air. The shot hadn't come from the man on the outside, but from her left. Joe's body jerked, and the gun fell from his hand, clattering to the floor. She heard Holder gasp behind her. Joe spun around, and before he could hit the floor, there was a neat hole in his forehead. His eyes were dead and glassy as he fell.

"Drop it, Holder. Move away from her." Leo stalked into the room, his feet moving silently across the floor. Wolf was next to him. They moved in perfect time, as though they had been partners all their lives.

They were the most beautiful sight she'd ever seen.

Holder tightened his hands around her and quickly shoved the needle in her neck. Shelley screamed at the pain. She could feel the burn.

Holder stood behind her, only paying attention to the men walking toward him. He used her body as a shield. "One step closer and I pump this whole fucking syringe through her system. It's too much. She won't be able to handle it."

"Yes, I can. I'll be fine." She didn't want him to push that plunger down. She wasn't sure what it would do, but she knew if Leo and Wolf dropped their guard that Holder could have a gun in his hand really fast.

"It's a barbiturate. I already pumped her full of ketamine. Do you want to see how she'll handle an overdose of this shit, too?" Holder asked.

"The cops are on their way," Wolf said. His eyes found hers. "Baby, it's going to be okay."

"Don't you drop those guns," she replied. "I'll be fine."

"She won't," Holder said. "I already killed one of your bitches, Meyer. Do I need to kill another one?"

"Ben, that's a confession. You're good to go," Leo said.

Shelley noticed the small device in his ear. Ben was the man on the ledge. Ben was the sniper, and he had his command.

"What the…" It was all Holder got out before Shelley felt something whiz by her head and then Holder's hands softened, and he fell behind her. The needle stuck in her neck, but Leo was at her side in a second, gently pulling it out and tossing it aside. She wanted to get her arms around him. She'd almost died. She'd almost lost everything.

There was another loud report, jarring Shelley.

"Hey, he was already dead, Wolf," Leo said, his hand on her skin.

"He stuck a fucking needle in her neck. He can't be dead enough for me." Wolf paced the floor, but his eyes didn't catch hers.

Tears streamed down Shelley's face. Her neck hurt, but it didn't matter.

Leo used a knife on the tape, and she was free in a moment. He pulled her into his arms. "Baby, baby, I was so scared."

She wrapped her arms around him.

Ben ran in the warehouse as the sirens wailed.

"How the hell did you get here so fast?" Chase asked.

"Kitten made Shelley swallow her GPS," Leo explained.

Chase smiled. "Kitten's getting a reward spanking. Oh, yeah."

Shelley held on to Leo like he was a lifeline, but her eyes trailed to Wolf. He glanced at her, but didn't move to hold her.

"I'm going to wait for the cops." Wolf nodded and walked out.

"Don't worry, baby," Leo said.

But she couldn't help but worry. Half her heart had just walked out the door.

Chapter Twenty

Wolf stared at the elevator doors as they closed, surprised at how nervous he was. He was bone tired, having slept next to nothing the night before. He'd managed a brief nap while waiting in the interrogation room of the downtown Dallas police station. It had been a long night filled with lots of questions. Julian and the legal brigade had shown up. Taggart had been there, and he looked like he'd pulled some of that hair of his out over the course of the last few days. He'd sworn Julian was the worst and then spent hours standing beside the man. Finn and Lucas had rushed around, smoothing over the fact that he and Ben had killed two men.

"You okay, man?" Ben asked. He looked past tired, with dark circles under his eyes and a deep slump to his shoulders.

He felt for the box in his pocket. It was there. Julian had worked a bit of magic, getting someone to open the store so early in the morning. Wolf had explained what he wanted, and one of Julian's employees had picked it up.

The right gift. He had it this time. Now he had to hope that she would accept it.

"I'm fine. How's Chase?"

"Already home. He's tough," Ben said. "Don't worry about him. I think he's already going through those files trying to find the one Holder was after. He was also able to identify a couple of the men who took him. They got into The Club with a man named Mitchell Cross. He's a US senator who was visiting tonight. He's either connected to Holder or Holder used him to gain access. Chase is determined to find out."

He turned to Ben, whose flat monotone let Wolf know that Ben still hadn't really processed. "Man, are you okay? You killed the man who murdered your woman."

A look of pain crossed his face. "She wasn't mine. She was never mine, but I'm glad she has justice now. Are you going after Shelley?"

Wolf nodded.

"Have you ever had a long-term ménage before?"

Wolf shook his head. "No. I've played around, but I've avoided it as a relationship. Where I come from, it's a viable option, but I didn't want a partner besides my brother." He laughed a little. "My mother is going to be surprised when we tell her about our wedding."

It would happen. He wasn't going to take no for an answer.

"You move fast, man. I don't think I'll ever find the right woman," Ben admitted. "I loved Ada, but there's no way she could have handled Chase. The two women we've had longer-term relationships with weren't really serious. Chase didn't want to marry one, and the other laughed when we asked her. Be careful. Shelley seems like a sweetheart, but not a lot of women want a ménage on a permanent basis."

The door dinged open, and Wolf looked at the long hallway that led to the condo. Ben stepped out.

"No way to know until you try, man," Ben said. He gave Wolf a tired salute and walked to the condo he shared with his brother.

Wolf walked down the hall. He could still see the moment that asshole had stuck a needle into her neck. It was right there, floating in his brain like a nightmare he couldn't shut off. He'd realized that she really could die, and his life would be over, too. He'd known he cared about her, but that one second had proven how much she'd taken over his soul. When she'd wrapped her arms around Leo, he'd realized how brutally he'd fucked up.

And how much it would hurt if he couldn't fix it.

Leo had been able to go to the hospital with her. Leo had been able to hold her and assure himself that she was fine. All Wolf had

had for the long hours of the night were short text updates.

He stood outside the condo. Fuck. He didn't even have a keycard yet. That was ironic. The love of his life was behind the door and he had to knock, had to beg to be let in. He had to hope they were even awake.

He took a deep breath and tapped on the door.

It opened almost immediately, his brother slamming it wide.

"Why the fuck didn't you call me? Do you understand we've been waiting up all damn night? We didn't know if you'd been tossed in jail or god knew what," Leo barked at him, making Wolf feel like he was a teenager slinking in after a stolen night.

"I thought Finn would tell you what was happening."

"I didn't want to hear it from Finn. I wanted to hear it from you. We need to talk about this whole partnership thing. If this is your idea of communication, it sucks." Leo moved back from the door, revealing Shelley, who was lying on the couch, a blanket around her. Even from here he could see the bruise on her neck.

Wolf pushed past Leo and got to his knees in front of her. "You told me she was fine."

Her eyes came open. "You're home."

He pushed her hair back, uncovering the vicious-looking bruise on her neck. *Asshole.* God, he wanted to get his hands around Holder's neck. It was wrong he'd gone down so quickly. He should have suffered. "You should still be in the hospital."

"She's fine," Leo said, calming down. "Though she might not be for long if you keep manhandling her. Maybe now she'll follow her Master's orders and get into bed. She refused. She wanted to go to the police station."

"I was anxious to tear off a piece of your hide, Wolf Meyer," she said with a yawn. "Now, I think I'll skip that part." She sat up. "I don't want you to leave me, Wolf. I should have said that. I should have been open. I love you. I don't know what idiot idea you have in your head, but I love you, and I want a family with you and Leo."

He felt his whole body sag in relief. "Baby, I'm so sorry."

His brother made a gagging sound. "Here comes the groveling."

"You stay out of it, Leo Meyer," Shelley said, her hand coming up to smooth back Wolf's hair. She pressed him to her breast. He snuggled in, the anxious feeling in the pit of his stomach dissolving.

"You little brat. I'm keeping track of every time you turn that bossy mouth on me. When you're physically able, we're going to have some punishment." Leo frowned down at her.

Wolf could hear the smile in her voice. She winked Leo's way. "I'm sure you will, you sadistic bastard. But until then, I think I would prefer something more pleasurable. After all, I did almost die. Shouldn't someone kiss me?"

Wolf pulled away and looked at her. "Just like that, baby?"

He wanted to believe her, but it seemed too easy.

She smiled that enigmatic smile that made his heart race. "Would you rather fight for a long time? I'm spent. I could yell and scream and act like the brat I am, but I would rather say it. I love you." Tears pricked at her eyes, pooling there. "This isn't the first time I've been through something terrible. My husband put me in a horrible position, and Leo is under the mistaken impression that I handled it beautifully."

"You did, sweetheart," Leo said, frowning. "You show no signs of having long-term emotional problems with it. Am I wrong?"

"I didn't care, Leo. That's what I never told you. That man held a gun to my head. He killed my husband right in front of me, and all I was worried about was whether Beth and Bo survived because I didn't care about me. I felt dead inside. I didn't care if he killed me because I didn't have anything to live for. I was almost disappointed when Trev saved me. There was a part of me that wanted it to be over. I'd lost my mom and dad. I'd married a monster, and I thought I maybe deserved it all."

"Shelley." Wolf's heart was breaking. He reached for her hand.

She shook her head, but her fingers threaded through his, accepting his comfort. Tears rolled down her face. "It wasn't the same this time. Leo's going to have to deal with some serious nightmares because I didn't want to die. I couldn't die, not when I just figured out what the whole love thing meant. Leo, I'm sorry. I should have trusted in what I felt. I keep trying to sacrifice myself because I think it's the only way to fix things, but I know now that I'm not alone in this. We're all together. We can't make decisions alone anymore. Holder put that needle in my neck, and I didn't want to die. I wanted to do anything I could to live."

"You told me to let him push the plunger," Leo said, his voice hard. "Don't think I haven't forgotten that."

She shook her head. "I know, but he was lying. It was truth serum. He didn't want me dead when he measured the dose. He wanted me talking. I was pretty sure it wouldn't kill me, but a bullet would have killed you."

"It doesn't matter, baby," Wolf said. "We need to set some serious boundaries. Look, we will follow your instructions when it comes to swatches and paint and furniture."

"Unless you try to wallpaper my office, and then we'll have a problem," Leo said.

Shelley laughed. "All right. I'm in charge of making things pretty, and you two handle the bad guys. I can agree to that."

Wolf hugged her, reveling in the feel of her in his arms. This was his place in the world. He'd searched for it, longed for it, mistakenly believed it was something like a career, but this was his place. Her arms. Her heart. Her soul. This was his home.

"I love you, Shelley."

She smiled brilliantly. "I love you, too."

He pulled the blue box out of his pocket. "This is what I wanted to get before I decided to do the martyr asshole thing."

"It seems to be a recurring theme in this family. We'll be in therapy for years," Leo said with a sigh.

She opened the box and touched the interlinking circles. "This is perfect."

"It isn't a ring, but I thought Leo and I should pick that out," Wolf said.

"I wouldn't dream of picking out a ring for her," Leo said. "I would screw it up. How about we take our woman and let her pick it out? After all, she's in charge of pretty things."

Shelley went still. "Is that supposed to be a proposal?"

Wolf knew when they had fucked up. "Nope. Not a proposal because when we propose, it's going to be beautiful and romantic and very memorable."

"And you'll say yes," Leo announced.

She grinned. "I suspect I will. Now someone better kiss me. I didn't take that stupid butt plug for nothing. I want my men."

Wolf felt his cock jump at the thought. He wanted it, too. He wanted to fill her up. Carefully avoiding her neck, he kissed her, his lips finding hers with the unerring instinct of a man coming home. Soft, she was so soft, his woman.

He let his tongue delve in, sliding against hers, dominating. She softened under him, giving him exactly what he wanted. He pulled her into his arms, pressing her chest to his.

He came up for air. "Are you sure you're up for this? I can be pretty rough. I'll try to be careful."

"Don't you dare," she said, her nails digging ever so slightly into his shoulders. "I want my Masters. I'm the world's worst sub, but I want my Masters. I want them rough and masculine and bossy. I want you and Leo exactly the way you are."

And he wanted to dominate her. His cock was swollen with need. "Strip."

Her mouth came open. "What?"

"You heard him, pet. My brother told you to strip. Let's make a quick amendment. We handle the bad guys, you handle the decorating, and we are definitely in charge in the bedroom." Leo's eyes had darkened.

Shelley obviously wasn't about to simply give in to that. "I get to pick the wine, too. And three times a week, I get to pick what we watch on TV or see at the movies."

His girl was a negotiator. And he foresaw a whole lot of HGTV and reality shows in his future. "Agreed. Now, strip."

He got to his feet and stood beside his brother as Shelley tossed the blanket off. She was wearing pajama pants and a T-shirt.

"No more clothes when we're alone. If I have to watch TV shows about people making food I can't eat, then at least you can be naked while I do it," Leo said.

He liked the way his brother thought. "And you have to let one of us shower with you every morning. You'll allow your Masters to clean you."

She snorted, an oddly adorable sound. "I bet there will be a whole lot of cleaning going on."

She tugged the T-shirt over her head, and Wolf's mouth watered.

She wasn't wearing a bra. Her breasts were round, with large pink-and-brown nipples that he loved to suck on. Her hands shook slightly as she pushed the pajama pants down and off her hips. Her pussy was such a perfect bud, a flower that bloomed only for them.

"I didn't want to die this time because I finally knew what it meant to be alive," Shelley said, standing in front of them. She didn't try to hide herself. "I knew what it meant to love."

Leo stepped forward, his hands finding her curves. Wolf walked to the back, pressing his pelvis to her round ass.

"I love you, baby. This is forever," Leo said, his lips kissing her forehead, her nose, her lips.

"Forever and a day," Wolf promised, nuzzling her neck. That might be enough time.

* * * *

Forever. The word meant something now. Shelley breathed in, letting the sweetness of the moment assail her every sense. This was the perfect place to be, between her men, her Masters. Oh, that part of their relationship might not be the dominant one, but it was there, and she would honor it. It was something they all needed.

"Show me what a good girl you are," Leo whispered, stepping away.

She knew what he wanted. She got to her knees as gracefully as she could. She vowed to practice until the move was second nature, a gift to honor her Masters. She spread her legs wide without the horrible inhibitions of before. There wasn't a place for self-doubt here. She settled her hands on her knees palms up and lowered her head.

"Very nice," Wolf said. "But I think I'd like to see you present yourself. Bring your head up, arms behind your head. I want to see everything that belongs to us. I want to see breasts and pussy."

With a deep breath, she did as he asked, lacing her hands behind the back of her head. It brought her breasts up, thrusting them into a presentation position.

"These are gorgeous. I love her tits. But I think I want to decorate them. The sub is in charge of decorating everything else, but I think we get to decorate her. I'm going to grab a few necessary items. Why don't you warm up her mouth?" Wolf asked.

"It would be my pleasure." Leo looked down at her, his thumb trailing across her lower lip. "How would you like that, my pet? Would you like to suck your Master's cock?"

"Yes, Leo. I would like that very much." She loved to watch him undress, that glorious body revealed to her inch by inch.

Leo pulled his clothes off with his natural efficiency. He folded each piece and turned back to her, cock in hand. She licked her lips. Leo's cock was a thing of beauty. Big and thick and long. There was already a pearly drop on the tip.

"Keep your hands behind your head. I like to look at those breasts bounce while I fuck your mouth." He took that massive cock in hand and stepped in front of her. "Lick me. Run your tongue all over me."

She leaned in slightly and did as he asked, licking the salty, savory fluid from the slit of his dick. She burrowed the tip of her tongue in, begging for more. She lapped at the *V* on the underside of his cock.

"Baby, you give great head," Leo growled, his hands in her hair. "You have the world's most fuckable mouth."

His words warmed her. For so long, she'd heard about how cold she was from Bryce, but Leo and Wolf made her hot. They made her feel like a sex goddess. They loved her and she loved them, and suddenly everything seemed open. What would have been dirty with Bryce was loving and affectionate with them. Love, it seemed, made all acts soft and emotional. Leo and Wolf could use all the dirty words they wanted to, but this was making love.

She sucked the head inside her lips, giving him just the edge of her tongue. She wanted to make her Master as crazy as he made her. She wanted a lifetime with both of them. When she was old and gray, she wanted her men to tie her up and spank her wrinkled ass because she would always be theirs.

"That's beautiful, love." Wolf's words were like warm chocolate poured over her skin.

Leo pulled his cock free. "I think you should have a turn, brother. Ma did tell me to share."

"Well, we don't want to go against Ma, do we?" Somewhere along the way, Wolf had lost his clothes. His enormous body was on full display. Every muscle and inch of skin was a testament to his masculine grace. He winked down at her as he took Leo's place in front of her. "Ma's going to want to meet her."

Leo smiled. "Ma's going to want to make sure she's alien free. You should understand that Ma has an obsession with alien probes."

Shelley felt her eyes get wide. "Alien probes?"

"There's only one probe you need to worry about, baby." Wolf's cock thrust against her lips. She licked him, loving the way he groaned. She licked at Wolf's monster, running her tongue over it. She lapped at the head, sucking it into her mouth.

"That's right. Use that tongue on me. Suck me deep. Get me hard."

Shelley followed his directions. Wolf loved to talk dirty. Every word that came out of his mouth had a direct line to her pussy, making her wet and ready. She felt a hand on her ass, cupping her. Leo. She was connected to them both.

She concentrated on the cock in front of her.

"I love the way that feels. Leo's going to get your ass ready, baby. He's going to fuck you with his fingers and then with a plug. He's going to open that asshole up for your Master's cock. Do you want that? Do you want to feel your Master's cock filling your ass?" Wolf groaned as she took his cock deep into her mouth. "Exactly, baby. That's what I'm going to do to your ass. I'm going to sink so deep inside. I'm going to fuck your asshole while big brother takes your pussy."

She felt Leo's fingers probing. He rimmed her asshole, spreading lube around, pressing in with an erotic pressure that had her panting.

He slapped her ass. "Don't you squeeze me out. This ass belongs to us. You let me in. You let me get you ready for a cock."

Wolf smiled down at her. "Relax. It's going to be okay. We're going to make you feel so good, baby."

Like they could do anything else. She sucked the cock in front of her and felt the head of a plug teasing at the edge of her asshole. It felt bigger than before. The pressure built.

"Press back," Wolf said calmly. He pulled his cock free of her mouth and got to his knees in front of her. "Bring your arms down and lean against me. When Leo presses the plug against you, take a deep breath and press your pelvis back."

She leaned into Wolf's strength. This was why she could submit. The minute Wolf had realized she was struggling, he was down here with her, lending his strength. It was the way he would live his life, giving her what she needed.

"Here we go," Leo said.

This time when she felt the press, she didn't fight it. She pressed out, and the plug slid in, stretching and burning erotically. She shivered as Wolf got her to her feet.

Leo kissed the back of her neck. "Very good, pet. I'm going to wash up and bring you another present."

Wolf put a hand under her chin. "I think it's your day for presents, baby." His face went hard all of the sudden, but Shelley knew it wasn't his mad face. It was his controlling-himself face. "You're going to marry me. You're really going to marry me."

Happy tears welled. She brought her hands up to cup his handsome face. "Oh, yes. I'll marry you, Wolf Meyer."

"I'll ask you every day. I'll wake you up every morning, and I'll ask you if you'll marry me."

"Oh, Wolf," she said, her heart swelling with emotion. "I'll say yes every day."

Suddenly Leo was behind her, his hands skimming down her back. "You better say yes to me, too. I'm the one who gets to sign all the legal documents. We'll have a nice wedding and even better honeymoon where we have to explain why the big guy's with us."

She loved Leo's smart mouth.

"The big guy's around to make sure our woman's needs get met." Wolf winked down at her. "Now, I see those pretty jewels in your hand. Did you pick them out special for our sub?"

Wolf turned her to face Leo, catching her arms in his hands. He held both her wrists in one big hand, forcing her chest out, putting her breasts back on display. Shelley looked at Leo and saw he had what looked like gorgeous emerald earrings in his hands.

But her man was a bit of a sadist. She was pretty sure they weren't what she thought. "Those aren't for my ears, are they?"

His decadent grin told her everything she needed to know. He fell to his knees in front of her, his mouth in front of her right nipple. "Not at all, baby. These jewels are for your pretty nipples. They're clamps to torture a disobedient sub. And don't you dare tell me you aren't disobedient. You're my sweet brat. I wouldn't have you any other way."

"Because then we wouldn't get to punish you," Wolf offered, his lips on her temple.

It was good to know her rebellious streak came in handy. "Are you going to stare, Leo? Or are you going to use those things on me?"

His eyes heated up. His mouth flattened into that Dom look he got when he was going to do something wickedly bad. "I think I'll take my time and play a bit."

Torture worse than any spanking. Waiting. It killed her. He slowly leaned forward and licked her nipple, making the thing pout and beg for more attention.

"I can smell her pussy, brother," Wolf said.

Leo traced the circle of her areola with the tip of his tongue. "That pussy is going to have to wait because I'm not giving her anything until she begs."

Begs? She could totally do that. He was way underestimating her need to get between them. "Please, Master Leo. Oh, please."

He stopped and stared at her. "God, you're a brat. I'll rephrase. I'm not stopping until I decide to."

"Don't push him, baby." Wolf's teeth nipped at her ear. "I don't want to prolong this. I want to get inside you. I want to know you're mine."

Leo set the edge of his teeth on her nipple, making her gasp.

"I'm yours, Wolf," she said on a breath. "I'm Leo's, too. I'll be good. I'll be good here."

She doubted she would be anywhere else. Now that they had built back her self-esteem, her men might find they had made a monster. She felt like she could take on the world. She was theirs. They were hers. It was all she needed.

Leo bit down, the pain a sharp reminder that her Master was hungry. He bit and played with the nipple before slipping the nipple clamp on. The tight bite skittered across her skin.

"Very pretty," Leo said before starting in on her other breast. He gave it the same treatment, lashing it with his tongue and teeth until it was a ripe red berry, and then he slipped the clamp on. "You're gorgeous like this, pet. One day I'm going to have these nipples pierced, and then I'll run a chain between them."

She wasn't sure about that, but Leo leaned over and put his nose in her pussy. It wasn't the time to argue with the man.

"You smell so good." His tongue licked upward, making her pant.

She wanted to scream in frustration when he got to his feet. He leaned over and kissed her, his tongue foraging deep. She could taste her own tangy essence on his tongue. He kissed her for the longest time before pulling away.

"Come on. Let's take our sub to the bedroom and show her what it means to serve two Masters."

She followed, her fingers tangling with Leo's. She reached back for Wolf, holding her hand out. He took it, completing the connection. She was the conduit, the reason these brothers would be close for the rest of their lives. The thought warmed her, made her aware of the awesome responsibility of her position. She held their hearts, and she'd given them hers.

"Come here," Leo ordered. When he turned, there was a brilliant smile on his face. He picked her up and hauled her close to his chest. "You never have to walk to our bed. One of us will always be here to carry you."

He looked younger than he had in months, as though his worries had flown away and he was the man she'd fallen in love with again. He tossed her on the bed and came down on top of her, his hands caressing, his mouth kissing. He turned them over, moving her in a position to straddle him. He looked up into her eyes.

"You said you wanted kids, right?" Leo asked.

The jewels on her nipples dangled down, tugging and making her breasts feel heavy and aroused. "Yes." She wanted their babies. "I do, Leo."

"I'm not getting any younger." The tip of Leo's unsheathed cock nuzzled against her pussy.

"Now?" She was shocked. She was sure she'd have to drag Leo

kicking and screaming into the baby thing, but here he was, offering her everything she wanted.

"Wolf isn't getting any younger either." Leo's hand tightened on her hips. "We need to take advantage of him while he's young and can keep up with all those kids. He's going to be Mr. Mom."

"Come on, baby," Wolf cajoled as he moved on to the bed. "Let's get this thing started. I don't know about Mr. Mom, but I would love to have a couple of rug rats to play with. Leo wants to get the raise Julian will almost surely offer him if he produces a playmate for his kid."

"Dude, you weren't supposed to tell her that," Leo complained.

She stopped that argument real quick. She lowered herself onto Leo's cock.

"Oh, fuck." Leo groaned. "I've never not used a condom. Oh, god, you feel so good, baby."

He felt like heaven, his big cock filling her pussy up as she slowly ground down on him. "I hope you still love it when I'm huge and round."

His hands ran up and down her back, making her feel precious and wanted. "I'll still want you, baby. You try to keep me off you."

"Lean over, love. I need to get in here." Wolf put his hand on her back, forcing her to lean into Leo. Her chest brushed his, the jewels dangling.

She gasped and felt Wolf part the cheeks of her ass. He gently eased the plug out, and she was shocked at the empty feeling there. She wasn't empty for long. Something far larger than the plug was fitted to her asshole. She felt the cool addition of more lube, and then Wolf began pressing in, using short strokes, opening her up.

"Relax," Leo said, his hands smoothing back her hair. "Let him in. We love you. Let us in."

She wouldn't keep them out. They were her everything. She took a deep breath and relaxed as Wolf's cock pressed past the ring of her ass and slid deep. She whimpered. They were so big, but they fit inside her like missing pieces of herself, fleshing her out, making her real.

"Love you, baby," Leo whispered.

"Always," Wolf said as he pulled on her hips.

And they were off. Wolf dove deep as Leo retreated. She seesawed between them, allowing them to push and pull her. Her body was on fire, lit with sensation. Her skin sang, completely enwrapped in their power. She was surrounded and consumed and finally whole.

Leo slipped his hand between their bodies and rubbed her clit as his cock surged up.

Shelley came apart, the orgasm overwhelming her.

Leo's hands tightened, and his gorgeous face contorted. He surged up one last time, and she felt the hot wash from his orgasm deep inside her pussy. Wolf shouted, a guttural, masculine sound before he lost his natural rhythm and plunged into her ass one last time.

They fell together in a heap, one man on each side of her.

She'd wanted a home. She'd finally found it.

Chapter Twenty-One

One week later

Julian waved them into the penthouse, a smile on his face. Leo looked at his boss. It wasn't often he saw pure pleasure on the man's face, but Julian was smiling brightly. It was far too soon for Danielle to have gone into labor, so something else must have happened. Leo got the feeling he was about to find out what Julian had been doing behind closed doors. All week long, Julian had closed himself in with Ben and Chase and Big Tag, plotting something that appeared to be coming to fruition.

"You three are just in time," Julian said as he hustled them in. "Please join the watching party."

"What are we watching?" Shelley asked, turning to look back at Julian. Leo watched as she winced the slightest bit. Her public punishment had taken place the night before. Leo happened to know his sweet brat's bottom was still a lovely shade of red. He and his brother had taken turns torturing their sub until they'd finally broken and given her the orgasm of a lifetime before formally placing a collar around her neck. And a diamond ring on her finger.

"God, please let it be football," Wolf said on a groan. He'd lost their last card game. He'd had to watch some show about grown women catfighting in an attempt to be models and a man looking for love on TV. Leo would never let his brother know it, but he'd totally cheated, and he intended to continue to do so until he was caught.

"Better than football," Julian said, walking briskly through the space. "We're watching one of my better plans come to fruition."

Oh, god, what had he done now?

Julian escorted them into the media room where he'd set up for a large party. There was a drink station complete with a bartender handing out champagne. Several of The Club's staff held trays full of elegant appetizers. Julian went all out when celebrating the successful completion of an evil plan. The room was full. Everyone had come in for the weekend's play. And to watch Leo and Wolf collar their sub. Finn sat with Dani, his hand rubbing her big belly. Jack, Abby, and Sam cuddled together on a small sofa, Abby in Jack's lap, her hands around her Dom's neck. She was talking to her daughter. Lexi O'Malley put a hand on her barely curved belly, and Leo caught sight of Aidan and Lucas beaming at her. That was baby number two for the O'Malley family. It looked like Julian was going to have a whole playgroup for his new daughter.

Charlotte Taggart stepped up and gave Shelley a hug. "I'm so glad you said yes."

"I can't wait to start decorating," his fiancée said. "I'm going to make Sanctum better than it was before."

"That can't be hard," Chase said with a shake of his head. "It was a pit of despair before."

"It was minimalist," Tag shot back. He'd been around a lot this week, making sure no one could ever get into The Club again. He hadn't counted on a team of trained ex-Special Forces invading, though he probably should have given what happened in his life. "And Shelley, I want to talk to you about a hamster wheel."

"No hamster wheel," Charlotte said, her eyes wide.

But Shelly was grinning. "I don't know. I think I could make that work."

Ian and Charlotte were bickering as they walked away. They would be making out in the corner soon enough.

Ben and Chase watched the screen, sitting apart from the rest. Ben had been quieter than usual for the last week, but he hadn't neglected his duties. Kitten sat between them, a new charm around her neck. Shelley had been utterly unwilling to give the old one back, though Kitten hadn't seen the problem. He really needed to work on her hard limits.

Kitten was without a leash this evening, and she looked shockingly normal in jeans and a sweater, her face free of the heavy makeup she usually wore. She seemed closer to her twenty-five years than normal. She looked young and happy. Kitten smiled up at him. "Hello, Mas...Hello, Leo."

Ah, progress, sweet progress. "Hello, Kitten. You look lovely tonight."

"Thank you. Kitten is...I am very happy. I'm ready to go back to work. I've even spent the week practicing answering the phone and taking messages. I'm going to be a good administrative assistant. And I found out happy news. I'm being rewarded for helping Shelley. Though I did it because it was the right thing to do. Master Julian is bringing in a new Dom for me to try out."

Chase looked up. "According to Julian, the man's a real sadist, but a controlled one. He intends to work with Kitten on her issues while meeting her needs. I believe he's going to call to schedule a meeting with you when he returns from his travels. You'll have to clear him for play."

Ben ruffled Kitten's hair affectionately. "Make sure he's a good one. She deserves it."

Leo was looking forward to meeting the man.

Julian stepped to the front of the room where the big screen was set up and held out his hands. "My friends, my dearest family, I want to thank you all for coming out to watch this news clip. My friends at the network sent it to me early in thanks for giving them the scoop. It's going to air tonight, but I wanted you all to be the first to see it. Shelley, dear, this is for you."

The tape rolled, and Leo felt his fists clench. Senator Mitchell Cross's smiling face came on in a box next to a thin, blonde newswoman in a perfectly pressed suit. Cross. If there was one thing he'd become certain of, it was that Cross had something to do with Shelley's kidnapping.

"This news station has received an exclusive tape of Senator Mitchell Cross making an under-the-table deal with the controversial security company White Acres. According to our sources, the deal sold out US security interests in the Middle East and Africa. The tape, received from an anonymous source, clearly shows the senator accepting cash for pushing through a multimillion-dollar contract on the taxpayer's dime. This tape also indicates that previously rumored shady business dealings with White Acres are rooted in fact. The company contact, recently deceased Steve Holder, plainly states that White Acres is involved in smuggling blood diamonds out of Africa."

The news anchor continued. Leo watched Shelley's jaw drop, and Wolf's arms wrapped around her. It was one of the things Leo had rapidly grown to love about the ménage he found himself in. Wolf was taking care of their fiancée so he could go and kick his boss's ass.

"Why didn't you tell me about this?"

Julian's eyes never left the screen. "You've been busy. I wanted this to be my wedding gift to you. I hear you're making it official sometime in the near future."

Yeah, and that was already causing him some trouble. "Don't even suggest The Club. I can't do it here. Ma won't get on a plane and driving through alien territory is dangerous this time of year."

Julian's lips tugged up. "Yes, I had heard you were having trouble."

"So we're going to elope. Shelley's not happy about it, but I don't know what else to do." Shelley had cried a little, but she'd agreed.

Julian sighed, a long thoughtful noise that Leo recognized as the sound of his mind plotting away. "Well, you could make your mother happy. And Shelley's brother."

"You think I should have the wedding in Bliss? Julian, have you ever been to Bliss? It's…it's Bliss."

"I think I can handle it. You know Stefan Talbot and I are quite friendly. He might have mentioned that Bliss is the perfect place for a wedding."

Having the wedding in Colorado would make everyone happy. Trev could give his sister away. Ma would be able to throw a huge party. Yes, Leo knew an opportunity when he saw one. He smiled. "You're going to take over this whole thing, aren't you?"

Julian shrugged. "If it helps, I intend to foot the bill. Oh, look, the

319

FBI had to drag him out of his office." Julian put a hand to his heart. "I feel warm inside. No one ever lets me do this anymore. Do you understand how deeply I enjoy screwing people like Cross over? I need to recommit. Marriage has made me soft."

Leo laughed. It bubbled up inside him. "I'll make sure to put that on your list, boss. More stabbing the bad guys in the back."

"I make no apologies for that," Julian admitted. "Stabbing people in the front is far too dangerous. I am a family man, after all."

The room erupted in cheers as the feds finally got the senator into a car, but Leo was stuck on two words.

Family man.

He'd run from his own, but they had blissfully refused to let him get too far. And now he'd found another. His wife, his brother. All of his brothers—Julian and Ben and Chase and Jack and Sam and Aidan and Lucas. Even Logan, who was working hard now, trying to find himself again.

Something odd was happening. His face felt puffy. His eyes watered. Oh, god, it was happening. Yep. He was going to cry. He fought it.

"Happens to the best of us," Julian said with a grin.

Shelley turned, her beautiful face smiling at him.

He didn't know about being the best, but he was damn glad it had happened to him.

* * * *

Ben, Chase, and Natalie will return in Siren Unleashed, now available.

Author's Note

I'm often asked by generous readers how they can help get the word out about a book they enjoyed. There are so many ways to help an author you like. Leave a review. If your e-reader allows you to lend a book to a friend, please share it. Go to Goodreads and connect with others. Recommend the books you love because stories are meant to be shared. Thank you so much for reading this book and for supporting all the authors you love!

Sign up for Lexi Blake's newsletter
and be entered to win a $25 gift certificate
to the bookseller of your choice.

Join us for news, fun, and exclusive content
including free short stories.

There's a new contest every month!

Go to www.LexiBlake.net to subscribe.

Siren Unleashed

By Lexi Blake writing as Sophie Oak
Texas Sirens, Book 7

Twin detectives Ben and Chase Dawson have been sent to investigate an unusual murder at a resort owned by Julian Lodge.

Natalie Buchanan came to the spa seeking sanctuary after escaping the clutches of a twisted sadist. Working as a massage therapist has given her a chance to heal. But when one of her clients ends up dead on her table, Natalie fears that the monster she escaped has come back to claim her.

As Natalie rediscovers herself with the help of Ben and Chase, all three will be forced to confront her past.

* * * *

She'd made some sort of horrible mistake. Oh, god. She'd slept with the wrong brother.

Chase snarled in his brother's direction. "She's not like that. She made a connection with me."

She still didn't know either one of these men. What the hell had she been doing? "Hey, you need to put me down. I need to go."

She needed to get the hell out of here. Her tiny apartment was across the resort in the employees' lodging. She could hole up and wait them out. They were visiting. They wouldn't be here more than a couple of days. She never had to see them again.

Ben frowned. "A connection? You made a connection with her? You don't make connections. You fuck and then you leave them to me to take care of. I skipped a step. Now she doesn't have to feel like you used her."

"I feel like everyone's used me. Put me down." She was starting to get pissed.

Chase's arms actually tightened around her body. "I wasn't using her, asshole. I was helping her. And if you'd taken two minutes to figure out who she was, you would never have touched her."

Ben stopped. "Who is she?"

Now she started to fight. The last thing she needed was a recitation of all the reasons she wouldn't be good for Ben. "Put me the fuck down, Dawson."

"Why are you mad at me?" Chase stared down at her, looking genuinely confused. And a little hurt. Like a boy whose favorite toy had turned on him.

"Put me down. I don't like to be manhandled. And I don't like to be tricked." She pushed at him, her heart thudding in her chest but for a completely different reason than five minutes ago. Five minutes ago she'd been in charge and happy and…she'd thought she was sleeping with Chase. But she'd slept with Ben, and now Chase was acting like a possessive caveman asshole.

"I didn't trick you," Chase said. "Nat, calm down. I'm not letting you go until you're calm."

She couldn't breathe. He was holding her so tight. Like a cage.

"Put her down, Chase." Ben crossed the space between them. "You're scaring her."

Chase went back to glowering at his brother. "Yeah, well, what did you do to her then? Do you know how long it's been for her? Do you know what she went through? And now she's blown that first time with a guy she just met. Except she didn't meet him because she doesn't even know your name."

"She knows my name, asswipe." Ben eyed his twin with a shit-eating grin on his face. "Which proves you can't know her too well since she didn't know my name wasn't yours."

Chase looked down at her, his eyes accusing. "You said you didn't want to know my name."

She finally knew what it felt like to be that bone two dogs were fighting over. "I know your name now and I am going to rip your balls off if you don't put me down."

Those lips she craved grew faintly cruel. "I would love to see you try."

"Nice. Threaten the girl," Ben said.

Chase stopped and set her on her feet. "I wasn't going to hurt her. I just can't let her leave."

What the hell did she do now? She straightened her way-too-short skirt and saw something peeking out of Chase's pocket. "You kept my underwear?"

He shoved them down further, as though trying to hide them. "They're a memento."

"He has a collection, sweetheart," Ben added.

"I bet he does." She clenched her fists. She couldn't really get mad at them. Well, she could, but mostly because they were gorgeous and she felt like such a mess. And speaking of messes, she needed a shower. It had seemed all hot and sexy before the Dawson brothers turned out to be doppelgangers, and pissy ones at that. Now the sweaty state of her body seemed like one more shitty thing in a never-ending, shitty day. "I'm leaving."

"Sit down, Natalie. We have things to talk about after I rearrange my brother's face." Chase took a step toward Ben.

Ben didn't back down, but he did seem calmer than Chase. "What the fuck is up with you? It was a mistake. No. I take that back. It wasn't a mistake. Not for me. She's beautiful and I wanted her, and I sure as hell didn't know you'd like hiked your leg up, peed on her, and marked her as your own. You don't do that. And since when do you have sex when I'm not around? I don't get this at all. I like her. Let's share."

Share? Chase didn't have sex without his brother around? God, she was a freak magnet. There was no other way to explain it. Somehow she found the weirdos of the world. She tried to walk out because it didn't seem like they needed her at all, but she was met with a solid wall of Dawson flesh.

"Sit down, Natalie." Chase pointed to the chair in the corner of the room.

"I want to leave now." She carefully pronounced each and every word because he seemed slow to understand them.

Ben stopped, his face falling. "Natalie? As in Natalie Buchanan?" He turned to her, taking her in as though seeing her for the first time.

Her hackles rose, that core of pride rushing in to protect her because he'd said her name like it was a curse. Obviously, he knew who she was. "That's me, buddy. Bet you didn't know you were fucking a certified killer."

About Lexi Blake

Lexi Blake is the author of contemporary and urban fantasy romance. She started publishing in 2011 and has gone on to sell over two million copies of her books. Her books have appeared twenty-six times on the *USA Today*, *New York Times*, and *Wall Street Journal* bestseller lists. She lives in North Texas with her husband, kids, and two rescue dogs.

Connect with Lexi online:

Facebook: Lexi Blake
Twitter: authorlexiblake
Website: www.LexiBlake.net

www.ingramcontent.com/pod-product-compliance
Lightning Source LLC
LaVergne TN
LVHW050412031225
826904LV00022B/181